CREW
PRINCESS

TIJAN

Edited by Jessica Royer Ocken
Beta read by: Crystal R Solis, Eileen Robinson, Rochelle Paige, Debra Anastasia, Heather Brown, and Heather Amber Pollock
Proofread by Paige Smith, Chris O'Neil Parece, Amy English, Rochelle Paige
Formatting: Elaine York, Allusion Graphics, LLC
www.allusiongraphics.com

CREW
PRINCESS

DEDICATED TO AMBER REYNOLDS MOORE,
HER FAMILY AND THOSE WHO LOVED AMBER.

To the reader,
Crew Princess is not a standalone. You must read *Crew* first!

Other books that are connected to *Crew Princess,* but do not have to be read before reading are:

Fallen Crest Series
(*Fallen Crest High, Fallen Crest Family, Fallen Crest Public, Fallen Fourth Down, Fallen Crest University, Logan Kade, Fallen Crest Home, Fallen Crest Forever*)

The Boy I Grew Up With (Channing and Heather)
(Can be read as a standalone.)

PROLOGUE

BREN MONROE
    RECORDED INTERVIEW, PART 1
    Fallen Crest Police Station
    Conducted by Fallen Crest Police Detective Broghers and
    Fallen Crest Police Detective Peyton.
    Duration: Five minutes.

POLICE: It's been established that Jordan Pitts, Zellman Greenly, Cross Shaw, and yourself, Bren Monroe, were responsible for the recent assault on Alex Ryerson, former leader of the Ryerson Crew. Is that correct?

BREN: *no response*

POLICE: After your crew assaulted Mr. Ryerson, he remained in the hospital for four weeks. Is that correct?

BREN: *no response*

POLICE: Do you care that you guys almost killed him?

BREN: We never touched him.

POLICE: *scoffing* You did, and we know you did. He was in the hospital for a month. Do you care about that?

BREN: *no response*

1

POLICE: You were given instructions not to harm him permanently. That's correct too, isn't it? Just give us that little bit, and we can move on.

BREN: I want my lawyer.

POLICE: *Sigh*. This ends police interrogation, part one.

CHAPTER ONE

YOU WOULD THINK one might outgrow violence.

At some age—after inflicting so much pain, seeing too much blood, hearing so many cries of agony—a person would be able to walk away, turn her back, and the need wouldn't be there anymore.

Right?

It never worked that way for me.

The urge just grew and grew until it was too much to handle.

There may not be a wish to die inside me anymore, that might've gone away, but a different desire rose up. I wanted to cake the streets in red. I wanted to put terror in the Normals' hearts, inflict them with some of the quaking we woke with. I wanted them to feel what it was like to have the power against them.

But I couldn't do any of that.

Or at least, it wasn't time.

"Bren."

The sounds around me permeated my mind, and I turned toward the voice amid the yells, laughter, shrieks, splashing, and glasses being tapped together.

Right. I was at a pool party.

No wonder I was feeling all murderous.

Who wouldn't be?

"Bren!"

A lot had changed in the ten weeks since a friend was assaulted, and particularly in the last month. *A lot*. One of those changes was heading toward me. Tabatha Sweets. One of the most popular girls in our school, one that used to fear me, and here she was. Coming up to me. Calling my name. Acting like we were buddy-buddy, which we actually had become. Hence the not-fearing me part.

She still should have.

She came to stand right in front of me. She wasn't blocking my sun because I'd been holed up in the corner of the backyard, lying down behind the grill, because let's face it, I wasn't the socialite here. I was here for very specific reasons: this pool party was at the Shaws' house.

Cross Shaw was my boyfriend.

Taz Shaw was my friend. She was also Cross' sister.

And the other two guys in our crew wanted to hang out. Zellman and Jordan.

So we were here.

I was here.

Unwillingly.

And daydreaming about violence.

Go figure.

I sat up, looped my arms over my knees, and sighed. "What's up, Tabatha?"

"What are you doing back here?"

Her voice was a little snippy with frustration, but also confusion.

Tentative was the best way to describe our relationship—and I'm being extremely loose with those words to describe whatever I had with Tabatha and her minions. You can blame all the hours I had to serve on their charity committee, which was renamed their 'event' committee as part of my community service. Stabbing our old principal had ended with me sort of having other girlfriends besides Taz.

I wasn't sure how that had worked out.

A couple had been after Cross, and I knew a couple still held a torch. As for Tabatha, she and Jordan were now a *couple* couple.

Yeah. I was surprised at how fast that happened too.

They went from one official date to being a couple, and now they were almost the lovey-dovey type of coupledom.

Anyway, right now, my crewmate's girlfriend who was also somewhat a friend of mine (depending on the day and my mood, to be honest) stood over me. She was staring me down, hands on her hips.

I couldn't lie, though. The urge to pull my knife out, just to hold it and know it would make Tabatha uneasy, was strong. But I didn't. I'd grown over the last year. See? Counseling and community service could rehabilitate us lower criminal beings.

"Where are the guys?" I ignored her question. Did she not know me by now?

Pushing up to my feet, I didn't wait for her to respond.

I took stock myself.

Zellman was on a back lounger, his on/off woman (Sunday) on his lap. Monica (one of the girls still holding a torch for my guy) was next to them, sitting on some other guy's lap (I think a baseball player).

Jordan was just coming out of the house.

He saw me staring at him and paused, beer in hand. He raised his eyebrows in question, but I shook my head.

I didn't need him for anything.

He kept moving, going to sit in another lounger by Z. And I knew where the fourth member of our crew was.

Jordan. Zellman. Cross. Me.

We were Wolf Crew, the smallest crew in the Roussou crew system, but also the most dangerous one.

There were other crews. Larger ones like the Ryerson Crew, or the Frisco Crew, which had popped up over the last semester. They were our neighboring town, and their high school had burned down. The town was too small to get enough funds to build a new one in time for their winter semester, so they were being bused to us. Well, half of them were. A few went to Fallen Crest Academy, and a good third went to Fallen Crest Public School, but the rest came to us. Frisco, Fallen Crest, and Roussou formed a weird triangle a bit inland in California, so those were the options.

We'd heard the Frisco students who went to the Academy shit their pants at how rich and fancy everything was. Most people in Frisco were poor like us. The Academy was for the rich. There were exceptions, but it's what it was.

A few of their girls had tried to follow Tabatha around. She only took in two of them, literally flicking the others away with her hand.

I guess that's what popular girls did? I didn't know.

All this is just to say: I'm not like them.

I'm not like Frisco. I'm not like a Fallen Crusty, and I'm not even like a Normal (our term for those who aren't in crews at Roussou). The ones I'm like? My crew. Zellman. Jordan. Cross. That's it.

And seeing Jordan laughing so easily with that sporty guy, I felt a twitch in my chest.

I didn't know what it was—jealousy, anger, or maybe I was just hungry. But the fact that I'd felt that twitch was enough for me. If I did emotions, it was never a good result, so I was gonna bounce.

"Oh, no, no, no."

I began to move around Tabatha, but she blocked me.

Her eyes flashed in determination, and she pressed her lips together. "I recognize that look on your face. You're going to ditch." She shook her head. "You can't ditch."

"I don't care." I started off again.

She blocked me again, flipping her hair as she did. The movement was enough to draw attention, and conversations around us started to wane.

I gritted my teeth.

Tabatha was in my face, and I hated when anyone was in my face, and I was two seconds away from—

"Sweets." The door opened again. Taz stepped out, a hand on her bikini-clad hip, dressed just the way Tabatha was. "Back away from Bren."

Tabatha started to turn, laughing.

Taz wasn't joking. She nodded at me. "She's two seconds from putting hands on you." She scanned the backyard. "Not a great situation to be in right now, if you get my drift."

6

There were phones out. Things didn't stay secret anymore, not since the Friscians came to town. And there was another development rumored as well, one that had most people seeing stars and Hollywood signs, but I can't even get into that now. I'd been given a heads-up and knew it was going to be a pain in my ass.

"You're close to losing it?" Tabatha asked quietly, easing back a step.

This was her redeeming quality. Sometimes she was clueless, but other times, she had learned to give me space. She backed down now, an apology flashing in her eyes.

I could move my jaw again. It wasn't encased in cement. "I don't like being cornered."

"Shit," she said under her breath. She stepped to the side. "Sorry. I wanted you to have fun."

I felt a little bad now, but not enough to keep me here, pretending to be a normal high schooler. I was literally itching, the need to be free and roaming alone making my blood boil.

Taz had stepped farther out onto their cement patio, and I could see the phone in her hand. Looking over, Jordan flashed me a grin as he put *his* phone away.

I got it now.

He'd called Taz, and that was a good way to handle it.

Taz was sweet to everyone, but as she fixed a look on me, I was getting that antsy feeling all over again.

"Bren." Taz started for me.

I knew what she wanted. It was the reason she threw this party.

And my jaw locked back in place. "No." My teeth were tight too.

"Bren, please."

"No." I moved around her, my hands in my pockets as I wove my way through the crowd inside.

Usually people moved for us, but I wasn't giving anyone time to notice I was coming. A few squeaked as I brushed past them.

"You need to talk to him."

I was at the stairs. I stopped, my hand on the rail. "I don't, actually."

"Bren, please." Her voice wobbled.

I paused. Really?

I gave her a look. "I know you were just drinking, laughing, and sitting on your boyfriend's lap two seconds before Jordan texted you to get Tabatha off me. Do not put on the waterworks and think it's going to work."

A tear fell, leaving behind a wet trail as she let it go all the way to her chin. She sniffled. "I miss my brother, Bren."

Nope. The tear wasn't real.

Or...

It could've been.

Cross hadn't stayed at their house for the last two months, not since—

"Stuff it, Taz," came a voice from behind her.

Relief.

I was no longer in the crosshairs.

Cross was heading down the stairs, his eyes firmly locked on his sister's and his jaw clenched. That strong, square jaw, the one I ached to kiss and touch and run my hands over. His hair was a little lighter than normal, but cut short, and if possible, he'd been hitting the weights harder over the last two months than before.

Jordan and Zellman liked to lift weights, but that was a pastime for them.

For Cross, it was different. There was a set of weights at Jordan's shed, and Cross was there a couple hours a day now. The results were staggering. At six-one, he remained lean, but he was much more defined than ever. His stomach was a washboard of abs, and if he turned to the side with his shirt off, I could see every cut of his muscles.

He'd been on a mission, and besides lifting weights and training with Taz's boyfriend (who was a boxer), his other outlet was me.

He turned those tawny hazel eyes on me, and I felt zapped. Just by that look, I knew he needed a release. I could feel my own need rising again.

"Cross," Taz began, flicking the tear away.

Her voice had suddenly firmed back up. *Shocker.*

She angled her body to block him as he came down the stairs, a bag over his shoulder. She had a hand on the other railing. "You need to talk to Mom—"

He stopped in front of her, staring down. "I don't, actually."

"Cross—"

"She cheated on Dad," he said coldly.

Yeah. This had happened over the last month.

Taz's entire body seemed to deflate. "I know, but he cheated on her first."

That happened too.

Then from Cross, "They're getting a divorce, Taz. Whether I'm talking to them or not won't change a goddamn thing."

And yeah, that was happening overall.

Times were now a bit tense.

Then Jordan came over and asked, "Hey. Are we going to the bonfire tonight? For District Weekend?"

District Weekend. I'd forgotten—and shit.

We had about a month left of school.

That meant prom was the following weekend.

CHAPTER TWO

WITH CROSS JUST two inches beneath him, Jordan was the tallest guy in our school. The only one who could've competed was our last principal, but he was gone.

Someone got him fired...

Cross came down the last few steps, moving his sister out of the way with a gentle hand, then stepped down so he was right behind me. His voice came over my shoulder, his breath caressing me. "We are?"

Jordan drew closer, some Normals behind him. The one lounger guy had tripled so there were three of them now.

I looked, but no Z. Where was Z? A few girls had come instead.

Sunday. Monica. There was another girl too. Lilac? She had a thing for Cross. I wasn't a fan. And I was pretty sure she loathed me. I didn't blame her. I'd feel the same.

See. More evidence of just how far I'd come.

I was all understanding now, not straight-going-for-the-knife Bren anymore.

Work in progress. That was me.

"Yeah. Why not?" He shrugged. "Fallen Crest and Frisco switched things around. Might be fun. That Quickie's place burned down. I heard they have a new place there instead of that one gas station. Wait. Is that where they put the new police station?"

One of the guys cursed. "Where's the bonfire going to be then?"

More than a couple phones came out, but Cross touched the back of my elbow. "Come on." He motioned to Jordan as well, so the three of us moved outside.

Cross walked to the street before stopping.

"Look," Jordan started, his hands in the air.

"I'm fine with it."

My eyebrows shot up.

Last semester, we would've been holding back for me. I was the one who always did my own thing, with Cross coming to find me later. But since his dad had moved out, since Cross had officially moved into my bedroom, he and I had switched roles.

Well, I was still one to do my own thing, but usually Cross was more vocal about how none of us needed to do *all* the parties. His being okay with this bonfire in Fallen Crest—*especially* there—wasn't... Then I got it.

"Your dad's new girlfriend is there, isn't she?"

Yeah. *Another* thing that had happened. His dad moved fast.

Cross had mentioned his dad having a new girlfriend. He'd mentioned she worked in Fallen Crest. I knew his dad had moved elsewhere, but Cross hadn't told me where. I was surprised Cross knew as much as he did.

The way all the cheating came out had been weird.

Usually, or maybe I was assuming wrong, but when someone cheated, there was a period where one spouse was upset. The other asked for forgiveness. The other didn't give it to them. The cheating spouse doubled-down, begging more, pleading more. And then there was a time when they tried to work it out? Counseling maybe?

But not with this divorce.

It came out that *she* cheated. Boom.

It came out that *he* had cheated, again.

The again part had been new because apparently he'd cheated a loooong time ago, before they even had Taz and Cross.

But then, I wasn't sure how the years of the marriage had been after his first affair (because it'd been a full-blown affair and not a single discretion, and yes, that mattered) until *boom*. He cheated again. And then apparently their mom had enough because she did her own thing.

Now they were divorcing. Final drop-the-mic moment here.

But back to Cross' dad. Cross said he'd been in the local motel at first, but this was the only thing that made sense.

"Damn," Jordan breathed.

We were all playing catch-up here. All that I did know I'd gotten from the first night when Cross came over and said he was moving in with me. And Cross not sharing with me didn't bode well. He should've told me this.

Cross' face tightened. "She works at Kade Enterprises, in HR." He cursed, low and savage. "He moved in with her last week. My mom—" He flung his hand toward the house. "—has some guy coming over and sleeping here."

"What's Taz say?"

His jaw clenched. "She doesn't know."

"The fuck?" Jordan muttered.

"Yeah." Cross' shoulders seemed to become even more tense than before. His voice dipped low. "I found a pile of his clothes in her room. She was hiding them, in a fucking laundry bag."

"Maybe they're your dad's?"

"His clothes are folded *under* hers in the drawers."

Well, there you go. That's a whole new level of hiding.

Jordan winced.

A loud cheer came from inside the house, and the volume suddenly got even louder as the front door shoved open.

"What the fuck?" Zellman saw us and came jogging down the sidewalk.

The door slammed shut behind him again, but then cracked back open.

Tabatha was there, her head poking out. "Are you all doing a crew thingy?"

Cross turned away, cursing.

Z and Jordan shared a grin, and Jordan hollered back, "Give us a bit, hon."

Hon.

As in honey.

Jordan noticed my grin and narrowed his eyes. "What?"

"You guys are nickname official now." I bit the inside of my cheek to keep from giving him too much crap. "Are you giving her a promise ring next weekend?"

Cross let out a brief laugh.

Z began snickering.

Jordan clapped Zellman on the chest with the back of his hand. "Keep chortling, asshole. You sound like a parakeet."

Z only snickered louder.

Jordan shook his head, rubbing a hand over his jaw. "You all are dipshits. And yeah." He shot me a look. "We're doing nicknames now. Is that normal? I just slipped one night while I was in her. *Baby.* God, I hate nicknames. I've always hated them. My dad calls my mom *sweetheart,* and she calls him *cupcake.* I never wanted to do nicknames, but shit—we're here." He groaned. "How do we get out of here?"

Z frowned, as if really pondering his dilemma. "Break up with her?"

"What?!" Jordan rounded on him, hitting him again. "What the fuck kind of suggestion is that?"

Zellman seemed undisturbed, just shrugging. "An honest one? I don't think you can go no-nicknames once you're there."

Cross snorted. "Especially when your dick is inside of her." He was speaking to Jordan, but his eyes were on me.

I knew where he was going with that one.

We'd been at "I love you" for a long while. The moment had come earlier than maybe it should've, but what do you do when your best friend/lover takes a gun to commit murder and you're trying to stop him? The L word had come out, and it wasn't one that could go back inside. And while we weren't public nicknamers, we were private ones. Like when he'd called me *baby* last night, and I'd gasped his name, driving my hips back against his. My nickname for him might've been along the lines of "Jesus, finish me, for God's sake."

"I hate you guys," Jordan announced.

Zellman was beaming. He clapped him on the shoulder. "I'm kinda proud of you. Look at us." He scanned the group. "I got a fuck-mate. Jordan's wifed up, and you and Cross, you're just you guys." He nodded to himself, growing serious. "We're all growing up. Holy shit." His face cleared, like a lightbulb switching on. "We graduate in a month. What the fuck are we all going to do?"

Annnnnd...now the pin could be heard dropping.

We all fell silent.

This.

Right here.

This conversation.

This was the elephant in the room.

Or maybe it was my elephant in the room.

Graduation meant change. Growth. We were done. We were moving. We were staying. We were—I didn't know what we were doing, and that was the problem.

Most crews disbanded after school, with only one still lasting, but even that one—and I'm talking about my brother's crew—had branched off somewhat with their normal leader, Channing aka my brother, no longer official, but still there. It was a gray area.

But back to us and the conversation we *weren't* having.

On cue, Jordan coughed. "So. We're going to the bonfire tonight?"

Z broke out in a wide smile. "Yeah?"

Cross nodded to Jordan, moving next to me. He brushed his arm against mine. "Yeah. I want to scope out this lady my dad's with, see what she's like."

"Got it. We can do that. A drive-by or are you thinking something else?" Jordan's gaze moved from Cross to me and back again.

Cross glanced at me too.

The hairs on the back of my neck stood up. "What are you really thinking?"

"Kade Enterprises is hosting an event tonight at their country club. I know about it because Race asked me if I was going. Both his parents are going. He was wondering if I could stop in since they're forcing him to go before the bonfire thing."

"Wait." Zellman held his hand up. "I thought they were getting a divorce too?"

"They are, but they're both still going."

"Race's mom moved there, and his dad is rich," Jordan added. "He's going to want to mingle with the Fallen Crusties for business."

"Shit. That's a good idea."

Then both Jordan and Cross looked at me again.

A stone thudded to the bottom of my stomach. I was fairly certain what he was going to ask, but I rasped out, "You gotta say the words. I can't do anything if you don't ask me."

Cross didn't hesitate. "I want to break into her house, scope it out as much as possible."

"Score," Zellman breathed, already nodding.

This was what we did, our crew.

One of us needed something, and we were there.

Only problem was me.

I was still on probation.

But I nodded. "When do we go?"

CHAPTER THREE

I LOVED CROSS.

Best friends since seventh grade, crew members—we'd been inseparable, but we kept things platonic while he'd been a slight manwhore. All that stopped at the beginning of the school year. Things went a way we could never take back, and that was the us we were now.

I rode alongside him in the truck. It was nearing ten at night. We'd talked Race into being our eyes and ears at the country club—because we'd helped him out last year, he returned the favor. He'd agreed to stay at the party (ignoring Taz's requests to leave for the bonfire) and keep an eye on Cross' dad and his date.

Cross' phone buzzed once again. It'd been going off since we left Roussou. Jordan turned in to a ritzy neighborhood, high up on some hill. All the houses were fancy.

"What's the latest?" Jordan asked.

"Thirteen," Cross replied.

We all grinned. Taz had asked Race for the thirteenth time to go to the bonfire.

Cross sent back a text.

"What'd you say?" Zellman stuck his head in through the back window.

Cross put his phone back into his pocket, glancing over his shoulder. "I told him to give us thirty minutes; then they can leave."

"Thirty?" I asked as Jordan paused in front of a mansion. "You sure about that?"

Just eyeballing the place, I could tell it had security. A lot of security. There was a gate, a camera at the top.

This was not a good idea.

"Shit." Jordan hit the steering wheel, leaning over to get a better look. "Cross. Man—"

I finished for him. "We scale that fence, I guarantee an alarm is going to the police, and they're not that far from here—just down the hill over there. We can't get in here."

Cross glared at the house, a vein sticking out from his neck. "This is the fucking address he gave my mom. It was written on the paper next to her computer in her office. What the fuck does his girlfriend do at Kade Enterprises?" He leaned out the window, as if the mansion or the ritzy street could give us the answers.

Me? I'd moved on. I knew we weren't getting into that place, but this neighborhood? I couldn't believe people actually lived here. Every lawn was manicured, at least the ones we could see through the gates.

There were no cracks in the sidewalk. A few trees had crystal lights on them. Palm trees dotted the streets. All their streetlights worked. A lady was walking a little dog on a pink leash, and I was pretty sure there were diamonds on the dog's collar. Maybe just sequins? Either way, they was rich. That was for damn sure.

I felt two inches tall.

The lady eyed us as she drew closer, and she looked right at me. Suspicion flared, her hand going into her pocket.

"Gotta go," I muttered.

Her phone was coming out, and she was going to call the cops. I knew it.

Jordan cursed, and he moved to put the truck in drive just as another lady stepped up. She slapped her hand down on the edge of the truck bed.

"The fuck?" Z almost fell backward, scrambling around to see who had got the jump on us.

It was a middle-aged woman, and she ignored us. She was solely focused on the pink-leash-dog-walking lady, the cop-calling one. She smiled wide and raised her hand high, waving, making a big deal out of it. "Hiya, Clara! How are you doing?"

Her voice was loud too, and she was doing it on purpose.

Z scowled at her. "Lady, let go of our truck."

Her hand tightened.

Jordan opened his door and started around to her side.

She continued talking, her hand still in the air. "How's Gordon doing? Did you call Brentworth's firm? I know they're excellent at defending their clients." She gave a forced laugh, but it was a hearty one. "It never matters if they're guilty, and don't you worry about your Gordon. Even if he goes in for a little bit, I'm sure they'll send him to a day-camp sort of place."

The dog-walking woman had frozen, but after the lady gripping the truck kept on, her voice getting louder and louder, the dog walker finally yanked her dog around and hauled ass back the way they had come.

"Lady," Jordan growled, now at her side. "You need to let go of my truck. Now."

She waited, her eyes following the dog walker until she turned a corner. Finally stepping away, she removed her hand and moved toward the front of the truck. She came slowly, her hands out like she was being arrested. Her eyes found mine and held them, until all four of us were staring at her.

She raised her chin in the air, her hands going to her sides. "I know you."

Jordan moved up, just outside of Cross' door. He looked at me. Z had jumped out, coming to stand next to Jordan. He looked over too.

Cross raised his chin in challenge. His tone was chilled. "Who the fuck are you?"

She ignored him, her eyes only on me. "You're Monroe's little sister, aren't you?" She nodded to herself. "Yeah. Yeah. You are. I knew your mother, way back when. She and I used to run around together. Got into all sorts of problems." She lowered her head, her mouth forming a somber line. "I've not told anyone that. You know me?"

I shook my head. "No."

Her chest rose, and her mouth turned down before her head bobbed again. "I figured as such. I didn't know if she'd say anything. I'm Malinda Decraw-Strattan."

She said that like I should know it.

I shook my head. "I don't know you."

Her nostrils flared. "You're Channing's sister, right?"

I didn't answer.

Her eyes narrowed. "Heather Jax's fiancé, right? He proposed."

I still didn't respond.

She huffed out, "Are you serious? Or are you shitting me? Heather's best friend is my stepdaughter." She waited again for a response.

I knew who she was talking about, but not until now. Channing knew everyone in Roussou. Heather knew a whole ton of people from both towns. Someone saying they knew them didn't mean shit to me.

But the best friend part clicked into place.

A person needed a family tree to understand all the connections, but I'd listened enough to know she was talking about Samantha Kade—the Olympic runner married to a pro footballer. Yeah, even someone like me who didn't care a lot about fame and names was a little awed by that. But that wasn't why I cared. Samantha was a good friend to Heather. That's what I cared about, and the Patriot was friends with my brother. They'd come to visit a few times. Every time, I vanished. That was their life, not mine.

"Yeah." Malinda had been watching me the whole time. "Now you're getting it all. Samantha's my stepdaughter. I married the daddy who raised her." She flicked her gaze over the guys, lingering on Cross before moving to Jordan, then Zellman. "You boys play sports?"

Jordan didn't answer.

Cross said nothing.

Zellman looked at me, then her, then the others. "Are we... she's a friend, right? Not an enemy? Can I answer that question?"

Jordan flicked his eyes to the sky. "Fuck's sakes, Z."

"What? B, you never said you knew Coach Strattan's wife." He held his hand out, striding over. "I play ball. I mean, not with our school because our team sucks, but I play in the summer leagues. We're starting up in May. And I know all about your husband. He turned around Fallen Crest Public's football team. They went to State after he transferred over."

Her lips curved up. Her eyes were twinkling. "You follow sports?"

"Oh yeah. What guy doesn't?" He looked back, saw all of us just watching, and cleared his throat. "What? Like Cross isn't going to ask about whatserface. You know he is. Stop glaring at me. I'm just beating you to the punch."

Malinda's grin turned warmer, and she moved closer to the door. "My house is the back one. Was taking my garbage out and saw your truck slowing down, and no offense, but you guys don't blend. And you really don't blend this time of night. I know you ain't a group of criminals, but a bit of friendly advice from a mama bear to someone who I consider connected through family. Because Bren, honey, Channing, and Heather are family to us, so that means you're family." She looked at the guys. "You all might want to head out. I'm fairly certain a call went to the police as soon as you pulled onto the street."

Jordan's lips thinned. "If you all are that stuck-up, why the fuck don't you have a gated community?"

She laughed. "Because that costs more money, and we all need to agree on the same rules. You really don't know this block, do you? We got a fair bit of enemies living across the street from each other. That means no rules are ever agreed on, so no gate. We all just do our own."

Cross' phone buzzed. He cursed as soon as he read it.

Jordan eyed him. "They took off?"

"Shit." Cross looked at me, indecision clear in his gaze.

We were in a bad spot.

But I didn't like asking for help.

I asked under my breath, "Can we come back?"

He lowered his voice. "You know we can't get in there, even if we wanted to." He held my gaze, but moved his head in the direction of this Malinda person. "Should you ask? Or should we figure it out some other way?"

Jordan's head was down. I knew he was listening, being the closest to our door and open window, but he didn't say anything.

Z was quiet too, until he threw his hands in the air. "Enough's enough. I'm deciding. All of us suck at computer stuff, and that's the only way we're going to find anything out." He nodded at the house we'd been scoping out. "You know who lives there? Can you tell us anything about her?"

Malinda glanced at the home, her eyebrows went up, and she turned back to us. Slowly. "You're asking about Marie?" She laughed. "Marie DeVroe. She moved here a couple months ago, divorced from her husband."

She was studying me again.

Those eyes. Warm, earth-toned, but damn smart too. Her brown hair was pulled up in a ponytail. She was dressed in jeans and a nice shirt—almost like us, but I knew she wasn't like us. I didn't know why she kept referencing me, as if we should know each other. That world she came from was a million miles from mine. Yeah, there was a bridge, Heather and my brother, but the bridge was long and slim. Not much space for even them to go back and forth, as much as they did. Heather was more on Malinda's side of the bridge than Channing, but I wasn't on the bridge. I wasn't anywhere close to it.

Cross was waiting for a signal from me, whether to press for more information or not.

I was torn.

Malinda's eyes danced among us. She straightened up, her arms crossing over her chest. "Okay. I think I'm starting to get some of what is going on. You want to know about Marie? I'll give you the rich-folks stats. And I'm doing this because I used to love your mama. She was the best kind of friend a girl could have, but back to DeVroe. She's got money. Rumor is that she comes from old money back east. Her net worth is around fifteen million, but that's all just gossip, you see."

She pointed to a gate farther down. It wasn't enough to hide the massive home behind it, which looked big enough to swallow up four or five homes. "She keeps to herself, is in her middle thirties. Nice, from what I've seen. Hasn't gotten involved in any scandal so far. She works human resources for Kade Enterprises, and she freelances as a decorator."

Cross scoffed, jerking forward.

At his reaction, her eyes lit up in triumph. She sized him up, angling her head to get a better view. "Oh, wow. Look at you. You've got a model face, don't you." She grinned, tapping her chin. "That jawline could melt women's panties across the nation." She looked from him to me. "You two a thing?" She stepped back with a knowing look. "I think I'm piecing things together. I heard Marie took up a new boyfriend, met him at a work event recently. She was called in to decorate a few new offices. Hmmm... Is that someone you know?" A smirk tugged her mouth. "Your father, maybe?"

That gorgeous jaw of his closed, and he straightened, staring straight ahead.

Cross' leg had been like cement when she first started, but the more she spoke, the more that cement melted to wet clay. He wouldn't look at her, but he was listening.

I knew he clung to everything she said.

We weren't the way she was.

She was warm. I couldn't tell if she was trusting, but she came up to us not knowing who we were to do us a solid. That meant something to us, even if we were being dicks about it. Zellman would've been halfway to being her best friend by now, but he was holding back because *we* were holding back. And I was holding back because she represented a world connected to mine that I never thought I'd step foot into. That was all. I didn't know how to proceed. Trusting adults wasn't our forte either.

I did remember Heather mentioning her friend's mother. There were two, if I was remembering right. One wasn't spoken about in warm tones, but the other was. I guessed this was the one who was.

Giving her a nod and a small smile, I said, "Thank you."

"There it is." She dipped her head in approval. "Heather's talked about you. I always wondered, knowing your mama, but I never said a word—not even your brother knows I knew his mama. You've got her beauty. I heard about your father. I'm sorry for what happened. You might not know it, but I am a friend." She winked at Zellman. "I ain't no enemy of yours, you can ask Heather, though..." She tilted her head to the side. "I don't think you will, will you? If I'm feeling you right, you keep your cards to your chest. These guys are part of those cards, ain't they?"

She was almost having her own conversation, but she was right. Each of her words pierced me.

She rapped softly on Jordan's hood. "You want to hear stories about some crazy adventures your mama got involved in; you look me up. I'll tell you all about her one night." She backed off, circling around us and giving a small wave. "I'll be seeing you folks, I'm sure."

And with that, as Zellman stared after her (the only one of us waving back), she made her exit. We waited a beat, and then Jordan started laughing. "Fuck. I don't know who that lady was, or any of the people she was talking about, but she owned us."

Cross was grinning along with them, which eased my shoulders. Air moved through my lungs more freely.

Jordan came back around and got behind the wheel.

Zellman hopped up on the back. He stuck his head through the window as Jordan started the engine again. "You don't know who Mason Kade is? He was drafted to the Pats and already has two rings. Can you believe that? Bren, you know him?"

"No."

I didn't.

"Channing's friends with him."

He said it as a statement, but it was more a question.

I didn't answer, sinking into Cross' side. "Let's just go to that stupid bonfire."

For the first time in a long while, I wanted a beer.

Cross said, "We gotta pick up some of our own shit. The Academy assholes roofie their dates."

For the briefest of seconds, I had forgotten.

But oh yeah.

I hated Fallen Crest Crusties.

CHAPTER FOUR

THE DISTRICT WEEKEND was a long tradition among the three towns.

Each town took an event. The Fallen Crest bonfire was usually Sunday, but things got switched around with Frisco. The street dance was tomorrow, but I wasn't expecting to have any merriment. The street they shut down was the one that ran in front of my brother's bar and his new bounty-hunting office. Channing would be there, probably busy kicking anyone underage out of his bar, while debating selling extra booze to make some cash.

Alas, Channing was on the straight and narrow too, which meant no booze to minors. I, on the other hand, would just take whatever was under the counter like always. Still, my big bro would be there, and he'd be keeping an eye out—his unofficial role in Roussou.

Tomorrow would be a day when I'd try to disappear from the watchful eye of his guys.

But tonight was a different matter. District Weekend used to have the bonfire up in a bunch of hills north of Fallen Crest, but this time, it was on the southside and overlooking Manny's, a popular place my future sister-in-law ran.

Heather had taken over Manny's from her father, and she was now talking about doing some other franchise spots. Sometimes I forgot about that other world Heather was connected to— Channing too since he was going in on one of the franchises. Or two, maybe. I tuned them out when they talked about that stuff, usually slipping out the door and finding Cross.

Tonight, things felt different.

Not Cross, but the rest. The future. It was lingering, ever since Zellman had mentioned graduating. And the same old paralyzed emotion crept up my throat, threatening to choke off my oxygen...

Cross' arm fell around my shoulders, and he pulled me back to his chest. He pushed a cold beer into my hand and lifted his mouth, pressing a kiss to the side of my lips. "You okay?"

We'd found a spot at the back of the party in the woods.

I'd settled against a tree that offered a view of Manny's below. We could see all the cars, hear the customers going in and out. Heather stepped out once to yell at her brother and went back in. The door slammed shut behind her a second later, the sound echoing in the valley around them.

That was normal.

The familiarity had eased some of my tension, but now I had Cross for that.

As I rested against him, his hand trailed down and began rubbing my arm. He lifted his beer, taking a drag and just waiting.

He knew I'd talk.

Sometimes it took a minute.

"What are you doing next year?" *Finally.*

He stiffened, his voice low. "What do you mean?"

"You know."

More tension, then his chest rose. "I don't know."

"Bullshit." I stepped away, turning to stare at him.

Cross never lied to me.

He held my gaze.

I'd picked this place for a reason. I liked my privacy, and most of the others respected me, staying away. Only a couple of the Ryerson crew had positioned themselves not far from us. There were a handful of other guys scattered nearby. I suspected they were Fallen Crest because they were obnoxious, and they were wearing polo shirts. No one I knew from Frisco wore fucking polo shirts. Some of them had been looking over, their looks lingering more and more until Cross arrived.

I'd have to deal with them at some point, but I'd been putting it off because of my thoughts.

They were dark—then again, that term could be used to describe me. *I* was dark.

Cross glanced at them, resting his head against the tree. "Let's talk about this later."

"Yeah."

He was right.

Right?

Now wasn't the time.

But...

"I mean it." I touched his shirt, fisting a hand in it. "We graduate in a month, and no one's talked about the after."

His hand went to my hip, slipping under my shirt, and he tugged me to him. My leg brushed against his, and I tipped my head back to see him.

He rested his forehead against mine, almost whispering, "What does it matter? We're staying crew, no matter what."

Lowering my voice as well, I said, "I'm staying."

He pulled me closer and nuzzled my forehead. "I know you're staying. We all know you're staying."

"But what about you guys?"

Cross lifted a shoulder. "You want to do this now? Here?"

Normally, no. But seeing Malinda had spurred something in me, an urgency I'd been ignoring for too long.

"I guess."

"Okay." He took another deep breath and watched me. His hand moved up under my shirt, starting to explore between our bodies.

Mine did the same. I couldn't help it. If Cross touched me, I touched him back. That's how it was.

"I applied at a few places."

My head lifted in surprise.

His eyes were waiting for me. "Some local that I can drive to, and a few not local."

Shit. My tongue felt heavy now. "Where did you decide to go?"

"I haven't."

"My counselor's ingrained in my head that I need to go to college or I'll die."

He laughed as his hand moved farther up. I tugged my shirt down so the others couldn't see, but I felt his finger tracing my bra before slipping underneath. He cupped my breast, his thumb rubbing over my nipple.

"That's what high school counselors do, but we have time."

We did, didn't we?

He leaned in, his lips finding my forehead. "We have lots of time."

"Lookie, lookie, such a happy couple. Hmmm?"

Cross stifled a groan, lifting his head, but I didn't need to ask who it was. I would recognize the smugness of my ex even if I were deaf. Lifting my head, I turned and stepped away from Cross.

Drake Ryerson stood, smirking at us, with the two of his crew beside him. A few others had congregated with them as well, and the Fallen Crest guys were more wary than earlier. They should've been wary before too, but they were arrogant and ignorant, just how we liked them. Their numbers were matched by our Roussou ones now, so they should've been scampering away. They weren't.

We'd see what unfolded. If there was a confrontation, more would come running—either to join in or record it.

"What do you want, Drake?" I asked.

We'd had to deal with Drake a few times since he came back to take the leadership role for the Ryerson crew. The crew was named after their family, but ironically the only Ryerson in the crew was their leader. Alex, their last leader and Drake's little brother by one year, had been kicked out then gift-wrapped for us to kick his ass.

He'd hurt one of ours, so the debt had been a long time coming. But since then, a tentative and uneasy truce had been called among all crews. There was no longer an unsettled rift between us.

But we didn't enjoy them. And we weren't quiet about it.

Drake's eyes moved between Cross and me. A wicked grin spread over his face. "I almost feel bad, breaking up a moment for the two of you."

He was right. We rarely showed that side. And it was over now.

I moved over, and Cross stood next to me, ready to square off.

I kept my hands at my side and raised my chin. "I won't ask again."

His eyes fell flat and his mouth pressed into a thin line. "You're not being fun, Bren. You used to be fu—"

"I'd consider whether you really want to finish that statement," Cross said.

A chill ran up the length of my spine.

That was not the angry Cross from his dad's divorce, or the quiet one waiting for me to decide something. This was the Cross no one wanted to mess with, the one who had stepped out and became our crew's leader.

He was dangerous when he spoke like that—calm, and eerily in control, with a veiled promise to back up the unspoken threat.

Drake had heard it too, and he stopped. He studied Cross top to toe, then lifted his lip in a sneer. "Fine. You're right. That was rude of me." He tapped the side of his head. "Silly me. I was responding to her as another guy who's been between her legs, not the crew leader I am."

I closed my eyes, just for a moment.

There it was. The taunt.

He knew crew law. He knew I wouldn't take that and not retaliate.

I opened my eyes and saw him waiting, staring at me. I smiled. "Really?" One step ahead.

We fought. It's what we did. The insult was to me, so Cross would wait for my move. I would make the decision to advance, when I wanted to do it. And if Jordan and Zellman found out, they'd come to help. Probably Race as well, because that's what had been happening this year.

Race had moved to Roussou specifically to fight in the underground rings. He'd been training Cross, and the rest of us were no slouches ourselves, so Drake coming up here, picking this place to start a fight—there was an angle.

"Why here?" I asked him.

He smirked. "Maybe I just want to feel your hands on me again." He looked to Cross, holding there a moment before sliding back to me. "Nothing? Neither of you?"

My grin wasn't hard-pressed. This was bothering him, so that meant I'd keep it up. I didn't give a shit about our reputation. Those who did had a reason they cared.

I slid my hands into my pockets. "I'm going to be honest; I'm enjoying how much you want me to take a swing at you." I narrowed my eyes, cocking my head to the side. "Why?"

Anger flashed in his eyes. He clenched his jaw, then took a step toward me. "Why does there have to be a reason? Maybe I'm harboring some resentment for what you did to my little brother."

Cross stepped next to me, keeping up. "You gave him to us on a silver platter. And we didn't permanently harm him, per your request."

His crew members shared a look, and a couple whispered behind his back.

Drake shot them an annoyed look. "You're right. That was stupid of me to bring it up. We all voted and decided that was the smart move." His grin was forced, baring his white teeth for a second. "No hard feelings on my little brother, but my cousin, on the other hand…" His voice trailed off, and as if on cue, Drake looked behind him.

I shifted over just enough to see that very cousin, Race, coming up the path. They'd been partying a little farther down. Along with him came a trail of Normals. Taz was right next to him, holding his hand. I skimmed over the group. No Jordan. No Zellman.

The back of Cross' hand brushed mine to get my attention.

We shared a look. If Race was coming, that meant our guys knew. They had something planned. Or I hoped so, because I didn't want to get my clothes bloody tonight.

"What are you doing, Drake?"

This time it was Race asking, and he sounded just as tired as I was.

Drake's grin widened. "Look, it's the cousin I sent to seduce my ex, and he failed."

Race swallowed, his eyes passing over to me.

I folded my arms over my chest. "He became our friend instead." I tilted my head. "You really up here hoping to start another crew war? Is that what you're doing?"

He stilled at my question, his eyes firm on mine. "What do you think—"

And then there was an explosion from down in the valley.

I whirled, my heart pounding, but it wasn't Manny's.

A few people screamed. Others gasped. Guys cursed.

"Holy fuck—it's our cars! Our cars!" The Fallen Crest guys took off, sprinting back down the hill. One turned and pointed. "You fucks. This is war. Don't think we don't know it was you!"

"Come on, D!" someone yelled.

Cross frowned, stepping forward. "That's what was going on?"

Drake rolled his eyes, shrugging. "Thought you guys were in on it. What happened? Zellman not tell you the plan?"

Cross met my gaze. Race had shifted to stand beside us, Taz still holding his hand.

Drake's eyes narrowed as he dipped his head toward Race. "This why you went to their side?"

Taz gasped quietly, pulling her hand away from Race. She hid it behind her back, averting her gaze.

Drake watched her with mild curiosity.

Race shifted in front of her, rolling his shoulders back. "What of it? You're the one who told me to come here." He gestured to Cross and me. "I didn't know what I was walking into. You did, and you didn't warn me. Don't get all pissy if I'm not joining the family crew like you wanted."

Drake glared at him, all pretense gone. This was his real adversary. He showed his teeth briefly. "I wanted you to take over for my brother. Love the kid, but Alex is a hothead. You, you're supposed to be smart. You were supposed to lead so I didn't have to come back."

"That's right." Race's tone was taunting. "You were at college, right? How's that going for you? Dropped out the first semester, didn't you?"

Drake surged forward, reaching for Race's shirt as he growled, "Listen here, you little fuck—"

"I don't think so." Cross stepped between them, using that same calm, controlled, and almost deadly tone.

Drake stopped, his hand in mid-air, and his eyes snapped to Cross.

He retreated a step, bringing his hand back down. He seemed flustered, and blinked a couple times to regain control.

I looked from Drake to Race, seeing a level of animosity I hadn't in a while, at least among family members. Then I remembered: Race's father had slept with Drake's mother. The fathers were brothers. It was messy all around.

I glanced at Cross beside me. As if feeling my attention, he shifted toward me and grazed my hand, sending tingles up my arm.

I wanted to be alone with him. Right now. Forget all the bad shit in life, just him and me. That's where it was good, where it was still right.

"Right," Drake snarled, raking his hand through his hair. He motioned to his crew. "Let's go. Cops will be fucking slow here, but they're on their way." He left with a parting shot for Race. "I'll say hi to your dad for you."

CHAPTER FIVE

"YOU DO THAT," Race growled at his back, moving forward, his head lowered like he was going to charge.

Taz caught his arm, keeping him with her, and we all waited until they were farther down the hill, out of earshot.

"Race." Cross jerked his head in the opposite direction.

Race nodded, running a hand over his face. The bags under his eyes showed his exhaustion. Taz started to go with, but Cross shook his head. "Just him. Sorry."

She let go of his hand, staying put.

Cross led the way. Race was second in line. I brought up the rear.

Once we got to another clearing on the trail he'd picked, Cross turned around. We couldn't wait around either, so he spoke quickly. "What was that about?"

"Drake and me?"

"The explosions."

"Oh." Race deflated. "That was my fault. I was supposed to pass the word and forgot. It happened fast and at the last minute. I'd come up here in search of Bren when word got to us that some of the Crusties were caught in Roussou. They were trying to burn our school down."

"What?!" Cross and I exclaimed.

Cross clarified, "Academy Crusties?"

Race nodded. "Yeah, and yeah. They were caught, and they're at the Fallen Crest police station now."

"Who caught them?"

Race glanced at me, and I knew. That look said it all. I'd gotten it every day of my life.

I stepped back. "Channing did?"

"One of his crew."

I gave Race a look.

He rolled his eyes. "What? They're still his crew, and you know it. Anyway, some of the Friscians are wondering if they were the ones who burned their school down too."

"Fuck," came low from Cross.

"I know."

A new thought came to me. A sinking thought. "*Who* did those explosions?"

"Who do you think?" Race motioned around. "Who sent us up here instead of coming themselves?"

Jordan. Zellman.

Now their absence was explained.

And fuck.

Race ran his hand through his hair, much like his cousin had moments ago. "Z was almost eager to do it, said he hadn't had a lot of action for a while." Race grinned. "Too much peace, huh? Is that a thing around here?"

Cross snorted and shifted back on his feet. "So we're in a town war now?"

"I don't think so. I don't know. It was the snob school who tried to do the school thing, not Public. We can exile all Academy Crusties from the weekend events and handle them."

Cross nodded at Race, approving. "Look at you. Talking like a crew member."

Race stopped, his face reddening in the moonlight. "Yeah, well. I like certain people in Roussou."

After his parents' affair came to light and the divorce was settled, Race's mother bought a home in Fallen Crest. His dad moved to Roussou, into Alex and Drake's childhood home to be with their mom. Their dad had moved out, and I wasn't sure what had happened with him, but judging from Drake and Race just now, things were tense.

We had to go. I shouldn't ask, but... "How are you doing? With all the family stuff?"

Race's head dropped down. "I don't know. We're dealing. My mom's still letting me attend Roussou. That's all I care about."

"If things get heated, you could be a target."

"I know." Race looked at Cross. "I'm driving back and forth right now—"

"You can have my room," Cross told him.

I was having a moment. Right here. Because while Race's family had been in disarray since the beginning of the year, Cross' family had been intact. Right now, both their lives were upended by family matters, and I, for once, was doing okay. I was living in Channing's house. And yeah, he hated that Cross was there with me, but he hadn't put in the extra effort to cause a rift between us. He hadn't banned Cross from staying with us, just grumbled under his breath every time he saw us.

We tried not to let him see us.

He kept a strict curfew for us. We had to be home at midnight. But Channing knew, I knew, Heather knew, and Cross knew, that if we were going to sneak out, we were going to sneak out. Channing couldn't do anything about it.

Things had been different this past week because Channing was gone a lot for his bounty-hunting business. His old crew members were around a lot more. Where Channing was, they were. If Channing was at the house, one of those guys was usually parked in the living room.

But for once, I was the one with the steadier household.

I didn't have the parent drama. My dad was in prison. My mom was six feet under. I had older-brother drama, but no divorces, no break-ups. Channing and Heather were both doing well.

Yes. I was loving this. Did that make me the good kid here?

I thought about it.

Nah. I was still messed up. It just wasn't coming out currently. I'd stuffed that bitch all the way deep inside.

Race was saying to Cross, "—be up for that?"

Cross' face tightened. "I don't think my mom's in any position to judge right now."

We needed to go. For real.

Race's head bobbed, his hands on his hips. He moved his feet apart, adjusting his stance. "I'll talk to Taz about it, see what she thinks your mom will think."

"Tell her it's for your safety, and she'll be fine with it." He started to walk away, but stopped. "Don't fuck my sister in my bed. Don't fuck my sister at all."

Race just smiled.

Cross grimaced. "You dick."

He held his hands up. "We've been dating for, like, five months."

Cross motioned to me. "Took us nine years. Aim for that." He patted Race on the chest, starting back down the hill.

Race barked a laugh. "You had a head start on me. I haven't known your sister almost all my life."

"Give it time. You'll appreciate it better in nine years."

Cross moved ahead of us, picking up the pace.

Race and I started after him, but I felt him trying to slow me down. I could hear people scattering farther down the hill. We needed to be there too. Then, having a feeling, I went with it and stopped suddenly.

"If you have something you want to talk to me about, get it out fast. We should already be driving away by now." I motioned ahead.

Race frowned. "Listen." He scratched his neck and tugged his collar away before letting it drop back in place. "I—uh...you're friends with Taz, and you're dating Cross. How do you handle that? I mean...where are the lines for you?"

I narrowed my eyes. "What's going on?"

"It's just a question. I mean, if something popped up that you think the other should know—"

"I'd tell Cross in a heartbeat."

He stopped, his hand still at his collar. Then he let it fall to his side. "Fuck."

36

"Why?"

He was rubbing his forehead now.

These were all signs of something coming down the pipeline I wouldn't want to hear. But better to get this dealt with right away than let it simmer and fester. That was never good. I should know. That's what I usually did.

"Out with it, Race. What's going on?"

"Shit." He drew a ragged breath. "You know their parents are divorcing."

"Yes..." Where was he going with this?

He twisted around, as if looking for an escape route. "Taz told me her mom might be moving with her, wherever she goes for college next year."

That topic again. The future. College and—screeching sounds. Halt. Back up.

I blinked a couple times. "What? Say again?"

"Taz heard her mom on the phone the other night. The divorce is going fast. Their prenup was pretty solid, and neither is really fighting it. I guess they've been struggling for a while. Anyway, their dad is officially moving to Fallen Crest—some girlfriend there or something—and their mom, well, she's going with Taz wherever she goes."

"Oh."

Cross would be left in Roussou with no family. No sister. No mother. His dad was already gone.

Race was watching me now. "Does he see his dad at all?"

Here was the hypocritical line with me. I demanded Race tell me things he probably had no right to tell me, but now he was asking about Cross, and my loyalties always lay with him.

I gave him a look.

He nodded, accepting that.

"Well..." Race jerked his head toward the path. "Not to lay that on your shoulders, but I'm guessing you'll tell Cross?"

He was going to be without his family.

Echoes resounded in my head. I felt them in my chest, my heart squeezing, bringing me back to when my dad was first arrested.

"Bren?"

"Huh?" I looked up.

Race had gone farther ahead. He stopped and saw I hadn't moved. "You okay?"

No, but I didn't matter.

CHAPTER
SIX

THERE WERE FIRES to be put out. Literally.

When we got to the bottom of the hill, five cars were in flames. Zellman had gone *all out*. Most people had scattered. We were behind the rush, so I couldn't imagine what it had looked like when everyone hit the lot. The cops were coming, I was sure—we were lucky they weren't there already.

As soon as I got to the parking lot, Zellman pounded the top of Jordan's truck. "Bren! Hurry up."

Cross was in the back with Zellman in the front, waving through the window. Jordan was at the wheel. They couldn't get to me. There were too many vehicles and people in the way, so I veered around, motioning to the north end of the lot. They met me, gunning the engine and jerking to a stop right in front. I grabbed hold of the bed and jumped. Cross reached for me and hoisted me up; I was over within a second. Then we were down, all the way against the bottom. Cross wrapped his arms around me, and we braced ourselves.

"Go!" he yelled, pounding on the side of the truck.

A second later, we were off. Sirens colored the sky behind us, the sounds getting closer and closer. We had to go the complete opposite way we needed to, but the drive wasn't too bad once we got out of Fallen Crest. Jordan slowed down when we hit the back roads, and Cross settled into me, nuzzling my neck. His hand smoothed over my shirt. "What'd Race have to say?"

Shit. Should I do this now?

I eyed him. I'd want him to tell me.

"He told me your mom is going to move wherever Taz goes to college. And that things are serious with your dad and his girlfriend." There was more. I couldn't pull my punches. "And that the divorce is almost done."

He was quiet for a moment and then rolled to his back. He kept one arm cradling me but stared up at the sky.

His hand rested on his chest, our bodies bouncing lightly from the gravel. "Fuck."

He was going to be without his family, unless...

God. I couldn't think that.

...he went with them?

Just the thought of that hit me hard in the chest. Pain sliced through me, and I felt tears welling up. If he went with them? I was supposed to stay here. That's how it was. Channing was here. Roussou was my home. I was ride or die, and that meant with my home too. I just knew it was not in the cards for me to move. Here, I could survive. Here, I could live. Somewhere else... That wasn't how it was supposed to go. I felt it in my gut, so if he went...

What would I do?

"Shit," he cursed again.

"Yeah."

"Shit."

"Yeah." I felt a tear forming. It hadn't fallen yet.

He ran a hand over his face, rolling back to me. Seeing the tear, he reached over and flicked it away. And because he knew me, his smile was so sad.

"I'm not going." He leaned in, his forehead pressed against my shoulder, into my neck. He wound his arm around me and held our bodies together. "I'm not going anywhere without you."

Fucking futures.

Who needed those things?

I felt another tear at the ready. I hated those things.

I didn't cry. I would bleed, but I wouldn't leak that way. I reached for him. I needed a different way to push away my sudden blind panic, because it was threatening to run over me, crushing me in its wake.

"Cross," I said quietly. I fisted a hand in his shirt and pulled him.

He lifted his head, his eyes surprised, but I know he saw my torment. His face softened. His hand came to my stomach, and he pressed a long kiss to the corner of my mouth. "I got you."

I mewled, needing something to drive away these feelings.

"Shhhhhh," he whispered, looking up to make sure Z or Jordan couldn't see. We were too close to the back of the window. Spotting a sweatshirt, he sat up, grabbed it, and laid it over me, then his hand slid underneath.

I grasped his arm, arching my back a little.

"Don't move." He pressed another kiss to my ear. "They'll know."

His hand was working as he spoke, finding my pants, undoing the top button, then moving the zipper down, just enough. He peppered kisses over my throat, and then with a groan, he pulled his mouth away. He sat up, propping himself up on his elbow, his head over me as if we were just talking.

But his hand. That hand.

It was inside my underwear, rubbing me, and I felt him searching for my entrance.

I grabbed his neck, my fingers digging in, just as his slid inside of me.

I gasped, but he dropped another kiss to my mouth, silencing me. His fingers moved in and out of me, quickly, but going deep, getting every groove. Sliding. Pulling out. Thrusting back in.

Pleasure pulsed through me, going to my fingers and toes, up my neck, and I groaned.

He grinned again, as he kissed me. "Shhh."

I bit my lip, nodding. I loved Z and Jordan like family, but I didn't want them to have any part of this. I closed my eyes, knowing Cross would keep up the act like we were talking, all while his fingers kept moving inside of me.

It was building.

Spreading.

I was close.

More dipping in, sliding out, thrusting, holding—his thumb pressed down on my clit, and I began to come apart.

A guttural moan left me, but I bit down harder on my lip. My eyes flew open; I needed to see Cross. He stared at me hard, fierce. His eyes gleamed with his own repressed need, and as if he couldn't help himself, his head dipped down, his mouth firm on mine. I opened and his tongue swept in, commanding, and he finished me. Sensations ripped through me, almost before I was ready, and I trembled in the aftermath. The climax took something out of me.

I sank down against the truck bed, but Cross' tongue swept against mine, gentling the aftermath until I was a puddle.

I moaned, cupping his cheek.

When I nodded to say I was okay, he moved to hold me again. His chin tucked into my neck, and we stayed like that the rest of the drive. I felt him; he had swelled up against his jeans, and I knew he needed release too. Once we were home, I would take care of him.

His eyes caught mine, and he smiled. He leaned in. "I'm never going to leave you. Know that."

Emotion clogged my throat, but I just squeezed his hand and rested my head on his chest.

Home. I just needed to get home.

CHAPTER SEVEN

A NOTE WAS taped to my door when we got home—not the main door, my bedroom door. The lights were off, Channing's bedroom door was open, and no one was inside, so I wasn't too surprised. I took the note off and read it aloud, "No fucking. Stay home. Shit went down tonight, and I want you safe."

Cross read it over my shoulder, a light chuckle warming my shoulder. "That's cute. Treating us like we're normal teenagers."

He swept past me, going into the room and dropping his bag on the floor. He touched my arm, his finger sliding down as he passed me on the way back out to the kitchen. "I'm hungry. You?"

"No."

After a moment, he opened the fridge, and I heard him rummaging around. As he moved around the kitchen, I read the note again. Channing knew about the Academy Crusties. One of his crew found them, so either Channing was at the station doing what he could to keep peace between the towns or he was at work. Oh hell. I didn't know where he was. There was a handful of places he could be, so I just pulled my phone out.

I heard loud sounds behind him when he answered, "Tell me you're home. You're both home."

"We're home."

"You and Cross?"

There was shouting behind him. I couldn't make out the words.

I frowned. "Where are you?"

"What?!" his voice came through loud.

I'd started to repeat myself when he spoke over me, still just as loud, "Yeah. I know. I'm talking to my sister. Give me a minute." He came back to me, "Give me a second." A moment later, the shouting faded, and I heard a door shut. "I'm at the warehouse."

The warehouse was technically his—a building set on a bunch of acreage outside of Roussou—but his crew used it to hang out.

"Why are you there?"

"Because some fucking high school idiots tried to burn your school today, and I know how this shit starts," he griped. "I was a part of it in my day, and I don't want bloody streets, people saying they're going to rape somebody, and exploding fucking cars, which I'm just now hearing happened at the District Weekend bonfire." He stopped, breathing hard. "Was that you guys?"

Cross came out of the kitchen, leaning against the wall as he folded his arms over his chest. I didn't even need to put Channing on speaker. I knew Cross could hear him plain as day.

I didn't answer.

"Bren!"

I locked eyes with Cross, but he just stared back. I knew we were feeling the same resignation. This was another day in our lives.

"What do you want me to say?"

Channing cursed, then cursed some more. He paused, and another savage litany came out. "You're fucking kidding me."

I sighed into the phone. "What do you want me to say? That we've suddenly become different people? This is what we do. This is what we live—"

"Then maybe you shouldn't live it anymore!"

I stopped. Six months ago, I would've taken those words a whole different way. Now, I just closed my eyes for a beat.

"Fine. Let's play that game. You leave, I leave."

"Fucking hell, Bren. Just—your crew did the cars? Is that what you're saying?" His voice cracked, but he was calmer.

"Yeah."

Another quiet curse under his breath. "Okay. One of those kids who tried to burn the school down, he's saying Alex Ryerson put him up to it. Now..." He barked out that word before I could process what he'd just said, and he gentled his tone. "I don't know if that's true or not. What I do know is that if the kid is lying, he's doing it intentionally. If he's not lying—"

Now I cut him off, my hand almost breaking my phone. "If he's not lying, Alex is going to be torn apart by everyone." Including me.

Cross' eyes narrowed to slits, like I knew they would at the mention of Alex's name.

Channing spoke, quiet and calm now. "Tell me about Ryerson—Alex. He's been in school again for a week, right?"

Channing knew Drake had handed his little brother over to us.

He also knew Alex had been in the hospital for a month to recover, and he came back to school without a crew and with a whole slew of people who hated him.

Besides trying to use his crew to beat up his cousin for family matters, not crew matters, he'd put Taz in the hospital when she got in the crossfire. Alex came back to school like a beaten dog.

I relayed all of that to Channing. "Yeah, he's been back a week. There were a few fights, but that's to be expected after what he did. No one who went after him like us, though. I think it was some of his old crew members pushing him around, maybe a couple jocks."

"Okay."

He didn't sound okay. I hissed as I relaxed my hand.

There'd been peace. Almost four complete months of minor hiccups, and now this? Out of the blue?

Cross pushed off the wall. He strode over, his hand out, and a settled look on his face. "Give me the phone," he murmured softly.

I handed it over. My gut was churning, but I couldn't do anything here. I knew that.

Cross put the phone to his ear and said, "All due respect to you, Channing, but if there's a town rivalry starting again, this isn't your watch anymore." His eyes held mine, fierce. "It's our turn now."

He was right.

Channing had run Roussou in his day. To an extent, he still did, but Cross was right. This was high school. This was ours.

I nodded, taking the phone back. I didn't give my brother time to argue, saying over him, "We'll let you know what happens."

"Bren! Cross—"

I hung up.

I stood there, staring at Cross. We had to let the realization of what we'd just done wash over us. Fully. Because right now, right here, we were breaking away from everything we'd done before.

We'd always followed Channing.

He was the crew godfather, and his crew ran everything, but this was different. This wasn't them pushing against a motorcycle club wanting to traffic drugs through town—that was their territory. This was ours.

This was right, what we'd just done.

I watched Cross' pulse ticking in his neck. "We can stay at Jordan's."

That felt right. More appropriate.

"What do we tell them about Alex?" I asked.

He thought about it. "We can interrogate him first?"

His eyes held mine, a darkness shining from them. I saw it, and I felt it rising up inside of me. All that chaos I had pushed down, all the healing at counseling I'd done over the last ten weeks, my community service—I was going to shove it aside, just because Cross asked me to.

I nodded. "Let's go."

But as he started for the kitchen. I reached out, remembering the truck, remembering how he hadn't gotten his release.

"Wait." I pulled him to me, feeling him line up right where he was supposed to. Just before his mouth touched mine, I said, "We have time. I owe you something." My hand slid down his chest, going to his jeans, and I unbuckled his pants.

He grinned, moving in, his lips grazing mine. "I'm thinking I like this something."

I found him through his boxers and wrapped my hand around him. He groaned, dipping to kiss me fully, harder, rougher.

"Fuck," he rasped.

I started to stroke him as he grew hard again, rising.

His hand wrapped around my back, then slid down to my hip. Lifting me in the air, Cross carried me to my room. We left the light off, shut the door, and went to my bed. He was over me until I pushed him off, my hand still moving up and down. "Back up."

"What?"

I pushed him, guiding him to stand before the bed. I grinned at him before pulling his pants down and lowering my mouth.

"It's my turn."

His hands caught in my hair just as my mouth closed around him, and he surged upward. "Oh, fuck."

Yeah. That was about right.

CHAPTER EIGHT

"YOU KNOW YOUR brother won't let this go. He's going to do something."

It was five in the morning. We were camped outside of Alex Ryerson's gym. We didn't want to take him when he left his house. Their driveway was too long, and Drake could've been there. Alex wasn't in a crew, so rules were different for him than if Drake got involved.

I grunted in response to Cross' low warning and shifted, resting my feet on his dashboard, coffee in hand. "I know. I figure we'll deal with him later, though."

Five in the morning was seriously too early to do what we were about to do, especially after Cross and I had not adhered to Channing's no fucking rule. We'd only gotten to sleep a few hours ago.

Cross yawned, rubbing his face. He shifted back, his arms crossed over his chest. "Remind me why we're not in bed right now?"

"Because..." I yawned. "Because we wanted to grab him first before anyone else got to him. Also, we wanted to avoid my brother when he got home."

"Oh yeah." Cross shot me a grin. "That's the real reason."

"Exactly."

But damn, it was early. I needed a coffee refill ASAP or I was going to get cranky. No one wanted that.

"Since we're here, we should talk about things."

My stomach twisted at Cross' somber tone.

I looked over to find him watching me with the resigned expression we'd both worn last night.

He pressed his lips together. "Your brother's been kind to let me stay at your house, but it was bound to end. He hates that we're screwing under his roof."

I grunted again. That's all I could do to participate.

I loved my brother. I'd always loved him, but our relationship was messy. We'd had more good lately than bad, but there were still bad times. He'd officially left the house when our mom died, but he'd been mostly gone for years before that. The fact that I was still in the house was an achievement, as far as I was concerned. All the bullshit about not having sex was just bullshit. Channing didn't talk about who he'd banged, but I knew he and Heather had started having sex way earlier than Cross and me.

Also, Channing was barely home lately. The strict curfew had slipped when his bounty-hunting business started taking off, and so did our family dinners. Cross had been sleeping in my room for almost a full month before Channing caught him, and he flipped out, but what'd he expect?

"You think he's going to do something if we start staying at Jordan's?" Cross asked.

"Yes." I ground my teeth together. "But it won't be the way most adults deal with runaway kids, like call the cops. He'll just sic someone from his crew on us."

I knew I was right. Moose. Congo. Lincoln. Chad. Any of them. They all looked like a mix of professional body-builders (except Lincoln, who was lean), members of a motorcycle club, and SWAT. And when they wore their bulletproof vests for bounty-hunting runs, those guys didn't mess around.

Cross laughed. "They wouldn't... They wouldn't burn down Jordan's shed...would they?"

We shared a look and groaned.

They totally would.

I shook my head. "We can't stay at Jordan's."

"Fuck."

Exactly.

But that was a problem for later on, because Alex's truck had just rolled into the parking lot. It was game time.

Cross and I got out, both knowing immediately how we were going to handle this. No words were needed. I jogged down to circle around from the rear as Cross went over the lot, coming at Alex just as he got out of his truck, a duffel bag in hand.

He shut the door, took one step, and stopped.

Cross was right there, his arms crossed over his chest. "Ryerson."

Alex just sighed, dropping the bag to the ground. "You alone?" But even as he asked, he was looking for me, coming up behind him.

I didn't cross my arms. My hands were at my sides.

Alex shook his head. "I should've saved my breath." He sighed, his shoulders hunching forward. "What do you guys want?"

The hospital stay didn't seem to have affected Alex. He was still stout, and almost as muscular as before. His round face seemed a bit harder, but maybe that was just my opinion. His eyes were a little close together, sunken in, but there was no scruff this morning.

"You sent those guys to burn the school down last night?" I asked.

Alex's head shot up, and his eyes bulged. "What? No—what?"

"Please. Like you don't still have loyal friends to tell you what happened last night." I stepped in, lowering my voice so we didn't draw attention and also for Cross, who'd gone to ice statue status.

We'd gotten our vengeance, but it'd never be enough for Cross, not after what Alex did to Taz.

"We're telling you one of the guys squealed and said you put him up to it." I raised an eyebrow. "Since when did you become so friendly with guys from Fallen Crest Academy?"

Alex shut down and leaned back against his truck, folding his arms over his chest. "I'm confused. Are you asking if I had someone burn the school down or for tips on getting better friends?"

Cross stepped closer, his eyes almost dead. "We can beat the shit out of you now, and no one would give a damn. Remember that."

Alex swallowed, his Adam's apple bobbing up and down. Wariness flashed over his face. "I'm giving you attitude because I'm not stupid enough to try anything like burning our school down. Why the hell would I do that?"

Easy answer. "So you're not forced to attend Roussou where you're hated, loathed, and detested?" I gave him a tight smile, narrowing my eyes. "It worked with Frisco. All those students are getting bused here or Fallen Crest. Our school goes down, and your family is wealthy enough to what? Homeschool you, if they decide not to have you attend somewhere else?"

Cross moved in. "Roussou's hard to survive if you're hated, but your family has money. You're one of the exceptions in town. It'd be easy for you to go somewhere else, maybe a private school. They like to pride themselves on being safer and a better education than anywhere else around here. Fallen Crest Academy comes to mind as one of those schools."

Cross' tone was slightly mocking. Mine was just cold.

Alex gazed between us before holding his hands up. "I'm not going to lie and say I enjoy going to Roussou now. Shit's different. I've got no friends, or yeah, maybe one or two who are scared to let anyone know they're still friends with me, but no one who'd do that shit. I wouldn't even roll the dice. Say I did do that, set someone up, I know word's gonna get out as to who was behind it, and what then? I'm more hated? By all of the crews *and* the Normals? Please. I'm dumb, but I'm not that dumb."

He bent to pick up his bag. "I'm just surviving the end of this year. I have to do some summer school to catch up on what I missed, but after I graduate, I'm out of here. I'm not in the crew life anymore."

He waited to see if we'd stop him, but neither of us made a move.

Going around us to the sidewalk, he stopped. "Listen. Watch my brother, okay? He didn't come back to take over the Ryerson crew, no matter what he said. I don't know why he's here, but it's not for them."

Cross' eyes flickered to mine, a question there.

I wondered the same thing.

Alex saw the look. "I don't think he came back for Bren either. He enjoyed meddling in your relationship before, sending Race here to try to get between you, but I'm sharing a house with him. If he cared about either of those things, he'd be grilling me about your crew and Channing, but he's barely home."

"Is he with the crew?"

"No. Half the time they're calling me to find out where he is."

Another truck pulled in, and Alex clammed up real quick. "I can't say any more. And do me one favor? If you're going to question me again, don't do it at school. I'm already a target there." Tightening his grip on his bag, he threw it over his shoulder and headed inside.

Two bodybuilder types strolled past, eyeing us, but they went by without a word.

Cross came over to stand next to me, facing the gym. "What do you think?"

I shook my head, my stomach twisting. "I don't know. When'd we ever learn we could trust Alex Ryerson?"

"True." His arm brushed mine. "I hate to say this, but we should get more information from your brother, find out what exactly he was told. Then, if we have to, we question Alex again, but in the crew way."

Which meant violence, lots of it.

I nodded, feeling like I was forty years old. "Not yet. Let's go bunk down at Jordan's and tell him and Z when they wake up what's going on."

"Okay."

⌒‿⌒

We didn't get the chance.

Word had spread by the time we woke up at Jordan's after a few hours. Jordan didn't even know we were there until we came down from the loft he and his father had installed last month.

We found him sitting on the couches with Race, Zellman, and Taz, talking about what Alex had done.

"Whoa!" Jordan did a two-step as we came down the stairs, jerking and spilling some of his beer. "What—when did you guys get in?"

Taz had a coffee. Ignoring Jordan, I went right for her and plucked it out of her hands.

"Um. Okay. There you go, yeah... I brought it for you."

I smiled and sank into the seat next to her. "I'm sorry. I'll go on a coffee run after I drink this. I promise."

Race chuckled, handing her his coffee instead.

Z had been tossing a ball in the air, but caught it and leaped over his chair to the kitchenette. "No problem. I'll brew a pot." He snickered, grabbing a filter. "We've even got flavored coffee. Bam. How about that?"

Taz frowned. "Huh?"

"Nothing." Cross yawned, rubbing the back of his neck before taking the seat Zellman just left. "You guys heard about Alex?"

Race grunted. "I'm not surprised either."

Taz turned her frown toward her boyfriend, reaching for his leg.

Jordan scooted to the edge of his seat. "Why are you guys here?"

Cross glanced at me. I glanced back, then sipped more coffee. I wasn't quite ready to get into all of this, but we'd heard Zellman's exclamation about how that "piece of shit Alex set the whole thing up," so we were already here.

Cross stood as Zellman finished the coffee and started back for the chairs.

"Nah, man. You looked wrecked." Zellman grabbed a stool and brought it over.

Cross rubbed his jaw, still standing. "If I sit again, I'll fall back asleep. We—" He indicated me. "—had an eventful evening. You guys heard the rumor, then?"

"Yeah." Jordan jerked his chin up. "What do you know?"

"We heard last night from Channing—"

I jumped in, feeling more alive now. "We caught Alex going

into the gym this morning. We didn't realize everyone would know about the rumor."

Jordan waved that off, scooting back in his chair. "The fucker is blabbing to everyone. They don't want the shit beat out of them, so they're putting the blame on Ryerson." He paused, glanced at Race, and amended, "They're blaming *Alex*, I mean."

Race glowered. "Too many of us, if you ask me." He slid his eyes toward me on the couch, a simmering heat there. "Drake should not be here."

I saluted him with his girlfriend's coffee. "Couldn't agree more."

Feeling Cross watching me, I waited to see if he'd share what else we knew. But though Race and Taz were close friends to the crew and family, nothing could make them a part of the Wolf Crew. That sanctity was still there.

Jordan gave me a questioning head tilt, and I shook mine in response. He knew there was more to say, but he nodded. The message had been received.

Zellman spun around on his stool.

"What's the plan then?" Race looked around.

"Since the rumor's out, your cousin better transfer schools already," Cross said. "Whether it's true or not, he's a target."

Race said, "I know, but that's on him. He dug his own grave."

"All fucking six feet of it." Cross moved toward the kitchenette and the coffee.

Taz looked down, but turned to watch her brother walk away for a moment.

"You never answered," Jordan said to me. "When'd you guys roll in here?"

"This morning, after we talked to Alex."

His eyes stayed narrowed. He was salivating to hear what we weren't saying.

I smirked.

He scratched his nose with his middle finger.

I laughed, and then coughed to cover it up when Taz frowned my way.

"So..." Zellman was clueless to everything, stretching his arms over his head. "Where's the party before the street dance tonight?" He looked from Cross, to Jordan, to me, and back again. "Party? Right? Or are we doing something else?"

Cross was coming back, a coffee mug in hand. "Do we have damage control after what you did last night?" He nodded to Z, then switched to Jordan. "People know it was you guys who did the cars."

Zellman harrumphed. "Fuck that. No way. Besides, that's payback for all those years ago. We still hear about that shit with the Broudou brothers. It's been a long time coming that we explode *their* cars."

Cross frowned. "Except those guys weren't from the Academy. They were from Public."

Zellman shrugged, going back to spinning his stool around. "Who cares? They're both the same."

I picked up a pillow and threw it at him. "My future sister-in-law went there. They aren't the same."

He caught the pillow, incredulous. "Seriously? You're vouching for the public school?"

"I'm not going that far, just doing my sister-in-law duties here."

"And Heather is right chill, but she doesn't go there anymore." He raised his hand, rubbing his thumb over his two front fingers. "She's busy making money now."

Jordan coughed. "Back to the matter at hand." He nodded to Cross. "I doubt we need to worry about payback. They were going to burn our school down. They got caught, and we didn't. That's on them."

I laughed. "We're better at being criminals."

Jordan grinned before resting his elbows on his knees. He cupped his hands together. "I've never heard of anyone from the Academy being a problem for us. We'll have to find out the truth, whether Alex set them up or not."

Cross nodded, resting a hip on the couch next to me. "That's what I was thinking. Alex said he had nothing to do with it, that he's stupid but not that stupid."

"You agree with him?" Race asked.

We all turned to him.

"Do *you*?" Cross asked

Race was silent a beat, his eyes downcast. "I don't know. As much as I truly hate my cousin, he was twisted up about hurting Taz. The fucker tried to kill himself, and he would've if you guys hadn't been there."

One of our rare "good guy" moments. Let's just forget the reason we went there in the first place. In the grand scheme of things, does that really matter?

"I can't see him stewing over it in the hospital," Race continued. "Drake told him he'd be back in the crew if he let you guys give him a beat-down for Taz. Then he went back on it and actually laughed in his face. That's what I heard, anyway. If he was going to be pissed at anyone, I'd think it would be his brother. Not our school. Alex was king of the dipshits at Roussou." He grunted. "He fit right in."

I pursed my lips. Was there an insult in there? Then I shrugged. I somewhat agreed with him. There were a lot of dipshits at our school, just not anyone in this room.

Zellman was still spinning.

Well, maybe one. Though we loved him immensely.

"Okay," Cross announced. "We'll ask around and see what happens."

Everyone nodded, and the matter was decided—for now.

CHAPTER NINE

RACE AND TAZ weren't in any hurry to leave.

They stayed until Taz's phone, Jordan's phone, and even Zellman's phone started blowing up. The girls wanted to party, but there was a rule. Jordan's parents were okay if he had our group here, but no big blow-out parties. So everyone was heading to Tabatha's.

I'd never been there, but it was a big Normal party place, and once we got there, I wasn't surprised. I had to laugh softly.

"What?" Cross asked, parking his truck.

"I always think of Roussou and Fallen Crest as an us-versus-them thing. We're the poor ones, and they're the wealthy ones." I gestured to Tabatha's three-story home. "But I think I'm getting it wrong."

It was obvious Tabatha's parents were doing well.

I knew Race's family was wealthy, and Alex and Drake's parents had a huge estate themselves.

Cross reached over and took my hand in his. "It's a mix. A lot of the Normals' parents work for companies in Fallen Crest, but yeah, I think it's a little more evenly distributed than it was a few years ago."

There'd also been a boom in business recently. I knew Channing's bar was drawing in local college students from a town thirty minutes away.

My chest constricted, just the slightest bit. "Ever get the feeling you're sitting in a car that's not moving, and everything is traveling past you instead?"

Cross was quiet, studying me.

For a split second, I was back in my old house. I could hear my mom throwing up from the cancer treatments. I could hear my dad's drunken yells. I could hear Channing cursing at him before the inevitable sound of something or someone being slammed into a wall, then feet stampeding, racing for the door, and that door slamming into silence.

Channing was the first to leave. Always.

My dad wasn't long after him, heading to the bar, and then silence. Maybe an occasional puke sound from my mom's bathroom before she crawled into bed, turned the light off, and went to sleep as if nothing were happening—as if our lives weren't coming apart.

Only after complete silence had transcended would I get up from the corner I'd been curled in.

I would pad down the hallway in my bare feet and make a ball at the end of my mom's bed, a blanket pulled around me. I'd stay there until my dad would tumble down the hallway, returning from the bar. Sometimes he'd trip over me and not know. Then I'd go back to my room, get in my bed, and wish Cross would come stay with me.

"Bren?" Cross ran his thumb over the back of my hand.

I blinked, startling and coming back to the present. "Sorry. I...uh..." Yeah. My throat had swollen. "We gotta tell Jordan what Alex said about Drake."

"I know. We'll find the time."

I nodded, still eyeing Tabatha's house. This whole party scene was not my usual thing. But my old derision for the Normals wasn't there, not as much anymore. It was more a flicker.

Things *had* changed.

"You want to talk about something?" Cross asked.

I shook my head. "Not at all."

He rested his head against his headrest. "You want to drink on our hill?"

Yes. But I wasn't ready. I hadn't been back in so long. I didn't want to feel the memories.

"No. Let's go to a Normal party." I grinned. "Words I bet you never thought you'd hear me say."

"No, not really." He smiled fondly, staring back at me. He cupped my cheek. "We can skip—the party, the street dance. J and Z have their girls. They'll be fine. There's no crew war now."

I knew what he was offering: an entire day for me to wallow. We'd go to that hill, drink a bottle of whiskey, and I'd look for a ghost I was never going to see again.

I shook my head. "I feel like something's coming, something big. We need to be with the guys until it hits."

"Okay." He leaned over, kissing me softly.

We walked side by side up to the house.

———

Tabatha greeted us at the door with a warm smile and glazed eyes. She was happy. She threw her arms around Cross, who stiffened and shoved her away. "The fuck?"

She blinked a few times, that sloppy grin turning sloppier. "Oh. Sorry." Turning to me, her eyes brightened. She reached out. "Bre—"

"Don't even think about it."

Her arms dropped, and she laughed. "You're so funny. I like you. I used to hate you, then I was just scared of you, but I like you now. I don't think you'd ever hurt me."

She was nearing dangerous territory.

"You're just all bark and no bi—"

Jordan stepped up behind her, his hand on her hip as he pulled her back to his chest. "Babe." He dropped his head down, nuzzling her neck a second.

"Hmmm, honey?"

There were the nicknames again. Except it wasn't cute this time because Sweets was pissing me off. I had a tendency to hate when people told me how I was, especially when I never asked for it.

He murmured, "Bren's not on probation for having no bark. You might want to remember that."

She jerked.

I waited. There was another thing she needed to remember: my hands on her. Violence might be distasteful to the likes of her, but it was our way—good, bad, dirty, or just bloody.

"Oh." Her smile slipped.

She remembered.

She blinked a few times before edging back a step, further into Jordan. He folded his arms around her, lifting his head to wink at Cross and me.

"How about you and me go somewhere private?" he asked her. "I need some time with my girl."

He pulled her away, nodding to us. "Z's outside," he said in parting. "He already did two kegstands."

"Shit." Cross' jaw firmed, and he started forward.

There were people everywhere. It was nearing four in the afternoon, and I wondered when this had started. Probably this morning. Normally people moved back when they saw us. Not today. They were everywhere, running, jumping, dashing, falling back, stumbling. Drunken laughter and shrieks, and slurred conversations. We caught the end of one girl telling her friend to just do it, "break the ass seal."

Cross shot me a grin over his shoulder.

I shook my head. Not solid advice, on any day.

Outside wasn't any better. Tabatha had a pool and a massive backyard. A small white shed stood in the far corner, with a literal white picket fence around it. A tanned, athletic guy came through the gate next to the house, a bong in hand and a long hose for funneling. His hat was on backward, and he wore a tank over beefy muscled arms and swim trunks. Behind him were about twenty friends who looked just like him.

"Hell yeah! This is where the party is." He bobbed his head. "Nice." He wasn't talking to anyone in particular, and at first, no one paid him any attention, but he kept on. He walked into the backyard as if it were his own. "Who's ready to party? We need to kick it up a notch. Yeah, man!"

Again, he wasn't talking to anyone. His eyes moved over the group, and one by one, people started noticing him. His grin grew, his head still bobbing.

I checked, but there were no headphones in his ears.

He spread his arms wide. "So this is a Roussou party? Where are the greeters? Where's the shots? Come on, people. I thought you all were so badass. I feel cheated."

Cross stopped beside me.

Zellman was off by the keg, but he moved closer now, his eyes on this guy.

"What the fuck?" Zellman growled.

I almost blanched, the beer smell was so strong.

That's when the Douche Guy saw us and did a double-take. He held up his funnel and pointed at me. "I know you. You're Heather Jax's sister, ain't you?"

Another growl from Zellman, but deeper. He moved forward a step.

My eyes narrowed. "Who are you?"

"I'm Zeke." He bounced his chin up as he said his name, and then nodded toward his friends who had started to fan out around him. "These are my boys."

Zellman went another step, one of his hands in a fist at his side. "You're from Fallen Crest Academy."

Zeke gazed at him a second, nonplussed, then his mouth broke out in another blinding flash of smile. "Hell yeah, we are. You heard of us, huh?"

Zellman, normally happy-go-lucky, just wants to drink and get laid, raised his head. His tone was ice cold. "I know you're the fuckers whose cars I exploded."

Had he...

No.

Wait.

He had. He went there.

I took a small breath. That cemented it. We were fighting.

Zeke's smile slipped, and he lowered his head. "The fuck? That was you?"

Three of his friends shoved forward. I could almost smell the tanning lotion coming off of them. They looked like surfers who enjoyed lifting weights, a lot. Zeke could've been a linebacker.

One of the guys jabbed a hand at Zellman. "That was you?"

He took another step forward. "Yeah, fucker. That was me. You guys sent your pals to burn our school down."

The big guy started to move forward, but Zeke slapped a hand on his chest, his eyes on Zellman before going to me, then Cross. "We didn't do that. That little prick's been dealt with, and he's insisting one of yours made him do it. Your fight's with one of yours."

Zellman growled again as the patio door slid open with a hiss. Jordan popped out from it, a bunch of other guys behind him. I looked for any Ryerson crew, but there were none. We were surrounded by Normals. Still. The jocks from our school matched theirs in size and muscle. They just didn't have clothing as bright as the Academy kids'. Those guys enjoyed their red, neon blue, and yellow shirts.

Jordan shoved through the crowd that had gathered to watch. "Get lost. You're not welcome here."

"Yeah?" Zeke's nostrils flared. "Who the fuck are you?"

"This is my girlfriend's house."

Tabatha came to his side, her arms crossed over her bikini-clad chest. "This is my house. You're not invited."

Zeke's eyes were still narrow, sweeping over Tabatha, Jordan, Zellman, Cross, and finding me.

Why me? Seriously?

A girl could only *not* fight back so many times before her parole office would get a call. I'd been good for so long.

"You," he snarled.

Yeah. There went that peaceful record.

I moved around Zellman and Jordan, staring right back at him. "I don't take kindly to being talked to like that. Change your fucking tune."

He got one chance. That was it.

"Where the fuck do you get the idea that yo—"

That was it. I slipped my hand in my pocket, brought my knife out in a flash, and I was across the yard the next beat.

He stopped talking because there was metal against his flesh.

He froze, his eyes popping out.

I leaned forward, my arm locked in place. "You want to finish that stateme—"

But it was too late for me too.

I made the first move, so the rest had to back me up. They did. The guys near Zeke were shoved back. I didn't look to see who grabbed who, but I waited until all the movement was done. Shouting. Curses filled the air. A girl yelled and harrumphed. All the while, I waited, my eyes locked with Zeke's.

I was letting him see me, the real me. The me Tabatha Sweets forgot sometimes. Because deep down, no matter how much therapy and community service had rehabilitated me, there was still a feral animal in me. It took a second to come back up, but it was there.

It was stretching, waking up, and I was starting to pant from the effort it took to rein myself in.

"You reading me right?" I asked, my voice low.

Because while I was letting him read me, I got a look inside him too. And he was nasty. There was a good chunk of sliminess and mean in him, but over it was shock and fear. He was mostly scared right now, and his Adam's apple bobbed up, pressing against my knife, nicking himself. A droplet of blood oozed out, sliding over the top of my knife.

I could get arrested for this. Right here. It was considered assault, and staring into this guy's eyes, I tried to gauge if he was the kind to run to the police or not.

"You gonna tell on me?" I asked. "You gonna narc?" And since he'd brought up Alex, I added, "You know what we did to the last narc in our midst, right?"

Jordan spoke up, shoving a big meathead. "He spent weeks in the hospital. That's what we did."

Zeke never looked away from me. His fear had faded, but he was absolutely still. "That was you guys too?"

I didn't answer him, just tipped my head back. "What are you going to do today, Zeke? Are you going to tell your boys to turn and walk out? Are you going to run to your rich parents? Tell on us? Tell them a little girl half your size got a knife to your throat? Or are you going to turn around, leave, and party somewhere else today?" I pressed in, just an inch, before releasing him and stepping back.

As I did, so did Cross and Jordan on either side of me.

I couldn't see Zellman, but I heard him behind me somewhere. "Walk. Don't come to another Roussou party."

Zeke swallowed, his eyes still on me. "We thought this was a District Weekend party."

"District Weekend is a street dance for Roussou. Always has been; never been a private party before," Jordan said.

"Then we'll see you there." Zeke's eyes closed a second. He visibly shuddered, but when he opened them again, he found me right away.

"Zeke," one of his buddies called. "Come on."

They were leaving, going back through the gate.

Zeke tore his gaze from mine, scanning the crowd behind us. He paused, seeing someone he knew, and his mouth flattened. "This chick speak for you too, Gramblin?"

One of the Normals broke from the crowd, coming to the other side of Cross, a beer in front of him. "You guys tried to burn our school down. That changes things."

"Thought you were better than your fucking stupid crew system." Zeke's tone was taunting.

Most of his friends had gone. Three remained, tense and eyeing the rest of us warily.

"That's what you say anytime we meet you on the field," Zeke added.

Gramblin rolled his shoulders back, one of his legs starting to tap. "Yeah. Well. I don't remember a time we got to really chat on the field. We're usually beating the shit out of you."

Zeke's lips thinned. "That right?"

That mean glint I knew was in there came to the forefront, rising, pushing aside the fear.

I knew what he was doing, but nope. Not going to happen.

I stepped between them, saying coolly, "You're not going to replace one opponent with another target. Your problem's with us, not with a Normal who, no offense, doesn't have a lot of say in this matter."

Zeke looked back to me. "That right?"

The adrenaline had bolstered his confidence. His head raised, and his chest puffed out. He was forgetting whose knife had caught his throat. I was about to remind him when Cross broke forward, his entire body tense and ready to fight.

"Your name is Zeke Allen," Cross said, almost sounding bored. "Your father is on the board of Kade Enterprises. He owns a small share, not enough to get a say-so, but enough that he can show up for board meetings for the free coffee and food. Your mom thinks she's a Fallen Crest socialite—wine for brunch, charity events, that sort of thing. You're the oldest in your family. You're hoping to go to Cain University, and you think you can be like Mason Kade. That's your goal. You've got his picture in your locker, and how do I know all of this?"

Now his voice was chilling. He looked at Zeke like a predator sizing up its prey. "Because we don't just fight. We do our homework. When I get told a bunch of Fallen Crest Academy kids are looking to burn one of our buildings down, you better be sure I find out who I'm going to be fighting in the long run."

Zeke's look was different now. A trickle of awareness came over him, his whole body stiffening. "I'm taking it you're the real leader here?"

There was more movement in the background, and then Race pushed to my side.

Zeke glanced over, his eyes narrowing, but he turned back to Cross right away.

"We don't have an official leader here. That's not how we work."

Except he was, and that *was* how we worked on some things.

I caught a small grin from Jordan before it vanished.

Zeke nodded, edging back. His hands went up. "Okay. I get it. You all are some sick badasses."

"Come on." One of his friends hit his arm, and the four of them walked backward, out through the fence.

We waited. One of the Normals went to the gate, watching. We heard a bunch of car doors slam shut, engines roaring, and tires peeling out, and he raised an arm. "They're gone."

"Fuck," Cross said, under his breath.

"How'd you know all that?" Jordan asked him.

"What the fuck were you thinking?" I asked Zellman.

"What the hell just happened?" Race asked, looking around for anyone with an answer.

Then, Cross sighed. "This is actually happening now. Shit."

He looked at me. I knew what he was thinking.

We were in a town rivalry. It was officially on.

CHAPTER TEN

EVERYONE WAS VULNERABLE.

That was the part of a town rivalry that sucked, but it was the truth. You didn't know what your adversary would do—if they'd go after someone considered innocent or weak, or if they'd step up and face off against someone equal to them. We'd never fought against this group from Fallen Crest Academy.

Cross explained that he had done just what he'd told Zeke. He'd called a few people and asked who ran their school. Everyone said Zeke Allen, so he'd gotten the details on him. I hadn't known he did that. No one did, but we were damn glad he had. Because we'd showed a small edge over them, they'd walked out with a prickle of fear. That small prickle could double, triple, grow and grow until we went against them again. Psychological warfare. I'd never known Cross to be good at it, but he'd just proven me wrong.

Yet another reason he was our "unofficial" leader, as he put it.

I was pretty sure after the Academy Crusties left, most the dudes in the backyard had a guy crush on Cross. When we walked back inside Tabatha's house, there was a new sense of awe and shock. And, of course, the girls weren't immune. I needed a moment myself, even though mostly what we needed was a crew meeting.

Rivalries required an organized effort, so all the crews were called, and an hour later we were meeting in the basement of Rossou's pizzeria. Even some of the Normals were there: Tabatha and Sunday were the ringleaders for the girls, and a few of the Normal athletes had come, plus one guy from the student council.

67

He kept adjusting his glasses and tugging down his sleeves. I was guessing he'd never been a part of something like this.

Moving up next to him, I asked, "You need the bathroom?"

He fixed me with a steady glare from behind his glasses. "Why? Because I look like I'm going to piss myself?"

Well, yeah, but also, "You look a little green in the face."

"Oh." He frowned to himself, his face twitching before he shook his head. "I'll be fine. I did have a touch of food poisoning, but that was two days ago." He fixed me with another look, swallowing tightly. "Do you even know who I am?"

That was easy. "You're on the student council."

"Yeah. That's why I'm here, but do you know my name?"

Roussou wasn't super big. I should've known, but I couldn't lie. "Don't take it personal. I make it a habit not to know. Just how I am." I gestured to my head. "Heed the rumors. I'm a bit messed up here."

He scowled. "Everyone has issues. You're no better than the rest of us with your issues."

That was... I wasn't sure what that was. "Okay. What's your name?"

"I'm Harrison Swartz. And I'm the student body president." He nodded. "Thank you very much."

Well then. "Thank you for your service?"

He bowed to me. "You're welcome." A cough, then he gestured around the room. "And thank you for this. You and your crew don't realize this, but Zeke Allen and his friends have been bullying other students at our school on a regular basis."

I frowned. "Why's no one said anything?"

"Mr. Allen's father is well connected in Fallen Crest. Who would they go to? The police? Our administration didn't care. Principal Neeon laughed at them."

Harrison was a good three inches taller than me, gangly, hair combed back with the ends frizzing up. I couldn't tell if he would be considered a good-looking guy underneath those glasses or if it was *because* of the glasses. Fair complexion. Hazel eyes.

Noticing me noticing him, he swiftly set his frown back in place. "I do know who you are, if that's what you're wondering. You're Bren Monroe. You're crew royalty. Channing Monroe's the one who started all of this devas—all of this..."

"Devastation."

He paused. "Hmmm?"

I saw right through him. "Devastation. That's what you were going to say." I could see more of him now. "You hate this, don't you? But you're also grateful. You don't like that there are crews in Roussou, but you're also thankful because now we're fighting someone who bullies *you*. Am I right?"

He paled.

"I bet a part of you wishes there were no crews, but a part of you worries what Roussou would be like without them. Am I close?"

A choked gargling came from him.

I turned to inspect the room, almost seeing it in a new light. I tried to see it from his point of view. The Normals looked more imposing. Tabatha and Sunday seemed prettier, but also bitchier. The leaders of each crew looked rougher, more dangerous. A trickle of fear slithered down my back, and I knew this was how someone like Harrison Swartz saw us all. I looked back at him, trying to feel the way he viewed me.

Dangerous. Deadly. And...what else was I feeling from him? Lonely.

Well, shit. That had me reeling. He was right, in some way. "You think I'm lonely?"

He blanched, another gurgling sound coming from him. "How did you..." He tugged at his shirt collar this time. "How did you know that?"

I shrugged. "A feeling. Do you?"

A helpless laugh came from him. "I feel like I'm going to get knifed if we continue this conversation."

Right. Knifed. Because that's what I did.

I knifed people. That's why all this was happening.

I felt a rock in my chest. "If you want, we can stop talking."

Except I didn't talk to strangers. Except I didn't open up. Except—why the fuck did I care?

I thought he was about to say something, but I moved away and went to find Cross. Why did I care about some kid like that? I felt his judgment. He looked down on me, on us, the crews. He'd been scared talking to me.

I didn't actually *know* if that's what he felt, but a part of me understood it. I judged myself all the time. Why begrudge someone else? I found myself watching Harrison again. If there hadn't been a crew system in place, what would his life have been like? He was being bullied by some rich prick from Fallen Crest Academy, so who's to say he wouldn't have gotten that in Roussou? But maybe, just maybe, it wasn't happening because of the crew system, because of us.

Maybe, just maybe, we weren't all so bad after all?

Then Jordan called out, "Okay. Is everyone here? Because we need to make a plan, for *everyone*."

CHAPTER
ELEVEN

THE PLAN WAS simple, but effective. Everyone had to move in pairs.

It was more of an encouraged guideline, but I noticed most everyone from Roussou followed it during the street dance that night. Moving through the crowd, Cross was my partner, and our job was easy: watch for trouble.

Of course, that didn't just mean from the Academy Crusties. Cross and I were crossing the main road, a block down from my brother's bar, when I felt him brush up behind me. "Moose."

Shit.

I veered right, catching sight of my brother's biggest enforcer on my left, but then I braked.

Congo, a smaller version of Moose, was there.

We went straight, and Lincoln was there, a scar running the length of his face, tattoos all around his neck and arm.

Backing up, I heard Cross hiss, "Fuck!" Then he was shoved to the side, and hands grabbed me.

"Heya, cousin."

I grimaced, hearing Scratch's voice before being firmly guided through the street and to the back alley. Once we were between two buildings, Scratch let go, but he shifted so his hand was on my back. He kept a lone finger there, prodding me ahead. "Big brother wants to talk."

I turned around and slapped his hand away. "Get off me."

Cross stood to the side.

Moose, Congo, Lincoln all fell in line, along with another one of my brother's guys, Chad. Big, red, and hairy, he was just shy of matching Moose's height. Seeing his fuzz, I rubbed at my jaw. "Growing this out?"

Chad grinned. "Maybe. I haven't decided. The nurse I'm dating is loving it."

I raised an eyebrow. "A nurse, huh? That's convenient."

He shrugged.

Lincoln stepped forward, the silent and deadly one of the batch. "Your brother's concerned. That's all."

Scratch threw him a side look. "Dude, that shit doesn't work with Bren. She's a Monroe. Ice-cold heart, this one has." He poked my shoulder.

I batted it away. "Touch me again, and I'll cut your finger off next time you're passed out."

Pride gleamed from his smile, his white teeth showing. He didn't even bat an eye. "There she is. Figured domestic bliss might've made you soft." He chuckled. "Nice to know my little wild cousin is still in there." He shoved his hands in his pockets and moved away, keeping an eye on me as he did.

It was useless to fight. Cross knew that too. These guys made up the oldest crew in Roussou.

My brother was just leaving his bar when he saw us coming.

He stopped in front of us, and his guys formed a circle, giving us a pocket of privacy. All around, people were coming in and out of his bar, most probably going to join the street dance. But it was nearing evening time, so the crowd was going to only get bigger. Channing's bar usually had a line wrapping around the corner and halfway down the block, especially on a weekend night.

"Ah." He stopped in front of us, folding his arms over his chest. His gaze moved from me to Cross and back again. "The two little ingrates who sleep under my roof, fuck under my roof, and eat all of my food." He tsked us, shaking his head. "I tell you one thing to do, and you do the opposite." His face hardened and his gaze settled right on me. "Where'd you go last night?"

"Technically, we stayed at the house."

"Fine." He moved a step closer. "Where'd you go this morning?"

"Alex Ryerson gets to his gym around five in the morning," Cross said. "We went to have a word with him."

Channing switched his gaze to my boyfriend, his jaw tightening. "A bird tells me your crew went and had a word with Malinda Decraw before the Fallen Crest bonfire."

Cross and I shared a look.

"*Technically*..." I was all about that word tonight. "Mrs. Decraw-Strattan had a word with us. We didn't go to see her, didn't even know her until she came to our truck."

"Malinda lives in a wealthy neighborhood. What were you guys doing there?"

"Fuck this," Cross said under his breath. "My dad's new girlfriend is over there. I was curious."

Channing narrowed his eyes, studying us again. "Did you get your curiosity satisfied?"

Yeah. My brother knew we weren't there for the 411 from the neighbors.

He added, "Do I need to remind you that my sister is *still* on probation?"

"It wasn't even like that."

Except it was. I turned, keeping my face forward as Cross glanced at me again. Channing wasn't stupid. He hadn't gotten to his position in Roussou by luck—fighting, being ruthless, and being smart were the main ingredients.

He needed to be distracted. "Mrs. Decraw-Strattan said she knew Mom."

Channing's gaze snapped to mine.

"Did you know that?" I added.

"Are you serious?"

I nodded. "That's what she told me. Said she hadn't told anyone who knew her. I'm assuming she meant you and Heather."

Channing eased back a step, his hand coming to rub his jaw. "Yeah. I mean, no. She never told me that."

I didn't really care what Mrs. Decraw-Strattan had said, but I knew Channing would. It would bother him the rest of the night, and it'd be enough to spur him to drive to Fallen Crest and ask her himself. I'd been so little when our mom died that I couldn't say what his relationship with her had been, and it was another thing on top of so much Channing didn't talk about.

He'd been wracked with guilt—guilt at leaving me alone in that house, guilt at leaving me in general until our dad went to prison and Channing took me in, and yeah, that was the ace up my sleeve because it worked. Consider him distracted.

Channing looked down, still rubbing his jaw. "I don't know Malinda that well, but I've been around enough. Heather more so. She told you and not us?"

I eased back a step, gave a small nod. "Warned us to leave the neighborhood, said someone probably called the cops the second we pulled onto their streets too."

He grunted, a brief grin showing. "Probably. Heather's more recognized, but man, we haven't gone over there in a long time. I think I was only at the house a few times." He turned to Cross. "Did you get the information you wanted?"

I eased back another step.

Cross shifted on his feet, bringing his hip in close proximity to mine, almost brushing against me. "I know about the lady, but that's it." His voice was tight, controlled. "I'll figure out the rest."

It was a nice way of telling Channing to stay in his lane. We all knew it. His guys too, and a couple chuckled.

Noting our close proximity and how I had moved away from him, Channing dropped his hand. His eyes flashed. "Okay, kid. I hear you, but the problem is you're taking too damn long figuring it out. You're in my house, and I understand the emotional need Bren has for you, and that's the only reason I'm allowing it. Got it? A year earlier and you'd be forced to bunk with Jordan or Zellman, and my sister would've been shipped out of state—"

"Fuck you!"

He ignored me. "So if you tell me to mind my own business one more time, I'm not going to care how pissed off my sister will be. I'll bust your head open. Got it?"

"Channing! Shut up!" I tried to move between them, but it was Cross who moved me out of the way.

74

He stepped up, coming eye to eye with Channing.

In that moment, I realized how similar they looked. Both tan. Both with dark blond hair. Both ripped. And both mean. Channing was more extroverted, while Cross liked to stay in the shadows unless he needed to step forward.

He was stepping forward now.

The air sizzled around us. The hairs on the back of my neck stood up, and I contained a shiver, reaching over my body with one hand to touch my other wrist.

"I don't care that your guys are here." Cross spoke low, quiet, but so clearly. He wasn't flinching, and he wasn't looking away. He was holding steady, staring right back at my brother. "I don't care how much respect we owe your crew—not when you threaten my relationship with your sister and not when you get involved with *my* family life."

"I told you—"

Cross tipped his chin back. "I don't care. All due respect, I'm handling my shit a lot better than you did at my age."

That was a direct slap in Channing's face, and he noted it, his nostrils flaring. "Really?"

Cross softened his tone. "I'm not saying that to insult you— just a reminder. You're coming at me as if you're going to kick me out, when we both know the real problem you have ain't me. Bren's birthday is coming up. She'll be eighteen, and if she decides not to rely on you for food and shelter, there ain't a thing you can do it about it. Except me. I'm the one holding her together."

Cross stepped back. Turning toward me, he added his last words, "And you know that too."

He had stripped everything bare and left us all exposed, because he was right.

Channing drew in a breath, his chest rising and holding before his gaze slid to mine.

I bit my lip. Yeah. There were still problems with us, and most certainly with me.

He blinked a few times, his forehead wrinkling before he tipped his head up, gazing at the sky. "Fuck. *Fuck!*" Exhaling, he focused on me. "Your boyfriend just owned me, and here I was, thinking I had the upper hand."

My throat swelled. I didn't know how to respond to that.

Apparently, neither did Cross, because he kept quiet.

Finally, Channing said quietly, "You remain at the house. You got it?"

Cross' eyes flicked up to his.

Channing nodded at him. "You too. Shit ain't ideal, but you're right." His eyes closed a moment, and an ominous threat hung in the air between us as he said, "Don't get pregnant, Bren. I mean it."

"I won't. I'm not. We're always safe."

I shifted on my feet, my belly heating up and rising north.

"Jesus." Channing glanced up again, just for a moment. "What do I need to know about this town rivalry?"

The tension in the air had eased.

My lungs could inflate once again. We were on to crew business. That was a good middle ground for us, a bonding ground even.

Cross spoke for us. "That's ours to deal with."

"Cross—" Channing said.

"It's high school stuff. That's our terrain. Not yours."

"It's mine if it's going to hurt people in the community."

"What? You're going to go fight a bunch of Academy Crusties? You need to loosen the strings, give us some freedom. We'll take care of it."

"People got hurt the last time this happened. Someone almost got raped."

"And that guy went to prison. I've heard the story, and that guy was one of ours."

"Broudou was not one of ours," Channing hissed right back.

"He was from Roussou. You know what I mean."

Channing stared at him, thinking. His hands dropped, and his shoulders loosened. "Fine. I'll back off if you do one thing."

Cross and I waited.

"You come to me before you step over a line you can't unstep from. You hear me?"

Cross nodded.

My brother's gaze pierced me. "Bren? I need you to give me your word."

I forced my head up and down. My throat burned.

"No stabbing people, especially school officials, and especially under video surveillance. You got me?"

Fine. I earned that one. "I hear you."

"Good." He let out a soft curse under his breath, eyeing Cross. "You're a scary little shit."

Then my brother rounded, slapping Cross on the back harder than it needed to be, but Cross barely moved. He took it, and with a nod, my brother went into his bounty-hunting office. His guys followed him, except my cousin.

Scratch stepped up next to me. "If there's a situation you can't go to him about, call me. Okay?"

I nodded.

He held up his hand, pinkie stretched out. "Promise me, Bren."

I hooked my finger around his. "Promise."

That was good enough for him. He turned around, his shoulder bumping mine, and he flashed me a grin as he moved around the beginning of the line, ducked behind the door bouncers, and slipped inside the bar he half-owned with my brother.

"Why do I feel I just escaped a grizzly bear's hold on my throat?" Cross murmured.

I grunted. "Because you did." I gave him a look. "That stuff about me..."

I stopped myself.

Cross waited, hearing what I couldn't say. He reached out, taking hold of my neck and drawing me close.

"I got you," he said softly before bending down for my mouth.

That was all I needed.

CHAPTER TWELVE

RELATIVELY SPEAKING, THE street dance was uneventful.

I say *relatively* because it was Roussou, it was a street dance, and you know how our lives go. But as far as the town rivalry, nothing happened. There were a few sightings of Crusties, Academy and Public, but they kept to their side of the town, and we kept to ours. Just like the old days, or that's what Heather once told me.

So now we were on day three of District Weekend.

The Frisco party was in the woods, similar to the bonfire Fallen Crest was supposed to do. Both had fires, but Frisco's put Fallen Crest to shame. Their main bonfire was as tall as a building, almost lighting up the sky.

"I think I'm in pyro-love." Zellman stopped in his tracks as we got closer. The parking lot was filled to the max, with cars lining the gravel road both ways for a full mile.

I glanced around, noting that there were no houses. There was a field on our right, and woods spread out on the left, with the bonfire in a clearing that attached the two. It had metal grates all around it to keep it contained. Trucks had been positioned around the field and near the woods, their gates down and the beds filled with coolers.

Rap music was playing, but not too loud. People were chatting, laughing, and drinking. As we neared the party, a guy was leading a girl into the field. Another girl was weaving around, her friends trying to hold her upright. A guy walked up to her, bent down, and threw her over his shoulder. Her friends started saying something to him, but he turned around.

"She's drunk. She needs to go home and to bed. Take her, or I'm taking her."

Two of the friends grumbled, but one grudgingly went with him. They passed us without a glance.

Zellman frowned at them. "I don't recognize them. They must've been shipped to Fallen Crest."

"Jordan!"

Turning around, we could see Sunday leading the charge, but it was Tabatha who had called out.

Sunday, Monica, Tabatha, Lilac?, and about four other girls had all come together. Taz was walking behind with Race next to her. More Roussou guys were behind Race, mainly athletes. I recognized Harrison trudging in the rear, pulling at his collar and frowning at his surroundings.

"Baby." Tabatha moved around Sunday and Monica, going to Jordan's side, snuggling into him. His arm rested over her shoulder.

Sunday stopped in front of Zellman, both of them sizing the other up.

She scowled at him, her arms folding over her chest. "I'm going on a date with someone from Fallen Crest next Friday night."

"Prom is Saturday."

She lifted a shoulder. "I'll still go with you."

He frowned.

Her scowl lessened to match his frown.

Then, he shrugged. "Fine."

"Fine," she snapped before pivoting on her heel and storming away. Monica was fast on her heels, muttering at Zellman, "You're such an asshole."

He watched them go before turning back to all of us. Seeing our attention, he stuck his hands in his pockets. "What? I'm not going to be forced into a relationship. She wants to date other guys, fine by me." He harrumphed, a very un-Zellman thing to do, and headed after them at a slower pace.

"Hey, Z! Wait up." A couple of the Normal guys hurried to catch up.

Jordan frowned after him, his arm tightening around Tabatha. "I'm his partner for the buddy system."

Tabatha groaned. "Be my partner." She smiled up at him, batting her eyelashes.

Jordan gazed down at her, his eyes softening before pinning Cross and me with a pleading look. "Please?"

We all knew what he was asking.

"Tab, who's your partner?" Taz sidled up on the other side of Tabatha, Race completing the circle as he stepped between Taz and Cross.

Tabatha's smile tightened. "Lila is."

Lila! Her name was Lila.

Lila spoke up from behind her. "I'm here! Buddy system here." She pushed her way in between Tabatha and Taz. She held a hand up. "Hi everyone. I'm here. I'm taking this whole rivalry thing seriously."

Jordan frowned at her. "You should, because it is serious. People went to prison last time because of this shit."

Her smile faded, and she blinked a few times. "Excuse me?"

The rest of the guys moved past us with Harrison behind them, walking alone.

"Harrison!" I waved him over.

He stopped, staring at me. "Me?" His eyes widened, and he scanned the rest of the group, lingering on Jordan and then on Cross, who watched him with his head tilted to the side.

"Yeah. You." I waved him over. "Come here."

He took a step, then stopped. "Why?"

"Who's your buddy?"

His mouth flattened. "At home."

"The fuck?" Jordan barked at him. "You shouldn't be here then. It's not safe."

Harrison's gaze grew wary. He knew full well how dangerous it could be, but that was for another day. I jerked my head toward Lila. "You have a new partner for the night."

"Excuse me?" Lila said.

I ignored her. "Meet Lila. Lila, meet Harrison."

"No way—"

I smiled. "If I see you without him five feet away, I'll put you in the hospital." And because I wasn't sure if she was narc-y girl, I added, "You won't know how you got there. You won't know who actually put you there, but you'll wake up and only have yourself to blame."

She seethed.

Tabatha was grinning, biting her lip.

Taz frowned.

"What?" Lila sputtered, pointing at Harrison. "Why aren't you giving him the same threat?"

"Because he's the student council president. Even drunk, I've got a feeling he abides every law and doesn't break any rules."

"He broke a rule just coming here tonight."

Harrison coughed, holding a hand up. "Uh. Technically, I didn't because I made sure to walk in with Roussou people, and I was planning to stick close to the Roussou crowd tonight."

"Why are you here?" Lila shoved out of the group, facing off against him. Her hands found her hips.

"Because it's District Weekend." He spoke as if that made perfect sense. "I'm the president of our student body. If something happens that could affect us at school, I prefer to have first-hand knowledge." He paused a beat. "Why are you here?"

Lila had no response.

Tabatha laughed. "She's here because she's hoping Cross and Bren suddenly break up and she can get lucky."

Lila whirled around, paling. "Bitch!"

Tabatha waved a hand. "Get lost, Lila. I don't think there's a place for you in my friend group any longer."

Blood drained from Lila's face, leaving her as white as a sheet. "What? Why?"

"Because I don't like how you talked to Harrison just now. He's already been accepted at Yale." Tabatha was smug with Jordan's arm over her. His hand curved around her hip. "Bet you didn't know that, huh?"

Lila's eyes bulged as she looked back at Harrison, her demeanor much more timid.

Harrison glared at Tabatha. "You weren't supposed to tell anyone."

Tab shrugged, stretching almost lazily under Jordan's arm. "Harrison, you've been my neighbor all my life. You never sing your praises. Let me have this moment."

He grunted, but tugging his shirt again from his neck, he started forward. "Let's go, Lidia. I suddenly need a beer."

She went after him. "It's Lila—"

Then they were swallowed by another group of students, ones we didn't recognize. They glared at us, and Jordan sighed. "Let me guess. Fallen Crest just arrived."

Sure enough.

Zeke Allen was smack in the middle, his beefy arms around the shoulders of two girls. His guys were lined up behind him, most with their arms around a girl as well. I was having déjà vu to a nineties high school movie.

Slowing down as he passed, Zeke smirked a frosty smirk until he got to me. Then it grew calculating. "We got people in common," he said. "Coach Strattan and Malinda Decraw are my neighbors. Did you know that, Monroe?"

"Piss off, Allen." Jordan let go of Tabatha, stepping forward to block me.

Cross stood next to him. Race came up beside me.

"We gonna have a problem tonight?" Cross asked, his voice quiet.

Zeke stopped in his tracks, his smirk falling as he took in Cross. "Nah, man. I mean, you guys might have a problem tonight, but not us. We're all chill."

His friends laughed, the sounds raucous and almost degrading somehow.

Zeke moved forward, the girls with him giving us nasty looks as well. He lifted his head in a nod. "Don't hesitate to reach out, Monroe. I can loan you my family lawyer. Since you tend to get in trouble with the law."

"The fuck?"

Now Cross was pissed. "I'm getting real sick of his obsession with Bren," he said so only the four of us could hear him.

Jordan lowered his head. "Yeah. Me too."

Race spoke up. "What's that about a lawyer?"

Jordan shook his head, watching the rest of their group trail past us. "Who the fuck knows. Maybe about her parole or something?"

Cross turned to face me. "You know what he's talking about?"

I shook my head. "No. I assume he's focused on me because my brother knows Mason Kade. Maybe? It's a stretch, but..." I shrugged, studying Zeke again as their group got refreshments from the first truck. "I have nothing to do with them. He'll figure it out, and that'll be it."

I hoped.

Cross grunted. "I doubt it. The guy wants in your pants."

I swung my head back to him. "You think?" That didn't seem right.

"I know so." He tapped my arm. "I recognize the look." He touched my chin. "It's the same look Harrison has."

It took a second. "No way!" I started laughing.

"Yeah, way." He stepped back, his hand lowering to his side. "Watch yourself with Harrison."

He knew I was already on high alert regarding Zeke.

I didn't agree with Cross, but I still nodded. He saw things I didn't sometimes. "Yeah, okay."

"I agree with Cross," Race added.

"Not you too." I groaned.

"Take it from someone who was interested at the beginning of school." He spoke quietly, and I knew it was so Taz didn't hear. "I see it in Harrison too, and the guy is smart, but he's not girl-savvy. A crush can develop into something more serious—depends on how scared he is of Cross."

Cross grinned. "The Yale fucker should be wetting his pants."

Race laughed. "Yeah. I know. I was too." He was lying...kind of.

I rolled my eyes, breaking from the group. "We gotta go find Zellman. Buddy system and all."

"Hold up." Cross grabbed the back of my pants. "Jordan, we'll watch Z tonight. Find us later?"

"Yeah." Jordan raised a hand in acknowledgment before folding over and nuzzling into Tabatha. Her hand slid around his neck. They would remain like that the rest of the night if they didn't slip away for some privacy later on.

"Wait." Race and Taz were coming after us. He tossed his arm around her shoulder too. "We'll come with you guys."

"Safety in numbers?" I teased.

Taz flashed me a smile. "More like I want to hang with my real friends tonight."

Sounded like a plan. I could do with some Taz time myself.

CHAPTER THIRTEEN

TWO HOURS AND three beers later, I was sober.

Taz couldn't say the same. She was beyond buzzed, which Cross and Race were shaking their heads over. I was more open-minded and accepting. Yeah, I surprised myself. Taz wasn't slurring her words, but she'd told me for the eighth time how she loved me and viewed me as a sister.

After the ninth time, Cross finished his beer. "Okay." He turned to Race, who was on a log parallel to us. "I'm thinking it's time my sister goes home."

Race gave Cross the slightest of nods. "Have you tried taking her home when she gets like this?" He raised his eyebrows. "Not so easy. Your sister gets feisty."

"Fuck yeah, I do!" She burped, raising her beer in the air, and surged to her feet. Jumping up on the log, she hollered just as she started to fall. "Hey, everyone!"

I grabbed her legs, steadying her.

I don't think Taz even noticed. She raised her beer higher, her shirt lifting from the movement. "Who's here from Roussou?!"

A cheer rose up.

"Hell yeah, we are!"

"Yes!"

"Us!"

"Boo."

She waited until they quieted, burped again, and yelled out, "Raise your beers, fuckers! 'Cause we're Roussou, and we're proud! Helllll yeah!"

Another roar went over the group nearest us, traveling to the other trucks, along with a few grumbles.

Cross groaned. "Like I said." He hit Race's leg. "Take her home, fucker."

Race glared back. "You take her home. She's your sister."

"She's your girlfriend."

"Boys, seriously." Tabatha sauntered over, sitting on the empty log across from our fire.

She was alone. "Where's Jordan?"

"Checking on Zellman."

I pointed to the next truck. Zellman was in the back, a girl on his lap. "He's right there. And the point of a buddy system isn't to leave while your partner is checking on someone else." I rose to my feet, already scanning the area.

I hadn't been taking stock while we were sitting, mostly because it was nice to relax and talk with Taz and Race. But now, seeing nine trucks spread out over the area, much smaller bonfires throughout and all the people walking around, I was a little taken aback at how many people were here. The lot was huge, and who knew how many were in the woods.

"Where is he?" I asked under my breath as Cross and Race climbed up on their logs.

I couldn't see him.

"What the fuck?" Race growled, shooting Tabatha a look. "You dropped the ball, Sweets."

She'd been all cool and relaxed, but now she stood with us. "What? How far could he get...?" She trailed off as she began looking too.

"What direction did he go?" Cross asked.

"I—" She gulped, starting to pale. She clutched her beer. "I don't know. He just said he was going to check on Z, then come find me."

I went truck by truck.

Truck one, no Jordan.

Cross moved to stand next to me. "Which one are you on?"

He knew what I was doing.

"I'm on two now, going to three next."

He pivoted. "Working on the last truck then. Race, check the parking lot. Tabatha, study the treeline."

We worked as a team. Taz had started a Roussou cheer.

Tabatha groaned under her breath. "Oh my God. What if something happened to him? Oh my God..." She wouldn't shut up.

Two was clear.

Three, the same.

Four, still no Jordan.

Cross was counting down as he cleared the end of the line. "Eight. Seven. Six."

We both were on five at the same time. Still no Jordan.

"He would stick out. He's the tallest guy here," Race said. "Fuck, guys."

It was decision time now.

I had my phone out, typing a text as Cross pressed his phone to his ear.

I spoke as my thumb moved over the keys, "Tabatha." My voice was calm, but my blood pressure was not. It was spiking all the way up.

"Yeah?" She rushed to my side. "What can I do to help? I'm so sorry, you guys. Honestly. He sent me over here. I didn't think—I trust Jordan. He usually knows what's best to do—"

I cut her off. Her rambling wasn't helping. "I need you to send a group text to as many people as you can. We need eyes on Jordan, now. Text. Then do group chats on all your social media."

"Okay. I can do that rush." She pulled her phone out and dropped it in her haste. She picked it back up and dropped it again. "Shit! Shit! Shit! Okay." She breathed out, exhaling deep. "I can do this. I can do this."

"YEAH, WE'RE ROUSSOU, AND WE'RE FUCKING PROUD!"

Since she was already shouting, I tugged on Taz's shirt and said, "Start cheering Jordan's name."

"FUCKING PROUD—JORDAN! JORDAN! JORDAN!"

Phones were lighting up. People were starting to look around. The word was spreading, and those who weren't checking their phones started in with her chant.

Cross turned to me. "Let's move. It's time to start looking ourselves."

I nodded, getting off my log.

"What should we do?" Race stepped toward us.

Taz was still thrusting her fist in the air, leading the chants. I gestured to her. "Watch over her. If Jordan's actually missing, pressure is good against whoever might be hurting him, but if he's not missing, we don't want to give the wrong people ideas. You know?"

He nodded, running a hand over his face. Bags seemed to appear under his eyes. "This whole rivalry thing is real, huh?"

Cross grunted, his hand touching my back. "'Fraid so. And our crew did those car explosions. We have to go."

Tabatha joined us, exclaiming, "Oh my God!" Her hand flailed in the air. "Someone said they saw him heading into the woods."

"Uh..."

We turned. Zellman had joined our group. He held his phone in the air. "Why am I getting texts about Jordan?" He glanced up at Taz, both her fists in the air now. "And when did your sister become a protest leader?" He looked around. "Where's Jordan?"

I fought the urge to clip him in the back of his head. "How drunk are you?"

"I'm sober. I was getting frisky the whole time." He grinned, wiggling his eyebrows. "If you know what I mean."

I groaned. We did.

"Tabatha, which side of the woods? Right or left?" Cross asked.

"Um..." She sank her teeth into her bottom lip, her fingers flying over her phone. "I'm asking."

And a second later, she jumped and pointed to the left. "Over there."

There were two main sections of woods, one that went up a hill and one that spread out over the back end of the field. There was a river beyond the treeline, but this was Frisco. We weren't familiar with the terrain here.

She pointed up the hill, close to the Academy Crusties.

A whole section of people were going up the hill. And as we were watching, a guy turned around, made sharp motions with his arms and everyone quickly ran back as if nothing had been about to happen.

"That's not good." Cross.

Tab saw the group moving back. "Oh, fuck."

"JORDAN! ROUSSOU PRIDE! JORDAN! ROUSSOU PRIDE!"

Taz had changed it up.

Zellman shoved his phone in his pocket. "What are waiting for? Let's fucking go. I ain't scared of some damn Academites."

Cross and I shared a look.

If something was going on with Jordan, he'd need a getaway.

"There's a road back there?" I asked.

Zellman grabbed a kid walking past us.

"Hey!" The guy squawked, beer sloshing from his cup.

Z ignored all of that. "You from Frisco?"

The guy swallowed nervously. "Uh, yeah. Why? I go to your school now, though."

Cross pointed toward the hill. "Is there a road back there?"

"Uh..." He looked, needing a second.

Zellman growled. "Answer. Now."

"Uh..." His eyes darted to Zellman before nodding. "Yeah. Yeah. There is. The river cuts through the hills, but yeah, there's a road. About a mile in, if you keep straight, you'll hit it."

"Thank you," Cross said.

Zellman shoved the guy away, growling again, "Thanks."

The guy fell back a few feet, more of his beer spilling on his shirt. His eyes were wide as he took us in. "Does this have something to do with your crew member?"

Zellman rotated, starting for the guy.

Cross grabbed Zellman's arm, holding him back, and stepped forward himself. "Maybe. What do you know?"

"Uh..." He looked at his phone, back to Cross, to his phone...

"Fuck's sakes." Zellman lunged, grabbing the phone out of his hands. He read what was on the screen, his entire body stiffening. "The fuck—"

We could see the blood drain from the guy's face. "I just got that text. Swear! I have nothing to do with it."

Cross grabbed the phone out of Zellman's hand, showing me as he read it at the same time.

Zellman lunged for the guy, but Race blocked him. "Hold up, Z. This guy might be useful."

The guy in question started to move for his phone. Race grabbed his shirt, holding him in place.

Number unknown: Holy f***ck! Wolf crew member just got attacked.

The guy pointed over Race's hold on him. "There's a video."

Cross clicked on it, and my stomach dropped, plummeting to the ground.

Jordan was on the ground. Guys I didn't recognize circled him, moving as one to punch and kick him.

"We have to go! NOW!"

"Get our truck," Cross told Race. "Pull it up on that road. If he's up there, we have to stop this. We'll need a getaway."

Race jerked his head. "Got it." He let go of Z and the guy.

"Hey! My phone."

"I need it. You can get it back at school." Cross was texting the person who'd sent the video, and we were already running.

We could hear Taz, "ROUSSOU—WHAT the hell?!"

Didn't need a guess to know Race had grabbed her, then dragged her with him to the parking lot.

Tabatha was running next to me, her face streaked with tears. "What can I do? Tell me what to do."

Cross threw the guy's phone at her. "Text with the person. Find out everything you can and relay us the information."

She caught the phone as we sprinted away at full force.

It was time to bash some heads.

CHAPTER FOURTEEN

TEARING PAST PEOPLE, I knew we were drawing attention. We didn't care. Swinging left, we headed for the woods. A trail of people were going up the hill, and as we broke past the first trees, we could hear their yelling.

I was straining, my heart pumping, but I couldn't make out Jordan's voice.

We kept going.

The trail was narrow. The trees blocked the moonlight, but there were lights ahead, and people on the trail had their phones out, helping to show the way. We sprinted past. A few people screamed, and a couple glanced back, then staggered out of our way. A girl gasped.

Another, "Holy shit!"

Then, "Slow down!"

And the giggles. Some people thought this was funny.

I wanted to pivot back and punch them, but Jordan needed us.

Thank God Zellman had remained sober tonight. Thank God all of us had.

Zellman and I were the ones who usually got into trouble. The rest swarmed in to save us or back us up, but not Jordan. Never Cross. This wasn't normal. Then again, I had a feeling Jordan was jumped.

It didn't matter. Whatever it was, we were flying in to fight. No matter who it was against.

Cross' phone lit up and he read the screen, still running.

"It's some of the jocks from the Academy," he said, not winded at all. "They're ahead." He put his phone away and picked up speed.

We were right behind him.

That was one thing I had going for me—I could run almost as fast as the guys. Long distance wasn't for me. No way, but I'd always been blessed with speed. We were getting closer to the crowd, and we could see the jocks ducking and dodging. A few were wading in for a punch, then darting back out of the way.

Cowards. All of them.

As we came to the clearing, we could see Jordan trying to swing at them. He was almost to his knees, but his head was up. His eyes were half-closed. Blood caked his face.

He swung, his fist almost getting a guy by luck before another stepped in from behind him and punched the back of his head.

He was going down.

My stomach churned.

A fist connected with the side of his chin. Blood splayed everywhere. His head jerked, and it was like I saw it in slow motion. His head whipped to the side. Blood. Sweat. Tears. All of it dripped down his face, and exhaustion.

I didn't know how long he'd been trying to fight them all, but his shoulders were dropping.

He fell to his knees, his head down.

It was as if he were asking for a break, a pause, so he could get a second wind. In some fights, this was granted. I knew it wouldn't be with these guys. They were cowards. Not one of them would stand a chance against Jordan one on one. They had to fight in a pack, like hyenas, and they were cackling like them too.

The closer we came, the more calm I felt.

The rage was there, the need for vengeance, to protect one of ours, but I dampened that down. A whole storm twisted my insides, but over it, I found serene peace. I needed it. It was a skill I'd been developing. Silencing the mind. I could do the most damage like this. I would see things they wouldn't see. Our opponents. Our enemies. Whoever was hurting us, they were going to be hurt. They were going to be ripped to pieces.

We were going to shred them.

We all moved to the edges of the pathway, coming in hot and fast, but silent—and on the side. If people looked back, they would look in the middle of the walkway. They'd look for a silhouette. The eye would automatically skip over the darkness.

I braced myself, waiting for someone to shout our arrival, but so far nothing. Maybe the people we passed didn't recognize us. Maybe we were just lucky.

Maybe we were supposed to have the element of surprise.

Maybe, just maybe, the universe was on our side with this one.

We were almost to them.

Jordan's entire body jerked as he tried to gasp for breath. As we cleared the last of the pathway, one of the attackers broke formation. He moved in, his fist up and cocked behind him. He was coming at Jordan from his right-side rear.

Jordan wouldn't know the punch was coming.

Then the guy looked up and saw us. His eyes widened.

I saw all of this in slow motion as well.

His mouth started to form a word, to yell and announce our arrival, just as his eyes skipped to mine. They caught and held, and I let him see the deadly calm in me. He got it. In that moment, he saw everything in me.

This was not our first day with violence.

We reveled in this.

We excelled.

I took another step, one more, and then I launched. Cross was taking down the guys with their backs to us, and as one started to go down, I used him as a stepping stool. I ran up his back, pushing off from his shoulders, and then I was flying in the air.

The guy saw me, horror and shock forming in his eyes, and he couldn't move. He was frozen, just watching me come. He tried to twist out of the way, but he had the thought to grab me at the same time. His hand came up in defense, but it wasn't enough. It was a weak deflection, and my foot found him, my heel making a clean hit. With the force of my jump and my entire body behind the kick, his body fell backward to the ground. I went with him, landing and going with the momentum to punch him in the neck.

He doubled over, gasping for breath.

But I was gone, pivoting and grabbing the arm of his friend coming in to save him.

I was smaller than most of these guys. They were athletes. Most worked at their bodies, lifting weights, and I couldn't fight them on that level. But speed, grace, and knowledge? I could fight them with those qualities. And smarts.

I was thinking, clear-headed. They weren't.

I'd look back later and realize there were no shouts. There should've been yelling, curses at least. There were none.

They'd been cheering on their pals as they fought Jordan. But we showed up, and nothing. They were quiet.

After I used the arm meant to hit me, I crawled up his body and threw myself backward so I could flip him over. Then I threw my legs up and scissor-kicked the next guy across the face—he was the third guy I knocked down.

After all of that, I looked up.

They ran.

They all ran, not one stayed to help their friends. That said everything right there.

"Bren," Jordan gasped, falling down.

"Jordan!" I ran to his side, catching him just as his face almost planted in the ground. I knelt there, holding him. I cradled him against me, but I was watching Cross and Zellman. Both were fighting, making quick work of the remaining two guys.

Zellman tackled his guy, throwing him to the ground and rearing back to land punch after punch. Cross' opponent tried to rush him. Cross caught his arm and twisted, tucking his shoulder into the guy's chest. He knelt, flipping him over, then landed one final punch. He knocked his guy out cold, then took stock. When he saw Zellman, he ran to tear him off of the guy.

"Z." He grunted, pushing Zellman back.

"No. Let me at him! I hate these fuckers." Zellman clawed at Cross, trying to break free.

Zellman was charged. He wasn't stopping, and seeing that, Cross yelled at the guy, "Get lost!"

The rest had run off, except for those unconscious on the ground. He was the last of his friends, and he nodded, barely. Pushing to his feet, he started for the path we'd just used. He staggered, falling down, pushing up, and going some more before repeating the process. After we saw him fall three times, he managed to catch his wind and went off at a slow jog, disappearing around a bend.

Cross let go of Zellman, who was still ranting and cursing. "What the fuck, man!"

Cross ignored him, coming to me and kneeling down. "Jordan?"

"Those assholes maced me. I didn't know what was going on until I was already on the ground. I couldn't fight back at first." His entire right eye was swollen shut. "Cross. Bren." His voice trembled. "I thought—I thought I was going to die tonight. If they hadn't stopped... If they'd just kept going..."

A shudder went through me. I held him tighter.

Not tonight. Not on our watch. Cross and I shared a look—not ever.

We were completely alone on the hill.

"God! Fuckers! I just want to—why'd you hold me back?" Zellman's arms were in the air. He was swinging them around, as if warming up for a race. His chest heaved. His eyes were wild. "I—"

I pushed Jordan into Cross' arms and stalked over to Zellman. "What the hell is your problem?! We fight with clear minds." I wanted to wring his neck, and my hands jerked up, forming fists.

Zellman saw them, the motion calming him for some reason, and he stepped back. His arms lowered to his sides. "Bren?"

"What the fuck were you thinking? You just kept railing on that guy." I remembered Zellman's hostility from the day before. "You've been nuts since Tabatha's party. What is going on with you?"

Ring! Ring!

Cross was helping Jordan stand up when his phone rang, silencing our fight. He pulled it out just as I saw the lights. Red and blue lit up the sky.

I muttered, "Shit," as Cross answered his phone.

"Yeah?" He listened to whoever was on the other end. "Got it. Taz can link up with my phone, so watch my GPS." He pulled the phone away and tapped a few buttons before sliding it back into his pocket.

Zellman stepped back into me, cursing under his breath.

Cross said what we all knew. "Cops are here." But then he added what we didn't know. "They have thirty cars down there."

My mouth almost fell open. "Thirty?"

His jaw was tight, his face grim. "Race saw them pulling in just as he turned onto the road up ahead. They saw the flashing lights, but not the actual cops when they were leaving the lot. My guess is that they got out just before the cops came over that last hill." Cross motioned behind us. "We can't go down there. They'll arrest us."

Which meant we had about a mile hike ahead of us.

I remembered what the Frisco guy had said. "He said go straight and we'll hit the road. Right?"

A mile hike was fine, in the daylight, when one of us wasn't struggling to stand.

As if reading my thoughts, Jordan grunted and shoved Cross away. "I can stand on my own."

He couldn't. He started to go down.

Cross grabbed him as Zellman, and I rushed forward.

"I got it. I got it." But Jordan was panting as he said it, and knowing he wouldn't listen to reason, Cross and I simply stepped up on both sides of him. We threw his arms over our shoulders, and Zellman took point. He had his phone out to light the way.

"Let's go."

There was nothing else to say, not until we got to the road and got Jordan to a hospital.

We'd gone ten feet when we heard the first yells, and as one, we looked back.

The red and blue lights were there, but they weren't moving. What *was* moving: flashlights.

Zellman sounded mystified. "They're coming after us."

CHAPTER FIFTEEN

WE COULDN'T GO fast. Jordan's leg was injured badly enough that he needed us to keep going.

Realizing that, he pulled out from under our arms. "Go, you guys." He waved us ahead, looking wrecked. "Seriously. Go. I might not get in as much trouble since I got jumped."

It was a valid point, but my gut was blaring loud and obnoxious alarms.

I shook my head. "No, Jordan. You gotta come with us." I shared a look with Cross. We'd have to carry him. Jordan was over two hundred pounds. It would take all three of us.

"Come on." Cross stood in front of him. "Don't jerk. Got it? You'll shit my back."

Jordan's eyes were wide, disbelieving, but Cross bent down, tucked his head to Jordan's side and whoosh. He scooped him up, fireman-carry style.

My mouth hung open.

The sight of Jordan wrapped around Cross' shoulders and body—yeah. It was wrong for my mouth to start watering. Drooling.

Jaw tight, face grim, Cross grunted. "Let's go."

He led the way at a light jog as Jordan groaned and held out the phone to light the way.

"I'm never going to live this down, am I?"

Zellman and I were both still gaping.

That was—that was hot.

Z closed his mouth with a snap. "Damn."

That was all he had to say. I was on the same wavelength.

"Guys!" Cross yelled. "Come on!"

A slight giggle escaped Zellman before he kicked off and sped to catch up. I was right behind him, my stomach doing all these fluttery jumping maneuvers. And those flashlights were still coming behind us.

Zellman ran ahead, his phone mixed with Jordan's to illuminate a walking path. I brought up the rear, keeping an eye on the cops behind us. They had stalled so far back so we knew they couldn't see our phones, but after ten minutes of running at a light pace, we heard a shout from the right.

I hadn't even been watching that side!

"THEY'RE HERE!"

More shouting and the flashlights began waving, almost frantically.

"Our 11! They're on our 11!"

"Oh, man." Zellman had come up beside me.

Cross never stopped. He just continued on, trying to pick up his pace.

We weren't going to make it. That shout jumpstarted them, and they were moving in and doing it fast.

"I don't want to leave Jordan behind," I whispered.

Z's voice was quiet. "I know."

But ...

"Hey!" A twig snapped, and Zellman and I jumped back, whirling.

Our lights swung up, and a girl was there. She was tall, long legs, slim and willowy. Her hair was pulled into a messy bun. She threw up an arm, squinting and blinking under the sudden light.

"Whoa! I come in peace, fellow earthlings. I swear. Book nerd. That's all I am."

We kept our lights pointed at her.

I stepped forward. "Who are you?"

"Um..." A strand of hair fell over her face, and she tucked it behind her ear, biting her lip. "Can we do the names later? I mean, don't murder me or anything, but I kinda see what's happening." She pointed to the incoming flashlights.

"Guys!" A hushed yell from Cross. "What's the fucking holdup?"

"Oh!" She turned, her hand going up in a Vulcan salute, her fingers spread wide. "I come in peace. I swear." She bit her bottom lip again. "Shit," she whispered. She looked down suddenly. "You all probably think I'm super creepy, don't you? Shit, shit, shit." She was hissing to herself, turning away, her shoulders hunching forward. "I'm so stupid. Why did I approach like this?"

"Weird girl." Zellman stepped forward, his voice firm. "What do you want?"

"Right." She snapped back. Her shirt was off-kilter, but she didn't seem to realize it. "I can help you. I mean—" Again with the lip biting.

My patience was wearing thin.

I growled, "Get to the fucking point because you're holding us up from trying to not get arrested!"

Her eyes bulged out, and she paled, but it worked.

The words tumbled out of her, "Iknowaplaceyoucanhideandtheywon'tfindyou.Imean,ifyoudon'tmindjumpingintowater.Iswearit'ssafe."

She said all of that. Yeah. One word. No breath.

Z and I shared a look, our eyebrows raised.

He grunted, a slight grin tugging at his lips. "I don't know if I should be impressed or weirded out." He thought about it. "I think I'm turned on."

Cross had turned back. "Guys, what's going on?"

She jumped onto the trail with us, waving her hands. "Okay. Yeah. If you guys don't mind jumping into water—I swear it's safe—then follow me. You can hide there, and it'll be totally safe. I promise. I mean, it'll be cold, but I think you'll all live. I hope, anyway."

"Who are you?" Cross barked.

Jordan raised his phone to peer at her too, frowning.

"Um... Let's do that later. I just, um... Just trust me. I was here yesterday with my parents, so I know where this water hole is—"

"A water hole?!" Zellman surged ahead.

She gave a nervous laugh that ended on a sigh. "We're running out of time."

I turned to Cross and Jordan. "I can't get arrested."

"We haven't done anything wrong," Zellman grumbled. "I mean, why are we even running? Jordan got jumped. Whatever. You know what I mean."

Cross started toward the girl. "Underage drinking and partying. If they raided a District Weekend party, they don't care. We have to go with the girl." His eyes flicked to mine. "You're right."

Zellman groaned. "Great."

Jordan's head lifted up. "Shut the fuck up, Z. You're not the one hurt or on probation."

The girl's eyes got big, her eyebrows crawling up her forehead. "One of you is on probation? Whaaaat?"

Zellman scowled at her. "No."

Jordan rolled his eyes.

Cross said, "No one's on probation."

I took a step toward her, gentling my voice. "Look, we have to go if we're going to go."

I prayed she wouldn't back out and suddenly dash off to the side, or worse, start yelling for the cops. Because she could've. She'd said it herself. She was a book nerd, and she looked the part.

I didn't care for stereotypes, but while she was gorgeous in the face, it was a fresh face. No makeup. She was wearing a long-sleeve hoodie over jean shorts and sneakers. Her speaking skills didn't give off the smoothest and most sophisticated feel. We were the criminals, and now she knew it.

"Oh, God." Her voice matched her hands, shaky. "Okay. Yeah. Okay. I can't believe I'm doing this. Okay." She turned and motioned for us to follow. "It's over here."

Cross nodded to me.

I needed to take point with her. She was a girl. I was a girl. She needed to be handled with care, or she could bolt.

I moved up next to her and asked quietly, picking up the pace, "So, you were here yesterday?"

She was leading in the opposite way of the road, back toward the police. She almost tripped over a log. I grabbed her arm, steadying her, and she managed a smile at me. "Thanks. Crap. I suck at this stuff. I shouldn't have come."

"But you were," I insisted. We were out of options besides dropping Jordan and making a dash ourselves. And that wouldn't happen.

"Yeah." A long, drawn-out sigh. "My parents were up here. They're working on a more hands-on project. I kinda got brought with them."

Four more steps, down a sudden steep incline, and she paused. "It's right here."

Here?

I lit my phone up, swinging it over the land. She was right. There was a hole smack in the middle, and it was just big enough for one person to jump in at a time.

Zellman and Cross came up behind us. He bent down, helping Jordan to his feet.

Zellman stepped up, shining his phone directly over the hole. "Shit." He looked up. "You can't see anything in there. You sure that goes to water?"

She took a deep breath, stepping forward. "Yeah. I mean, I saw it yesterday."

"Yesterday? You've never jumped in it?"

"No..." Her head suddenly popped up high. "But I'll be the first now. I promise. I'm just..." She was still wavering.

"What's the problem?" asked Cross.

"I'm, uh..." A laugh hitched on a slight sob came from her. "I'm scared of heights."

"Oh. I'm sure jumping in a dark hole at night is totally helping." Zellman was sarcastic.

I hit his arm.

He shot me a glare. "She's a stranger, and now she's trying to get us to jump into who knows what? Is that a bear hole? Could be a bear hole."

Jordan frowned. "Are bear holes a thing? Really?"

"Oh my God! I'm going." And without further ado, she did just that. She rushed forward and disappeared into the hole. A second later we heard a splash and then, "I'm okay. I'm swimming to the side."

Now we really did have to jump.

Cross' arm brushed mine. "Our phones."

I finished for him. "Will be destroyed."

"Nope! Nope! Hold on." Zellman was reaching into his pockets, fishing things out. "Aha!" He produced three condoms. He waved them, grinning. "I knew these would come in handy."

"Are you serious?"

"Yeah." He shrugged, already ripping open one and stuffing his phone inside it, then double tying the end. "I might even have more to double wrap them. We gotta try, at least."

He was right.

I hated that he was right, but I didn't know why.

It was wrong, putting our phones into condoms, but desperate times, desperate measures.

"Oh!" Jordan dug in his pockets now too. "Wait. I have a baggie. Hell yeah!"

"Uh... guys?" Her voice rose up from the water. "What's going on?"

"We're coming," I called, handing my phone to Jordan. "Here. One of us has to go down there with her."

As soon as he took it, Cross grabbed my hand. He pulled me in, his lips brushing mine, and then I grinned, stepping backward. I was airborne for a second.

"Oh!"

Splash!

I submerged in the water, and it was freezing, but with a kick, I shot up. As soon as I surfaced, I began moving to the side. "I'm good. And clear."

"I'm over here."

I moved toward her, hearing her teeth chatter. "What's your name?"

"Aspen."

Her teeth were clanking together.

That wasn't good. "Are you going to be able to handle this? We might have to hide for a bit."

"Uh-huh." She didn't sound so sure, though.

"Coming!" A big splash followed, the water rippling from the weight.

"Z."

He popped up and swam over, grabbing my arm.

"We're clear."

Another splash, a bigger splash.

"That's Jordan."

Z swam back to pull him over.

"I can swim, douchebag." Irritation was thick in his tone, but I heard the pain too. "Ah. Leg cramp. Fuck!"

A last and final splash.

A second later, Cross didn't sound affected at all, "We're all good?" He kicked off, coming over to me. "Bren?"

"Here." I felt him tugging on my shirt and twisted around, linking our hands, drawing him forward. "We gotta move. The girl's already really cold."

"I'm fi—i—ine!"

Even Zellman snorted. "Yeah. Right. You're going to get hypothermia."

"I—have—a—bag—of—dry—clothes—on—the—bank." She gulped for breath. "Just ahead."

"Say what?"

I growled, speaking over whatever Jordan or anyone else might say. "We don't have time for this. We have to go." I grabbed her shirt. "Everyone link up. You lead the way." I patted her arm, and once Zellman and Jordan were holding on to each other, and Jordan was holding Cross' shoulder, we started.

We were silent, swimming for about thirty seconds when we heard voices above. Lights shone down into the hole.

"Hey! Here's a river hole."

"Over here!"

We could hear them crashing through the brush above, their voices growing clearer. More and more light came shining down, but we were far enough ahead. They couldn't see us.

"They're not there. No way. They'd head for the road. Let's keep sweeping the ground."

Cross' hand squeezed mine. He tugged me back, ghosting his lips over my forehead, before we were back to swimming.

Whoever this chick was, we owed her. Big time.

CHAPTER
SIXTEEN

WE LEARNED TWO things when we swam up to the bank farther down the river. One, Aspen had been camping. There was a tent, and she hurried inside to change clothes. Second, two of our phones still worked: Zellman's and Cross'. The two that had been double-bagged and put inside Jordan's baggie survived the trek. Mine and Jordan's, both only in one condom, hadn't made it.

We'd need to have a phone funeral, but we had more important things to handle. Job one being getting the hell out of Dodge. The cops had descended back down the hill, so Cross turned his phone on to call Race. He strolled down the river, looking for the road.

His voice traveled down to us. "Yeah. Is Taz's synced with me? You see where we are?" A pause. "No. We had to go in the river to hide from the cops. Did you see them? They might do a sweep down the road where you are." A longer pause. "Yeah."

He turned.

Headlights were starting to grow, coming from the south.

"I think I see you. Park up there. Jordan's hurt. We'll bring him up." A beat. "You got any clean clothes up there? Or blankets?" A nod. "Okay. Be up in a bit."

Cross hung up, coming back. He started to relay his conversation. I beat him to it. "We heard."

The tent unzipped, and Aspen stepped out, pulling her hoodie up over her head. "Sound travels over the water." She glanced back to where we could still see the glimmer of the cops, their flashlights had dwindled, but the squad car lights were still flashing.

Everyone was quiet a second, all of us—sans one—on the same wavelength.

Then, Jordan asked, almost gently, "So, um... You were camping here tonight?"

Zellman interrupted, "Alone? And dude, why here?"

"Zellman." I cursed under my breath.

He shrugged, not looking at me. "Just saying what we're all thinking." He gave the tent a cursory look, his mouth lifting in a slight sneer. "This shit's weird. Who camps alone? Or what chick would camp alone?"

Jordan sighed.

I wanted to hit Zellman. Again.

Cross shifted back on his feet, standing close to me.

"It's weird, you guys. And not safe." Zellman was on a roll. "Are you socially not there or something? Were you camping to spy on the party?"

She stiffened at the last question. Her eyes blazed, widening. Her mouth pressed tight.

Oh. God.

She was.

That was weird...or sad.

Zellman had violated so many etiquette rules...an awkward silence fell over the group.

Then Jordan murmured, "Ignore our friend. He's a moron ninety percent of the time and ignorant the other ten—"

"Hey!"

"We have a lot to thank you for tonight. If you hadn't helped us, we would've..." Jordan glanced at me.

I would've been in trouble. A lot of it.

I nodded. "Yeah. Thank you. Zellman doesn't mean to be offensive. He's just not saying it in the right way." I shot him a look. "In a sensitive way."

"Oh." She laughed, but it was hollow, forced. "It was nothing. I mean, I saw the cops coming and figured I should try and do what I could to help."

I glanced at her tent, and my stomach dipped over itself. The whole place looked sad. Solitary. Then again, who was I to judge? Someone watching me watch my old house could think the same thing. They could judge me too, and they'd be right.

Headlights flashed behind us before turning off.

Cross cleared his throat. "They're here."

"Finally!" Zellman huffed, going over to Jordan and ducking to put his arm around his shoulder. They started heading up the bank.

Cross touched the inside of my wrist, nodding to Aspen, who had quickly turned to look back out over the river. Her back was to the truck, her arms crossed over her chest.

I nodded and lingered as he hurried to go get under Jordan's other arm.

"Do you—do you need anything? Food or...?"

"What?" She twisted back to me, her mouth in a fierce frown. She cocked her head to the side. "Wait. You think I'm homeless?"

I had no idea. I said as much. "I, uh...are you?" I exhaled a ragged breath. "I mean, if you are, I'm not trying to judge. Where do you go to school?"

She stepped backward, her face pinched as if I'd committed the biggest offense possible.

I swore under my breath. "If you're not, I'm sorry. And if you are, I don't care. We owe you—I owe you. You can come with us, stay at my place. My brother would be a bleeding heart for you. Trust me."

She was quiet for a moment, not looking at me, and then she said tightly, "I'm good. And I wasn't lying about anything. I just wanted to help."

I was the worst person there was.

I wanted to make things right, better with her, but I could also read the signs that she was done with me. She wanted her space, so I nodded and started to turn around. "Okay. Thank you for everything. I mean it."

She didn't respond, but I saw her nod slowly as she turned her back to me, again facing out toward the river.

With a heavy heart, I trudged over to climb up to where Race's SUV was waiting for us. Taz was in the back, and as the door opened, she had a blanket ready for me. Heat blasted me, along with the smells of family.

"Who's that down there?" Race asked.

Zellman snorted. "Some wei—"

I cut him off, firmly, "Someone we owe. She helped us."

"That's good." Race eased the SUV back onto the road, but instead of turning south, he headed north. We'd have to go all the way around Frisco before going east and then south toward Roussou.

We traveled a bit, warming up, before Race spoke. "You guys should know the shit show that happened back there."

Cross looked over. "What shit show?"

Taz leaned over the seat, draping her arm between her boyfriend and brother. "The cops. Word already got out. They didn't arrest any Fallen Crest Academy students, or the public students from FC."

"What?"

"They rounded everyone up and asked them which school they attended," Race said. "All the Roussou students were arrested."

"What?!" Jordan jerked up, then grimaced and fell back.

Zellman shot forward. "You serious?"

Race nodded. "Yeah. And there's video of it. The same account that got Jordan's attack got the round-up. That's what they're calling it."

"What about the Frisco students who go to Roussou now?"

"Same. The ones who were transferred to Roussou were arrested. Ones who went to Academy or FC Public were all let go."

"How can they get away with it? Is that even legal?"

Race shrugged. "Who knows? I mean, they could say anything to justify it."

Shock ran through me, spreading wide. People could get arrested at high school parties. If you were drinking or high, yes. If you were in a crew, you were targeted. But the rest...even the ones who weren't drinking?

"All of them?" I asked.

Race nodded. "All of them. Sober or not. They were all arrested."

Cross looked over his shoulder at me, but what was there to say? It felt wrong. It felt unjust. It felt—something was up, that's what it felt like.

I hardened inside, and the whole feeling that something was coming just grew. I didn't know what kind of storm it was, but I knew it would be big, and I felt like it was on our doorstep, ready to blow down our home at any moment.

I only hoped we'd all survive it.

"We gotta tell your brother," Cross said.

I agreed, my neck stiff. "I know."

CHAPTER SEVENTEEN

THE COFFEE AROMA woke me, but it was the smell of toast and the sound of eggs being fried that had my stomach growling. Slipping out from under Cross' arm, I used the bathroom, brushed my teeth, and slipped on a pair of lounge pants and a shirt before heading down the hallway.

My brother's tattooed back greeted me first. His tattoos covered most of his body, and he twisted around, a glare on his face.

"I can't handle this anymore, Bren." He raised his spatula. "If Cross is going to live here, he needs to move downstairs. You know, where there's two guestrooms? And a couch. Or, at the very least..." He focused his glare over my shoulder.

I had a second's warning before a hand curved around my waist.

"At least wake up before I do and sneak back downstairs from now on? What do you say? Can you do that?"

Cross stepped into me, pressing a kiss to my forehead before moving away. He padded barefoot to the kitchen counter, pulling out a stool and taking a seat.

Channing watched him, still glaring. "Right. Sit there, Cross. I'm just here to make you breakfast and *also* serve it to you."

Cross grinned, raking his hand through his hair. He left it sticking up, but it looked good.

"Do me a favor." Cross lowered his head, still smirking at Channing. "Maybe inform us when you're coming home at night, and I'll be happy to set my alarm so I can sneak downstairs before you get home."

Channing shot to his fullest height. He pivoted, setting the spatula down on the counter.

A buzz filled the air. Cross had never challenged Channing before. He had smarted back once or twice, but never like this. Not with a ring of disrespect.

My brother grew taut and rigid. "Are you fucking serio—"

Cross started laughing, dropping his hands and leaning back. "No. God, no. I'm just giving you shit. Yes, I'll sleep downstairs from now on."

"Oh." The fight fled from my brother, but he was slow to pick his spatula back up. His eyes narrowed, he swept me and Cross with a stinging look. "It grates on my nerves." He pointed the spatula at me. "And don't give me shit about what I was like when I was your age. I don't care if I was worse than you. I'm the adult now. This is my house, and..." His irritation was fading. He turned back to the eggs, speaking normally. "You're better than me, anyway. You're going to be better than me too, when you're my age. You'll have your shit together long before I did."

Cross and I shared a look, frowning.

"Uh, okay." I was too tired to argue or ask what he was talking about.

My brother was doing quite well. He hadn't gone to prison. In my book, that was doing really well. Moving past him, I went to the fridge and grabbed some milk. "Cross, you want juice?"

"Please. Orange juice."

After that, we did our breakfast routine, or the routine we had when all three of us were in the kitchen together.

It was a small space, so one person typically stayed out. Cross was that person this morning. I pulled out plates and handed them over. Cross took them to the table. Silverware came next. He set the table, getting everything ready for the pan of eggs. I poured the juice, and he set his glass at his spot. I poured the coffee, added milk. Cross put the cups at Channing's and my plates. I added the condiments, and we'd just sat when Channing finished with the last of the toast. He brought over the heaping plate, carrying the pan of eggs in the other hand.

He sat at the head of the table, and Cross and I sat next to each other.

"No Heather?" I asked as Cross started taking some eggs. I reached for a piece of toast.

Channing pulled two onto his plate. He shook his head, reaching for the honey. "Nope. She had friends come into town last night, so she's in Fallen Crest."

Cross stiffened. "Speaking of Fallen Crest..."

He filled Channing in on what happened the night before.

"Are you sure?" Channing asked once he was done. His eyebrows were pulled together, low. "They only arrested Roussou kids?"

"That's what they said. We haven't gone to school to question anyone, but if Race said it, I believe him."

Channing swung his gaze my way. "And that girl, her name was Aspen?"

I nodded. "You know her?"

He shook his head, raising his toast to his mouth. "No, but... there's something about that name... You get a last name?"

"No. She closed up when I offered to have her come home with us."

"I'll swing over there, see if I see her tent or not. If she really is homeless, I can't let her stay out there."

I couldn't imagine what she'd think, seeing a tattooed guy coming around. "Maybe take Heather with you?" Though neither gave off warm and fuzzy feelings.

Channing grunted, grinning. "Yeah. Maybe. I can enlist Ava. She looks like a lamb compared to us." He sighed, sitting back in his chair. "I don't like it, any of it. Cops never show up at District Weekend events. It's a respect for tradition. They used to like when the three towns got along, for the most part."

"I was thinking it was a setup."

Channing nodded, picking up his coffee. "Seems like, which means a part of this is my business." He tossed Cross a raised eyebrow. "Hear that? Handling the cops is what I do. That's *not* high school. That's *community* shit. That's *my* place."

Cross shook his head, flicking his eyes upward but not completing the full roll. "Whatever." But he was grinning. "Still old, in my opinion."

"Old, my ass." Channing grinned back before he grew serious again. "For real, though. What's your plan on the crew front? I know you guys are going to do something."

Cross glanced at me.

I said, "We'll figure it out."

We hadn't talked about it. Everyone was exhausted after taking Jordan to the hospital and having him looked over. The rest of the night had been somber. Seeing him in the emergency room, being poked and prodded and questioned by a nurse who knew us by name was so normal that it shouldn't have been. But that was this life.

What happened to Jordan, we were mad about it, we were already swearing vengeance, but underneath all those emotions was something that shouldn't have been there. Acceptance. And that made me buzz a little, but I didn't know why. And not a good buzz, a bad buzz. The kind of buzz that was a warning.

The easiest thing to do was shut it down, ignore it.

I was in the ignoring phase right now.

Channing lowered his mug slowly, his eyebrows pulling together. "Something else I should know about? Jordan's assault doesn't normally get this no-reaction from both of you."

Cross lifted his head. "Huh?"

I looked over. He was blinking as if he'd been lost in thought as well.

"Jordan. Your crew member. He was attacked last night."

"Oh." Cross leaned forward, resting his elbows on the table. "Yeah. We'll figure out what to do, our next plan of action."

Channing leaned back. "Okay..."

It was obvious he didn't believe us, or he was troubled by the way we weren't reacting. I was too—in a dark part of me, I was.

And after finishing breakfast and getting ready for school, that thought continued to plague me.

I'd been out for blood the night before, my heart racing. We couldn't have gotten to Jordan fast enough. We needed to get there, save him, then rain damage on those who'd been hurting him. But my brother was right—retaliation hadn't been the first thing on my mind this morning—and that was just now setting in. Fleeing and then hiding from the police had taken precedence. Then the ER trip. And I kept remembering the last time we'd been to the emergency room, when we took someone in to save his life.

Round and round.

Cross and I were heading out to his truck when he asked, "You okay?"

I nodded as he started the engine. "Yeah. Just having weird thoughts." I remembered he'd been out of it earlier too. "How about you? You okay?"

He paused, glancing at me before jerking his head in a nod. "Yeah. I'm totally fine." Then he pulled away from the curb, and I knew one more thing that morning.

Cross was lying.

CHAPTER EIGHTEEN

CROSS GRINNED AS we parked at school. "Look. We have a greeting party."

Taz, Sunday, and Tabatha were all standing on the curb, backpacks on, purses in hand, and the school in their background. Students milled behind them on the sidewalk.

We parked across the lot, and as soon as we got out, the girls headed over to meet us halfway.

"Finally!" Taz exclaimed, skewering us with a heated look. "We've been waiting for thirty minutes, and that's thirty minutes we'll never get back—"

Tabatha settled a hand on Taz's shoulder, a calming smile on her face, "She's had three espressos this morning."

"But she's not wrong," Sunday muttered, turning away from us and glancing across the lot.

Following her gaze, I saw the rest of their friends, including Lila and the other girl from Frisco who had joined Tabatha's group. Right up in the middle of them were Jordan, Zellman, and a bunch of jocks.

Cross stepped close to me, and I said under my breath, "Why do I feel like we're being swallowed by the Normals?"

He laughed shortly, his hand grazing mine. "Uh, because we are." He nodded at the group. "I'm heading over there. The crew needs to plan later."

I nodded in response. He was right, and so was Channing. The weird arrests aside, heads needed to roll for what they did to Jordan.

"Jordan couldn't make a fist this morning. He couldn't brush his teeth this morning. He called me over so I could help him." Tabatha said as soon as Cross was a few feet away. She swallowed, blinking away a few tears. Her voice grew hoarse. "I have that video burned in my head. I can't get it out of my mind. I know I've believed the crew system is reckless and stupid at times, but my God, if you guys are looking for temporary members, sign me the fuck up." She stared at me fiercely, her eyes sparking, her chin raised.

Sunday shook her head. "Are you kidding me? Your boyfriend got attacked. Big fucking surprise. He's in one of the toughest crews here. They're a walking target. Welcome to my life the last year, constantly worrying about Zellman. And also, get over yourself. Are you forgetting that other thing we all went through? You know." She stepped closer to Tabatha, crossing her arms. "When we were all arrested, except these guys." She clipped her head toward Taz and me.

Tabatha exhaled deeply, closing her eyes. She touched her temples, rubbing in a circle before taking a step back. Looking up, she coughed. "I've not forgotten. I'm just worried about someone besides myself." And with that said, she surged forward, getting right into Sunday's space. "And what is your problem? We all signed the same piece of paper. We all took the same deal. It's not even a hardship. We were all excited about it anyway—"

"Wait." I held up a hand. "What are you guys talking about? What deal? What piece of paper?"

Both girls froze and moved apart. Tabatha's eyes swam with guilt, and Sunday refused to look at me.

Taz asked quietly, "Sunday?"

Sunday looked up.

"We can't talk about it," Tabatha said. "No one can talk about it, but trust me. You will find out..." She cut off, her eyes moving over my shoulder.

I was just turning to look when someone cleared their throat.

Mrs. Cooke, the front office secretary, raised a thinly penciled eyebrow. "Miss Monroe, your presence is requested with the principal."

"When?"

She sniffed, looking down at me with near disdain. "Now."

Taz laughed as Mrs. Cooke went back inside, walking around the clusters of students as if she were walking through a field of manure. She kept tugging down her suit coat and smoothing her hands over the sides of her skirt.

"Um... I was with you last night and since you arrived at school today," Taz noted. "I know you didn't get arrested, so my question for you: what'd you do to get into trouble?"

I snorted, adjusting my backpack strap over my shoulder. "Who the hell knows? Breathing, maybe?" I jerked my head toward the school. "I'm gonna head in, stash my things first."

"We'll come with you." Tabatha moved to my other side. "The bell's going to ring soon anyway." She looked back for Sunday, but she was gone.

Sunday was halfway across the lot to where her other friends were still standing and laughing, draped over the guys. Cross was watching us, and he tilted his head in question.

I shrugged in response, mouthing, "Principal."

He frowned, but I motioned to Taz.

He nodded.

"Do me a favor?" I asked her as we went inside. "Tell your brother where I was summoned? He's wondering."

"Oh yeah. Oh hey!" She touched my arm.

Tabatha stopped, but Taz tucked her chin down. "Um... Can we, uh..." She motioned between us, then rushed out, "It's about my brother."

"Oh!" Tabatha moved back, hands up. "Yeah. I get it. I'll see you guys in class."

Taz and I continued down the hallway. People noticed me and moved aside, clearing a path all the way to my locker. Taz didn't move to open hers. She fiddled with her backpack, looking down.

Finally, she sighed. "Fuck it. My dad called and left me a message. He's been trying to get in touch with Cross, too. He..." She looked up, biting her lip. "He and his girlfriend, Marie." Her nose wrinkled. "But whatever. They invited Cross and me to dinner."

"When?"

"The first dinner was a few weeks ago. Cross didn't show up, and you never said anything..." She shrugged. "Anyway, Dad wants to try again. This time, he thinks he has a better chance at having Cross show up if I invite you. He asked Race too."

I narrowed my eyes. "Are you asking me to go behind Cross' back?"

"What?" Her eyes widened. "No! God, no! I'm—I don't know." She shook her head. "Look, Cross is handling this whole thing how he's handling it, but I have to show up. You know me. I can't not show up if my parents ask me for something. Cross, on the other hand, can literally say 'fuck you' to them, and he's still their favorite." She groaned. "But whatever. That's beside the point. If Cross doesn't go, can you still come? For me? I need support. Race, though I love him dearly, is still a boy, and he's clueless sometimes. He adores his mom and hates his dad, so he doesn't get the in-between right now. I could just do with another person there to support me, you know?"

Crew code was clear in a situation like this. I couldn't say or do anything except report to Cross. Girlfriend code...a bit different.

I sighed. "Look, I can't guarantee Cross will come, but I can come as *your* friend."

"You will?!" She shot forward, her hands latching onto my arms. She shook me in excitement. "Are you serious?"

I already knew this was a bad idea. My gut was already backing away. "Yeah. Sure, I will," I said anyway. "When's the dinner thing?"

"Oh my God! I'm so happy you'll come, and it's next Sunday. They wanted to wait till after prom."

"*Ahem.*" A throat got cleared, sounded like it was cleared on the regular too. We looked up. A teacher had been watching us from an opened classroom. "I believe your presence has been requested elsewhere, Miss Monroe."

Taz and I shared a look. Since when did a random teacher know about my principal visits?

But stowing my bag, I grabbed a pen and shut the locker.

"You don't want your first class' textbook?" the teacher asked.

Taz now opened her locker, acting as if she suddenly wasn't paying attention.

She was.

"Nah. You never know how long I'll be there. Thanks for the concern, Mr. Ortega. Means a lot that you care."

He huffed, going back inside his classroom.

Cross and the rest were coming in, and he stopped in front of me. "What's going on?"

I jerked my head to the left. "Your sister will fill you in, and make sure to ask her about next Sunday too."

"Jerk off!" Taz called once I started forward.

I gave her a grin over my shoulder, then picked up my pace.

CHAPTER NINETEEN

"BREN." PRINCIPAL BROGHERS waved a hand toward the chair across from his desk.

He must've dyed his hair because his normal half-white frizz with a reddish tint was dark red now. And he'd learned how to manscape. His eyebrows were usually bushy, but today they were trimmed.

He was still skinny, and he was distracted this morning. Though freshly colored, his hair seemed more harried than last week. It was literally sticking up. His gaze was focused on his computer, and he cursed softly under his breath, running a hand over his pointy chin before clicking something, then sitting back and focusing on me.

"Miss Monroe."

I'd recently watched *The Matrix*, and I was tempted to correct him by saying, "Mr. Anderson" in return. Or maybe I was just missing Principal Neeon. Who knew. I doubted the latter.

Instead, I gave him a closed-mouth smile. "Let me have it. What am I in for?"

He frowned. "What?"

I motioned from him to me, then around the room. "You. Me. This room. I get called here when I'm in trouble. Remember?"

"Oh!" He blinked a few times. "You're not in trouble. Well, it's about your probation, so I guess it's about what you're still in trouble for."

Oh. That.

I stabbed the last principal.

Fun memories.

"I see." I didn't.

"Um..." He cleared his throat, his eyes darting back to the computer screen. "So, I'm reading about what happened last night." He looked at me, his eyebrows arched up slightly.

He didn't say anything more.

I didn't either.

He leaned forward. "Do you want to fill me in?"

"About what?"

"Last night?"

Uh...pretty sure I'd watched enough documentaries on Netflix to know what this was. Entrapment. I was going to play the dumb card.

"What are you talking about?"

"I'm sure your friends have already updated you about last night."

Again. En*trap*ment. Did I need to give him the definition?

"Yeah..." I leaned forward as his eyes lit up in triumph. Resting my elbows on his desk, I shook my head. "I'm still not following you, Mr. Bro."

His mouth thinned. "Are you kidding me?"

"Seems like you're going to have to give me the 411 this time."

He'd forgotten who I was. Crew royalty. My pops was in prison. My resume was packed with experience dealing with authority figures like him. I was on *probation*.

He muttered something under his breath and leaned back in his chair. He steepled his fingers over his chest. "I'm aware that you and Ms. Bagirianni—"

"The Badger."

He continued, ignoring me. "—had a discussion a few weeks ago. You expressed interest in fulfilling the rest of your hours through a different means than counseling and the events committee. Correct?"

Oh.

Crap.

That.

He read my face and chuckled. "I can tell by your expression that you remember the conversation."

I'd tried to wipe it from my memory, actually. I swallowed over a lump in my throat. I hadn't told anyone. Not Cross. Not Channing. No one. Though somehow, word had gotten out because I'd heard the Hollywood whisperings myself.

"That thing went through after all?"

"Did *that thing*, as you refer to it—a documentary series that came to Fallen Crest to shoot—get the clear for production? It did, indeed, and..." He leaned forward, his chair squeaking. "They've asked to come to Roussou for further footage and interviews."

This. This whole thing he was talking about was my worst nightmare.

The Badger had brought it up to me a month ago. The original production had been about Mason Kade and his wife, Samantha—their story. She was an Olympic runner. He now had two Superbowl rings. The project ran on ESPN, and it was a hit.

That was fine, dandy even. It wasn't my problem. It had nothing to do with my life.

Then Badger had said there was enough interest in the town dynamics that another project had been greenlit. The film crew was coming back, but to do a new story on the rivalry between Roussou and Fallen Crest.

Principal Broghers cleared his throat. "Ms. Bagirianni asked to have you to help one of their production teams, to assist with the locals because of your unique connection to Mr. and Mrs. Kade."

I gritted my teeth. My arms crossed over my chest, and every fucking muscle in my body stiffened. "I have no connection to them."

He started to speak, but no.

I jerked forward, my arms still crossed tight over my chest. "I have no problem with the football guy or the big-time runner, but I don't know them. He is friends with my brother. She is friends with my brother's fiancée. *They're* connected to *their* lives, not mine. Not me. Not my crew. And I told Badger thank you, but no thank you. I asked for a different option because I'm done with counseling, and the events committee is finished for the year. Prom was their last event, and I had nothing to do with that."

Without waiting a beat, he picked up right after I finished. "And I'm telling you that Ms. Bagirianni is no longer offering counseling as part of your probation hours. And because you chose not to assist with the prom planning, you are ten hours short of fulfilling your obligation."

Oh...

He wasn't finished. "I have looked into all the other options, and none of them has an opening for you. So that means you have a choice: fulfill your hours by helping out one of the production teams or go to juvie." One of those manscaped eyebrows curved. "Your decision."

I glowered at him. "My brother can find an alternative—"

"No, he cannot." He was so smooth now. "That would take too much paperwork. I would have to sign off on all sorts of things, and I'm telling you I am unwilling to do that."

I opened my mouth, an argument ready to spill. I didn't know what I was going to say, but my God, it would be a good one.

The principal held up a hand. "And I just got off the phone with your brother. I explained the project, the connection to his friend, and sorry to burst your bubble, but your brother's actually on board with this one."

Consider my fucking bubble popped. He'd strapped a grenade to it and pulled the pin.

My mouth snapped shut.

My brother. My own flesh and blood. Channing sold me out.

Mr. Bro chuckled again. "I can see you're upset, but I don't get it. I really don't. Why don't you want to help this camera team?"

I skewered him with a look.

He had to get it, and he was playing dumb right now.

Mr. Broghers might've been tentative when he'd first replaced Principal Neeon, but he'd come long strides over the last few months. I saw the calculation in his depths.

Production teams meant attention. I didn't care who they talked to; if they came to Rousson, there'd be comments and statements about the crew system. It was inevitable, and what then? More attention.

I didn't know what the cameras would pick up, how it'd be edited, but I did know there was already an audience waiting. The ESPN program had been national. Would this be too?

Having a national spotlight on us was not good, not at all.

"Bren?" he prompted.

A different thought came to mind, and I sat up straight. "Did you do it?"

His mouth dipped down, just a bit.

I scooted to the edge of my seat. My hands curled around his desk. "That documentary was about my brother's friends. This, Roussou, has nothing to do with them. Did you do it?"

He swallowed.

"Did you ask them to come do another series on Roussou specifically?"

The dots were starting to connect now.

The school had used cameras last semester to shut down the crew system. Not much had happened, but we worried they were going to target us. Nothing came of it.

Now this. The production team. Me being forced to help them, one of only two girls in a crew...

Maybe I was jumping to conclusions, getting ahead of myself. Maybe it had nothing to do with the crews at all.

"I don't know, Bren." Mr. Broghers' face was devoid of expression, giving nothing away. "I can just tell you you'll be meeting Miss Sallaway in a moment, because you *will* be helping her team, and we both know it."

"Who's Miss Sallaway?"

Someone knocked on his office door just as he stood up.

"She's one of the producers you'll be assigned to," he said. "She'll be your go-to for instructions on how to help, and a word of advice?" He went around the desk to the door, but paused before answering. "I would be very helpful to her. If she's not happy, I'm not happy. You need me happy considering you need *me* to sign off on your probation papers. I believe the wording in your documents is that you must 'fulfill all hours to the expectations of your school supervisor,' and since Ms. Bagirianni has signed off, that person is now me."

He opened the door, and all I could think was that it was official.

I needed to stab this principal too.

CHAPTER TWENTY

I WAS KIDDING.

Kinda.

"And no time like the present," Mr. Bro said.

I'd started to stand, and hearing the smugness in his voice sent a chill down my spine. I went slowly, but I knew I had to play ball. Courts and juvie were not things I wanted to deal with during the rest of my year.

"Is this a bad time, Kenneth?"

Kenneth.

I turned to see a woman shaking *Kenneth's* hand. She looked young, but I'd guess she was five years older than me? My height, slender, sleek auburn hair. Her roots were more red than the regular mane, so it looked like she dyed it darker.

She was dressed in jeans and a white shirt, with a blue infinity scarf wrapped loosely around her neck.

Broghers was pumping her hand, his smile way too eager. "No, no," he gushed.

I fought hard not to roll my eyes, but kudos to me, I hadn't yet yearned to pull my knife. Rehabilitation—it was real and at work.

His cheeks were filling with color. "This is perfect timing, actually. You requested a local assistant, and I have the girl right here. We were just talking about the documentary too."

The woman's eyes drifted toward me, and I saw a keenness in them. I also caught a flash of a few other emotions, but she masked them quickly. Her eyes narrowed, and she studied my face as Kenneth kept on talking.

Once he was done, she held out her hand. "Hello! I'm Rebecca. You can call me Becca."

I didn't say a word.

I also didn't shake her hand.

An embarrassed gargle rippled up from the principal's throat, and he took my hand, fitting it into hers manually. "This is Bren, Bren Monroe." He laughed nervously, complete with a slight hiccup at the end. "And she is delighted to be helping, right, Bren? Right? Or..." He dropped his voice low. "You can always choose the other option."

"Option?" Rebecca stepped farther into the office, her gaze flitting between us. She pulled her hand back. "Is everything okay?" There was a sharp edge to her tone.

"Yes. Yes! Everything is okay. Right, *Bren*?"

I needed to have a minute with myself.

There was a storm brewing. My bones rattled with its impending doom. The old Bren was railing against her cage, where I had stuffed her down, locked her up. I hadn't let her out—not after stabbing Principal Neeon, not after Taz's assault, not after seeing Cross with a gun in his hand, not after talking him out of doing something that would've taken him away from me.

My life had flashed in front of me in those moments, and I'd prayed. I'd bargained. I'd promised.

I did everything possible to talk Cross out of what he was going to do.

He went into that house anyway.

But he'd saved Alex's life instead of taking it, and it had clicked with me. I'd gotten my bargain, and after that, I'd committed to changing.

It had worked.

Until now—until I was pushed into doing something I didn't want to do. I knew, I just knew, that somehow this was going to backfire on me and hurt my crew. I knew it, but it was this or juvie.

I'd promised I'd never go to prison. And I didn't care what the name on the facility was, juvie was prison.

Fuck Kenneth. I made my decision, but fuck him.

Glaring at him, and vowing that when I got the opportunity to hurt him, I would, I cleared my throat and forced a smile to my face.

I felt like I was breaking plaster as I shook my head. "Yes. Everything is fine. Hi. I'm Bren."

"Hi." Becca's smile was easier, relieved. She tucked a strand of hair behind her ear. "Monroe's your last name? Any relation to Channing Monroe?"

"No." I shot my principal a glare. If he was forcing me to do this, I was forcing him to keep quiet. And it wasn't actually that I wanted to keep Channing a secret. I just didn't want to deal with anything else. My brother had been a rakish asshole when he was younger. If she knew him...

"Oh," she said. "I knew a Max Monroe when I went to school in Fallen Crest."

Oh... All the fight left me.

"You did?"

She nodded. "He'd be half-brothers with Channing. I didn't know there were so many Monroes in this area." Then she upped the wattage of her smile and pulled out her phone. "Okay. Well, I was told that everyone signed their waivers?"

"Yes. They did," Mr. Bro chimed in. "Everyone. You should have a list of the students in your email. I sent that earlier this morning."

"Great. Perfect. Can we set up in a back room? Privacy is important for these interviews. We want the students to feel comfortable."

"Oh yes." He was close to gushing again, and grabbing some keys, he gestured ahead. "If you go on out, I'll close the door and show you the way. We have the room already set up."

I moved aside once we were farther into the front office area, I saw Jordan at the desk, a slip in hand and bruises all over his face.

Becca saw him at the same time, and she gasped.

He didn't react, just looked at me, his gaze moving to where the principal was locking up.

"What's going on?" he asked.

I opened my mouth, but Mr. Bro swooped in. "Ah, Mr. Pitts. Your mother called ahead with your doctor's note." I felt him moving behind me, and Jordan's eyes widened, panic flaring as I registered what was about to happen.

Pivoting around, I saw the principal's hand coming down. He'd been about to touch me on the shoulder, and instantly, the need to fight swept over me. My teeth bared, and my fists were up.

Jordan was at my side in a flash. "Don't touch her."

Principal Broghers reacted, following his command. His hand balled up and retracted to his side. He seemed flustered, as if he didn't know what to do for a moment.

Becca watched the exchange. She had moved to the side, with a bag I hadn't noticed before now pulled to her front. She held it close, but she didn't seem scared by what had happened. Just curious. She tilted her head to the side, taking me in, and then because Mr. Bro still hadn't uttered another word, she took over.

Her hand outstretched, she crossed the space, a polite smile on her face. "I'm Miss Sallaway. You can call me Becca. What's your name?"

Jordan glanced at her hand, shifting more firmly behind me so I was a barrier now.

Noting the movement, Becca cleared her throat, but her smile didn't dim. She nodded and murmured to herself, "Interesting."

"This is Mr. Pitts. Jordan Pitts."

Mr. Bro had finally recovered. He tugged at his tie and moved to stand beside her, his eyes flashing to me. He seemed to have remembered what happened the last time someone touched me against my will.

He tried to muster a smile. I knew that was his apology.

The old Bren, she'd been there. She was getting sick of being tested, and I let out a deep sigh, pushing her back down. She needed to take a seat.

"Is, uh..." Becca asked Mr. Bro, with a discreet nod in Jordan's direction.

"Ah. No, unfortunately."

"Is, um..." Another discreet nod at me.

He shook his head, silent. "But she is supposed to assist you in any way."

Assist?

"She is?" Jordan said. Then he nudged the back of my elbow, dropping his voice so only I could hear, "You okay?"

I gave him a small nod. "Later."

He nodded back.

The principal had moved around us. He was talking to the secretary, and I knew I'd been right not to bring my first-period textbook. Apparently, we were going to the back of the library, a room barely anyone used unless they wanted to get their rocks off during school hours.

"Camera team?" Jordan asked. "What the fuck?"

"Mr. Pitts," admonished the secretary as she picked up the phone. "Language."

Jordan grinned at her, wiggling his eyebrows. "Come on, Miss Marjorie." He gestured to his face, winking and groaning. "Pity points. I'm thinking and moving slower than normal." He nudged me again.

Becca shouldn't have been able to see the motion, but I had a feeling she wasn't missing anything.

He bent down and whispered in my ear, "Cops want to question me about last night. Cross said to wait to talk to everyone before deciding the story."

I couldn't give him my opinion—not my real opinion. Nosy people were overhearing, so I hissed, "What story? We were home last night, remember?"

Jordan was silent, and Mr. Broghers had grabbed whatever he needed.

"Okay. Right. Off we go, Miss Salla—" He moved around us toward the office door.

"Becca, please." She began to follow, casting a furtive look over her shoulder to Jordan and me. "Or Rebecca."

He paused, a genuine smile on his face. "Rebecca, then. And I'm Kenneth, as I've already said." He added a nervous little hiccup laugh.

"That's disgusting." Jordan groaned behind me. "He's, like, thirty years older than her."

Agreed.

Becca stepped past him out into the hallway.

Mr. Bro almost let the door close, so eager to please, but then he remembered me and ducked back in, a cloud forming over his face. "Miss Monroe?" There was no question to his command. He was just playing the part.

"What is going on?" Jordan whispered.

"I'll tell you later," I whispered back, starting forward. "Don't say anything. I already lied to Principal Moron about last night."

Jordan's head moved back. "He was asking?"

"Bren!"

I could only nod before stepping out into the hallway, and then we were off to the library.

But bright side, I knew Cross had study hall in the library, and double bonus, it was during first period. If Miss Becca was intrigued by Jordan and me, she'd be consumed by Cross.

I was kinda looking forward to that.

CHAPTER TWENTY-ONE

I WAS RIGHT.

As soon as we swept into the library, I spotted Cross at the desk. He turned as we approached, and Mr. Bro groaned at the same time Becca ground to a halt.

"Oh my," she said. "Is that what high schoolers look like nowadays?" She narrowed her eyes, as if musing to herself. "Then again..."

"Mr. Shaw." Principal Broghers' shoulders rose, held, and fell. So dramatic. "What are you doing here? Why aren't you in class?"

Cross left the desk, stepping to the side so he could see me better.

Mr. Bro stepped between us. "I don't think so. Miss Monroe is here to assist Rebecca today. She's been excused from her classes."

Cross' eyebrows shot up. "She has?"

"I have?" I echoed.

Becca stood silently, taking it all in.

"Mr. Shaw. The reason you're here. I'm waiting for it."

If he could've stomped his foot and gotten away without looking like a toddler throwing a tantrum, I had no doubt the principal would've done it. There was a slight whine to his voice too.

"I'm sorry." Becca stepped forward, holding her hand out. "You are..." She shook her head in amazement. "You are gorgeous. Holy crap."

Cross didn't shake her hand, but she didn't seem to notice. She stepped back, taking him in from head to toe. "Has anyone told you you could be a model?"

My thoughts exactly.

"You play sports?" she added.

"Uh..." Cross turned to me. "What are you doing here? What's going on?"

"Mr. Shaw!" the principal barked.

"Chill, Kenneth. He's got first period here. Study hall."

"*Kenneth?*" Cross mouthed at me, a grin teased at his lips. "We can't use the cafeteria. Someone in the administration said it was too much like social hour. You know, with all the talking and snacks. You sent us to the library since there's no empty classrooms. Remember?"

Becca pointed between us. "Wait. Are these two in a..."

Kenneth rolled his eyes ever so slightly. "They are a couple, yes."

Becca stopped talking, but her mouth remained open. Her eyes pinged between us. As if coming to a decision, she folded her hands together and took a step backward.

I could read Cross' thoughts: *What the fuck?* I wondered the same thing.

"Is the back room ready for us?" Kenneth asked the librarian, who had perched at the counter, waiting.

She grabbed her keys and moved around, stepping through our little circle. "I'll unlock the doors."

Becca started to follow, but the principal waited, his beady eyes on Cross and me.

I didn't move. Neither did Cross.

Then Cross sighed. "Really? We can't even talk? She's not going anywhere."

Kenneth chewed the inside of his cheek, seeming to think it over. "Fine." He sighed, surrendering. "But make it quick. Miss Monroe is finishing off the rest of her hours with this project. It's important, and I don't want anything to mess this up."

His threat was clear. He didn't want *us* to mess anything up, our crew.

He stalked off, and Cross moved next to me, still watching our principal weave through the tables of students. "What the hell is going on?"

I filled him in as quickly as I could and with as much I could say. Mr. Bro was going to come barking for me to follow him any second.

"Kenneth?" That was Cross' first question.

I grinned. "Yeah. Isn't it awesome? I didn't know his first name."

Cross smirked. "Okay, but *Kenneth* aside, you're worried about this show?"

I gave him a look. "Aren't you?"

He shrugged, leaning against the front desk. "I don't know. I mean, why would we? It's nothing to do with us, right? It's about your brother's friends. Right?"

"I don't think so."

"What do you mean?"

I stepped in closer. "They already did that show on the Kade people. Why come back? And why do I have this feeling it *does* have to do with the crews?"

Cross straightened up. I had all his attention now. "You think this is a thing against us?"

"I don't know if it's us specifically, but the crews. Yeah. I mean, we know they were starting to make moves against the crew system last semester."

"Yeah, but..." Cross cut himself off, thinking, his jaw clenching. Then he cursed under his breath. "You're right. They haven't been able to get rid of the system. What's a last ditch-effort someone might take?"

A sick feeling had taken root since I was called into the principal's office. "Shine a spotlight on us?"

"We look like fucking gangs to the outside world. People don't like gangs. They hate them. That's how they'll spin everything. They'll talk about the violence." His gaze centered on me. "They'll talk about you. But..." He stepped back again. "Who'd actually talk, though? If you're a Normal, you keep your mouth shut. If you're crew, you keep your mouth shut. We shouldn't have to worry."

But I was worrying. And I could see he was now too.

He cursed again, raking a hand through his hair. "This is not good."

"Speaking of not good, I saw Jordan in the office. He mentioned the cops?"

"Yeah—"

"Miss Monroe!"

There it was, that bark I knew was coming.

Kenneth stood between two bookshelves, his tie thrown over his shoulder. He jerked his hand toward me. "Are you coming?"

Cross shifted to stand behind me, brushing up against me. "Why am I having bad thoughts about Broghers?" He clarified, "Things we could do to shut him up."

I grinned. "I don't think egging his car would do it."

"We saw how well the last principal reacted when Jordan dated his daughter."

"Bren!"

I had to go. "Yeah, but he is gone after all," I called over my shoulder.

Cross didn't respond, but he watched me, and those tawny hazel eyes softened before smoldering. I could read his mind. He needed me, and I was there with him.

I suppressed a groan. Desire could roar through me at a moment's notice, and it was spreading wide and fast, all through my body.

His eyes darkened. He was reading me too, and his lips twitched. He mouthed, *Later.*

I nodded, forcing myself to turn and walk away from him.

Kenneth huffed in impatience and stepped aside as I entered the aisle that went to the back section.

"I am going to have your boyfriend moved to a different class during this hour," he informed me. "And do not push me on this, because I *could* get him banned from the library for the rest of the year. And yes, while you're helping Miss Sallaway, you will be spending most of your time in the library."

I didn't know what to think about that.

That told me Cross' presence would be a huge threat to this project and also how invested Kenneth was. All facts we needed to know for whatever was coming.

"What about my class time?" I asked.

"I've talked to your teachers. Given that we only have a few weeks left in the school year and that you are not attending college, they've agreed to give you modified work to complete. There will be extra tests for you to take, which you will need to study for, and they will provide the specific learning materials you'll need."

"But—" I was reeling. Was that even legal?

"This is a special scenario, and yes, I did get permission from your guardian," he snapped. "I explained the general scope of the project and the extra studying you would have to do to pass your classes. But let's be honest. You are intelligent. You do minimal work in the classroom to pass your exams, and most of you seniors have already completed the majority of any requirements you need to graduate. The last month is a cake month for you, and seniors will be released within two weeks anyway. So no, you will not find a loophole to get out of this project. You are on probation. The law requires you to be here, I require you to be helpful, and I am your judge, jury, and possible executioner. Got it?"

With that, he stormed back to the room where I could see a camera guy standing in the opened doorway, the lens pointed our way.

Yeah.

Two things hit me at once:

One, whatever he'd recorded there was going to be destroyed.

Two, I *really* needed to start bringing my knife to school with me again.

CHAPTER TWENTY-TWO

BECCA HAD A stool just behind the camera, to the right.

After seeing the entire camera setup in its entirety, I was awed but also nervous about the direction of this whole thing.

Becca talked to the librarian a bit more, then Kenneth. Another older couple, probably in their early fifties, were there as well. They all conferred.

The librarian left first.

The principal next.

Becca remained in that circle, her head bent with the other two, and I had a feeling maybe they were the real bosses. They kept going over a list and pointing at items on there, speaking to Becca. She nodded until they asked a question.

She pointed at me. "Her," she said.

They looked at me.

The woman's hair was almost silver, but it didn't look old on her. It looked regal. With her thin frame and her hair pulled up in a loose bun to frame her angular face, she could've been a model in her day. Long arms, long legs. There was an intense perusal in her gaze as she looked me up and down.

She didn't speak for a long time. The man didn't either, but it was her that pulled me in and held me captive. I wanted to shift around, adjust my shirt, scratch my face. But under her gaze, I couldn't. Kenneth was a bonehead at times. Becca was young and smart, but with this woman, there wasn't anything. She was an impermeable wall. It was as if she was reaching inside of me, and she could sense my inner thoughts and emotions, though. And just like that, the old Bren sprang to life.

I almost sighed.

She'd been getting teased awake more and more today, and I was not liking it. I had a balance going. Yank too deep inside of me, and that old Bren would come out, and no one wanted that. Me included.

Fuck this. Fine. If this old broad was going to psychoanalyze me—because that's what I felt she was doing—I was going to let her see me completely. I'd been standing back in the corner, but under the weight of their focus, I stepped straight out, almost to the center of the room. I stood facing them directly—arms at my sides. Shoulders back. Head up.

The woman straightened as well, her chin lifting. She wore a long, loose skirt with a cashmere sleeveless sweater. She also had an infinity scarf, but it was a whole lot richer than what Becca was wearing.

I caught a brief glimmer of a grin, her eyes flashed, and then she nodded. I was dismissed.

I felt like an animal at an auction. Someone gave their measly last bid on me, and the sale was decided. Exit left for my slaughter.

"Okay. That sounds like a good plan," Becca said, and the other two left through the side door.

Becca turned and came toward me. "Let's bring in the first girl, shall we?"

An excited buzz filled the room, and Becca clapped her hands together. "Let's get this started." She neared me, lowering her voice. "The first girl we're interviewing is this one." She pulled up a file and Tabatha Sweets' face stared back at me. "We have a general list of questions to go through with her, but while we're warming her up, getting her comfortable for the camera, I'd like you to jot down some more personal questions. You know, questions only you might know to ask her—the questions she won't want to answer. You can write them as the interview goes too, just anything you think we should ask."

The fuck?

She stepped away, speaking to her team, and I was half aware of the door opening again. Someone stepped in, and I heard Tabatha's voice.

I'd started reading over the questions but looked up, hearing how so not-Tabatha Tabatha was sounding. She had her arms wrapped around herself, and she was tugging fiercely at the bottom of her shirt. Her hair had fallen forward to cover one eye, and she swung her gaze all around the room—as if she couldn't fully see anyone but was trying to pinpoint their location through sound.

Until her gaze found me. She halted, back-tracked, and then the blood drained from her face

"Oh no." Her teeth found her bottom lip.

I looked from her reaction to the questions, and that's when I knew my gut had been right.

There were general warm-up questions about what she'd had for breakfast that morning, general questions about her, her age, her family, and then a whole other list of notes. *If the subject is tense, find common ground. Annoying younger siblings? Have them laugh. Favorite hobbies. Talk about what makes them light up at first. Move to harder questions once trust is established.*

My heart had fallen past my stomach, all the way to my feet.

I got to another section.

Are you in a crew?

Tell us about the crew system.

What do you dislike about the crews?

What do you enjoy about the crews?

This was my worst nightmare.

I looked up at the name of the entire goddamn project: *The Crew Gang World.*

I felt dizzy, seeing spots. Air particles were swimming around, and my skin was too hot for me. I had to get out of there. I had to—

"Are you ready?"

Becca's chirpy voice grated through my panic, and I lifted my head. My hands gripped her clipboard. My knuckles were white. I was going to break it if I didn't get myself controlled.

What to do? What to do?

This was going to happen with or without me.

I had to stop it. I had to. They would get us wrong. We'd be crucified, vilified. I gulped, a lump forming in my throat. I saw the hate that came out against Channing's celebrity friends. There was love and adoration, but so much hate too. We'd be worse. We weren't a success story, an adoring couple that had beautiful children. *Gang World*. That's the title they were going with.

"Okay." Becca was so fucking calm and smooth. Why was she calm?

I swallowed, feeling myself starting to choke, and then I heard a murmur of voices and the lights went off. The spotlight flashed on and smack in the middle, on a tall chair perched in front of the camera, was Tabatha.

"It's roll time."

Becca leaned forward on her stool, and she was so warm, so soothing, almost seductive as she asked her first question. "Are you a little nervous?"

———

I shoved Tabatha up against the dryer in the bathroom. "What the hell was that?!"

I was in her face. I didn't care.

I was the bully. I was threatening. I was fulfilling all the stereotypes, but I was livid, and underneath all of that...I was scared.

Terrified.

My hands shook—the aftermath of having to sit there the whole time as Becca took her time. She chatted with Tabatha. Made her laugh. Made her sigh. Little by little, Tabatha relaxed. She got comfortable. She felt sorry for Becca as she told her stories about her childhood. She felt connected to Becca, and I caught the gleam in the young producer's eye. All that shit she was saying, I didn't think any of it was true. It didn't matter. It served its purpose, and after building rapport, Becca started in with the real questions.

Once they were done and Tabatha left, I announced a need for the bathroom. I was hot on her trail, and I'd grabbed her arm and shoved her into the bathroom as soon as I got a chance.

The third-period bell rang, and someone tried to open the door. I shoved it back, kicking the door stand underneath it.

"Hey!" came a voice from the other side.

"Use a different bathroom. This one is busy."

"I'm going to be late."

"You're already late. Get lost!"

She did. I heard her bitching, but she left. The squeak of shoes faded, and I turned, feeling like a predator with my prey. But I didn't want to eat Tabatha. I wanted to rip her to pieces.

I stepped back. "You have one minute to spill everything. One minute!"

Tears were already rolling down her face, but she wasn't wiping them. She had balled her sleeves into her fists, and she raised them, then slid down the wall until she hit the floor with a thud. I didn't think she even noticed.

"I—I had to, Bren! You weren't arrested! They didn't make you sign that paper! I had to sign it! I had to." She was blabbering, just the way she had been for the last hour, spilling secret after secret of the crew system to those cameras. I'd grown nauseous as I listened, but also cold and hard. I was a murderous robot by the end, and my anger had found its target.

"What paper?" I demanded.

"I was arrested! You weren't."

She started to scramble to her feet.

I pushed her back down, standing over her. "Explain everything, or I swear, Tabatha, I will turn Jordan against you in five seconds. And I won't be making anything up. I will tell him the truth." I pointed toward the library. "What you did in there should get your ass beaten by any one of us. No one talks. No one! You're not exempt because you're Jordan's girlfrie—"

"THEY MADE ME!" She heaved for air, her tears continuous. She hiccupped, gasping for breath. "I can't—"

I growled.

Her head hung low. "They made us sign confidentiality agreements and non-disclosure documents. With me telling you this, they could sue my family."

I kneeled down. I didn't give one shit. "I am running out of patience. Talk, or I will do things you and I both will regret."

When she lifted her head, her eyes searching, she saw the truth.

I would rain holy hell over this school if she didn't tell me what was going on.

"That's why they arrested us at the party last night."

Finally.

Surrender.

My rage simmered down, just a little bit. She was talking.

"Go on," I said.

Her head folded back down. The fight had completely left her. Her voice was so weak, small. "Every student at that party who went to Roussou was offered a deal. We were separated. Half of us went to the Fallen Crest station and half went to ours. I don't know—maybe to cut down on time since they were running short? But I know every student was taken into a room. A police officer, an attorney, someone from school, and then their parents were escorted in. They were in there for twenty minutes, the longest was forty, and when that door opened, the parents were shaking hands and the student was signing a bunch of papers."

"You said a school representative?"

"Yeah." She sounded so tired. Her head lifted, resting against the wall, but her tears still flowed. She sniffled, wiping the back of her sleeve over one side of her face. "I recognized Principal Broghers, and then the superintendent came in. That teacher, Ortega, came in later. They rotated, like they were giving each other a break."

I was sick to my stomach. The need to expel whatever was in there, as it was rising, piercing through my rage. I knew what they did. I had it all connected, but I needed her to say it out loud. I needed to know it was real, that it was all actually happening the way I'd feared it would.

"Keep going." My voice was raspy now, hoarse.

She sighed. "I got my turn. My parents walked into the station, saw me in handcuffs, and my mom just broke. It was messy and embarrassing, and she was blaming Jordan before she even knew what happened."

She paused, her bottom lip trembling.

I waited until it stopped, until she stopped swallowing past the pain.

"What did happen?"

"They offered me a deal: full disclosure and participation in this project to get off. No charges. No fines. Nothing on my record."

"What charges did they have for you?"

"Does it matter? They'd find something. Underage drinking? There were drugs at that party. You know Frisco is still dealing. Trespassing even. The cops said the landowner called in the party, complained about all the teenagers vandalizing his field." She snorted. "That's bullshit. Anyone arrested has to talk to the cameras and work with them. Otherwise, charges. I don't want to deal with probation or even community service. Not this summer. Not right before college. If my college found out about this, they could kick me out. I'm going to a private school next year. They might feel I'm not right for them, and bam, I'm out. What then? Community college?"

I shifted back on my heels and stood, grinding my teeth together. "My brother's girlfriend went to community college. She's doing just fine. Don't think your future would be ruined if that was your last possibility."

I started for the door, not needing to hear anything else. She'd spilled the details. What was next were the justifications, the excuses, the victim-talk. I wasn't going to feel sorry for her. She chose to sign that paper. They all did.

They all could burn in hell.

I'd ripped out the door stop and started to open the door when she spoke up.

"What are you going to tell Jordan?"

I didn't look back.

Tabatha was a Normal. I had melted, halfway forgetting over the last few weeks. I remembered now.

"The truth," I told her. "You're a sellout."

I got three steps before Taz was in my face. A bathroom pass in her hands, she stopped in surprise, then rushed to me. "Hey! I was just thinking—we haven't talked about prom at all. Like, at all. That's weird."

I glanced over my shoulder.

If Taz went in there...if Tabatha came out, I wasn't sure what I would say. Or do.

I was still pissed, beyond pissed.

These cameras were here to mess up our lives—my life—and they didn't get that right.

"Bren? Hello." Taz waved her hand in front of my face, stepping around to face me as I tried to evade her. But I couldn't do that, not to her.

"I—what?"

"Prom." She frowned at me, waving her bathroom pass in the air, distractedly. "It's this Saturday. I know we're all doing a limo together, but what are you wearing? Monica asked about the salon that morning, and I assumed you were in, but then I realized we've never talked. That's super weird."

I wanted to groan. This *conversation* was super weird. I gave two shits about prom.

"Uh, yeah. Maybe. I don't know."

I needed to find Cross. I needed to tell the guys. I needed to figure out my next steps because Becca would come looking for me, and what would I do then? I wanted to burn this school down, but I was fairly certain the guys wouldn't be on board with that. So what? Sit tight? What could I actually do?

"Bren." Taz lowered her voice, stepping closer. Concern filtered over her face. "Are you okay?"

"You want the short answer?" *No. Hell no.*

But I lied because I knew what I had to do. "I'm fine. Just... worried about prom. You're right."

I needed to go back to that room. I needed to sit there for every interview.

They wanted me to give them specific questions for each person, so I would do that—questions that had nothing to do with crew life.

I would sit. I would stew. I would spy.

And then I would decide what to do—with the guys, but only with the guys. I wouldn't react. I wouldn't put anyone in jail or leave the school in handcuffs. *That's* what I would do.

"Bren. Prom. Do you or don't you have a dress?" Taz was trying to be funny. "That's the big debate going on here."

A dress? Fuck.

Prom was a big deal to Normal girls. That wasn't me, but we were going. Taz had begged and pleaded, and we all gave in a while ago. I'd put it out of my head, and no. I didn't have a dress.

"I—"

"I'm just kidding!" Taz swatted my arm, bouncing backward. "Of course you do, but for real, the salon day. Are you in? Monica's mom made the appointment. It's at the Fallen Crest Country Club. Her mom knows a manager there or something, and they have that spa now. We're booked there that morning. You want to ride together? We're supposed to be there at nine."

"Uh...yeah. Sure."

Prom. Shit.

CHAPTER TWENTY-THREE

SILENCE. TOTAL AND complete silence.

I forced myself to walk back to that library, back to that room, and sit there as they brought in another student. Then it was lunch, and I couldn't hold back any longer. The four of us met on the bleachers by the football field.

No one was out here during lunch. If they were, they saw us and turned away. Survival instincts.

I'd just finished telling the guys everything.

Crickets.

"She talked about us?" Jordan finally asked, his shoulders bunched tight around him.

I nodded. "She didn't name us, but she didn't hold anything else back. They asked for her thoughts on the crew system. She gave them. And I'm quoting, she 'didn't like the system in the beginning, but recently had a change of heart.'"

His voice was raw. "Did she elaborate?"

"Did she tell them she had a boyfriend in a crew? No. She talked about the Ryerson Crew and the new Frisco one, but she kept quiet about us." But I knew it was only a matter of time. "They'll find out. You know they will. She said everyone has to give full cooperation."

"The Ryerson Crew isn't here today." Cross looked around us. "They didn't sign those sheets."

I hadn't even noticed.

As if reading my mind, he said to me, "You've been sequestered in an office or the library this whole time. You only would've noticed in the morning, and who notices then?"

That was true. I'd been standing to deliver the shitty news, but I sat now, turned toward the others.

Zellman was quiet, half turned away.

"Z?" I asked.

"Those Academy Crusties were a part of this. They had to be." I shared a look with Cross. Jordan frowned.

Z shook his head. "I don't know what it means, but they had to have been in on it. They attacked Jordan in front of us. We were there. Ryerson Crew was there. Only reason I can think of that they would've done it then and there is because they knew the cops were coming. They knew we couldn't retaliate, and hell—maybe they thought we'd get arrested and wouldn't have time to think about revenge." He growled. "I hate those Academy assholes. Rich pricks who think they can get away with anything."

I was out on a limb here, but ... "Any chance the guy Sunday's going out on a date with goes to that school?"

He shook his head. "Not anymore. Not after I tell her what they did. She's going to drop him in a second. She got arrested too. The prick didn't warn her."

"I don't get the connection," Cross said, more musing than angry. He stood, starting to pace with his head tipped back. "I get the administration working with the police. I get that. This all makes sense on their end, but—"

"Why would Principal Moron insist on Bren helping them, though?" Jordan interrupted. "I don't get that. Do they know Bren is in a crew?" He looked at me.

"I don't know. I can't imagine someone not telling them, but this Becca person isn't acting like she knows I am."

"You said she knows Channing?"

I glanced up at Cross. "She asked if I was related to him. I said no, and then she said she knew Max."

"Wait. Who's Max?" Zellman asked.

"My half-brother. We didn't really know him growing up."

"Oh." Z frowned. "I'm sorry, Bren. I didn't know."

"I don't talk about him."

The guys shared a look, and Jordan coughed. "And you talk about everyone else in your life?"

I grinned. "Touché. It's not a big deal anyway. Max had a different mom, and he went to Fallen Crest Public. She didn't let him see us, hardly ever."

"Still. That sucks. I'm sorry, B."

Jordan rubbed a hand over his jaw. "I know Bren's dropped a bomb on us today, but I got the cops waiting to talk to me after school. My parents ran interference, giving me the day to go to school, but we know they're going to show up in a cruiser if I don't head over there as soon as the last bell rings." He looked at all of us. "What do I say?"

"Nothing." Cross grunted, dropping down to sit next to me. "Usual protocol. Why's this even a question?"

"Because there's video of those assholes getting the drop on me. That's why."

Zellman pointed out, "And those guys were at the party—"

"No, they weren't," Cross countered.

Everyone turned to him, waiting.

"If they were there, they would've been arrested. They weren't. Why discriminate against only one group? Therefore, no one's going to say they were there."

"Dude. The video," from Zellman.

Cross shrugged. "It'll get used if something legal happens, but I bet they'll just ignore it. If they know about it."

"So what should I say?"

"Say you don't know who got you. They dropped you, and everything after that was a fog."

Another beat of silence as Jordan digested that. "Okay." He nodded. "I can do that."

He turned to me. "Kenneth asked you about me?"

Zellman snickered. "Kenneth. I love it."

"He was fishing about last night in general, trying to see if I'd roll over. He didn't specifically mention you."

"Well, there's that, I guess."

"We're doing something, right?" Zellman hopped to his feet. Shoving his hands in his pockets, he took up the pacing for Cross. The snickering was done. I recognized that look on his face. Everyone did. He was antsy, and he wanted action.

I stayed quiet.

Cross was the smartest of all of us, so I'd do what he said. And since last semester's hierarchy fight, Jordan adhered to Cross' instructions as well, so it was really Cross' decision.

Z knew this. He stopped pacing, and all of us watched our officially unofficial leader.

Cross shook his head. "I don't know, guys. I think there's too many moving parts and unanswered questions. We need more information before we do anything."

"What about the buddy system we had going for the town rivalry?"

Cross shook his head. "I mean, they got you back for the cars. If Z is right, they got all of us back. I think everyone should stay in the buddy system, just to be safe, but am I worried Fallen Crest Academy is going to hurt someone else? No. Am I going to broadcast that? Also no."

Zellman growled, kicking at a rock on the bleachers. It pinged off another bench before falling. "Fuck that. I want to bust someone's head."

Cross' mouth flattened, and he stood up. "Why don't you go get laid instead? Assert your dominance over Sunday?"

He wrinkled his nose. "I don't want a relationship."

"Is it worth losing her? 'Cause it sounds like she's going."

Cross raised a good point, and Zellman knew it. He didn't have an answer, but he burst out with a myriad of curses, his hands balled into fists, and he tore out of there, heading back to school. The bleachers shook from his momentum.

Jordan waited until Z was halfway back to the school, far out of earshot. "He's not messed up over Sunday pressuring him to be in a relationship. She's pregnant." He met each of our stares. Not a blink. "Z's not in love with Sunday. We all know that, but he cares about her. The baby daddy is an Academy kid. The prick wants her to abort it."

Oh. Whoa. I hadn't seen that one coming.

"Wasn't she drinking this weekend?"

"She was acting. You know the drill. Fit in to get by, and all that." Jordan sighed, standing. "What do I do about Tab?"

Cross and I shared a look.

"She's not in our crew." I was extending a forgiving olive branch here. See? Strides. This was a big one for me. "I don't like what she did, but she was vague. That helps."

Jordan didn't respond at first. But his shoulders slumped. "Yeah." He sounded exhausted. "She should've told me, though. I can't get around that." Pain flared in his eyes, and he blinked a few times, a mask falling over his face. "I'm going to need to drink tonight. Heavily."

Cross leaned forward, his elbows resting on his knees. "Then we'll do that. No one except Wolf Crew."

"Goddamn. Sounds perfect."

Jordan stood. "I'm off to catch up to Zellman, make sure he's not doing anything stupid."

I asked, "Are you going to be okay?"

His eyes met mine, the pain flaring up again. "No, but that's why I have you guys. Tonight."

Cross and I echoed, "Tonight."

I waited until he'd gone down the bleachers, heading toward the school.

"I act normal in there?"

Cross expelled a deep breath, leaning forward once more. "Shit. Yeah. Why'd they target you?"

I shrugged. "I'm sure I'll find out."

He glanced over at me. My hand lifted to rest on his back.

"Talk to your brother about this Becca chick," he said. "See what he has to say."

"Okay." I rubbed his back in circles.

There was deeper shit happening now, though. Zellman was hurting for someone he cared about. Jordan felt betrayed by someone he cared about. Our other two members needed us.

"Tonight," I murmured.

Cross sat up, lifting his arm around me and pulling me in. He nuzzled my ear and pressed a kiss to my forehead. "Tonight." He ghosted a kiss down to my lips. "Why do I feel like I always need you? Why can I never get enough of you?"

I pulled back, just enough to look him in the eyes. "Because you do?"

He grinned. "I love you."

"I love you, too."

CHAPTER
TWENTY-FOUR

AFTER SCHOOL, AFTER a quick trip to get phones, I reported to Zellman and Cross how the rest of the day went. How I took note of every single thing anyone said in their interviews. How once they saw me taking note, they clamped up. How that was a *good* sign.

Zellman slouched down in the truck, his leg up on the dashboard. "I'll say that's a good sign. Maybe people will just shut the fuck up. Crews ain't no one's business but our own."

Cross didn't respond. Neither did I. There was really nothing more to say so instead, we resumed waiting for Jordan. We were outside the police station, and he'd gone inside to make his statement.

His parents went in with him.

We weren't allowed, and when he came back out, both parents just shook their heads at us. He headed over, gave us the run-down, which was that he said nothing. He couldn't remember how he got his bruises and cut-up face.

Cops weren't happy. His parents weren't happy. No one was happy, except us.

Well, technically because Zellman wasn't happy.

He wanted to drive. Jordan said no.

Zellman said Jordan looked like a hospital patient.

Jordan didn't care.

The argument was resolved when Cross took the keys and tossed them across the lot.

"First one gets the keys, drives."

Zellman surged forward.

Jordan grabbed his head in the palm of his hand and shoved him backward. Z fell back, and Jordan was halfway over the lot by then. He swooped up the keys, but Zellman was in a mood about it all. I got it. It was a dick move that Jordan did, but it was also kinda nice to see some of that dickhead part of Jordan was still in there.

After *all* of that, we headed out of town.

We had a spot north of Fallen Crest and Frisco. We'd found it by accident one time when we were out for a drive, and we'd only been back a handful of times. But tonight was a night for the beach.

We had booze. Blankets. Lighter fluid for the fire. Food to grill if the guys got ambitious, but if they didn't, we went through a drive-thru in the last town before our spot.

Jordan and Zellman were in the front. Cross and I took the back, and it'd been a rough drive, but we were there. Jordan pulled onto the gravel road that took us closer to the beach. From there, it was a hike down the cliff to our little alcove.

A small creek joined the ocean, sidewinding between two ridges of rock, and it was there we usually sat.

"We're here," Jordan said, the truck rocking to a stop just before he and Zellman got out.

They came around the back, and everyone grabbed something to carry. With our arms full, we started the trek down.

It wasn't long, but it was steep enough that we needed to go slow or risk breaking an ankle.

"God." Jordan stopped at the bottom and tipped his head back for a deep breath. "Why does the air feel lighter here than back home?"

Z went past him, grumbling, "It shouldn't be. We learned why in school, but fuck if I know. I just know it's not. You can breathe easier because Tab's not looking for you here."

"Ah." Jordan's tone was wry, watching Zellman stomp ahead of us. "Right. The voice of logic, that one." He smiled faintly. "Who's the scholar of our crew now?"

"Fuck you, dude!" Zellman held up his middle finger. "Google that shit. I'm right." He paused a beat. "About both things!"

Jordan didn't respond. His head lowered, his eyes closed, and then with a soft sigh, he started forward.

Cross and I followed. Zellman chose the spot by the creek and threw his items down. Shoving his hands in his pockets, he yelled over his shoulder, "Gonna look for shit to burn."

"Now that's the Zellman I recognize."

Jordan's voice was loud enough to be heard, but Zellman didn't react. He just headed down the beach.

Jordan began rifling through the bags as Cross started to unfold the chairs, setting them in a circle. My job was to grab some rocks and outline where the fire would go, but I knew there would be a conversation. I was slow to get going. I wanted to hear it.

Cross' eyes flicked to mine, and I gave him a small nod. Now or never.

"Why are you and Z fighting?" he asked.

Jordan didn't look up, still rifling through the bags. He pulled out lighter fluid and matches. "Because we spend all our fucking time together." A beat. He glanced up. "I mean, you and Bren are actually fucking, but he and I ain't. You get my drift."

"Har har." I stepped in, slapping his shoulder.

Jordan chuckled, pulling out the food we'd grill. Guess he was feeling ambitious after all.

He shrugged. "I don't know. We're both just pissed, and taking it out on each other. That's all. We'll be fine. Give us booze, something to grill, something to burn, and let us bitch tonight. We'll head back later feeling all refreshed and shit."

I didn't like my crew members hurting. It tore me up inside, but damned if these weren't situations I could do nothing about it.

"I'm sorry, Jordan."

He looked up at me. A small smile. "Thanks, B. We'll figure it out. Always do."

I wanted to believe that.

I didn't.

Cross' phone buzzed, and a second later, mine did too. I glanced down. It was Taz, and looking up, I didn't even ask the question before Cross reached over and pressed the reject button.

As I put it back in my pocket, Jordan's phone started going. "That about the Sunday dinner thing?"

Cross pivoted back. "What?"

Jordan rejected his call too, shoving the phone back in his pocket. "What's going on? Sunday?"

I opened my mouth.

Cross spoke over me, his eyes hot on mine. "Really? You're going to tell them?"

I closed my mouth, hurt searing my lungs for a second.

His eyes flashed a warning, and I felt pain slice my chest. He didn't trust me? For serious?

"Uh..." Jordan's eyes were narrowed, a hardness flashing there. "Wanna tell me why I'm supposed to deal with a girl I love talking about things I normally wouldn't want her talking about, while you're telling your girl to keep quiet about something maybe we should know? Hmmm?"

Yeah. He wasn't happy. Not at all.

"It's nothing serious."

"Fuck you."

Cross gave him a look, but Jordan wasn't backing down. He stepped up, looking down at Cross from the two inches he had over him.

A shiver went down my spine, setting all the hair on the back of my neck upright.

I could've used Zellman right about now.

"Hey." I stepped forward, my voice soft.

I maneuvered until I was between them, and then my hands went to Cross. He was like cement, and his chest muscles twitched under my hands, but his eyes never left Jordan's.

"Hey."

I pushed Cross back a foot before turning to peruse the scene. Both were heated, but Jordan wasn't as mad.

I spoke to him first. "You're hurt."

"Damn right I'm hurt." He thrust his finger at Cross. "Maybe my patience is wearing thin. You've got shit happening in your household, and you ain't saying shit to us about it. What the fuck's that about, huh? Huh?! We're here tonight 'cause of me. 'Cause I told you the shit going down with Z and myself. And you—you ain't saying shit to us. Where's the trust there, *bro*?"

Damn.

He had a point. He had a lot of points.

I kept quiet and glanced to Cross.

He had moved his gaze away, glaring at the beach now.

"Bren?" Jordan asked. "Can you fill me in? What. Sunday. Dinner?"

I closed my eyes. Just needed a second here.

I was officially being asked to choose crew over a relationship, and just like that, Cross' words came back to haunt me, something he said last semester. *"Your first loyalty is to the crew, but mine is to you."*

I felt my heart being ripped out, just as it had been then. He had it in his hand. It was still beating, pumping, but he was holding me captive.

As if sensing what was going on inside of me, Cross finally made the decision for me.

"You know my parents are divorcing," he said.

"Yeah. I mean, is that what this is all about—"

"My dad has another kid."

What?! Shock ricocheted through me, pinging back and forth until I was almost swaying on my feet.

"What?" I moved toward Cross.

He moved away, shaking his head. "I can't even explain everything because it's all so seriously fucked up." He drew in a sharp breath. "My dad had an affair a long time ago. He's always been on the road for his job, but I didn't know about the affair until a month ago."

A month... He'd known a month and hadn't told me.

I tried not to be hurt by that.

But that stung.

Jordan cast me a pitying look. That didn't help.

Shit. Shit. Shit.

"My parents' relationship has been all fucked up for an entire year. I don't know. I don't know what happened. A part of me doesn't want to know, but I know that whatever happened back then, they got over it. Things were all good, and then my mom cheated. And I don't know..." He turned toward the ocean, his voice so raw.

I felt a tear welling up, and I blinked it away. I shoved down a lump in my throat.

"I don't know the details, but I know his new woman is the woman he had an affair with, and the kid is in Fallen Crest. He's a senior this year."

Jordan looked like a statue.

Neither of us could speak.

"Taz doesn't know."

Oh... I was almost falling down at this point. I sat instead.

Jordan let out a strangled laugh, sinking down next to me. "That's..." He leaned forward, resting his arms over his knees. "Holy shit, Cross. That's—I don't even know what that is." He turned his head, angling back to look up at Cross. "You got a brother, man?"

Cross didn't respond, still staring at the ocean.

He blinked a few times, and I saw a tear slip down. He ignored it, looking back at us. New emotion shone through him. I saw it break past a wall, and the torment there had the lump in my throat doubling in size.

I surged to my feet. I just had to hold him, have him in my arms. Unlike the last time, he stepped into me. His head went to my shoulder, my neck, and he wrapped his arms around me.

We stood that way a long time before he pulled away, his thumb flicking at the corner of his eye. "Sorry. I—fuck." He let out a ragged breath, sitting at my side.

"That's rough," Jordan said softly.

Cross nodded. "Yeah."

"Hey!"

Jordan turned around. "Ah. Z's coming back."

Zellman was scowling and waving his phone in the air. "Why's Taz all pissed at you guys? You wouldn't take her calls or something?"

Cross laughed, and Jordan rolled his eyes, standing again. "Yeah." He ignored the question, gesturing to Z's empty hands. "I see you brought a lot back to burn, huh?"

Zellman lifted a middle finger. "Burn this."

Jordan laughed, smacking Z's shoulder. "Come on. I have stuff in the truck. Safe stuff we can burn. Help me carry it down."

"What? Why?"

"Just *come on.*"

We could hear Zellman arguing, but he went with him, protesting the whole way.

Once they were out of earshot, Cross leaned forward, his head dropping down, almost between his knees. "Fuck, Bren."

I couldn't take away his hurt, but I wanted to. So badly. Instead, I could only rub his back. "I'm sorry about your brother."

A wry laugh ripped from him. "Dad had a kid, around the same time he got our mom pregnant. Can you imagine that? Two lives almost."

"Has he known this whole time?"

He stiffened. "I don't know." He sighed. "Shit. I should know that before judging him, right?"

I didn't know how to respond. Cross had been quiet about his family for so long. The little bit I did know had just slipped out over the years. But I knew it tortured him. I knew there was so much anger, and now it made sense, but I had no idea how to talk to him about it.

Did he want me to ask questions? Offer words of comfort? Scheme how to send this half-brother away?

I had no clue, so I turned off my mind and went with my gut.

I started low, in a quiet voice, and moved so our legs were touching. "I can't speak to finding out your dad has a secret kid, or there was an affair, or how your mom had an affair of her own. I have no clue how that all works in a family. I'm guessing there's trust that's been ripped away. Hurt. Pain. Anger." I was trying, but I had no clue what I was saying.

"Look, I—from what I've been hearing, it seems like your parents are both okay with the divorce..."

Cross shoved to his feet. "But *I'm* not okay! Who the fuck decides on dissolving a family? Taz and I didn't get a say in that. It was—I thought they were good. I think..."

But he didn't, and I knew he didn't.

"Cross." I caught his hand, tugging him back down. "What—"

"They were forcing it. Faking everything."

I closed my mouth.

"Looking back, I know the exact moment they stopped. And it's not when they started fighting. It's when they stopped pretending to be this happy solid unit." He leaned forward again, his hands catching his head. His fingers slid through his hair. "I've been trying to remember a time when they weren't so stiff around each other, when they didn't seem like they wanted to tear each other's heads off, when the smiles weren't forced, and I swear to God, I can't remember. There's always been this undercurrent of hate between them, and I felt it growing up. *Growing up*, Bren."

He looked at me, his eyes haunted. "Taz has no idea. She's hurting, but she's trying to do this whole charade that she's 'being there' for Mom and Dad, that 'if this is what makes Mom and Dad happy, we need to support them.' And fuck that. Fuck her. Fuck THEM!"

"I'm sorry, Cross."

He shook his head, sighing. "You ever grow up and find out most of your life was a lie? 'Cause that's how I feel right now."

That I could feel. That I could understand.

"Yeah."

One word, so simple, but Cross remembered. A wall fell from around him, one I hadn't realized was there, and he reached for my hand. "God, Bren. I'm sorry. I'm pissing and moaning about my family when—"

I stopped him. "I grew up in a house where there were no lies. It was obvious Channing hated everyone. My mom was dying. My dad was an alcoholic. I mean, I have no idea how to relate to your situation except that you're losing your family, and that..." I laced our fingers together, squeezing. "That I can relate to, and that sucks."

He nodded. "I'm sorry for not letting you in." He motioned in the direction the guys had gone. "Them too. It wasn't really a decision to keep you guys out. I was trying to keep myself out. I didn't want to deal. You know?"

I understood. "Yeah," I whispered as I rested my forehead against his. "But don't do it again."

He cracked a grin. "Deal."

"Oh-kay!" Jordan's voice boomed behind us. He and Zellman were suddenly there, marching over the sand. Both had their arms full of wood and coolers. "We were waiting, but saw you two about to start macking, so we figured it was safe again."

Zellman frowned down at us. "What's going on? Asshole wouldn't tell me, so you have to. Now." He tightened his hold on the logs against his chest. "Tell me, or I'm dropping a log on your shoes right now, and I may not be talking about the wood I'm holding."

I scowled. "That's the grossest threat I've heard from you."

Zellman didn't break. "Spill the beans, or I'm spilling different beans." His fixed us with a blank stare. "Don't think I'm bluffing."

We didn't.

Which is why we loved him.

Cross stood, taking some of the logs. "How about we make a fire, grill some food, drink some booze, and I'll fill you in during the process?"

Zellman grunted. "Why didn't you just do that in the first place? Do you think I enjoy resorting to threats? It hurts my soul."

We all snorted. That was such a lie.

Zellman grinned.

CHAPTER TWENTY-FIVE

"IS THAT HIM?" Zellman popped up from the back of Jordan's truck.

"What?" Cross looked, leaning forward, then rested back again. "No. I told you, I only saw one picture of him, and it was when he was little—like twelve or something. He plays soccer." He paused a beat. "And he has brown hair. That kid has bleached blond hair."

We weren't at school. We weren't where we should've been. Nope. After telling Zellman everything, Z had suggested we stay up all night drinking, then come to Fallen Crest Academy once our buzz had worn off to scope the half-brother.

"I want to see him." That's what he said, and that started off the chain of events.

And because both Jordan and Cross had been feeling a buzz already, they'd heralded it as the best idea ever. So here we were. Scoping.

My phone rang, and seeing Channing's name on the screen, I muttered a curse.

Cross looked and laughed. "You didn't tell him we'd be out last night?"

I groaned. "You know the answer to that. I just got this thing yesterday."

It kept ringing.

Jordan shook his head, still watching out the window. "Just answer it. We don't want your brother tracking you here and having Moose or Congo showing up to haul us back."

"Yeah." Zellman's head pushed in through the back window, narrowly missing mine. His breath wafted over my ear. "Especially when we're trying to do espionage shit."

I moved my head away, scowling. "Pretty sure you hocked a loogie in my ear using that word. Don't."

He wrinkled his nose. "Thought you were chipper as long as you got your coffee. What's with the attitude?"

I was ready to kill him. My hand formed a fist as I ignored my still-ringing phone. I started to turn around. "Really?"

Cross grabbed my wrist at the same time Jordan took my phone out of my other hand. "Bren."

Jordan answered the phone. "Yo, Godfather. What's up?"

I snarled at Zellman. "This 'attitude' came from being woken up by your farts every five fucking minutes. Do you realize how loud you are when you're sleeping? 'Let's all stay on the beach, guys.'" I imitated him. "'We have sleeping bags, guys. It'll be fun, guys. Bonding crew moment, guys.'" I shot forward, almost hitting him with my face. "Back off of me right now. I love you, Z, but I want to kill you."

He huffed, easing backward. "I just fart when I drink too much and have too many hot dogs. It's not all the time."

"That's what you got out of that? Really?"

Cross chuckled, easing me back around. "Simmer. We'll get more coffee after this."

"...yep. She's here." Pause. "Nope. She's about to kill Zellman. I don't know. I think he breathed on her." He held the phone out, a smirk on his face. "Your brother wants to talk to you. He ain't too happy."

I took the phone, raising my eyebrows. "Really? You don't say."

He laughed, settling in his seat. "He's the godfather. He calls; we answer. That's how it works." He shrugged. "Besides, I endeared him to us since you didn't ignore his call. You're welcome."

My fist was working again, itching to go in Jordan's direction now.

Cross sighed, taking the phone from me. "Hey, Channing." A beat. "Yeah. It was a crew campout last night. We're good, just scoping someone out right now, then heading to school." Pause. A longer pause. "Yeah. She's, uh...she's in a fighting mood today. Maybe later?" He nodded. "Okay. Yeah. Dinner sounds good. Bye." He hung up, handing the phone over, and without looking at me, he said, "You're welcome. We're having dinner with your brother." He slid a cocky smirk to me. "Payback for next Sunday night."

I pocketed the phone. "If you don't want to go, don't. I said I'd go as Taz's friend."

He shook his head, focusing on the school across the road. "My sister has you whipped."

I was friend-whipped.

I considered it, and shrugged. I think I was.

"Is that him?" Zellman shoved his head through the window, again narrowly missing mine.

"Z!" I growled.

"Wait." Cross grabbed my wrist automatically, but leaned forward. "I think it might be."

All the fight left me, and I looked, seeing a guy with an athletic build getting out of a—

"Jesus!" came from the window.

"Zellman!" I yelled.

"That's a Mercedes G Wagon. Dude." He slapped my shoulder in excitement, his eyes wide. "That's new this year. Holy fuck."

Jordan whistled. "Your half-brother's a rich prick."

Cross grunted, folding his arms over his chest. "What do you expect? He goes to the Academy, and you heard that lady—his mom's worth fifteen mil. Not surprised."

The truck's body was white with a black rim and a black top, and while it did look pretty, my eyes were on Cross. For once, he wasn't aware of my attention. He was always aware of me, but this time, he couldn't tear his gaze away from his brother. He'd gone silent and still, his jaw clenching a tiny bit, and I felt the tension in his body.

"You don't know if your dad knew about him all this time?" Jordan was watching Cross as well.

"I don't know. Only reason I know about him is because I heard my parents arguing one night. Taz was at Race's. I slipped in to grab some things before heading to Bren's, and I heard 'em. They were so loud. I could've rang the doorbell, and they wouldn't have heard me. I was going to ignore it. They'd been fighting all year, but after I grabbed my shit and was heading out, he dropped the bomb. 'I have another kid.' His exact words. My mom gasped, then started sobbing, and he stormed out. I left after that—didn't feel like staying to comfort her. Either of them."

"Where'd you see the picture then?"

"My dad's office." Cross broke, a sly grin pulling at the corner of his mouth. "I went in and snooped another night. I took a whole folder he had on him." His eyes flicked up. "Can you imagine? Having an actual folder on your kid? Like he was a patient or a client or something." That sly grin turned to a hard smirk. "His name is Blaise."

"DeVroe. That's what that lady said your dad's new woman's last name is. Blaise DeVroe."

Z shook his head. "Even his name sounds like money."

They were all watching this kid, but I was still watching Cross. His eyes followed the kid as he walked across the parking lot, all the way inside.

It was almost eight. Fallen Crest Academy started earlier than the other schools. That gave us thirty minutes to get to Roussou and stroll right into our own classrooms.

"Well." Jordan sat up. "There he was. We saw him, if that was him."

"That was him." Cross hadn't moved, his jaw still clenching. "He looks just like my dad at this age."

We all fell silent.

Cross' hand had formed a fist, resting on his knee.

Zellman bounced when he was agitated. Cross got still, super still, when he wanted to tear someone's head off.

"Oh, fuck."

I was about to suggest we head out when Zellman swore, surging to his feet in the back of Jordan's truck. That was all the warning we got. He pounded his fists on the top of the cab as Jordan jerked forward, swearing too.

Everything stopped as we saw Zeke and a whole group of his friends heading for us. They were pointing, and there was no mistake what they intended.

"Not this time, assholes," Jordan breathed as he pocketed his keys. "It ain't twelve on one, and I ain't maced." He looked over at us. "Let's go."

Zellman was already yelling, "You want some of us, huh? Odds are more even this time, fuckers."

Cross didn't say a word. He was out of the truck in a flash.

I stopped, just for a second, thumbing off a text before shoving my phone back in my pocket. Then I scrambled, because we weren't waiting this time.

Zeke paused as he drew near, like he wanted to have words first.

Not us. Not this time. Not after Jordan.

Zellman jumped down from the cab, howling, "Let's do this!"

Jordan stalked ahead of us. Zeke was focused on him, and I could see his snarl forming in slow motion. He was totally and completely captivated by Jordan, his friends too. They were huffing and puffing up their chests, pounding their fists together in front of them.

Cross was the one no one saw coming.

He came at them, running behind Jordan and Zellman. Then he weaved around, cutting in.

I darted to the side as he veered the other way.

Zeke never saw him.

Cross was on him, nailing him with a right-cross, using his entire body behind the hit. He was shorter than Zeke, more leanly muscled.

Time seemed to stop, and we all watched together.

Zeke's eyes flared wide, shock and fear flashing, and then his head snapped to the left from the hit, and he couldn't react. His body was going, going, falling, and *bam*. He was down, and he was out.

Cross had knocked him out with one punch, and as everyone was watching Zeke, Cross went on to the next guy, using his momentum.

The second guy had a split second's warning to step back, so Cross' fist didn't hit him in the face, but instead got him smack in the neck. The guy doubled over, gasping.

Cross went down—it was inevitable after the way he'd used his body for both those hits. But no one had hit him or shoved him. He was just unable to fight gravity. But after a moment he scrambled to his feet. Jordan came in behind him, catching the second guy with a second hit, and that guy fell right next to Zeke.

Then it was on.

We all waded in, because this was our crew. Jordan was one of us.

As we fought—hitting, ducking, taking hits—a part of me basked in this. That old Bren, the one locked away in a cage inside of me, she was the one controlling me now.

She was the one smiling as blood trickled from a cut on my face. She was the one finally breathing, and she was the one basking because underneath the roughness of fighting, there's something beautiful about violence.

The ugliness of it, the harshness of it, the realness of it.

It's simple.

With violence, someone gets hurt. It's going to happen. You're on one side or the other. There's no in-between, because that's the bottom line for violence. Your mind is allowed to shut off. Your body takes over. And your body knows to protect its own.

This moment, this day, this morning, we chose.

They'd gotten one of ours before, but not today. Not now. Now was our time.

This was our retribution.

You either hurt or you get hurt. We chose to hurt first.

CHAPTER
TWENTY-SIX

AN AIR HORN sounded, ripping through the air.

Everyone stopped.

The fight had just seemed to start, but that wasn't the truth. As soon as it began, half their guys ran off, and an audience surged forward.

Someone had yelled, "FIGHT!" So when that horn blasted, I wasn't shocked to see an audience, or the phones pointed at us.

What surprised me was who had the air horn.

Cross' half-brother.

And now I was getting a better view of him.

He was...shit. Cross was right.

I straightened from where I had jumped back to avoid an arm. Cross stopped too, a guttural sound coming from his throat.

"Bren," he said quietly, moving the guy he was holding in front of me to block me from the phones. "Run."

Jordan heard him too, and it clicked for both of us. He shoved a ball cap down over my face.

I was on probation. It wasn't the first fight I'd participated in with that status, but this one was more televised. I was in trouble, a lot of fucking trouble.

"Bren." Another whispered order from Cross. "Go. Get to Roussou so you have an alibi."

It was a little late for that, but I whispered back, "I'm covered. I sent a text before we started."

Cross and Jordan both looked at me, eyebrows pinched.

His brother came wading through the crowd.

"EVERYONE, GET THE FUCK BACK!" he yelled. "And delete those fucking videos! We're not fucking narcs!"

To his credit, a lot of the students seemed to move to mess with their phones. A couple showed him their screens. A few hesitated, and he seemed to sense who they were, zoning in on them. Pointing the horn at them, he barked, "If I see one of those online, I will find out who put it up, and trust me, I will destroy you. DELETE THE VIDEOS! NOW!"

He was seething, his chest rising up and down, and when a few didn't run fast enough, he lunged at them. Sweeping the horn out and pressing the button again, he yelled, "Get the fuck in school! Now!"

"Yeah, Blaise."

Another hurried off, running for the door. "Sorry, Blaise. Sorry, man."

A few of Zeke's guys were still there, and the one Cross was holding jerked away. Cross shoved him for good measure. Zellman was interlocked with another guy, and they pushed at each other to get away. Jordan stepped in front of me, Cross closing in on the other side as a shield.

Blaise scanned the ground. Three guys had been knocked out, and another two were trying to stand up, bleeding from their faces.

Blaise shook his head. "Are you fucking serious? This shit?" Then he swung his gaze around, finding Jordan. "You come over here to start a fight with us? You know who we are? HUH?"

I went ramrod straight. This guy...

Cross erupted with his own savage growl and took two quick steps to push into his space. He got right in his face. "Who the fuck do you think you are? Do you not know who *we* are?"

Blaise got a good look at Cross and stumbled backward a step.

Cross was right with him, keeping pace. He was furious. "You know who *I* am? You know *my* name?"

Holy. Fuck.

My jaw was on the ground, and I let out a breath to calm my sudden nerves.

Jordan reached back, his hand finding my shoulder. He spoke quietly, "We got him. Don't worry."

"Get gone." Zellman kicked at the air, near one of the guys still on his knees. He flung a hand out. "Take your pals and don't fuck with us again."

He was scanning the rest of the guys, and I knew who he was looking for: Sunday's baby daddy. I didn't know who to be more worried about, Zellman or Cross.

Jordan squeezed my shoulder. "I got Z. You take Cross."

Decision made. I stepped forward, pulling the ball cap even lower.

At first glance, Blaise DeVroe was another golden boy. Classic handsome features, high cheekbones, square jawline. Blaise's face was leaner than Cross'. His nose was a tiny bit bigger, and he had a rounder forehead. His hair was a little lighter than Cross' but the undertones were caramel brown. Cross' hair was just lighter from the sun. Cross was taller, but Blaise had broader and rounder shoulders. Cross was leaner than Blaise.

The eyes were different.

Cross had tawny hazel eyes, which made everyone take a second, third, and sometimes fourth look. Girls swooned for those eyes. Blaise had dark almond eyes, almost black.

But damn. Cross' dad had some strong genes, that's for sure.

"No, buddy." Blaise got ahold of himself, his mouth snapping shut, and his eyes flashed. He stepped right back at Cross, angling his head to try to look down on Cross. "I don't know you, actually. I'm new this year."

"You don't act like you're new. You act like you have weight to throw around here."

Blaise grunted. He was preparing for a fight, but everyone knew that had passed. "I'm here to help out my best friend."

"Your best friend?" Cross' eyes were cold, his tone even chillier. "There ain't no best friends here. Walk, pal. Walk back into that school."

"Not without Zeke."

"The fuck?" Jordan and Zellman moved to my side.

"Allen is your best friend?" Jordan asked.

Zellman scratched behind his ear. "This is the guy, right? Cross?"

Cross surveyed everything and made a decision. He took a step back, clearing the way, his head cocked to the side.

"Yeah, this is the guy," he said tightly. "You heard him. Let him help his *best friend* out of here." He arched an eyebrow, silently issuing a challenge to his half-brother. "Let's let him get his buddy. We got places to be anyway."

One of the unconscious guys was coming around. His eyes opened with a groan, and he pushed himself to a sitting position.

Blaise motioned to him. His eyes never left Cross as he walked over to Zeke. "Can you give me a hand, Darby?"

The guy was still trying to clear his head. "Yeah. Uh... Hold on." He kept blinking. "What happened?"

"You knocked one of ours down," Zellman told him. "We came back twice as hard."

Jordan tapped his shoulder. "Let's go, Z."

Still eyeing them, his top lip curled up in disdain, Z began walking away backward. "Yeah." He flipped a finger in the air. "Until next time."

Cross tore his gaze away from his brother, his hand catching mine. He turned and began walking us to Jordan's truck. Then it was like a spell lifted, and reality rushed at us. We'd just fought Fallen Crest Academy students, near their campus. They were sure to have security cameras, and though we were across the street, they could've captured everything.

We needed to jet. Now!

"Come on!" Jordan pounded the top of his truck, the engine revving, and his window down. Zellman had jumped in the back, still glaring at the guys.

Cross jumped in behind him, and I lunged for the front seat. Jordan took off, his wheels spinning up dirt even before I shut my door. Then we were off, and I had no doubt we'd just put another problem on our pile to tackle, but I couldn't ignore the thrill inside of me.

I felt alive.

It shouldn't be like that, but I couldn't deny it.

I turned, making eye contact with Cross, and he read my need. He nodded, splaying his hand on the window between us. I moved, fitting mine against his on the other side of the glass. I figured I'd tell them once we got to school that I'd already texted ahead. Race was going to cover for us, putting the word out that we were at school if people started asking. The attendance office might show we were late, but word in the hallways would be that we were right on time.

It'd have to do if anyone questioned us.

Just as we turned the corner, I saw three school officials heading out across the lot.

We got to school five minutes after the last bell rang to start the day.

Separating at the bathroom, I rushed in and did a quick clean, but I still smelled like booze, campfire, cold sweat, and blood. Plus, dirt. I groaned, washing my face and pulling my hair up into a braid. I couldn't do much else except slip on a different sweatshirt. That wouldn't disguise the smell, but I had deodorant in my locker, and Taz had some body spray.

When I came out, Cross was just finishing at his locker. He stopped, book in hand, and leaned back against it. He gave me a cocky smirk as he folded his arms over his chest.

"Look at you," I almost cooed.

He laughed, but that smirk just grew. I opened my locker, and he waited for me to rifle through, get what I needed, and step back.

Spying the new sweatshirt in my hand, he asked, "What are you doing?"

"I stink."

I pulled the sleeves back through so they went the right way.

"So?" He leaned over, sniffing me. "And you don't."

I did. "It doesn't matter. Girls don't like to smell."

"Uh, girls usually don't smell. They think they do, but they don't."

I wasn't going to have a gender debate with him about my olfactory senses. Nodding at Taz's locker, I asked, "Can you open it? Grab her body spray? I know she has some in there."

As he did, I used my deodorant and put my sweatshirt on. I zipped it up, pulled off my other shirt, and tossed it in my locker.

Cross caught it just as it was going in. "What are you doing?" He handed over the spray, still eyeing me like I'd lost my head.

"That shirt smells like campfire. My hair reeks. I'll make do with this thing."

He tsked me, going to his locker. Punching in the code, he bent inside as I sprayed myself and put the body spray back in Taz's locker. Cross had a shirt in his hand when I turned back.

"What's that?"

"A shirt."

"Is it clean?"

He lifted it to his nose, took a big whiff, and started coughing. Then, cracking a grin, he handed it over. "I'm kidding. Yes. It's an old shirt of mine I put in there last week. I've not worn it. Take it. It's better than a sweatshirt. You know the librarian has a thing against sweatshirts."

I shuddered. He was right. She thought they were coats. All coats and hats had to be off to step inside her library.

I did the whole switcharoo again, pulling it on under my sweatshirt.

Cross' smirk was now a shit-eating grin, and his eyes were latched onto my chest.

I paused, drawing a circle over my breasts. "You're watching me like you're sex-deprived."

I knew he was not.

He grinned a happy little grin, transforming his face from hot and smoldering to an adorable puppy my arms were aching to grab.

God, I loved this guy.

"I'm just enjoying the show. And thinking how I'm going to buy an oversized sweatshirt to zip around both of us. Your mission will be to change your clothes inside." His grin was wicked again, his eyes darkening. "That image is going to get me through the rest of the day."

We were late, in the hallway. We were bound to get in trouble, but I couldn't stop myself. I reached over, touching his lips. I said softly, "You're happy."

It wasn't a question.

He paused, catching my hand, and considered my statement. He hugged me to him, but he didn't lean down for a kiss. He continued holding my gaze.

"Yeah. I think I am."

I leaned back a little, tilting my head to the side. "Because of your brother?"

Cross shifted his book to his other hand and dropped it on the floor. Then both of his hands splayed out on my back, slipping under my/his shirt. He rested his chin on my shoulder, and I wound my arms around him, my fingers sliding up to his hair.

I knew without looking that his eyes were closed.

"I don't know," he whispered, kissing my shoulder where the shirt's collar had slipped to the side. I felt his entire body seize up in a breath and exhale. "He didn't know who I was."

"Didn't seem like it, no."

"You think he was lying?"

"I don't know."

I drew circles on the back of his neck. In this moment, we were boyfriend and girlfriend. No crew. No beef. No siblings dared interrupt.

"I don't think he knows."

I nodded. "Are you going to tell Taz?"

Cross stiffened and pulled back. I lifted my head to meet his gaze, and he gave me such a sad smile. His hands moved to my hips, keeping me anchored against him.

"I don't know. How do I not, though? He looks so much like me."

I grinned crookedly. "Almost like you. You're way hotter."

"And Zeke Allen is his best friend. How the hell did that happen?"

I shook my head. "Who knows, but your half-brother is rich. Zeke Allen seems like a tool, who likes to collect all the right tools in his shed. You know? Maybe it's one of those things?"

"Maybe." His hands flexed, digging into my hips before he let me go. "We should get going."

"Hey."

He was about to pull away, but I stopped him, a finger to his chin.

He paused, waiting.

"Whatever is going on, you and I are good. Crew's all that matters at the end."

He nodded. "I know." He straightened and kissed my forehead. "Walk me to the library?"

CHAPTER
TWENTY-SEVEN

THAT AFTERNOON, AFTER school, I descended into hell—*my* kind of hell, not a normal girl's kind of hell, but most definitely mine.

I was shopping for a prom dress, and I still stunk. I knew I looked a nightmare—bags under my eyes. I'd gone through three energy drinks, and I'm talking the big-ass ones, not the little cute can ones. So I was half acting like I was on something too, which maybe I was.

My phone buzzed in my pocket. Seeing it was Cross, I answered. "Hello, my penis."

Silence.

I pulled the phone away, checked to make sure it was him, and prodded, "Cross? Hello?"

"Did you just call me your penis?"

I kept moving down the line. How many colors of black were there? Off black. Midnight black. Lead black. Jet-black. Onyx. And I wasn't even looking at the different cuts of the dresses or the fabrics.

"Well, if you think about it, you kind of are."

Ooh. I never thought I'd be the girl who liked black lace, but I tucked the phone between my neck and shoulder and reached up to take the dress from where it was hanging. I stepped back, holding it up in front of me. "I don't have a penis, but you do, and you're my guy. There you go."

Did I like the ruffle sleeves?

I put it back. I wasn't the ruffle sleeve type.

"Okay. You sound weird. Where are you?"

"I'm shopping."

And I was distracted again. Pink? Why was I feeling pulled toward this pink contraption? I didn't even think it was a dress. It looked like a scarf, something I'd hang around my head. It'd be perfect as a weapon. I could wrap around it someone's neck, climb up on their back, and then twist... I forced myself to move on. Those kind of thoughts weren't healthy, not for this new and updated Bren.

I chose not to focus on the last two fights I'd been a part of.

"Shopping?" Cross swore into the phone. "Are you on something? I can't believe I'm even asking that question."

"Which? Shopping or the other?"

He was silent a moment. "Uh, both?"

I grinned, feeling flushed all over my body. "No, but I'm thinking I need to not drink so many energy drinks after a crew night. It's either coffee or a nap." A yawn worked its way up, and I waited until it passed before murmuring, "Maybe I should've done the shopping tomorrow."

"Um." He was so confused. "*Why* are you shopping? I was looking for you after school."

"Oh." Yeah. I forgot. "I'm shopping because prom is this weekend."

He was quiet. Again.

Then, "Oh, shit."

"Ha. I see I'm not the only one who forgot."

"Do I need a tux for that?"

I shrugged, though he couldn't see, and headed toward this glistening creature. I would look like a mermaid in it.

"Ask Race. Do whatever he says. *Don't* tell him I'm just now shopping, though. That'll get to Taz, and she'll freak out. Apparently, I was supposed to do this ages ago."

He chuckled, sounding strained. "Okay. I'll talk to Jordan and Z too. Where *are* you, though?"

I gritted my teeth, knowing he wasn't going to be happy. "I'm in Fallen Crest."

"What?!"

"Before you get mad, I'm incognito," I rushed in.

And I was. I'd stopped at home, not to shower like I should've, but to swipe some clothes. Heather had left a few of her things in Channing's room, so I pulled on one of her leather jackets with a white tank under it, and a pair of my jeans. My hair was still in a braid, but I had one of Channing's ball caps pulled low.

No one would recognize me, especially here.

"Roussou does not have good shopping," I continued. "Fallen Crest does. There's one store in Frisco, and it's a Dollar Store. It's either here or make the trek to the big city. I don't have time for that."

He groaned. "I don't like this."

I didn't either. "Shopping is not my thing. Trust me. I'll make it quick."

I snagged another dress off the rack. It was white tulle, with pink sparkles lined in the fabric, and it wasn't too long.

Tulle.

I hated tulle.

Usually.

Gah.

Why couldn't I put this down?

It was so girly. It was *so* not me.

"That would look perfect on you!"

I jumped as a store clerk magically appeared beside me, her eyes wide in wonder and her mouth open. "Oh my gosh," she said, taking it from my hands. "I'll find you a dressing room. You have to try it on. Your body, you'd look magnificent, and I'm so extremely jealous right now. I've been eyeing this since we got it, but I don't have the body for it. My sister either. You, though." She looked me up and down, shaking her head. "You'd be ready for the Pinterest board. Lucky."

She turned, heading for the back.

"What just happened?" Cross asked. On the phone. He was still here.

"I—I don't really know."

He snorted. "Okay, I'm not going to fight you on it, but get your dress and tell me when you're leaving. The buddy system is still in play, and you're violating it." He dropped his voice. "It's their turn for payback now. I really don't like the thought of you being there alone."

I knew this. I knew this, but it was a dress. One dress.

I grumbled into the phone, "Can I go to prom in fashionable sweatpants?"

"Is there such a thing?"

There had to be. All those fancy airport shots. "Celebrities fly in stuff like that."

"Yeah. Okay. I don't know what you're talking about. Get the dress. Text me or call me when you're leaving the store, then when you get in your vehicle, and when you're driving back. Don't forget we have dinner tonight with your brother."

I winced. I'd forgotten that too. This is what happened on not enough hours of sleep, and a full day of zoning out while two Normal students were interviewed. When they were asked about the crews, I snapped to attention and glared. I did my best glaring.

Once word got out that I was taking note of what everyone was saying, I didn't have to do much more than the occasional glare. But I got really good at it. A few times I pulled my knife out. And I had to do it when I was in the back and when I knew no camera guy would turn and see me. Cause, shit would be bad for me if that happened. It was worth it. Eyes got real big once my knife showed even for a second, and the rest of the students got through their questions without revealing much of anything after that.

"I will. Love you," I told him.

"Remember, stay incognito."

The store's bells rang behind me as someone came in.

I nodded. "Consider me a chameleon. No one will recognize me. Trust me."

I hung up and turned around, coming face to face with my ex.

"Oh, fuck. It's you."

Drake Ryerson grinned down at me, cocky. "You might be blending in with the dresses behind you, but I'm pretty sure it's Bren Monroe standing before me."

"Look at me, laughing. A comedian has entered the building."

He chuckled, but some of his cockiness faded. He moved around me, scoping out the place. His hand traced over some of the dresses. "Imagine my shock, driving down this street in Fallen Crest and seeing one of your brother's trucks."

See? I really had tried for the incognito, even swiping the keys for one of Channing's vehicles.

"And I'm pretty sure the girl I saw leaving that truck and heading in here was not Heather." He touched on the end of my braid. I smacked his hand away, "Your future sis-in-law does not have dark hair." He skimmed me up and down, the same way the store clerk had, but a whole layer of dirt followed his path. "And Jax shows more skin than you do—not that I'm complaining. You could show *way* more skin."

God. That grin.

I wanted to punch his throat, wipe it clean. "What are you doing in here, Drake?" I looked behind him. "And alone?"

"Why are *you* alone?" he countered.

I didn't think Drake was my enemy, currently anyway, so I really needed to get this damned thing and go. The clerk hadn't come back. I kept looking, just for more options.

"I'm shopping, and hiding from Taz since she thinks I should already have this dress. My excuse is justified. Why are you alone? You're a part of the buddy system, you know."

He followed along, pulling out a dress for me. "This would look good on you." He pointed out the short hemline. "Lots of thigh. Cross would thank me."

I took the dress, hung it back up, and squared against him. I guess I shouldn't be multitasking here. One opponent at a time.

"You are here for a reason. You *followed* me in here for a reason." And I wasn't forgetting what Alex had warned us about him—that Drake wasn't here to lead the Ryerson crew.

Was Alex wrong? Was Drake actually here for me? That didn't feel right. Drake would've been pestering me long before now. Too much time had gone by when he was scarce.

Drake went after what he wanted. I'd once thought it endearing. Now I used it as a warning sign.

No. Drake didn't want me, but what then?

I pinned him with a look. "Just say it, whatever you came in here to say."

He hesitated, and I knew I was right.

He dropped all pretense, his eyes scanning the store once again, lingering on the street, before he lowered his voice. "Did you know your previous principal remarried last summer?"

I frowned. The fuck? "Principal Neeon?"

He continued as if I hadn't spoken, "That his new wife is your new principal's sister?"

A female Kenneth?

I asked softly, more cautious, "Where are you going with this?"

Again he ignored my question. "And that Neeon's daughter suffered a breakdown over the holidays. She had to be shipped to a boarding school, one that's not just about basic high school education."

He was trying to tell me something. His eyes flared, hidden meaning there, but I wasn't following. He was dropping hints, wanting me to follow the trail.

"Drake."

"Did you know Broghers' sister is a cop?" That lone eyebrow rose again. "She's a cop here, in Fallen Crest." His gaze went flat after that.

He was done. He'd said what he came in to say, and I wasn't surprised when he walked around me, almost in a complete circle.

"Think about all those tidbits. Aren't they *interesting*?" With that, he left.

One last look at me before he turned and strolled out, just as I heard the store clerk coming back.

She clapped, still beaming. "I hope you don't mind, but I pulled a few more dresses for you. They're all ready." She leaned in, whispering, "And between you and me, I talked to the manager. I told her I might've found a local model for our store fashion show. You'd get paid, and of course, we have to make sure the dress looks right on you, but I think anything will look amazing. Are you ready? Aren't you excited?"

Yeah. *Excited*. Not the word I would use right now.

But, I still needed a dress. "Where's the dressing room?"

CHAPTER TWENTY-EIGHT

MY HOUSE WAS in chaos when I walked inside.

When I'd texted Cross as I was heading back, he'd said dinner was almost ready. I expected Channing, Cross, maybe Heather.

But I heard voices from the curb where I had to park. The driveway was full. Walking up the sidewalk, I glanced back to the street. Five Harleys were parked, along with Taz's Ford, Jordan's truck, and I was fairly certain Race's car. What was going on?

I walked inside, and the noise bombarded me at the same time as the smells. Grilling. Hot dogs. Burgers. Voices giggling, shrieking. Some deep laughter and baritone murmurs. All with low music underneath: Beastie Boys, "Sabotage."

A party. That's what was happening.

Zellman was playing air guitar when I went to the kitchen. Jordan was doing air drums, sitting at the table. Two wooden spoons were his drumsticks.

If "Make Some Noise" came on next, I was going to kick them out to the street.

"Bren!" Taz waved at me from the basement stairs. "Come down here. We gotta talk."

The guys stopped their air concert and waved at me. "Heya, Bren."

"Where's Cross?"

Jordan pointed to the patio with one of his wooden spoons. "I wouldn't go out there, though. Your brother has his hand on Cross' shoulder. His crew are all out there too."

I nodded, saying to Taz, "One second."

My dress hung over my back. I wasn't sure if she'd seen it yet, but I didn't want to advertise how late I was in being prom-prepared.

She frowned. "What's that?"

"Dry-cleaning. For Channing." Uh... "He has a favorite shirt." I hurried backward. "I should go hang it up."

"Come down after that. Something serious happened with Monica. You need to know about it."

Oh, dear. Monica. I was quaking in my boots.

I turned at the same time Heather was leaving the bedroom. She stopped, cocked her head to the side, and narrowed her eyes. "Nice jacket."

My smile was stiff. "Yeah."

She eyed my shirt too. "And tank top."

"Thanks."

She was looking at my jeans as we passed each other.

"Those are mine."

She nodded. "I gathered, but I'm also asking myself, why don't I have a pair as well?" She fixed me with a look. "Is this going to be a problem? Sharing clothes?"

"Not unless you start sharing mine."

She grunted. "Touché, little Monroe. Touché."

Heather moved past me, giving Zellman and Jordan the sign of the horns, bobbing her head with the music.

"Hey! Yeah!"

Jordan set off on a drum solo as Zellman threw up his own sign of the horns to Heather. Then he was back to playing right alongside Jordan.

Heather grinned at them, snagging a bottle of rum before slipping outside to the patio.

I was just putting my dress in the closet when a soft knock sounded on my door. It opened, and Cross slipped inside. His eyes warmed, seeing me. He came right over, his hand sliding around my waist. "Hey." He moved in, and his mouth was on mine.

I could taste the rum. Pleasure and warmth filled me, and I swear, my toes curled. So cheesy, but it was the truth. I wasn't prepared for this kiss.

"Hmmm. Whoa." I pulled back. "Where'd that come from?"

He shifted, pulling me firmly against him.

I grinned, feeling him. "Oh. There."

He laughed, nipping at my lips again. "Yeah. There." His mouth moved over mine, demanding, hot. "I want you."

I was tempted. And I shouldn't have been. There was a full house, literally, but Cross pressed me into the closet, his mouth growing commanding, and *fuuuuck*. His hand slid inside my jeans, finding exactly where I was throbbing, and my mind started to shut off.

Then the doorknob rattled.

"He—what?"

Taz. She pounded against the door. "Bren? Bren! Are you in there?"

Cross cursed, his mouth ripping away. "Shit. Sorry. I'm..." He grinned, a little sheepish. "Feels weird to say this, but we were sneaking booze in our drinks."

"Right." I said dryly. "'Cause I'm sure my brother was clueless."

He shrugged, dipping his forehead to rest on my shoulder. His hand smoothed over my stomach, pulling out from my jeans. "It's a copacetic relationship. He didn't ask, I didn't volunteer. There you go."

"Bren!" The entire door was rattling now. "Are you in there?"

I sighed, pulling out of her brother's arms. "I'm here. A little busy right now."

"What? Why? I just saw you five seconds ago."

"Taz." Cross' voice teased my skin, his forehead still on my shoulder. "Go away."

"Oh—oh my God! Are you having sex?"

"Not anymore." He sighed again before lifting his head. Two steps back and he unlocked the door and swung it open. "My sister. Cockblocker extraordinaire."

Taz wasn't alone.

Tabatha was beside her, biting her lip to keep from laughing. Sunday was next, a mix of disgust and something I couldn't place on her face. They had another girl with them, but I didn't recognize her. No Lila and no Monica. I was relieved. They still had the hots for Cross.

Taz *pffted*, striding into my room, shoving her brother aside. "You get her all the time. It's our turn now." She turned, folding her arms, her legs apart.

Was she? She was. She was squaring off against her twin.

"Get lost, brother. I want my friend tonight."

A couple of the girls laughed.

Cross narrowed his eyes. "Don't forget, I'm the reason you were invited tonight."

"I was invited because you wanted a buffer between you and Bren's brother. We all know you shit your pants when it's just the two of you."

Cross' gaze flicked to mine, and I suppressed some laughter. Cross might've been a bit wary, but Taz was way off.

He shook his head. "You're right, sis. I'm terrified of the guy I'm living with." His tone was taunting. "You got me there."

Taz's mouth clamped shut, and tears welled up.

She'd forgotten, for a moment there, that her brother was not living with her anymore.

"Right," she continued after a moment. "Well, I don't care. Get out. I want Bren right now."

Cross looked ready to argue, probably just because he was enjoying needling his sister, when Tabatha stepped forward.

"We got chick things to discuss. Can you go make sure I still have a boyfriend?"

The playful look in Cross' eyes fell flat. I was right.

A mask took its place. "I don't do your bidding. Fuck off." His eyes met mine for a second before he walked past the girls.

A full beat of silence followed him. Then Tabatha's hands went to her hair. "Jordan's been distant to me, and that confirmed it." She turned to me. "You *did* tell them."

I shook my head. "You thought I wouldn't? You serious?"

Sunday mocked, "Crew code, Tab. Remember? There's no girl code with Bren."

I pivoted to her. "You have a problem with me?" My tone was ice.

The girls shifted on their feet. When they forgot who I was, I showed them. I let some of the old Bren peek out, and Sunday eased back a step.

She coughed, her eyes looking anywhere but at me. Her voice tight. "Look, whatever. Tell her what happened."

"Right." Taz took over. "We're calling it the Monica Mutiny."

"Monica Mutiny?"

"It's insane." She waved her hand in quick, sharp motions. "And I'm so pissed off about it."

"Just tell her. She needs to know." Sunday looked ready to explode.

"Right. Okay." Taz took a breath. "Monica left the group. She took Lila and Angie with her."

"Who's Angie?"

"Good grief," Tabatha muttered. "It's like you don't know anyone. She was one of my best friends for the last three years."

Noted. Angie was important to Tabatha. I frowned. "Why do I need to know this?"

"Because the code is out. Gone. Destroyed."

"What code?"

"Girl code!" Sunday snapped, then held her hands up in surrender. "Sorry. I just—it's a thing. Not just crews have codes. Girlfriends do too." She gestured to Taz. "Yours. Sorry."

"Yes." Taz turned to me. "So this is a problem for you, because she has her interview scheduled at the end of the week with that show. We know you're supposedly helping them—"

Tabatha snorted. Sunday tried to smother her own laughter, and she turned all the way around, facing the hallway. The girls there were giggling.

Taz rolled her eyes. "Yeah. Supposedly. Everyone knows you're really just scaring people out of talking about the crews, but anyway. Monica. She's going to go in there, see you, and not give a shit. It's war as far as she's concerned."

"War? Why?" Was I missing something else?

"She's tired of playing by the rules." This came from the girl I didn't know.

"Who are you?"

She flushed, her face growing red.

"Oh my God. See? This is what I was saying. She doesn't know anything!" Sunday's hands flew up in the air. "It's so aggravating. We're people too, Bren. Not everything is about the guys."

I couldn't help myself. "You seem upset."

"Agh!"

I laughed. "Relax. I know, but what rules are you talking about? The girl code again?"

"No. The friendship code."

There were so many codes.

"And yes, the girl code...not really. Never mind. The friendship code. She broke from the group because she's dating someone from Fallen Crest Academy now. He said the crew system is stupid, so therefore, of course now Monica thinks it too. He's brainwashed her into thinking you guys are the enemy. She believes it's her mission to help destroy the crew system. You guys are in a lot of trouble because she's going to talk. She's going to say everything, and I mean *everything*."

"But what could she even say? We get into fights?"

"That you guys hospitalized Alex Ryerson!" Sunday's hands were up again. "That Cross took a gun when you guys went to find Alex. She's going to talk about how you stabbed the principal, and how your brother runs the town and fixed it so you didn't get any jail time. She's probably going to make shit up too. You're not hearing me. This is big, like, *big* big. Everyone knows that documentary is about the crews. Principal Broghers wants the system gone—like, evaporated. You guys are cockroaches to him. Shine the light, and the roaches scatter. That's what he's hoping will happen, and it's working. Did you even know two crews disbanded this week?"

She moved toward me. "The Frisco crew is dunzo, and that other one. I never remember their name, but they disbanded too. It's you guys and the Ryerson crew. That's all—oh, and your brother's, but they're not in school. And aren't they more bounty hunters now anyway? Are they even still a crew?"

That was the forever debate, were they or weren't they? I lifted a shoulder. Even I couldn't answer that.

I was hearing her, noting everything. Monica would be dealt with, but one thing was bugging me. "Why are you so upset about this?"

"BECAUSE I CARE ABOUT YOU AND YOUR STUPID CREW AND ZELLMAN AND I CARE!" Sunday yelled. "Okay?! I just do. I just care. I don't even know why, and it's so FRUSTRATING, but I do. Okay?!" She was shouting in my face, her breath blasting me.

I had the sudden impulse to hug her, but that was insane. Instead, I cracked a grin. "Thank you."

She stopped. Her cheeks puffed up, and then she yelled, her hands in her hair. "OH MY GOD! SHE'S SO FRUSTRATING!"

"Hey, hey, hey." Jordan waded into the room, his hands up as if to smooth things over. He turned, coming to stand beside me. Zellman remained in the hallway, frowning. I caught sight of others coming down the hallway, but Z shook his head at them. They stopped, but didn't move away.

"What's going on back here?"

"Your girl is so fucking frustrating!" Sunday was still shouting. "That's what's going on."

"Tabatha?"

"NO! Bren!" She stabbed at me in the air.

"Yeah. I understand friendships," Tabatha said. "Bren doesn't. You're either family or not with her. There's no in-between."

"Hey." There was too in-between with me. "We're...friends... kind of?"

"You blabbed about me to my boyfriend."

My head inched back. "There's a hierarchy. You're beneath Jordan."

Zellman started laughing.

Sunday twisted around to him. "This isn't funny!"

"It kind of is."

She got in his face. "It so isn't! Have you not been listening? Monica and Lila broke from the group. Lila's going to make a move on Cross, and Monica wants to destroy everything now."

"Okay!" Jordan raised his voice to talk over Sunday. "We'll handle Monica. Lila's not really a problem, but who's the guy Monica is dating?"

"Why?" Sunday stuck her bottom lip out, her hands on her hips. "So you guys can go beat him up?"

"What? No." Jordan crossed his arms. "So we can have Channing's crew go beat him up."

One of the guys down the hallway heard and barked out a laugh. "Yeah. Right. Thought this was a high school thing to handle."

Another guy started snickering before they moved away, their footsteps going to the kitchen.

The patio door opened, and I could hear Heather's voice. "What's going on in here?"

One of the guys said, "High school drama."

Hearing this, Sunday screeched, "OH MY GOD! NO ONE IS TAKING ME SERIOUSLY!"

"Oh my GOD, Sunday!" Zellman touched her arm. "Settle the fuck down. We are, but we're also fucking with you. Jordan is. Bren, too. Calm down."

"Oh." Her eyebrows pinched together. "You are?"

Jordan and I nodded. "It's just really easy right now," I added.

She stared at us, and we could almost see the steam rising out of her ears. She was winding up, getting ready to blast us again.

"Z," I said.

He clapped a hand over her mouth just as she screamed. "Got it."

He took her hand and pulled her from the room. They went outside a second later.

"Okay, then." It was Tabatha's turn. She was much calmer. "The Monica thing is a real problem, whether you guys are taking it serious or not."

"She's dating someone from Fallen Crest. That, by itself, is a big fucking mistake," I told her. "So yes, we're taking it seriously, but we just handled shit over there. We'll deal with her, but we'll do it our way."

"So physical violence?" Tabatha swaggered over to her boyfriend. Her head tipped back. "You're going to beat him up, right? You might've laughed off Sunday, but that's how you handle things. That's what you've been doing. Why would you suddenly change tactics?"

Jordan shared a look with me. "We don't only use violence."

I nodded. "We've threatened torture. That's different."

"You're right. We have." Jordan perked up, fighting another grin.

Tabatha shook her head. "I give up. Whatever. You do what you're going to do." She started to storm out, but stopped suddenly and wheeled back around. "It's just that violence is not going to always work. It's just not. Why do you think the cameras are here? Because that's going to work, and it kinda bugs me to say this, because while I used to think the crew stuff was stupid—but hot and dangerous at the same time—I hate it now. I hate that my boyfriend is in the most dangerous and tightest crew there is. And I hate that I constantly worry about him. I hate that I have nightmares a 'beatdown' went too far. I hate that I wake up screaming sometimes. My mom runs in. And I *really* hate that I have to lie all the time so my boyfriend isn't hated by people who love me, who worry about me. And I really, really hate that no matter how much I love him, three other people will always take precedence over me. That's what I hate, but even with all of that, there is a need for the crews at our school. Because it *is* dangerous out there, but because I know when I'm in Roussou, I'm safe. I'm not going to get raped, or jumped, or robbed even. And it might only be in Roussou that I know I'm safe, but that means something. My cousin was raped at a party last year, and my first thought when I heard about it wasn't about her. It was about me." Her voice wobbled, growing thicker. "It was *Thank God that'd never happen here.* And I thought that because of the crews, because *you guys* wouldn't let it happen. Everyone's too scared of you. I mean, the Ryerson crew was scary for a minute because of Alex, but he's fine now. They're fine now. You get my drift. Alex got crazy for a couple months, but you guys put a stop to him. That's my point."

Alex. *Drake.*

I'd forgotten about him, what he said. I needed to tell the others.

I glanced at Jordan, but he wasn't paying attention. He was fully focused on his girlfriend, and I touched the back of his arm. He looked down. I nodded toward her. *Go to her.*

His shoulders dropped. I hadn't realized he'd been tensed up, but then he went to her.

"Baby," he said softly, gathering her in his arms.

He pressed a kiss to her forehead, and she began to sob.

She grabbed the back of his shoulders and held on, burying her head in his chest. He cradled her, smoothing a hand down her hair and back.

Taz was the first to edge out of the room. I was behind her.

Jordan mouthed to me, "Thank you."

I nodded, feeling déjà vu because we'd been here before.

People were congregating in the living room, except Channing's friends. They were outside.

Cross and Race sat on the couches, waiting for us, elbows on their knees.

Cross lifted his head up as we came in. "Everything okay in there?"

I sank down on the couch beside him, patting his leg. "Later. Crew meeting." Taz went to sink down on Race's lap, and I met her gaze. "We've got a Monica problem to handle."

CHAPTER TWENTY-NINE

CROSS HOVERED ABOVE me, his lips on my throat as he moved in and out of me.

He'd snuck up when Channing and Heather snuck out. I assumed they went to her house, probably so they didn't have to be so quiet. Her brother technically stayed with her, but I knew there were nights he wasn't there. Tonight was probably one of those nights, and they thought they could wait till after three, making sure we kiddies were good and asleep and ignorant of them creeping out. But they were idiots—idiots I wasn't going to educate.

No way.

Cross slid right back inside, moving nice and slowly—delicious. He moved his mouth to the other side of my throat, his hand and thumb rubbing over my breast. When he'd slipped inside, I thought it'd be a rough and hard ride. He'd been hungry earlier, but I was surprised. It was a slow and tender, making-love encounter, one that made me cry just before I crested, and I'd already done that. Twice.

I groaned as he began picking up speed, his hands sliding up my arms to entwine with mine. He held them pinned above my head, and he looked into my eyes. I was already being a girl, and when he did that, a couple more tears slipped out. He could see inside of me, be inside of me, and I almost couldn't handle it.

"Show me," he whispered, his lips nipping mine. He thrust harder at his command. "Show me you. I want to see you."

God.

He tore a hole right in the middle of my chest, where I kept her buried. She was in there, along with all the pain from my past, all locked up nice and tight. He knew where I had her caged, and he wanted her to come out.

"Cross," I whispered, a plea in my voice.

"Show me." He let go of my hand, capturing the side of my face. His thumb rubbed over my lips. "I need to see you, Bren. Not the you in my arms right now, not the you you show everyone else. I need the real you, the one I know you hide. I need you."

I gasped, and my back arched.

I felt her rising.

I couldn't keep her down, not when Cross called.

I broke out, my voice hoarse and raw, "Only you. Only for you."

He groaned, his eyes closing as he thrust again, pushing deep and holding. Then, the pain flooded me. Everywhere.

It wasn't just pain. It was everything. I felt it all.

Love.

Agony.

Hurt.

Anger.

I could smell the sweat on our bodies. I could smell that Channing or Heather had laundered my pillowcase recently. I could smell the lilac perfume Cross had bought me as a gift and I was obsessed with. And I could taste my tears—not the ones from when he brought me to climax, only to have my body climb once again for another, but the tears from the past. The tears of missing my mother, of missing my father, of denying myself visits with him, the tears of holding back from my brother and not fully loving him as family, the tears of seeing Jordan hurting, of seeing Zellman ripped up about Sunday, and most of all, the tears of feeling the torment inside of Cross over his family being ripped apart.

I experienced it all.

And I could see inside of him too.

He was right there, staring back at me, and I saw the deep yearning he kept checked because he knew I held myself back so much.

But I had to. I couldn't endure life if I lived it like this, feeling everything. I couldn't, but right now, with my legs winding tighter around his hips, this was the only place I had to be.

His lips found mine, holding, claiming.

He began moving harder, deeper, then paused and rotated his hips, moving so he touched every part of me, and I almost screamed. Pleasure nearly blinded me. My back arched again. I was almost off the bed, only my head and hips keeping me there. Cross lifted with me, his mouth moving to taste my nipple as he growled and grabbed my waist, holding me down. He began shoving, and I was a frenzied mess, pushing back just as hard.

Tears slipped down my cheeks.

He moved up, tasting them, and found my lips. "I love you," he breathed.

A deep groan left me. "I love you."

As we both pushed over the edge, he found my hand, his fingers sliding against mine, and thrust once more. Both of us came down, our bodies jerking from the ferocity, and then, calm.

Utter. Complete. Quiet.

It filled me just as much as everything else had, and I lay still, totally still, savoring it.

I felt him. I felt us.

His lips were at my throat, and then I felt them brush over my face. He was tasting more of my tears.

I gasped, the inevitable pain slicing me as my climax moved along and living filtered in.

"Cross," I cried, my voice still hoarse. "Cross."

He shifted, gathering me in his arms. He feathered kisses over my cheeks, my forehead, then lingered on my lips.

"I'm here. Don't, Bren. Please. Stay with me. I know you'll lock her back up, but not tonight. Not till the morning."

I couldn't. The denial was quick on my lips, but seeing his agony, knowing how much he needed me, I stifled it. I held on, and I pulled him back to me. "Okay."

"Okay?" He searched my eyes.

I nodded. "Okay."

And I stayed.

I'd put her back in the morning.

He wound himself around me, his head against my neck, his hand on my breast, and one of his legs between mine. We went to sleep.

CHAPTER THIRTY

I COULD GO to jail for what I was doing.

I didn't care. Waking in Cross' arms, I'd started the process of shoving her back down. I'd numbed myself, only feeling a third of what I could handle, but I'd stopped halfway. I didn't know why. Normally, I couldn't wait to turn off my emotions, but this morning, after feeling that with Cross, knowing how special it was, there was an ache I hadn't felt in a long while. Months maybe.

It was nearing seven in the morning now. The timing was stupidly close, but I couldn't stop myself.

Crawling over the fence, I didn't unhook the latch because I saw they'd finally smarted up and bought a full fence that went all the way around their lawn. Who knew what other changes they'd made. They'd gotten a dog since my last visit, but the toys were the same.

I'd watched them before. It seemed like another life ago, so much had happened. So many changes, but I had to come. I had to see if I saw her.

Sneaking over the fence, not wanting to risk them having an alarm or squeaky hinges, I dropped over, and then I was officially trespassing. Didn't matter that this had been my home growing up, or that this was where my family had been pulled out from beneath me. At one point, the two-story home had been mine, and I knew it was irrational, senseless, but I still wondered if I could catch a glimpse of my mom walking the hallways.

Creepy, I know.

I was so far past caring.

A Barbie doll looked at me from the grass. A small tricycle. A plethora of trucks and trains. A dinosaur. Some superhero figurines. Large plastic pieces for a puzzle.

I picked up every one of them, taking them to the front patio and laying them just in front of the wooden steps. I knew those creaked. The home hadn't been renovated, and I could see they hadn't touched up the stairs or patio area, so I saved that trip for last.

One trip after another, I picked up a toy, took it over in front of the deck, and laid it in the grass. A second trip. A third. More than six until I had all the toys collected. Then after that, I moved into stealth mode. They had two large toy chests next to the window. Both were open, the tops off, and why not? Their fence was high enough to deter people from invading their space, giving them a modicum of privacy even though it was the front lawn. Roussou wasn't big on homeowner associations.

I knelt and quietly placed every single toy through the deck's railing. There was enough space through the smaller posts. The tricycle I left for last. It was too large. Once everything was on there except that, I skipped the steps and climbed up over the middle banister. It was the sturdiest and the only one that wouldn't creak under my weight. Then, stepping down onto the middle plank— another one I knew would remain silent—I began putting the toys into the chests. One by one. When all was done, I closed the tops and leaned back over, lifting the tricycle clear. Rotating on my heels, I rested the trike between the chests.

It was done.

The lawn was clean.

This was when I should go.

I should turn and sneak back out the way I came, because I wasn't the type to break in and steal stuff. But I couldn't bring myself to go.

Swallowing thickly, my instincts were quiet. I liked to listen to them, but I couldn't move. Heaving a quiet breath, I edged farther over the deck, making sure to touch lightly on the planks, so only two protested under my weight and I was at the swinging bench.

Easing down, sitting with my back against the far edge, I could see the house, and I only needed to turn my head to see the street.

I watched the house.

I wasn't even lying to myself, saying I'd only stay for a little while.

I never once looked at the street. My head was on the house, my eyes trained for a glimmer of a shadow, a movement in the curtain. If I was asked what I was looking for, I wouldn't be able to explain it. How can you look for a ghost? But that's what I was doing, still doing.

I just wanted to see her. One more time.

Bark!

I tensed, freezing for a split second. I forgot about the dog.

"Yeah. Yeah. Okay, buddy. I'm coming."

A light switched on.

I heard paws on the floor inside.

Before I could leap from the bench, the dog was on the other side of the door. He froze, catching my scent. A low growl began, followed by loud and angry barking.

Shit. Shit. Shit.

I was off the bench, jumping over the banister, but instead of going to the front gate, I darted to the side of the fence between their house and the neighbor's. Scaling up and over, I dropped down on the other side just as I heard them open the door.

"What is going on with you?" The husband was half griping, half laughing as he stepped outside.

There was a rush of feet on the patio, and I heard the dog growling and sniffing on the other side of the fence. A desperate whine came from him, and he tried to dig at the bottom.

"Groot! Stop it."

They named their dog Groot. I smiled.

"Hey, boy. What are you smelling there?"

He was getting closer.

I headed out, running over the neighbor's grass. They hadn't put up a fence. The dog followed me, and I heard the owner say, "Oh. Whoa. What the hell...?"

Then I was at the sidewalk, and after darting past a few vehicles, I slowed to a walk, hunching my shoulders forward. I tugged the hood of my sweatshirt up and dug my hands into my pockets. It was the end of April, but it was still fucking cold in the morning.

I'd gone a few blocks when my phone started buzzing, and then I heard an engine behind me.

I knew, like I always did, because he always came after me, that it was Cross.

I didn't even look.

He slowed down, and I reached for the door handle. I got inside, breathing in his scent of sand and pine, and I crumbled. The tears wouldn't stop, and I wasn't only crying because I missed my mom.

"Bren." Cross parked the truck and slid over, pulling me into his arms. "Baby."

I just cried harder.

Life was hard, almost too hard sometimes.

That's what I cried for.

CHAPTER
THIRTY-ONE

THE NEXT MORNING, thirty minutes before the school doors opened, I was still raw.

After Cross picked me up and held me during my breakdown, I hadn't been able to put all the emotions away. That made me volatile, and no one liked a volatile Bren—me in particular. So after discussing things with Cross (and by that, I mean we just waited till Channing came home, changed, and headed back out), I took a day off. Cross called in for me because he'd been perfecting his Channing imitation. Then he went to school, and I stayed home to get my emotions in check.

It hadn't fully worked.

But I was better today, and after having a crew meeting to bring everyone up to speed on the surprise Drake visit and the tidbits he'd dropped, we'd decided to deal with Monica first.

It was going against my bones to be at school this early, but here we were.

Zellman looked ready to piss, grimacing. "I don't think this is the right way to deal with her."

We were going to confront her.

I frowned. "Why not?"

"First, you look like you want to rip someone's head off."

The guys glanced at me.

I nodded. "True." Monica's would be preferable.

"Two, Monica is not scared of us. She knows we're not really going to do anything." He paused. "To her."

I held up a hand. "I might."

Zellman gestured to me. "You just proved my point. But three, what are we really going to do? Threaten her? Monica's a little nuts, and she's more nuts than normal because she doesn't have her friends to reel her in anymore. Also..." His eyes flashed to Cross. "Monica really, really hates Bren." He coughed. "Because of you."

We all understood that. No one was arguing that point.

I frowned. "Is Monica seriously that crazy?"

Cross and Zellman said at the same time, "Yes."

Huh. I hadn't realized. Okay then.

"New plan." I held up a hand. "Cross talks to Monica—"

His eyebrows shot up. "You want to pimp me out?"

I kept going as if he hadn't said anything, "—and pretends he's jealous of who she's dating. Then we can find out who she's dating."

Jordan tilted his head. "Why can't we just ask Tabatha?"

"Because they don't know. Monica wouldn't tell them."

Cross nodded. "Taz said Monica wouldn't give them a name, but they know it's someone from Fallen Crest Academy."

Zellman growled. "I really hate those fuckers. Wait!" He tensed. "What if it's the same asshole that got Sunday pregnant?"

"Double reason to bash his head in?" Jordan mused.

"It doesn't matter. I don't think she'll tell me. She knows I don't give a shit about her."

I had such a good boyfriend. Pride swirled around my stomach, making it flutter.

"Monica's nuts, but she's not like that.," Jordan said. "She and Sunday were best friends. She left their group because of Sunday's ties to us." He gestured to Zellman, who grinned. "Not because of a falling out."

"My boyfriend is Zeke Allen," a voice piped up behind us.

Oooooooh.

Shiiiit.

We all turned as one, probably with varying expressions. We'd heard nothing. Not a sound, not a car, not a footstep.

Zellman grunted, his eyebrows shooting up.

Jordan grimaced, stepping backward.

I didn't know what Cross looked like because he was silent, like he always was, unless he needed to step up and kick some ass. But me? I was all about this.

I started smiling, and I knew Monica was taken aback. She blinked a couple times, her scowl flattening.

I stepped toward her. "Really? It's Zeke Allen?"

She moved her bag to her other shoulder and edged away from us, toward the school. "Why are you happy about that?" She motioned around us. "And don't bother. I can tell you're gearing up for a 'crew intervention' or something, but it's not going to work. I know you guys don't hurt girls, and I'm not really doing anything to you anyway."

The guys were hesitant. I *sooo* wasn't. I was almost salivating. Yes, the old Bren was back, and she was rising to the surface and having a *great* time.

"You mean you're not going to blab to the interviewers today? 'Cause you're scheduled for this morning. Becca emailed me the schedule in case I was sick again."

Monica's mouth closed with a snap. She looked rocked.

"You're not planning on saying anything about me, Cross, Zellman, or Jordan?"

She swallowed. Her voice came out small. "I don't have to, about you guys."

"But the Ryerson crew, you will?"

She opened her mouth, but then she paused and closed it again. She didn't say a word.

"What are you going to say when they ask about the crews?" I asked.

Her facial expressions shifted until she settled on something and a smug grin came out. "Did you know none of the Ryerson crew had to sign a deal with the cops?" She watched all of us, that smug smirk deepening. "You all have been wrapped up in your own lives, so I bet you didn't notice that. They were arrested. Just like us. They were offered the deal. Just like us. They didn't take the deal. And yet, unlike us, they were released the next day. Not one has charges being brought against them. They all got off free and clear. Wondering about that? I would, if I were you."

"They posted bail. Same shit would happen to us," I said.

"No." She said it so calmly, with such confidence. She knew. She knew something we didn't. "They didn't. They were released. My aunt works for the Fallen Crest Police Department. She could tell me that because there were no restrictions. They all walked free. And they've been quiet. Have you noticed that too?"

"Because Drake's their leader," Zellman said, but he wasn't as cocksure as she was.

That wasn't a good sign.

"Really." She laughed, mockingly. "Are you sure about that? Are the Ryersons even still a crew?" Her eyes found mine and settled. "Have you guys noticed the lack of crew activity? I mean, they've pulled the glue out of yours. If she's at school, she's locked up in the library doing her helper duties."

She was right.

A thudding feeling took root in me.

"I overheard the conversation Broghers had with Badger. She didn't want to give up her counseling sessions with you. It got heated. And yet, look who else has been absent the last couple weeks. We haven't had any committee meetings. I'm here for early prom decorating, which you knew, which is why you're here."

Another thing was she right about.

Fuck.

I sensed a theme here.

As if making our decision for us, she began walking backward toward the school. "And one more thing, you might want to talk to that producer you're helping. She's got some ties close to you." She was speaking right to me. "I would know. Zeke's a huge Mason Kade fan. He's obsessed with him."

I raised my chin. "Those guys have nothing to do with me."

"Not you, but your brother, your future sister-in-law..." She let it hang between us before she turned and walked into school.

"Man." Zellman sighed once she was gone. "I wasn't sure if I wanted to see Bren pull her knife or not."

"It wouldn't have worked," I said faintly. I turned to the guys. "She's right. Monica's right. We can't do anything physical. We need to do something else, something—"

Cross said it for me. "Not crew."

I felt sick to my stomach.

Zellman swore under his breath. He was speaking for the rest of us.

"So what are you going to do?" Jordan asked.

I shrugged. "Talk to Becca. That's the only thing I can do."

———

"You want to do what?"

Becca Sallaway's disbelief was evident.

We'd put together a small plan after talking to Channing, then Heather, and I was incorporating phase one. The rest of the camera team were getting ready. Monica was due to walk through the door any second, but I wanted her on pause.

I said it again. "I want to be interviewed."

"You?" Her eyebrows were up. "We were told you would not be a part of this documentary. In fact, your principal told us not to even entertain asking you or that gorgeous guy I've seen you snuggling up with." She sounded wistful. "Though, I can tell you the camera would love him. It would be *amazing* exposure for him."

"Him too."

"Excuse me? What?"

"Him too. And Jordan. And Zellman. And I'm fairly certain I can get a few others to redo their interviews."

Her head lowered. She clasped her laptop to her chest and peered at me. "Why would people have to redo their interviews?"

"Because of me."

"What do you mean?"

"They weren't as honest as they could've been, and that's because of me."

"I don't get it. Why because of you?"

"Did *Kenneth* really not tell you guys?"

"Tell us what?"

"That I'm in a crew."

"You're what?" She staggered back a step, almost dropping her laptop. "No. He didn't say a word. Though..." She shook her head, sighing. "Part of that was because of us. We were asked to come in and do a somewhat more personal piece on the history of Roussou—how it is now versus where it came from."

I was lost.

"We're not the only team working in Roussou. There are two others. We're just the ones assigned to interviewing current students."

I gulped. A large boulder had wedged its way into my throat. It was painful as fuck. "Excuse me?"

"The other team isn't totally based here. They're interviewing older students, and one's in prison now. Another team is doing sweeps around the towns. It's a more in-depth piece about Fallen Crest and Roussou. Frisco as well. We wanted to get here in time for District Weekend, but we were unable to."

"You..." I couldn't talk. That boulder was expanding, squashing my entire throat. "Why? I mean, what's so important about this area?"

"Well, I mean, there's a few factors. One, Mason Kade is still a big story. He's won two Super Bowls, and he's only been playing professional football for two years. Mix that with who he's married to, and that's news. The first piece on Mason Kade just whetted their appetite, to be honest. The audience wants more about him, and if we weren't here, others would be coming in. There's a personal stake for the executive producers too. They have—I shouldn't be telling you this—but they have their own motivation for making sure the piece about Fallen Crest and Roussou comes out well, that old dirt isn't being stirred up. Believe it or not, that's not our focus."

"I thought you were here for the crews? Your project is titled *Crew Gang World*."

"Oh!" She started laughing. "That's just for Kenneth's sake. His agenda is pretty obvious, so we're playing along. We're asking the questions we want to, but still others for him, and who knows, maybe we will focus on the crews. It's not been fully decided."

I mulled this over. "You said a few factors. Those are two."

"Yeah. The third is that Roussou has their own famous person, and no one here talks about him."

"Who?"

"Brett Broudou."

"The guy in prison?"

"No, the brother—who also knows Mason and Sam, and who realized he's really fucking good at football in college. He has his own story, but no one is talking about him. That's really weird."

Oh.

I was stunned.

"The Broudous aren't really talked about here at all."

"I know, because of what Budd tried to do. I was in school then. I know what happened."

"I do too."

She frowned, wrinkling her nose. Her hair was normally flawless, but as I said that, she reached for a strand. She began twisting it, as if it were a nervous habit. "What do you mean you know too."

"I know the history, who Budd Broudou tried to rape. I know who stopped him. I know who his intended target was."

She swallowed, blinking a few times. "I—that's not publicly known. Some people would know, but the general public..." She shook her head, as if trying to convince herself.

I dropped my last card. "I lied to you about not knowing Channing Monroe."

She stilled. Frowning. "Say again?"

"Channing Monroe is my brother. Heather Jax is going to be my sister-in-law. And I talked to both of them this morning. They told me you usually go by Becky Sallaway. They told me a whole bunch of stuff about you."

She was silent, her eyes complete saucers. Her chin trembled, but after a moment she let out a deep breath and rolled her shoulders back.

Five seconds passed.

Thirty.

Her forehead was wrinkled. An entire chunk of hair fell over her forehead, hanging in her eyes.

Still. Nothing.

Then she seemed to decide something, and her eyes found mine, crystal clear, and she started.

"The executive producers asked for information only from people who agreed to be interviewed. Your principal and your counselor both approached me. They both offered to have off-the-record interviews. I turned them down. It was obvious they wanted to give us information we weren't sure we wanted to know, and anything we get off-record, we can't use. They were both adamant about it being off the record. I'm wondering now if they both, in their ways, wanted to tell me about your relation to someone I used to consider a friend." Her voice broke. "I messed up a while ago, more than a few times, and I have some burdens to bear because of that. This documentary is my apology to her. The executive producers of this project—I think it's their apology too. We came in with our own agenda, but it's not what you're thinking. It's not what anyone is thinking, so while I can't tell you fully what's going to end up on the editing room floor, I can say that you want us here. Other projects were in the wind about coming here, and those wouldn't have been as favorable. We got here first. That's big in our industry. Those other pieces won't be so kind."

Her eyes were swimming in unshed tears, but her head was up. Her chin was rock solid.

"I was engaged to someone who wanted to hurt Samantha and Mason. Sam tried to tell me, but I chose him. I chose wrong. I'm trying to do right by *them* this time."

I glanced away.

Thinking.

Weighing the pros and cons.

I decided.

"I still would like to be interviewed, because whether it was your intention or not, I know my principal wants attention drawn to the crew system here. I need to make sure both sides are told."

She was nodding before I'd finished, and she tucked that strand of hair behind her ear. "I think hearing both sides would be good." She coughed, clearing her throat, getting herself back in check. "We would love to interview you and *your crew*."

I looked back at her.

She flinched. "And everyone else who needs to redo their interviews, apparently."

CHAPTER THIRTY-TWO

AFTER TALKING TO Becca/Becky, I was officially let go as her helper.

I'd fulfilled my community service hours by then, so it wasn't that big of a deal.

Monica came in just as Becca was saying she needed to have a "talk" with Principal Broghers. I didn't know what that was all about, but it wasn't my problem. None of this was my problem anymore. As Becca swept out the door, Monica bit her lip, seeming to wait for whatever I was going to say to her.

I didn't really have much in me, surprisingly. "You can say whatever you want."

Her mouth opened. "What?"

I started to move past, pausing right beside her, my words quiet and just for her ears. "You don't have anything on us. Not anymore. And about Allen..." Now I looked at her. She turned, and I saw the beginning of fear in her gaze. "Have a great life with that one."

That was it. A good luck and goodbye.

Prom was in two days. Maybe it was because I'd been hiding from so much this year, maybe it was because I felt I was standing still as everyone went past me, maybe it was because I now had to talk about my crew publicly, maybe it was because today was just another threat against us, and I knew it wouldn't be the last, and I knew we would survive no matter what. Maybe it was all of those things, or maybe it was just because I was *feeling* again, but whatever the reason, I felt hope.

I felt a new beginning coming. And while I used to look to the future with panic, wondering who it would take from me, I didn't this time.

As the bell rang, I walked through the library and saw Jordan walk out, his arm around Tabatha. Zellman was already in the hallway, already bickering with Sunday, and waiting at my locker was Cross.

I was almost looking forward to what the future held.

Or maybe I was just growing up.

Whatever it was, I smiled at Cross as I drew near, and he looked behind him. "I don't see someone you want to beat up. That must be for me." His eyes warmed. He reached up, brushing his hand over my cheek and drew me in, his forehead resting against mine.

He said it softly and simply, "I love you."

Oh yeah. Life was good right now.

"I love you too."

"Oh, gawd! You two. Stop with the public displays of cheesy shit." Zellman was groaning. "We can only take so much before we start seeing Bren's face when we jerk off to the nudie magazines."

Everyone stopped.

No one said a word.

Then:

"Gross!"

"Ew!"

"Oh my God! Are you serious?"

I felt sick.

Cross looked sick.

Even Jordan was eyeing his best friend. "Dude. That's disgusting."

"What?" Zellman scanned the group. "No one else does that? Really?"

Cross stepped toward him. "Do you and I need to have a talk?"

Zellman swallowed. "It's a compliment. Bren's hot."

Sunday didn't say a word. She cocked her arm, and the back of her hand came swinging. *Smack!* Right into Zellman's head.

"Ow!" He ducked a second swing, glaring at her. "Woman. Stop."

"That's gross. You think of your crewmate when you jerk off?" she asked.

"What? Like you don't?" He shrugged. "Come off it. Like you've never imagined Cross when you're playing with yourself?"

"No! I think of you!"

He perked up. "What? You do?" He surged for her, capturing her hand. "'Cause ninety percent of the time, I think of you. I mean, if we're all being transparent here—"

"No one's being transparent here. Only you." Cross cut in. "Please. Stop."

Zellman ignored him. "Bren's like two percent of the time, and it's enough where I get uncomfortable about it. That's why I said something."

"And the other eight percent?" Sunday folded her arms over her chest.

Zellman rubbed at the side of his jaw. "Do I have to be transparent about that too?" He leaned forward, dropping his voice, though everyone heard. "Because, babe, you shouldn't know those. I'm a guy. We're crude. A lot of the time."

"Stop while you're ahead," Cross suggested.

Zellman turned to him. "I'm ahead?"

"No, but your girl doesn't want to stab you right now."

"But I might," I growled.

Zellman threw me a carefree grin, as if he assumed I was joking, but as Sunday stalked off and he went with her, he glanced back. There was a twinge of uneasiness there.

He stopped halfway down the hallway and yelled back, "We're good. Right, Bren? You're not gonna slice me when I pass out Saturday night? Cause I'm 98-percent sure that'll happen."

I flipped him off. "Since we're all about being transparent right now, yes."

He hurried to catch up to Sunday. "Okay. I'll—please don't murder me. Crew mates don't murder crew mates."

I tipped my head back. "Crew mates don't say about crew mates what you just said about me!"

"Yeah. Okay. I see that." Sunday was turning the corner, with Zellman hot on her heels. He raised his book in the air. "Sorry, B!" Then they were gone.

Jordan coughed. "I'm noticing you're here. In the hallway."

I knew what he was asking. "Yeah. I told her. It's getting set up."

"About all of us?" Cross asked.

"She's salivating over you especially."

"Great."

I laughed.

And like before with my smile, Cross' own grin appeared. Jordan grinned a little too, and even Tab softened at the sound. It's like I never laughed.

Did I laugh?

Crap. I might never laugh.

I sighed. I'd have to work on that. But not now.

"How's Sunday doing with the baby?" I asked Tabatha.

She straightened from Jordan, shrugging. "I don't know. I bring it up sometimes, but she doesn't want to talk about it." She looked over her shoulder to where Sunday and Zellman had gone. "I was at her house the other night. Z came over, and I heard them fighting. I don't know what he's all told you guys, but he's trying to find out who the guy is. She won't tell him. Me either, because..." She leaned back against Jordan's side. "For obvious reasons."

Cross frowned. "I don't like knowing one of those pieces of shit has hurt one of ours, and he's getting away with it."

"Yeah." She chewed the inside of her cheek. "I know."

Jordan was looking down at her, but glanced over to me.

Cross noticed the look, and the three of us were on the same wavelength. Or I was pretty sure we were.

"Her phone," I started.

"That's a good idea," Cross said.

And Jordan clarified for us. "Take her phone."

"What?"

"You know her passcode to get in her phone?" I asked.

Tabatha shook her head. "No."

That was easy enough. "Watch her one day. Like, watch her open her phone, get the code, then take the phone. We can snoop through it, if you want."

"Are you guys suggesting we break into her phone?" Tabatha seemed shocked.

Jordan grunted. "Yeah. Why not? She's protecting a piece of shit. We should know who it is."

"But that's her right—"

"Not about this." Cross shook his head. "Or just watch her for the passcode. We'll do everything else. When her phone goes missing, you can be honest and say you have no idea where it is."

"Oh, boy." She chewed her other cheek. "What are you guys going to do?"

I lowered my head, my eyes still on her. "Do you really want to know?"

She gulped. "Maybe not."

The warning bell was about to ring. We all knew it, and since I was no longer needed as the camera team's helper, I guessed saying I wouldn't glare during future interviews wasn't enough. I had a class to go to as well.

The bell rang.

Jordan held up a hand, walking backward. Tabatha lingered.

Cross waited for me to get my books.

"Just get the code," I told Tabatha as we passed. "Do it sooner than later, just to be safe. It's better to know with a situation like this than not know."

We weren't normally a PDA couple, but Cross lifted his arm and put it around my shoulder. I didn't care.

I was a PDA girl in that moment.

CHAPTER
THIRTY-THREE

"OH, WOW."

I tensed, tucking the last strands of my hair into the braid before looking to the doorway. Heather stood with a stunned look on her face.

She shook her head. "I mean, wow." A flurry of eye blinking. "Bren, you look amazing."

Oh, fuck.

I looked like a girl.

I was in the white tulle dress with pink sparkles. The store clerks had a bunch of fancy names for how it was designed, but it was strapless. The top was sleek, dipping down just a little between my breasts. There was a minimal amount of tulle at the bottom. It didn't puff out or anything. But what sold it for me was when I put Heather's leather jacket on again.

The look. The feel. The vibe. It was me.

"Thanks?"

She started laughing. "You hate it, don't you?"

I lifted a shoulder, moving to my closet. I grabbed a clutch. Taz said we had to have clutches. And they had to match. I looked at mine. It was black. My dress was white and a soft shade of pink.

My clutch didn't match.

Taz was going to have a breakdown.

"Bren?" Heather moved closer, her voice quiet.

The clutch was supposed to match.

Why didn't I do this stuff ahead of time? How hard was that?

Dresses. Purses. Even fucking bracelets. Makeup. None of that was natural to me. I knew I was pretty, or pretty enough. No one made fun of how I looked. And Cross loved me. He wasn't a shallow kind of guy, but would he love me if I was ugly?

Taz. Sunday. Tabatha. I knew those girls would be all decked out. Dresses that molded perfectly to their bodies. Their hair was always good, but I knew they'd be masterpieces tonight. They understood mani-pedis and blowouts. All that was second nature to them. And jewelry—who knew there were so many kinds of earrings.

I didn't have my ears pierced.

"Bren." Heather was right behind me now.

I knew it was coming. I was prepared, knowing she'd feel how tense I was.

When her hand touched my shoulder, a soft curse slipped out. "Oh, babe."

I was crying. I'd felt tears coming all day, and I'd pushed them off.

Prom was a rite of passage, right? Not for me. This was a nightmare.

"Aren't you supposed to learn about makeup, nails, the difference between flats and stilettos? Sisters. A mom. You learn that from them, don't you?" I looked at her. "Where'd you learn that stuff?"

Heather was beautiful. Always had been. She had a sexy tomboy look to her, and she never seemed self-conscious. She was confident, strong as hell, and used her sex appeal like a weapon at times.

I grew up watching her, watching how she handled her brother, how she handled my brother, how she was a badass boss at her restaurant.

She hugged me, her lip trembling.

I'd never seen Heather's lip tremble. Never. I never saw Heather cry, choke up. She wasn't weak, not the way I was right now.

"Bren, hon." She smoothed a gentle hand down my back, then picked at some strands and tucked them into my braid again.

I looked at my clutch. "I went to the Fallen Crest Spa this morning. The other girls all wore button-down shirts. Someone explained later they did that so they could take the shirt off and pull their dresses on and not mess up their hair." I sighed. "I wore jeans and a tank top. A tight one. The hair stylist looked at me in horror, but I didn't know. No one told me. I don't do girly shit. Taz goes to the salon, and I go cave diving with the guys. That's how I grew up."

"Bren."

I heard the tears in Heather's voice. She hugged me once more, and tucked her head against my arm. "I lost my mom when I was young, too, but not as young as you. I don't know who taught you about tampons, but I got my mom for a while longer. She did teach me some of that stuff. But I had Rose, Marie, Theresa. They worked when my dad still ran Manny's, and those ladies were like second moms to me. They *tsk*ed me if my pants were too tight, but that was my style. Just how I was. I don't know why, but I never cared. Never bothered me, but you know what did bother me?"

I raised an eyebrow.

She smiled. "Fitting in. That's something you've always had that I didn't. Chan was in Roussou. I was in Fallen Crest. I never felt like I belonged in one place or the other, so I was kind of a loner. There were friends, acquaintances, but not a crew like yours. Then I hooked up with a good friend, she brought along a couple baddies, and somehow that evolved into years of friendship."

I knew who she was referring to. "Now you're going into business with them."

"Yeah. And it's going to work because everyone in our group loves the person first over the business. That's the only way it'd work for us."

I motioned around the room. "I didn't know anything was wrong in here until Taz asked one day why I didn't have any pictures. Guess that stuff is normal to other girls. I never knew." I wasn't making sense. "You're—"

We didn't do emotional talks. Heather or me.

In some ways we were so alike, in other ways, so different.

Remembering that, I closed up, pulling away. My words dried up, and I swallowed them. Restlessness settled in. I wanted to get this shit done—go to Cross' parents' house where everyone was meeting for pictures. Go to the pre-dinner thing. Tabatha was hosting a shindig for more pictures, and then we were off to the dance.

And after the dance, I could breathe.

I could slip away.

I wouldn't have to see all *their* moms taking pictures anymore. I wouldn't have to see *their* dads grudgingly there, or proudly there.

Even Cross would belong to his mom, his dad's during the picture process. He might stick to me, but they would be there—hopefully playing nice with each other—wanting his attention, wanting to talk to him, hug him, love him. And deep down, he would love it. That's what he needed.

Cross was normal.

I breathed out, catching myself only after I'd started. "I don't know why Cross is with me sometimes."

A choked gasp came from Heather as she sat down. "Excuse me. What?"

Shit. I'd already said it.

"Nothing."

"Oh, no, no, no." Heather's chair scraped against the floor as she shoved right back out of it. She was across the room, trapping me.

I was going to bolt, but she caught my arm and sat beside me. "Hey."

I didn't look. I couldn't.

I couldn't believe I'd even said that. I mean, it wasn't my place to question Cross' decision, but...I was.

"Hey!" Heather tapped my chin. "Look at me. Talk to me. What is going on in that head of yours?"

The floor creaked.

I froze.

Heather cursed.

We looked up.

Channing stood in the doorway, his eyes pained and one hand resting against the doorframe.

"Why'd you say that?" he asked.

"How much did you hear?" I asked over a lump in my throat.

"All of it, but that—why did you say that, Bren?"

He stared at me, knowing. He knew why I'd said that. Why was he making me say it again? Explain it?

"You know," I hissed.

"No." He shook his head. "No. Not that. I don't know that. Tell us, Bren. Now."

"It's noth—"

"It's not nothing! Tell us. Tell me! Let me in!"

"Channing." Heather jumped to her feet.

He flung a hand out, silencing her, but his eyes never left my face. "No, Heather. This is brother and sister shit, and Bren is about to say something real and significant and something that'll make everything make sense. I can feel it in my bones, and I am also feeling this huge red alarm saying to push her. Make her talk. Make her open up, because if you don't, she never will."

He took a step forward. "I don't know why this came up, but there's a crack. You opened it, just slightly, and I'm here. I'm pushing my way in, all the way in. Let. Me. IN!"

My emotions swirled inside of me, picking up speed, power, like a tornado trying to shove out of me.

Then, silence.

Heather didn't dare talk.

The room was so small, so heavy.

Channing was breathing hard, but he grated out, "Bren. Please."

I crumbled. That last *please*. It was soft and delicate and so unlike everything else, and he was right. There was a crack. It had formed this morning and grown all day long, and I couldn't deny what was staring me in the face.

I was different. I was not like those other girls, but it wasn't because I chose it. That's what I'd told myself. I grew up brainwashing myself into thinking I was better, elevated above them, but that wasn't the truth.

I was just a girl, hurting, and I didn't know why, but today I could see it. I couldn't put my head down and ignore it, not anymore, and the reason for that—I wasn't sure. I just couldn't hold myself back anymore.

Channing was in my face, breathing hard, his eyes pleading, so stricken, and I—I felt her.

The hairs on the back of my neck stood up.

She was here, and as I stared at Channing, his eyes widened too. The hairs on his arms stood up. He could feel her too.

"You..." he started.

A surreal warmth oozed into me. Calming. Peaceful.

"Channing," I whispered.

"Shit," he cursed softly.

Two steps and I was in his arms. He wrapped me tight, pulling me to his chest.

I could hear Heather's soft crying.

She was here. I knew it. I could feel her.

"Oh my God," Channing breathed.

Words would've cheapened this moment.

I knew and I knew Channing knew, and that was enough for me. I was supposed to meet Cross at his parents'. That's what everyone planned—meet there for the first round of pictures. And Taz had gotten involved when Cross said he was going to get ready at my place. She insisted, with full-on sobbing and her face looking like a puppy dog's, that he needed to do it at home. For her. This was the last prom for both of them, and I'd been fine with it.

That was then.

This was now.

Leaving my house, I felt raw and unsettled. For the life of me, I couldn't fold in on myself this time. I assumed I was healing. Maybe?

Who gave a fuck?

Well, I did. Because I felt exposed and vulnerable, and I was trying my hardest to pretend otherwise. No one could know. No one.

As I headed out the door, I heard Heather whisper to Channing in the living room. "What was that? What happened?"

He didn't answer, and I froze, unable to make myself leave. I needed to hear what he would say, if he would say it.

"It was—I don't even know what to say. Something happened." A pause, and his voice dropped even lower. "I can't stop feeling her. Is that normal?"

"Who?"

"My mom."

Our lives, the way we were—tough. We either bled or we made others bleed. We didn't share or cry on each other's shoulders, not unless we were so broken that it was the only way back. If Heather made fun of us or said something mocking, I was going to stab her. Straight up.

"I feel my mom sometimes," she said after a moment.

I waited, but I didn't hear anything else, and knowing the time had come and I couldn't put if off anymore, I opened the door. Stepped out. I closed the door and went down the sidewalk to my vehicle.

It meant something, hearing Heather take what had happened seriously. It meant a lot.

And somehow, it made me less vulnerable than before.

Maybe I should've thought more on that, but I was past the emotional breakthrough limit for today. I was exhausted, and the night hadn't even started.

I had a picture session to get through.

CHAPTER THIRTY-FOUR

PARKING AND WALKING up the sidewalk to Cross and Taz's house, I heard them all inside.

I stepped up on the front porch and stood there. I waited. I savored. The feel of my mom was still with me. And when I went inside, I would lose her. She'd fade, replaced by Cross, the guys, Taz, everything else.

A car door slammed behind me.

I was jerked out of my trance and looked to see who was coming, my mouth opening in surprise.

"What are you doing here?"

Heather laughed, tossing her hair over her shoulder. She cut across the lawn as Channing rounded the back of his truck. He tossed his keys in the air, catching them and throwing me a grin.

His eyes sparked. "You really think we'd let you deal with this alone?"

Heather drew up beside me and squeezed affectionately.

Channing strolled up the sidewalk. I rolled my eyes, but his smirk just deepened. His phone rang, but reaching into his pocket, he didn't even look to see who it was. He silenced it and put it back. He stopped in front of me.

"You're a Monroe. You're going to prom." He leaned in, his forehead pressing against mine for a second as he laughed. "Where the fuck else would we be? We're your family." He stepped back. "You don't have Mom and Dad today, but you have us old folks instead. Deal with it."

Heather moved in, hugging me, and she whispered, "I know I'm usually not like this, but will you bear with me?" She stepped back, and Channing's arm came around her shoulders. "I'm feeling a mom moment coming up."

"Plus." Channing jerked his head up, indicating inside. "We'll enjoy scaring a few of those parents in there. Some don't know how to react with us breathing the same air."

Heather shoved her elbow in his side, but the door opened just then, and Cross was there.

"Bren?"

Then Taz yelled his name, and he cursed, stepping outside. Shutting the door, he moved aside. "Fucking hell. She's worse than our mom. I swear."

His voice trailed off as he looked at me.

And I had no voice because I was looking at him.

He was...

"Bren. Holy shit. You're—"

...HOT!

"—fucking gorgeous." He blinked a few times. "Wow. Holy, just—wow."

Channing snorted, clapping a hand on his shoulder. "Yep. You use that education, son. We're going inside." He tugged Heather behind him, and as the door swung shut, we heard Taz asking where I was.

Channing murmured something, but the door shut, leaving Cross and me on an empty porch.

I suddenly felt self-conscious again and crossed an arm over my chest, grabbing my other arm. "Hey."

He was still taking me in. "Bren." Cross lifted his head, his voice rough. "We're not going to prom."

"What? We aren't?"

"Nope." He took my hand, digging in his pocket for his keys. He pulled them out, leading me to the sidewalk. "We're getting a hotel room. I'm getting us champagne, wine, roses, chocolate dipped things, and we're spending all night there. No one else. And condoms. I'm getting a fucking Easter basket of condoms."

I laughed, tugging him back. "Stop."

He whirled, his hands coming to my hips. Breathing hard, looking all fierce, he peered right into my eyes. "I'm not joking. I'm totally fucking serious." His hands flexed. "I do not want to share you right now. Or, like, ever." He groaned as he kissed my forehead. "You are fucking beautiful. I don't have any other words. I just want to keep you all to myself and—"

He stopped.

I pressed a hand to his chest, smoothing it down.

"Bren?"

I wasn't looking up anymore. There were tears again, and I was trying to keep them at bay, but he was making it tough.

I loved him so much.

I needed him so much.

I yearned for him so much.

And hearing these words, feeling his need emanate from him, I couldn't talk.

Finally, after a few breaths, I choked out, "I told Channing and Heather today that I didn't know why you were with me."

"Bren. What?" His hand came to my arm. He pulled me close.

"All day today, I was missing having a mom. I was dreading coming here tonight because I'd be the only one without a parent. And I've thought it for a while, wondering why you're with me. I thought it was because you had parents. Normal parents. Even their divorce is normal. And a sister. You and Taz are so close, but you're normal." I lifted my head now. I wanted him to really hear me. "I'm not normal."

"Bab—"

"No, listen to me." I should've moved out of his arms, but I couldn't bring myself to do it. So I stayed and poured out my heart, within his shelter. "I'm not. But you are. I used to think I was above the Normals, but today, tonight, I had to stop believing that lie. I'm not above them. I'm not special because I have your love, and Zellman and Jordan's friendship. I *act* it. We act it, but we're just tougher. We're meaner. We're loyal to an extreme. That's how we're different, but we're not above them. I think in some ways, we're what's wrong. Not the school. Not the Normals. Us. The crews."

"Bren." He shook his head. "Where is this all coming from?"

An image flashed in my head. Jordan with Tabatha. Zellman following Sunday. Taz and Race together. Then Cross and me.

I was holding everyone back.

"You guys never talk about college." It was the elephant in the room. "I know it's because of me. You're protecting me, but I know you guys have all made plans."

"No, we haven't. We—"

I stopped him. I had to say this, standing separate. My body against his defeated the purpose.

I took a step away. "I'm holding you guys back. I know I am. I am terrified of moving into the future. I'm terrified of losing you guys, but I will. People change. Lives evolve. And I am too. I *will* too."

I looked away, my throat swelling with emotion. "Maybe it's the counseling. Maybe I'm truly healing, but...we can't be a crew if we don't grow as individuals." *Fuck.* The Badger would be so proud of me. "That interview I'm going to do, it's going to be me letting you guys go."

"Bren!"

"Not letting you go as a crew, but releasing you from putting your futures on hold for me. That's all. I'm not being a good crew member if I don't deal with this stuff inside of me. I cannot stand still, paralyzed about who or what I'm going to lose while you guys are all growing. That's it. You're growing. I've refused to grow. But I can't, not anymore. I would be selfish to hold you back. Do you understand what I'm saying?"

"Baby." He tucked his head down and kissed my neck. His entire body shuddered. "I've never been more in love with you." He tipped his head back, staring deep at me. "I love you. YOU. No one else would fulfill me. No one else would make me feel excited for the day, grateful for the day. No one else makes me feel like I'm half a person. My other half is in my arms. No matter what happens in the future—where we go, where we don't go—this stays."

He touched my chest, his palm just under my throat. "You. Me. This stays. Because it has to, because I need you that much, because I'm not Cross without Bren. It's that strong for me, and I don't give a shit if you want to grow separately. We can both grow. Zellman. Jordan. They can grow too, but we grow together. That's how it'll be, or I'm not letting you go." He shook his head. His arms tightened. "You and me, we're going to die standing here. I'm that committed. Fuck prom."

I grinned at him, and I realized I'd been wrong.

The love and warmth and peace that I'd felt from my mom, I still had it.

Cross made me feel those things too.

"I love you so fucking much."

He smiled at me, resting his palm to my cheek. "I love you so much fucking more."

"Please. Shut up," Zellman whined from the door. "We're crew. We're tough. Shut up. People could hear you. We have a reputation to uphold. Jeez." He knocked his hand against the doorframe. "Oh, and get your asses inside. Taz's order, not mine. I guess your mom got into the wine, and she's about to pass out on the couch. Taz wants the pictures done before someone pukes or makes an inappropriate pass at Bren's brother. Sunday's mom is drooling. It's embarrassing."

CHAPTER
THIRTY-FIVE

WE POSED.

We did *Charlie's Angels* poses. We did funny faces. We did let's-pretend-we're-ninjas poses. Animal poses. Sultry. Sexy. Mysterious. Sunglasses on, sunglasses off, sunglasses thrown in the air.

I wouldn't have been surprised if Tabatha's mom requested we do a cheerleader triangle pose, but she didn't. They did bring out pompons, which I refused to hold.

Zellman did a cheer all by himself.

Jordan banned Zellman from ever touching pompons again.

The next stop was Tabatha's house, where she got text alert after alert. Everyone hugged and kissed. Cross and Taz's mom was tipsy, with pinot grigio breath. Tabatha's mom blinked back tears, smudging her eyeliner, and also sending Channing a hungry side-eye. Heather eventually put a stop to that, literally standing in front of him with her arms crossed and her chin raised in challenge.

The Normals had joined us here, and there were food and booze on the low-down, handed out in coffee mugs and prepackaged in juice bottles. One guy kept walking around with a loaf of bread, and I only saw the alcohol when he opened the bottom. An entire bottle of Jack Daniels had been stuck in there.

Taz complained about the waste of bread.

Race's mom was out and out crying. She wasn't even trying to contain herself. Race kept going over to her and hugging her, and that'd just make her cry harder. After the pictures, he stood with her, her head buried in his chest as he patted her back with a pained expression on his face.

Sunday's mom just had a perpetual frown. I heard her whispering to her husband about "getting pregnant on prom night." I guessed Sunday hadn't broken the news yet.

Then we piled into a party bus to go to the restaurant. As we entered, Taz informed me that she and the girls had decided against the limo. It was "so millennial" of them, and we were trying to go against the millennial theme. Party bus it was, and I couldn't complain. More leg room, and more room to get out of the way when Jordan and Zellman started humping the stripper pole.

Some of the Normals came with us, and that's when I saw Lila had infiltrated our walls. She was sitting on a guy's lap, wearing a low-cut black lace dress. His hand was on her hip, but her gaze was on Cross. It was all Cross, and seeing me looking, she licked her lips and adjusted her legs, opening them wider. The dress barely covered her, and it covered her less now. The guy's hand dipped down, smoothing up the inside of her thigh. He didn't look or stop talking to his buddy, but there was a secretive grin on his face.

Yep. He thought that move was for him.

Cross laughed in my ear. "You know I don't give a shit about her."

I glared at her as I said, "It's the principle of it. She should instinctively fear me."

He laughed again. "Not respect you. Fear you."

I leaned against him. "You know it."

He moved so my back rested against his chest. His arm came around me to rest on my stomach, and he looked down as I was suddenly tipped up to him. Our lips were inches away—and who was that girl again? She fled my mind. I focused solely on Cross, so much that Taz had to hit my leg to get our attention.

I felt the hit and reacted without thinking. I had her wrist in a hold before either of us registered what had happened. A blink of an eye, and I had her in my grip. She hadn't enough time to sit back.

Race's eyebrows went up. Taz's mouth dropped.

Even Zellman noted it, and he was blitzed already. That said a lot.

Letting her go, I leaned back into Cross. "Sorry, Taz. I—"

"Nope. That was on me. I know not to hit you, and I forgot." But she was uneasy about it. I could tell when she wouldn't meet my gaze right away.

Race pulled her close. He lifted his chin in greeting. "So, the girlfriend didn't come for pictures today. I'm sure you were relieved to see that?"

It took a second, but he was speaking to Cross. Not about Cross' girlfriend, but Cross' *dad's* girlfriend.

Oooh.

I glanced up at Cross, who had stiffened beneath me. His free hand went to my leg, and he began fiddling with my dress.

"Yeah. A nice relief."

"But you'll meet her tomorrow."

Why was Race bringing this up now? I threw him a frown, but it clicked. Taz's eyes were glued to Cross, who was not looking at her. She seemed to be studying him to get some answers, and I was starting to think maybe she knew about their half-brother?

Race's gaze jumped to mine, and I jerked back. Oh yeah. They were looking for something. That something flared in his gaze at my reaction, and I bit the inside of my lip. Fuck. Cold-as-ice crew member I was not at that moment.

Well, fine. Two could play that game, and I smiled at Race, who visibly tensed.

"How's it going with your dad?" I asked. "I haven't seen much of Alex lately. Everything good there?"

Taz sucked in her breath. The people around us stilled, listening in.

Cross lifted his head, glancing between me and Race. He noticed Taz then, a slight sheen of tears in her eyes.

"Why would you ask that?" she asked.

"Why do you think?" I shot back.

Race lowered his head. He slouched in his seat and angled his body, so he wasn't fully facing us anymore. Taz reached out and laced their hands together.

She looked down, playing with his thumb. "That's not cool of you."

I raised an eyebrow. "And his question was?"

I expected Taz to drop it. I wasn't trying to be hurtful. I just wanted my message sent and received, but she spoke again, surprising me.

"There's more to the story. Things my brother needs to deal with, and you can't always jump in for him. It's family stuff." She lifted her gaze, looking sad but also defiant. I saw a flicker of fire in those eyes, same as her brother's. "And I miss my brother."

Her look was for me. Her words were for him.

Cross noted it. "Enough," he said. "Drop it."

She opened her mouth, but Zellman chose that moment to stagger over and stumble onto our laps. He winked before pushing himself up and stealing a place between Cross and me.

"Hey, guys!" He lifted his arms around Cross and me. "I miss my guys. Bren, you're a dude now to me. No more of that other stuff." He waggled his eyebrows, but I saw some sober in him. He knew what he was doing.

"Z," I murmured.

"Dude?"

"If you don't slow down on the Jack, you're going to pass out," I told him. "You'll miss prom."

"Yeah." He sighed, sinking down in the seat. He kicked his legs out. "Jordan switched me to water. Stupid water. Sober water. No-booze water. You get my drift?"

Oh, we were getting it.

"So, who's going to do a body shot on me?" he asked, lifting his shirt.

We got off the bus at a nice restaurant in Fallen Crest. It was new, recently opened, and I knew Heather had been worried at one point about how Manny's would be impacted because of it.

Looking around, noting the fancy glasses, the rest of the customers and how they stiffened and threw horrified looks our way, I knew she didn't need to be concerned. People were people.

People liked to let loose and get drunk, not be prickly and stuck-up. Her place would continue to kick ass.

I recognized one of the servers when she came to our end of the table.

Slender, her blond hair pulled up in a tightly wrapped bun, absolutely perfect. Her uniform was a white button-down shirt over black dress pants.

"Ava?"

She paused, looking over. "Oh, hey, Bren." She looked around the table. "You all look great."

I shared a look with Cross. Zellman and Jordan glanced at me. They recognized her too.

"What are you doing here?"

Tabatha laughed, reaching for her water. "She's obviously working, Bren. How much have you had to drink?"

I ignored her. "You're working three jobs?"

Ava stiffened, biting her lip. "Uh... It's not that bad. The money is good."

Fuck that. She worked nearly full-time at Heather's place, and she picked up shifts at the pizzeria in Roussou. Now she was here? Was she trying to work herself to death? I remembered Heather talking about her, how her last boyfriend had been a jackass and now she had a nice new guy.

Ava also went to our school, the school that had prom tonight, and she was working.

I didn't push it, and Ava seemed to relax as she filled the rest of the waters, then returned to take orders.

When she came to me, I lowered my voice. "You're not going to the dance tonight?"

She froze. "I'm not a big dance person."

I called bullshit on that. I hated dances, and I was even going.

Cross touched my arm, shaking his head just slightly. I knew what he was signaling, but it was wrong. I wasn't going to let it go. I liked Ava. We weren't friendly, but I knew she was a good worker. She was quiet, did her studies. She didn't have a lot of friends, and thinking on it now, I didn't know who she hung out with at school. She didn't seem to hang out with anyone outside of school either. She worked.

"Roy."

She lifted her head from her order tablet. "Hmm?"

"That's your boyfriend's name. Roy, right?"

Her eyebrows lowered. "Uh. Yeah." An uneasy laugh. "He's working too. What would you like to order?"

I told her, handing over my menu, and when she left, Tabatha asked, not so quietly, "You know her?"

Ava paused, her shoulders stiffening.

Jordan elbowed her. "Tact, babe." He nodded toward me. "She's Bren's friend. Obviously." Then he got pulled into conversation with the guys on his other side.

Tabatha was still frowning. "Yeah. I know, but that girl's a loser. She used to be on mock trial." She snorted, laughing by herself. "Can you believe that? Mock trial."

This. Right here. This was why Tabatha and I were still a work in progress.

Taz had been quiet since the party bus, but she jerked her head up now. "Fuck off, Tabatha."

Tabatha gasped.

Jordan turned back, his eyes wide.

Zellman had been mid-belch, but quieted it, pressing a fist to his mouth.

"What did you say?" Tabatha asked.

Race started to speak, but Taz leaned forward, her arms crossed tightly over her chest. "I said fuck off. If you want to be friends with us, you need to pull the superiority stick from your ass. We don't put up with that shit."

Tabatha sat up in her seat. Her neck was red, and it was moving up her face. "Are you fucking kidd—"

Race started to say something, again.

He was interrupted, again.

Cross beat him to it this time. "Are you delusional?"

Tabatha looked like she'd been slapped in the face. The red drained, and she paled.

"We're not like that. I don't care if you're dating Jordan. You're about to say the wrong shit to my sister. You're stepping wrong. What you should've done is stepped right the first time by realizing Bren was talking to that girl for a reason. Bren cares about her, and that means she's good people. Back off and learn your place."

Tabatha's mouth hung open. A gargled sound escaped, and she turned to Jordan. "Are you going to let him talk to me like that?"

"Babe."

"I'm your girlfriend—"

"Babe."

"I don't care who they are to you! They didn't suck your dick before pictures today!"

Zellman snorted, lowering his head, his shoulders bouncing up and down. The other guys weren't as considerate. They outright laughed.

Tabatha shot them a dark look. Sunday smacked Zellman's chest with the back of her hand.

"Sorry." He coughed, reaching for his water. "Everything's a little funnier right now."

"Shut it, Zellman!"

"BABE!"

"What?" Tab rounded back to Jordan, fisting a fork.

Calm. Cool. Definitely smoothing it over, Jordan nodded toward our end of the table. "What you did was wrong. Taz is right. Cross is right. And Bren's probably second-guessing your friendship right now."

It penetrated. You could see it. Tabatha still had the stung look on her face, and her cheeks puffed out like a blowfish, but after a few seconds, she suddenly deflated.

About that time, Ava came back. She was placing a plate of appetizers in the middle of the table when Tabatha started.

"Um…"

Ava paused, her hand stretched out, stepping between Sunday and Zellman's chairs.

When Tabatha didn't continue, Ava asked, "Did you need more water, miss?"

Miss.

Shit.

Zellman started laughing again.

"Shut it, Z!"

"My friends call me Z. I'm Zellman to you."

Tabatha looked rocked, actually weaving in her chair. Her eyes filled with tears. "Ava."

Ava had stepped back by now. "Yes?"

"As my friends have pointed out to me just now, I don't know if you're aware, but I have this problem..." She rolled her neck, lifting her chin, and shifting on her seat. "I'm a reformed stuck-up bitch. Or I'm trying to be, and I still have flare-ups when the stuck-up part shows it's ugly head. I had one of those moments with you just now, and I am sorry." She bit down on her lip. "For being a bitch to you."

Zellman gave her a nod of approval.

"Uh. Okay. Thank you, but you were fine, miss." Ava ducked her head. "I'll be right back with the second appetizer."

Once she was gone, no one moved for the food. They were waiting.

Tabatha looked down, her hands in her lap. "I'm sorry. I meant what I said. I'm trying to change." She sought Taz out first, then Cross, then me. "Becoming friends with you guys is important to me. I wasn't expecting to change, but after Jordan and I began dating, I fell in love with him. It just happened. But I have a ways to go, and I'm sorry again."

Now I felt uncomfortable.

Being in a fight was my terrain. This—calling someone out and having them not only apologize, but be genuine—was foreign fucking land to me.

Taz was smiling, beaming even.

Race shrugged, reaching for his soda.

Cross was eyeing me.

Then everyone turned to look. I lifted my hands. "Okay?"

Zellman started laughing. "There's our girl, not knowing how to function. She's used to beating the apology out of bitches like you."

"Dude," Jordan admonished.

"Right." Zellman raised his water toward Tabatha. "You can call me Z again, and *dude*," he said to Jordan, motioning to me. "That's Dude. We've gone over this."

Everyone started laughing—even Tabatha, a little red in the face again. "You're such a goof, Zellman."

He grinned. "That's Z to you."

She smiled back, the lines around her mouth softening. "Z."

"And I won't hear anything besides it."

Zellman was teasing, but he wasn't wrong.

I felt a lingering sense of unease through dinner.

Tabatha had looked down on Ava for what? Working three jobs? Being in mock trial? I didn't know what mock trial was, but it sounded better than anything I'd done in school. I was in a crew. That was it. These guys fulfilled both family and friend roles for me, but things were changing. I'd talked about growing with Cross, and I meant it, but that made me uneasy too.

How far could you stick your neck out—trying to learn, push yourself, adapt, grow—before it was chopped off? It was different for Tabatha, for the Normals. Going to college was expected of them. I'd been in The Badger's office when they came in, asking for help with college applications. They rattled off their options, weighing where they wanted to go. No problem at all.

Not for me. Even the conversation filled me with terror, but I knew it was going to happen. Growing. Moving on. What then? If my guys left and I stayed back? What bitch like Tabatha would I have to deal with, looking down on me because I'd need to work three jobs too?

When we finished dinner, we went back out to the party bus, headed for the dance this time.

Cross came up behind me, placing his arm around my shoulders. "You were quiet in there."

"Yeah."

"What's going on?"

What was going on with me?

I didn't have an answer for him. It was the same stuff I'd started talking about before, but I didn't want to get into it here.

"I'll tell you later," I said.

"Okay." He pressed a kiss to my forehead, and we got on the bus.

Turns out, I spoke too soon.

CHAPTER THIRTY-SIX

MY SIDES HURT from laughing.

My feet hurt from dancing.

My ears were ringing from the music.

My head pounded. My dress was a mess. My makeup was nonexistent. My hair was a nest.

But prom had been everything.

I was shocked. All those years I'd avoided life, school, classmates, dances—maybe I shouldn't have? I came out of the bathroom and headed for the parking lot—like I'd just texted Cross—as I considered that.

No. It had been fun now because I was ready. *Now*. Not then. I'd needed only my crew then, and now, I was opening up, trying to accept others, not be so guarded.

I was just passing the guy's locker room when I heard the door open.

I didn't think anything of it. I didn't think anything of the empty hallway. I didn't think anything of the low lights until I heard, "Bren."

A chill shot up my spine. My gut clenched. This wasn't good, whatever was coming, because I felt it happening. It was like a train departing the station. It was heading right for me, and I knew no matter what, I couldn't get off the tracks in time. And. That. Train. Wasn't. Going. To. Stop.

I turned and read it on his face.

"Alex?"

His face was haggard—bags under his eyes, and it seemed he hadn't shaved in a week. He was dressed in a tux, but the coat was gone. His shirt was half unbuttoned, the tails pulled out. His pants were dirty, scraped at the bottoms, and in his hand, a full bottle of Jim Beam. He wasn't even standing still. He staggered back into the door, hitting his head, and he didn't say a word. He didn't react.

He didn't feel it.

But his eyes had a storm in them, and they wouldn't leave mine.

I should've gone. Walked away.

But I took a step toward him. "What's going on, Alex?"

He shook his head, raising the bottle and peering at it as if it had magically appeared in his hand. "I warned you."

"Warned me? About what?"

"About Drake." He shook his head, and once he started, he couldn't stop. He started to fall, then slammed into the wall by the door. Now the door could swing shut behind him, and he stepped back, but the door wasn't there. He backpedaled rapidly, slamming into the wall now.

A hard hit. And still no reaction.

He just raised the bottle again and pointed it at me. "I told you he wasn't here for the reason he said he was here. Crew's gone. They kicked Drake out. I'm out. It's no longer a Ryerson crew."

I frowned. "They're still a crew?"

He shrugged. "Who knows. I don't. I'm out, been out since Taz."

Pain sliced over his face, and he closed his eyes. "I'm so sorry for what I did to her. Shit went south. It went north, sideways, east, west. It was going all around, and I couldn't get a handle." He gulped, his voice thickening. "I should've gotten a handle. I ain't bad, not all the way."

He pressed that bottle to his chest, hugging it. "I got bad parts, good parts. I'm trying to have more good than bad. I'm trying, Bren. I really am."

I took another step toward him, but I was tentative. My insides were on full alert, yelling at me to leave.

"Alex." I sighed. What could I actually do? "What's going on? Just tell me."

"Drake." He looked down. "It's been all about you, and you never knew. You were supposed to be there. They were supposed to arrest you, but you weren't. Or if you were, you got away. You hid. You messed up their plans."

God. This didn't sound good.

My phone was buzzing. That would be Cross, wondering where I was, but I couldn't respond. This. This was important. If I pulled out my phone, it would break whatever this was. It was delicate, like thin ice. Any wrong move, a wrong word, and Alex would close up.

It buzzed again.

I ignored it.

It started ringing, and I shifted my hand to my clutch and silenced it. I did it with as little movement as possible.

"Alex," I urged. He had to keep going.

"Crew Princess. That's you. You're the glue."

My eyebrows bunched. "What does that mean?"

"That party when everyone was arrested? They only wanted one person."

His eyes were gleaming, suddenly sober, though I knew he wasn't.

"They only wanted one person, but they couldn't find you, so they took everyone else."

"The District Weekend party? But—"

"Plan B." He hiccupped, swinging the Jim Beam around before tipping back and taking a long drag. Wiping his mouth with the back of his hand, he added, "That was plan B. Arrest everyone else, make 'em sign that sheet. The cameras were plan B, but you were plan A. You were first priority."

"How do you..." My head was swimming. It wasn't making sense, any of it. "How do you know this? Why did they want to arrest me?"

"So they could lock you up, hurt the crews. You stabbed Neeon. He got vengeful, started hating you, your crew. His daughter had a breakdown. She's in some mental facility now. That added to Neeon's anger, enough to make him motivated." Alex started out hot, but slowed down, his words getting lost.

"Alex! Snap out of it. Tell me the rest."

God, please. Tell me the rest.

His eyes blinked, bulged, and then settled back. "Yeah. Um... yeah." He was thinking, remembering. "You're the glue. You. Channing's the king. You're his sister. They wanted to hurt you, put you away, hurt your brother." He stopped again, flinching from some invisible pain. "Hurt your dad."

"What?" My dad?

"Red Demons took over in Frisco. They can't sell in Frisco if the Demons are there."

Who was *they*?

The Red Demons were a motorcycle club, and my brother had battled them not long ago. We'd been a part of it. Our dad joined their club, but he was in prison—had been this whole time. All of this was coming out of nowhere. I knew it had happened, but Channing protected Roussou. I never thought any of that life would come into school, into *my* school.

"I thought the documentary was about putting the spotlight on the crews?"

"Plan B. They want to wipe the crews out, get rid of them, bring in dealers and start selling here, the only place your brother isn't policing 'cause he knows your crew is here, dogging it. Like I said, hurt you, hurt your brother, hurt your dad. It all spreads out. Your brother would be distracted, your dad too. They wouldn't be focused on what was happening in your school, just focused on saving you, 'cause they both want you to have a future."

He started to slump, his back hitting the wall, and down he went, all the way to the floor. He mumbled, his words slurring, "Drake's their point guy. They brought him in, forced him in, and he knows all about it. His job? Make our crew go away, which he did. And his other job..." He looked up, opening his eyes with some effort. "You. Set you up."

"Set me up?"

Alex nodded again, but his head hung lower, and when he didn't look up again, I raced to him. "Alex!"

I shook him.

He didn't move.

I jostled him.

Nothing.

"Alex!"

And then it happened.

What he'd been here to warn me about.

The doors burst open as flash bombs were thrown. Tear gas. Smoke filled the hallway, and I could hear their footsteps. It was a stampede.

I couldn't move, but I had to.

They'd have night vision goggles.

But fuck it. I had to try.

I pushed off the wall, surging to my feet, and I kept my eyes closed. I moved across the hall, my arms stretched out, until I hit the opposite wall. It tore my skin, but I bit my lip, holding in the cry. They were coming in the doors, down the main hallway too. They were circling me, but there was a side door. It wasn't far, and I just had to get there.

Everything inside of me was screaming to give in. Sit down. Wait.

I couldn't do that.

Inch by inch, I moved along, feeling the wall until it gave way. My hands touched glass and moved down to the door handle.

Success!

I pushed on it. It was locked.

I wanted to cry out again, scream, but I kept it in. Rearing back, trying not to breathe in the smoke and gas, I threw my body at the door, kicking it with everything I had, and it opened. Then I was on my knees, outside, and I pulled in air until lights shone down on me.

Legs.

There were legs upon legs, lights shining behind them until one stepped forward. A woman with her gun drawn.

She came over, knelt down, and sheathed her gun. "Bren Monroe?"

Really? Could I lie at this point? Even try to pretend I wasn't?

I didn't answer. I didn't have time because another cop came to the door. He spoke without emotion, like he'd just stepped on an ant.

"Body is Alex Ryerson."

Body!

Body?!

"DOA?" she asked.

"It just happened," he said.

"Resuscitation?"

"Unsuccessful."

DOA.

Alex.

Dead on arrival. He was dead.

I couldn't process that. We had saved his life months ago and now...

And then those cold eyes turned my way, and she pulled her hand from her side. She held a pair of zip ties.

"Bren Monroe, you are under arrest."

CHAPTER THIRTY-SEVEN

Cross

THE FRONT DOOR to the police station flew open.

I knew he was coming. I'd made the call, knowing this was no longer a fucking high school thing. Cops were involved, and that meant there were bigger fucking things in play, and I wasn't messing around. Seeing Bren led to that squad car, her hands in zip ties, by some fucking stone-cold bitch was one of my nightmares come to life.

Fuck that.

I mean it.

Fuuuuck that.

I was done playing by the rules, playing nice, doing shit so the least amount of damage was inflicted. I was ready to throw a bomb, grab Bren, and haul ass after that.

Jordan and Zellman held me back. Race had gotten involved, and the three of them were still standing guard.

I. Was. Furious.

I was seeing red.

Blood.

I wanted to fucking taste it, and as soon as that door flew open, I was ready. I was more than ready.

Channing came in like a fucking lightning storm, not even wearing a shirt. That's how fucking badass Bren's brother was, and he was my goddamn salvation in that moment.

Scanning. Finding me. He pinned me in place and stalked toward me.

Everyone knew Channing was there. It was like a wave swept the building, and everyone came to attention. The cops behind their desks were watching, wariness building. It'd been there since they brought Bren in, since we'd stormed in, since I'd tried to deck the first cop who told me to "Take a seat."

I was hauled back before I could make contact, but fuck that. I was tempted to get arrested, just so I could go back there and see Bren.

It was only Race telling me to chill out and that Bren was probably already in an interrogation room that penetrated. The only goddamn fucking thing.

I needed Bren. I needed to save her, whatever it fucking cost. I didn't care. Me for her. I was ready to offer the switch, but Channing was here. He had pull. Or he did with the Roussou department.

His jaw was clenched, and rage simmered just under his surface. "Why the fuck are we in Fallen Crest? She was arrested at the school?"

I clipped a nod. That was all I could get out because the need to hurt someone raged in me. Seeing Channing, someone who loved her almost as much as I did, ready to do whatever he needed to do had unleashed a fucking monster inside of me. I literally wanted to peel someone's head off, and I had to force a calming breath. It wasn't working.

Channing's eyes narrowed. "Get a handle on yourself. You can't help Bren if you're like this."

"Fucking easy for you to say," I seethed. "You didn't see her walked out to that cop car."

Shit. The image was searing my mind again. I flinched, unable to unsee it. "They gassed her. They smoke bombed her. They went at her with SWAT, in SWAT gear, holding their fucking guns at her." My voice rose. "They pointed their guns at her!"

Channing swore under his breath, then motioned for the door. "Take a walk. Tear something up. I don't give a shit what you have to do, but do it. I need the Wolf Crew leader with a clear head in about an hour."

"Why an hour?"

"Because they're not going to let us get to her before that, and I have the cavalry coming in for this."

He turned away and headed for the front desk like he was squaring off against the opposing team's goalie, score was tied, and he was skating to win the gold medal. No. Not even that. He was heading for them like they were between him and his sister.

I felt a smidgen of pity... No, I didn't. That was a goddamn lie, one I was trying to tell myself so I'd calm the fuck down, but it wasn't working. I growled. I didn't even realize it until Channing twisted back to look at me.

He scowled, snapping his fingers at Jordan and Zellman. "Get him out of here. He needs to calm down."

They nodded, but Race was there before either of them could touch me.

He started to push me for the door, but I resisted, planting my feet.

"Cross. Come on."

"We got him."

Jordan and Zellman were here, but I still wasn't fucking going. I couldn't. Everything inside of me was screaming to stay, be here for Bren, just in case they walked her past the desk. I had to be here. I just had to be—but the guys had a different thought.

"Take him out," Channing yelled. "Now!"

All three of them were on me, and I was up and in the air. Throwing myself backward, I clambered over Zellman, shoving off of Jordan's shoulder, but then two more guys were there, grabbing me. They fucking carried me out. Twisting, wrenching, vowing I'd kick all their asses—they ignored me until we were back in the parking lot.

They set me on my feet, and Jordan grunted, "Hold him down until he can think clearly. He's goddamn nuts right now."

I waved my arms. Bren needed me. I had a primal need to be back in there, as close to her as I could. I was almost rabid. I couldn't see straight. The air was humid, weighing me down. I had to get free. I had to fight bac—

"SETTLE THE FUCK DOWN!"

That was Jordan. Screaming in my face.

"Cross! Oh my God!"

That was Taz. My sister. Her voice got through, but I couldn't stop. I just couldn't.

"Holy fuck."

Someone grunted in surprise. A car door slammed shut.

I was fighting. I didn't care who I was hitting. I could taste tears, sweat, blood. Mine. Someone else's. I. Did. Not. Care.

Bren was all that mattered.

Then footsteps pounded, and I was shoved down to the cement. A two-ton truck was on top of me, and I couldn't move. There were hands on my arms and legs, pinning me down.

But

I

Was

Still

Fucking

Fighting!

My head scraped against the cement. More blood. It was the only thing in my nostrils now, the only thing I could smell.

"Shit," someone breathed.

"Oh, Cross." My sister. I recognized her voice. She was crying. "I got him. I got him. Let me..."

They shifted around. The feet blocking my vision moved, and Taz was there, kneeling down to look right at me.

"Cross." Tears streamed down her face. Snot too. She wasn't paying any attention. She was pale, so pale.

She was scared.

It started to sink in then.

My sister was scared. For me. Of me.

Because I was acting like a rabid animal.

"Cross," she said softly, soothing me.

She reached out, slowly, until she had my hand in her grasp. She linked our fingers. And then she began to speak, but she didn't get it.

I'd never felt this monster in me, but he was here. He was angry. He was threatened. He wasn't human. That was me now, and I could still think, recognize what was happening, and I was scaring myself. But I needed to know Bren was okay. I couldn't breathe. She was the only thing that would make him go away.

Taz didn't know this. I couldn't tell her because I couldn't talk. I had to—

"That's it, brother," she said, still soothing.

She took in a breath.

I felt myself doing the same, going with her. Syncing.

"Another."

Together, we breathed.

In and out. Holding. Exhaling, still slowly.

And after a long while, I started to taste my fear. No one had told me that could happen. It was revolting, and my stomach cramped up in protest.

"Cross," Taz whispered, squeezing my hand and pressing it to her cheek. "I need you to calm down. I'm scared too, but I need my brother. I need him. Remember when we were little? We'd lay like this, side by side, watching each other until one of us broke and started laughing. Let's do it again. But let's calm down. Okay? Just calm. That's all."

I couldn't be calm.

She didn't get it. No one was getting it.

Bren.

It was all about Bren.

Panic burned my chest, searing me.

"Cross. Please." She was crying again.

I tried to shake my head. I tried to signal her, because I still couldn't talk.

White-hot, blind panic was taking me over, and I began to fight again. I needed them off of me. I couldn't breathe. I couldn't move. I couldn't—I could only rage in my head, and they weren't helping me.

"He's scared." Taz said it like she was just realizing something. She pushed to her feet. "Get off him. Get off him! He needs to move around. He needs it. I can feel it in him! Get OFF HIM NOW!"

Things began moving.

There was a sudden push down on me, and it was gone, but I still couldn't move. Not at first.

I had to get my bearings.

Then I jerked upright and gasped for breath. Taz threw her arms around me, her head buried in my shoulder and neck.

"Please," she murmured. "You gotta calm down. You gotta calm down."

I moved my head up and down, or tried to.

She was still crying into me, and I lifted my hand. It was all bloodied, but I tried to pat her back. Feeling it, a whole new wave of sobs took her over.

"Babe."

That was Race. He reached for her, trying to take her away from me, but I looked up with a warning in my eyes. *Back off. Back off now.*

Seeing it, he nodded and edged back a step. But he didn't go far.

I could lift my arms now. The feeling had come back, and I wrapped both around her. Feeling the other arm, Taz broke down. She wasn't trying to soothe me anymore. She was breaking down and cursing.

All my shit started to clear.

This was my sister, and she needed me. I began soothing her, comforting her.

I rested my head on her shoulder as she continued to sob.

"What the hell?" someone wondered.

I knew. I didn't have to wonder. This was about my family, her family. We'd lost it, and I hadn't been there for her. Fuck. Shit. Goddamn. I hadn't been there for my sister.

"Taz, I'm so sorry."

She curled into herself, forming a ball as her arms slid away from my neck.

I felt Race coming back, and I nodded this time. I looked up and saw a cut on his face, blood running down his cheek. I winced because I knew I'd been the cause of that, but that was for later. He started to bend for her, but paused, waiting for me.

I nodded. "Yeah. She needs you now."

His arms slid underneath her, and he picked her up, cradling her to his chest. I expected him to take her away, but he didn't. He just sat down beside me, holding her, and she reached for me.

I took her hand, lacing our fingers, and she seemed to settle a little from the contact.

She had her head resting against his chest now.

"Sorry," I told him.

He raised a shoulder. "Can't say I wouldn't lose it if it were Taz in there."

True. Still, I should've had a better handle on myself.

I finally looked around, feeling my eyebrows rise.

Jordan, Zellman—and they weren't alone. I knew some of the Normal guys had come out to help, but so had four members of Channing's crew. Moose—the big fucker who'd been sitting on me. Seeing my glare, he just grinned. Congo, Lincoln, and Chad, the big red-headed asshole. I scowled at all of them, but the only one who reacted was Lincoln.

His face impassive, he said, "Relax. You were psychotic. Chan said to contain you, so we contained you."

"Fuck off." That prick had been part of trying to squash me. I didn't give a shit about the semantics of it. My chest still felt it had been deflated inside of me.

He grinned, just like fucking Moose.

But then there was another surprise, because behind our crowd was another one. They were standing toward the end of the lot, and I couldn't think of a reason they'd be here unless they'd been part of setting Bren up.

Shoving to my feet, I felt my blood spiking again.

"Hey, hey!" Jordan was in front of me. His hand against my chest. Z was right next to him.

"What the fuck are they doing here?"

Zeke Allen and his jerkoffs were down there, their bitch girls next to them, and I didn't give a shit if they weren't looking ready to fight. I was ready. I was more than ready, and they were the perfect target—until Blaise stepped out from behind them, a whole different look than the last time on his face.

Then I knew. I *knew*.

He fucking *knew* too. He looked between me and Taz, seeming all sorts of twisted.

"No! Get the fuck out of here. No! You don't get to come here, not now, not when my girl was taken from me tonight."

"Shit," said Jordan under his breath.

Zellman grunted. "I need a drink. I don't care if it's an adrenaline shot or straight Jack."

Blaise kept looking at Taz, looking at me, still giving me that look.

I was seeing red all over again. I started to climb up over my brothers. I didn't give a fuck. No way was *that* brother going to get in, no fucking way in hell.

Jordan cursed, catching me as I leaped. Congo, Moose, Lincoln, and Chad all scrambled. Two of them ran around Jordan to catch me. The other two were coming up behind me. I glimpsed them from the corner of my eye, and then Moose reached up, grabbed my shirt, and yanked.

The material tore, but I was ready for him this time.

Launching up, kicking off from his massive chest, I jumped between Jordan and Zellman. Chad and Lincoln went to grab me, but I landed and shot off from the ground, ducking and dodging them. It was a desperate, last-ditch effort, because I was only going to get one shot at him, but it worked. Luck was fucking on my side, and then I charged my half-brother.

He just braced himself.

Zeke Allen shouted. Their group tensed in surprise, but I was already there. My hands found him, and I hauled Blaise around, slamming him into the vehicle beside them.

"You don't fucking come near her! You got that?! I will end you if you try to hurt her. I swear!"

He wasn't even trying to fight. He was barely paying me attention, his head turned, his eyes still on Taz.

"STOP LOOKING AT HER!"

That's when people clued in. I heard a few gasps. More curses. Sudden silence fell over the crowd, only interrupted by the sound of tires pulling into the parking lot. A door opened. A second.

Then, "Cross?"

A door slammed shut. "Cross! Get your hands off him."

A different voice, a feminine one, "Get off my son!"

They were running over, but all the while, he kept looking at Taz.

I had two options. Finish this later, or do it now.

I chose now. I reared back, ready to throw the first punch, but my dad was there. He shoved in between us, growling, "Goddammit, Cross. GET THE FUCK BACK! NOW!"

"Dad?" Taz asked. "What are you doing here?"

"We got a call, said our children needed us."

"Blaise. Honey."

A woman launched herself at him. As soon as I stepped back from him, she was there, holding and hugging him. He didn't move, didn't lift his arms. His face was expressionless. But she kept mauling him, smoothing his hair, down his arms.

Taz came up next to me, her eyes glued to his.

I growled again.

My dad smacked me on the chest. "Stop it. I know you know, so calm down."

And in the middle of all of that, a black SUV pulled into the lot and parked. Two doors opened, and two guys got out. One was famous, and the other was infamous around here.

Zeke Allen gasped, his eyes bulging. "NO WAY!"

The bigger of the two, with jet black hair, gave us a scan before heading inside. The other one had brown hair, still just as pretty, and a cocky smirk.

He stopped and stared at us, then sighed. "Aw, fond memories. Remember the times we beat people down, just for the fun of it?"

The bigger guy was at the door now, and he yelled back, "Logan! Get in here."

I knew who Channing now meant by the cavalry. He'd called in the Kades.

"Why'd he call them?" Jordan asked, shifting to stand next to me.

I grunted. There was only one reason. "Their dad is the biggest benefactor for this police station."

He and Zellman both looked at me. So did my dad and Blaise. I felt their attention.

"How do you know that?" Z asked.

I gave him a look. "Police arrest every student from our school and not theirs? You bet your ass I'm doing my homework. I've got a list of who has the power to pull strings, and James Kade is at the top."

Jordan grinned. "And there's our fucking leader. Always two steps ahead."

I broke free from everyone. Channing had called in his fancy friends. That told me one thing: Bren was in more trouble than I'd thought.

CHAPTER THIRTY-EIGHT

Bren

THE DOOR OPENED and the two detectives from before came in. The woman carried a folder.

"Let's try this again."

The other cop didn't sit. He moved against the wall behind me, his arms folded.

She sat, her head down as she skimmed through the papers.

One, I knew what they were doing.

Two, they'd already tried the friendly, we're-just-trying-to-help-you act.

Three, this bitch knew exactly who I was, because I knew who she was.

Four, I'd asked for my lawyer, so the most I had to worry about was curbing the inner feral Bren I turned into when I was feeling cornered, which no doubt was their new agenda. It was in my files. I'd undergone counseling. It was well-documented that I lashed out when I felt pushed into a corner. So we were now on to their second attempt: emotional and physical intimidation.

Detective Broghers was making me wait, and she was doing it intentionally.

A full minute. Three. Then, after the fifth, she pretended to be done reading up on me. She closed the file and lifted her head, a smile on her face. She angled her chair toward me, at the side of the table rather than not across from me.

"Bren," she said. "Would you like a water? Soda? Something to eat?"

"Water."

"We can do water." She nodded behind her, and that cop left the room.

While we waited, she looked me over and winced. "We didn't let you wash up, huh? Would you like a washcloth?" She indicated my hands. They'd been scraped, the skin torn.

I pulled my hands down to my lap. The zip-ties were gone, but red lines from them remained. They'd pushed the line, pulling them tighter than was comfortable. In a sense, I knew they were just doing their job: push the line, make them uncomfortable, lean on me, get me to give up what they wanted, and then the case would be wrapped up.

"So." She pretended to be bored, even tired. She yawned. "You were at prom earlier?" She gestured to my dress. "I bet the pictures are beautiful."

All their tactics were working, but I knew what they were doing, why they were doing it, and I had to remember that. I had to keep a cool head, no matter how long they kept me in here. Had to, or I'd give them some reason to hold me. That's the real reason they were pushing, because they hadn't asked about Alex again since I'd said I wanted a lawyer. There were no pictures in that file. I'd been looking. Just papers with words, numbers, and signatures.

I had to wonder a few things.

Why would Alex take the time to tell me all of that about Drake setting me up, if he was going to die? The way he went down, he would've had to be drugged. For him to say Drake set me up would indicate he knew Drake was setting me up for killing *him*. Alex wasn't pleading for help. And he would've, if that had been the correct scenario.

Which meant he didn't know he was drugged, and he was telling me Drake had set me up in another way. That's the only thing that made sense. I hadn't felt for his pulse, just saw that he passed out.

They'd told me Alex was dead... No, they'd *implied* Alex was dead.

Alex might not be dead.

It was ironic in a way. Here I was, hoping once again that Alex Ryerson wasn't dead.

A knock at the door. The other detective came in and set a bottle of water in front of me.

Detective Broghers reached forward to take off the cap. She pocketed it, pushing the opened bottle to me. And again, she offered that same fucking friendly smile. "There you go."

I didn't reach for it. Not yet. "I asked for my lawyer."

"You did."

I hated how condescending she was.

She lounged back in her chair, fingers drumming on the table as if she were the impatient one, as if she were the one who wanted this over with. "We're just waiting for them to arrive."

There was no clock in this room, another thing they did on purpose. Take everything away from the criminal. Shove them in a room with no windows—a tight and confining room, and make them yearn for the bare necessities. Like time. Like water. Like conversation. You took it for granted until you lost it. That's what they used against you.

"So you're in school?'

I didn't answer.

She didn't care. Still friendly. "Senior, right? That's what your file said. College? Plans after graduation?"

Again. Silence. But they weren't expecting me to talk.

"I was so worried about what I was doing next when I was your age. Thought I had no time. A lot of pressure, right? Even more so now, these days with the internet. The Gram..."

She was talking, but I tuned her out.

I looked up, staring at the point between her eyebrows. It was a trick I'd once heard. You could look there, and the person thought you were making eye contact. It was a nonverbal cue that you were interested in what they were saying, and they'd keep going.

I was banking on that because I had my own thinking to do.

First: Drake.

She droned on. I never wavered from that point between her eyebrows.

Drake had found me when I was in Fallen Crest. He wasn't using the buddy system. He hadn't been on the crew scene. Months before that, he'd announced that he was back in town, texting us where Alex was waiting for a beatdown from me. He gifted us vengeance for what Alex did to Taz, and we took it.

But Drake had known where, he knew how, he knew when.

He could've rigged a video to record us.

But we had his texts gifting us his own brother.

What else did he have on us or know? He knew when District Weekend was. All those cops being there, it was an organized event. That meant they were alerted in advance. Someone told them where the party was, but it could've been the Academy Crusties. Was it them? They'd attacked Jordan up in the woods. Did they do that knowing the cops were coming and we wouldn't have time for retaliation? They could've...

Someone burned down the Frisco school. According to Alex, it was this secret group who wanted to sell drugs.

When the Fallen Crest Academy students were caught, intending to burn our school down, they claimed it was Alex who told them to do it. That could've been a lie said to cover their backs. We'd never questioned them. Shit. We should've questioned them.

Instead, Zellman blew their cars up.

They'd tried to come to Tabatha's party. We kicked them out. They found out who did their cars.

The next night was when they beat on Jordan.

Since then, we'd showed up at their school. They came at us, waiting for a fight. They'd been expecting a fight. We hadn't been there for a fight, but when it presented itself, we took it.

In that same moment, Blaise saw Cross face to face. He'd acted like he didn't know who he was. That could've been real or could've been a lie.

But since then, there'd been nothing except Drake's visit with me in the dress store.

He was the one who'd told me about Neeon marrying Principal Broghers' sister, who now sat across from me.

I glanced at her ring finger. There was a white line there. "Broghers—is that your maiden name?" I asked, stopping whatever she'd been saying,

Her lips parted.

I'd surprised her. She'd been expecting a different question, but I didn't ask her if she was related to my principal.

She cleared her throat.

I noted that reaction, and at the same time the guy behind me pulled his hands out of his pockets. I caught it from the corner of my eye, but her eyes flicked up to his and he put them back in.

She gave me that smile again. "Why do you ask?"

I nodded toward her finger. "You're married."

Her lips didn't part this time. They pressed together. She wasn't happy with me.

She wasn't going to answer. I saw the wall come down, and I tuned her out before she even started. I had my answer.

Drake had told the truth. About that part.

I remembered what Alex had said, that the group recruited Drake to come and be their person on me. If that was true, Broghers was either in that group, or she was being used by that group. And then what? Alex said the group wanted to push drugs through Roussou's high school. How would they get that going?

The answer came at me, startlingly and fast. They had someone else in my school, someone ready to start pushing their drugs for them.

They could've used Drake, but according to Alex, he was kicked out of their crew. That meant Drake was out. I'd been arrested on Alex's supposed death, so that meant Alex was out. Who then?

I could've kicked myself, because we hadn't been paying attention. No one had been paying attention. The documentary wasn't there to threaten us with national exposure. It was there to distract us from what was really going on.

The Ryerson Crew.

If Alex was right, if Drake had been kicked out, that meant there'd been a mutiny. Someone rallied their crew. Someone stepped up to be their new leader. That someone was going to push the drugs. Had to be. It's the only thing that made sense.

But Fallen Crest? I was here. How was I here? What part of this was I missing?

Principal Broghers had wanted the documentary to be here. *Kenneth* had asked them to be here. But he was kissing Becca's ass. Why was he kissing her ass if the end goal was just to distract us? That didn't make sense. A person kisses someone's ass because they want something. The documentary crew was already there. But if Kenneth was already getting what he wanted, he wouldn't have kissed Becca's ass.

He wanted something else.

I felt it in my bones. The documentary *was* there to distract us, so that meant the principal didn't know.

He was a puppet.

And this cop? Was she a puppet too?

Who was pulling her strings?

Neeon? Drake had talked about Neeon's daughter.

If Drake wasn't in on pushing the drugs, he was being used too.

Alex knew. Drake didn't. Who was using Drake? How would Alex have known?

Then I realized something. What brought them together? Their family. Someone in their family was behind all of it. That would make sense. Use the Fallen Crest police station to pull attention away from Roussou. Make us focus here, not in Roussou. Everything was a distraction. Everything.

That meant I needed to find someone who was active with the Fallen Crest police station, find someone who was connected to Drake, to Alex, find someone who was in communication with the new Ryerson Crew leader—the mastermind of all of this.

Drugs. It all came down to fucking drugs.

I was here because of goddamn drugs.

"Why am I here?"

Detective Broghers stopped, blinking once. "Why do you ask?"

"Was it a joint task team? Roussou and Fallen Crest together?"

She didn't answer, but she was listening.

"Who put that together? Whose idea was it?"

She wasn't going to answer. I knew she wasn't, but I was betting she knew. Follow it back. Always follow it back, and there would be one person who connected everything together.

We just had to follow the right string.

Someone knocked on the door. It opened, and a guy's head poked around.

"Her lawyer's here."

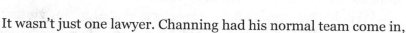

It wasn't just one lawyer. Channing had his normal team come in, along with another guy who smiled wide at the detectives when my bail was posted.

Broghers sighed. "Keep it up, Kade. I'm sure we could find something on you while you're in town. And don't think we don't know you're still in law school. You ain't a full lawyer yet."

The guy's smirk just deepened. "Keep it up, huh? Is that a challenge? An innuendo?" He shifted, facing her. "You coming on to me, Detective Broghers? You sure you want to do that? Pretty certain your entire force is well aware of how I handle challenges. I always *rise* to the occasion."

Broghers cut to my brother. "You called *these* guys in? Your normal lawyers weren't enough?"

Channing had been still, eerily still when I was led out, but now he turned his cold eyes her way.

"You don't want to ask me the lengths I'll go for my sister." He shifted, deadly power radiating off of him.

There was another guy standing with him, but in that moment, no one could look away from Channing.

"You took SWAT in. *SWAT*."

The cop in the back shifted. "We got a tip there was a shooter. That's protocol—"

"Stop!" Another cop shut him down.

Channing's eyes were slits now. "I can't help but wonder, who really pays your salary? If something gets shaken up, who'll fall out from the bottom of the bag."

He wasn't asking, and she wasn't answering, but his message was received. Her eyes went flat, and she straightened, her hand falling from her hip.

The cop at the front desk finished with my paperwork, sliding the sheet over to me. "Signature, please."

I lifted my wrists, zip-tied once again.

Channing snapped, "Are you serious? Even I didn't have cuffs on when I was leaving."

Broghers lifted a shoulder. "Just following protocol. You know us. Every rule of the book, we follow it."

Well, in that case... I finished signing, waited for my zip-ties to be taken off, and looked at her. "You know there's video of when you arrested only Roussou students and not the Fallen Crest students at that party. Was that protocol?"

Her eyes narrowed to slits. "What are you saying to me?"

Fuck it. I stepped toward her. "I heard a rumor that someone was pushing drugs in Frisco. That someone didn't like it when the Red Demons focused only there, so they burned down the Frisco school to send students to Roussou and Fallen Crest, and they had me assigned to that documentary to distract my crew from noticing a new leader stepping up in the Ryerson crew. I also heard Drake Ryerson was pulled in to set me up, that Alex was used as a pawn to arrest me, and that whoever is pulling all the strings is pulling yours too."

And my last one. "I also heard a rumor that Alex Ryerson is completely fine. He's just sleeping off his drunk in the tank."

I waited. Watching. Studying.

Her eyes flared. Her mouth dropped, just a bit, but it was enough.

I swept my gaze over the rest of the station. Most were watching and listening, but only one reacted—a guy in the back. He snapped his eyes to mine, then disappeared into a side hallway.

I looked at Channing to see if he'd been watching him too. He had.

As we left, Channing said softly, "What was that about?"

"Pulling a string. You know who that cop was in the back?"

He nodded. "Yeah."

"You think you could get his phone, see who he called?"

His eyes flashed. "Why?"

I stepped outside. "I want to see if I pulled the right string."

His gaze didn't move from me, only intensifying. "I'm thinking we need to have a long discussion tonight."

That was a given, but a crowd had formed outside. Not around us or me, but around the two guys that had come with Channing. Or one of them, to be specific. And it wasn't just Roussou people, but also Fallen Crusties. Zeke Allen looked like he was pissing himself.

"Bren!"

Cross.

I picked up my pace, going to him.

The famous guy yelled over the crowd, "Channing."

My brother's hand was on the small of my back. "I know," he called. "Come to the warehouse."

The guy nodded, going back to signing an autograph.

But Cross was in front of me by then, and his arms were around me as he lifted me in the air. Everything—all the strategizing, all the worrying—all of it was gone in that instant. It was only Cross and me, and I didn't want to let go.

"Shit," he gasped, peppering me with kisses. "I was so worried. I lost it. Totally fucking lost it. I could've killed someone."

If that was supposed to scare me, it had the opposite effect. I just hugged him harder. Then Jordan and Zellman plucked me out of Cross' arms to hug me, one by one. Then came Taz and Race.

I whispered to him, "They told me Alex was dead."

He jerked backward. "What?!"

"You haven't heard?"

"No. But—what?"

I patted his arm. "Find out. We have to talk later."

He nodded before stepping back, already pulling out his phone. His hand in Taz's, he led her to his vehicle.

Tabatha. Sunday.

Then came Moose, Lincoln, Congo, and Chad. A truck pulled up, and rather than find a parking spot, it just stopped, and the driver ran out, coming around the front to pick me up. Scratch.

"Heya, cousin." He swung me around. "I heard you been starting trouble." He set me down, grinning, and smoothed my hair. "Why am I not surprised?"

I laughed, pulling back and softly punching his shoulder. "You just got here? Slacker."

He barked out a laugh, then spoke over my shoulder. "Heather called. She's holding down the fort, but wants to know the plan."

Channing stepped up beside me. "We're going to meet at the warehouse, but I need a moment with Bren and her crew alone."

"Got it. I'll let her know. She'll meet us there."

Scratch headed back to his truck, and Channing bent down. "I'll put Lincoln on the guy, but do me a favor," he said softly. "Meet me at the office before we go to the warehouse. I want to know everything that's going on before I step inside that warehouse."

I nodded as Cross took my hand.

No one said a word.

I was out. Now it was time to regroup, make a plan, and execute.

CHAPTER THIRTY-NINE

OUR ENEMY STRUCK us down.

We rallied.

Now we were off to defeat them, conquer, win.

I wanted to think that was our next course of action, but something—a nagging something in the back of my mind—was telling me otherwise.

In a way, what they did was simple, though it appeared complex. Distract, then throw a ton of shit at us to keep us distracted. *Then* move in. Sell drugs. Keep the profits going. But in another way, it wasn't simple at all. It was actually very dumb because they were banking on no one figuring it out. And they were banking on all those different factors they'd used as a distraction to go away.

They weren't going to go away.

Halfway to Roussou, a text came in.

Race: Alex is fine. He's at the hospital.

I was right. They were told to arrest me. At least one person inside the department knew this was a setup and was acting on outside orders. We needed to find who that was.

A second text came in.

Channing: We know who that cop called. Change of plans. You and your crew go home. Lock up. Be safe. We're taking over.

I wanted to curse, throw something, argue; but I did none of that. In a way, Channing was right, and I knew it. I knew my role. I was in high school, soon graduating, and I still hadn't decided what my future would look like.

Once I figured out this whole mess had to do with drugs, I knew I was out of play. I knew my brother would step in, and I knew he would handle it. He always did. He's the one who had contacts inside the Roussou Police Department. He had contacts everywhere. Becoming a fucking great bounty hunter in such a short time said a lot. He wasn't just good; he had relationships.

But Alex, Drake. Those were our problems.

Jordan was turning onto the road leading to Channing's office when I told him the change of plans.

"What?" Z twisted around. "No way. We helped his crew with the Demons. He can help us this time. Come on. This is our fight."

But it wasn't.

I shook my head. "Do you actually want to wade into that world? Drugs? Territory war? I don't. I want to remain a high school student, worrying about what I'm going to do next year. They told me Alex was dead. They pointed guns at me. They came at me in SWAT gear. I don't want that life, at least not yet."

Not yet.

Jesus.

Wasn't that the key phrase here.

"Then *we* don't," Jordan said. "It's your call. Your brother. Your arrest. We do what you want."

What I wanted...

What did I want?

My hand brushed over my dress—more than a little worse for the wear now—and I wrinkled my nose. "I want to change clothes. I want to shower. I want to do simple shit."

I didn't want to be crew right now. And I hoped they didn't think less of me, but I was tired. Plain and simple, I was just tired.

"Then that's what we'll do," Jordan confirmed.

Zellman started to say something, but there was a movement and he grunted. "Ooomph. Yeah, Bren. Yeah. Simple shit."

We went to my house. Cross went with me to the bedroom to make sure I was okay. There were hugs, kisses. He kept wanting to make sure I was okay. We might've fallen to the bed, ignoring the others in the house. But when the doorbell rang, Cross cursed and pulled away.

I heard a lot of footsteps, Taz's voice filtered down the hallway to us.

Cross groaned, pushing up and off of me. "I have a feeling everyone's coming over here. I'll deal with them." He paused, looking down at me. "Are you okay?"

I touched his face, my palm smoothing over his cheek. "I will be."

His eyes clouded over. "You sure?"

I nodded. "I'm sure."

Straightening his shirt, he shot me a dark and rueful look. I found myself grinning as he pulled the door open and headed out.

I stopped listening after that and went into the bathroom.

I *did* want a shower, but I mostly wanted to clean off the feel of those zip ties, those accusations, that hallway, seeing Alex slump down.

I wanted to wash away that image.

I stepped under the shower, and once that water hit me, I lost it. Head buried in my hands, water pounding down on me, I almost fell apart.

But I didn't.

Stay strong, Bren.

I heard my mother whispering in my ear, and I stopped myself. I just stopped.

I took a breath and then washed and stepped out.

The water was still going. I was reaching back to turn it off, but again, I just stopped.

Cross was standing inside the door, his eyes heated. His jaw clenched.

My body started trembling, reacting to the need I saw from him. It rose up, swiftly, almost threatening to choke me.

I thought I fell apart in the shower, but this—it didn't compare to this.

I needed him. Being arrested, hearing those words about Alex, being interrogated, and then walking out—all of it came back to me, pounding me one memory at a time, but there was a surge of renewal. I was fine. I would be fine. They couldn't destroy me and here Cross was. I saw all of it in him, a mirror reflection. And whoever was in the house, be damned. Forget them.

In this moment, it was Cross and I.

I dropped my hand and he started for me. Stark hunger flaring in him, then he was in front of me. His hand curved around my waist. He stepped in, his head bending. His mouth grazed over my shoulder, and I trembled again. A full-body shiver because that felt so fucking good.

He murmured there, "I couldn't—I need this."

I was nodding, already relaying how I needed him too even before he finished.

"—I need you," he finished, gutting out.

I reached up, grasping the back of his head, and I lifted his mouth to mine.

Then I didn't need anything else. His mouth opened over mine, and all was gone.

Moving into the shower, he was soaked in an instant.

He pushed me against the wall and I was pulling at his shirt as he was kicking off his jeans. Everything was tossed out until it was just him, just me, and then he was lifting me up. My legs were around his waist.

Mouth on mouth.

This moment, it was just us.

No one else existed.

Nothing else existed.

There'd been no arrest.

There'd been no police station.

We were wiping it all away.

Him. Me. And then he was inside me, and we both stilled from the contact.

He groaned, his mouth moving to my throat. "I love you so much."

I wound my arms tighter around him. I couldn't talk. My throat was full with emotion, so I moved my hips. His hands grasped under my thighs, and he began to move with me. We rode each other until both of us came, and even then, I didn't want to release him.

"Cross," I whispered, not able to speak again.

His head was buried into my neck and shoulder. He shook it, just hugging me to him. "Not yet. God. Not yet."

We stayed.

Long after the water was turned off, long after both our bodies grew cold, long after the air began to dry us.

We stayed.

Then we heard the doorbell ring, and I knew the world had come back to us.

Groaning, Cross let me back down, and without speaking, we both dried and dressed. I was combing my fingers through my hair as we walked out into the hallway.

I could hear Tabatha's voice and Sunday's laugh. Race. The gang was here. All of them.

I headed for the door. Cross was right behind me, then I opened it and heard Cross swear behind me.

Blaise stood there. A few steps back stood Zeke, with more of them waiting in vehicles on the street. I saw a few girls, but mostly the same guys we had fought with before.

Cross stepped around me, taking point. "Are you *fucking* kidding me?"

"Just wait." Blaise stepped back, his hands in the air. "Wait. Please."

Zeke jerked forward.

"You take one more goddamn step, and I'm coming out there to remove your head from your body," Cross said.

Blaise turned. "Stop. I believe him."

Zeke lowered his head. "I believe him too. Doesn't mean I'm leaving my best friend up there alone."

I cocked my head.

Zeke had a submissive air to him, but he was still defiant. I believed *him*. If Cross took a step out, Zeke would be coming in, no matter how much of a beatdown he was certain to get. He was loyal. I hadn't seen that one coming.

"Look. Let me talk, okay? Just a minute." Blaise still had his hands in the air. He lowered them and shifted to look behind us, into the house, but Cross moved to block him. "Okay. Okay. I didn't know. Okay? I didn't know about who you were, who—" He jerked his head up, indicating behind us. "About her. I had no clue."

Cross was rigid, tension seeping from every pore.

I moved closer, leaning against him, and I placed my hand on his back. He sucked in a breath, releasing it slowly. Some of the tension left him. Some. Not enough.

But he was listening.

Blaise spoke faster, wetting his lips. "I was always told I was an only kid, that my dad was some jackass who didn't give a shit about me. I had no clue. Honestly. Then my folks are suddenly getting a divorce. We're moving back here where my mom grew up, and she's got some random dude coming around."

Cross growled.

"No offense, but can you see it from my point of view? My mom *just* divorced my dad. My dad doesn't give one iota of caring any-fucking-thing about me anymore, and this new guy is coming in and acting all fatherly. It pissed me the fuck off. Who's this guy? I wasn't told shit. Nothing. Nada. Then I know Zeke from way back. We reconnect. That's great and all. My old best friend is still here, so things aren't great, but they're decent, and then *bam*. He tells me about the crews in Roussou. You guys blew up some of our buddies' cars out of nowhere—"

"You sent two of your assholes to burn our school down."

Zeke took two steps to the side—not toward us, but onto the lawn for a better vantage point. "We *really* weren't behind that. Swear to pussy. We weren't. Those two assholes don't go to our school. We don't even know who they are. *You guys* told us about them. That was the first we'd heard about it. So yeah, we beat your boy down, but we knew you were close by. We knew you'd intervene. We wouldn't get too bad on him. That's what we were thinking, and it worked. You guys showed up. You beat our asses. And then that was going to be it for us. You exploded our cars. We beat your boy down. It was done, as far as we were concerned."

"Then you guys came to our school," Blaise said.

Zeke made a frustrated sound. "Yeah. I mean, fine. You show up at our school? Our campus? Our girls are there? You bet your fucking ass we're going to fight. You brought the fight to us, man."

"We weren't there to fight," Cross said.

I still hadn't said a word. This was between Cross and his brother, but I wanted to tell them we were there to see Blaise. I didn't. I couldn't. That was Cross' decision, but a part of me yearned to shout it out.

Family was precious. Fuck. All the shit I gave Channing, and he was right now out there, fighting for me.

I bit back tears, knowing I had to make things right with him. All the anger from growing up, that was done. It was time to start new. Clean slate. I pressed my hand harder against Cross' back because I wanted the same for him.

"What's going on?"

I whirled. Z was there, and his eyes got wide seeing who was at the door. "Holy—"

I was at him in two steps. My hand clamped over his mouth. "Stop. Don't say a word." I looked over his shoulder, to the kitchen, but everyone was outside. My shoulders sagged in relief. If Taz came in, Cross would go nuts, and that wouldn't be good.

I motioned behind him. "Go out there. Shut the door. Act fucking normal."

"But—" He pointed over my shoulder.

"I know. Do what I say. Trust me."

"Bren!"

"Trust, fucker."

His eyes flicked upwards. "Trust, my ass."

269

But he went, and he shut the door, and I saw how he rolled his shoulders back. He was trying, but I knew Jordan would see through his act.

A second later, Jordan opened that patio door, coming in, and I sighed. There was nothing I could do right now, so as Jordan came over, I let him see who was standing on our doorstep.

Unlike Z, Jordan just pressed his mouth in a firm line and moved behind me. We went back, ready to have Cross' back if he needed us.

He needed us. I could tell. I moved behind him again, my hand on his back, moving up between his shoulder blades.

He twitched, settling back into my touch.

"I'm just saying, I was told a Roussou crew was out front, beating my best friend, and I'm hauling ass out there. Then I saw you, I really saw, and—" Blaise stopped, shaking his head. "—my world was fucking rocked." He looked down. "People not looking for a connection, might not see it. People look similar all the time, but you? Me? Not like this. I tried ignoring it. I did. No fucking way was I related to some Roussou scum."

"Fuck's sakes," Jordan muttered over my head.

Blaise glanced up. "Sorry, but that's how I was feeling. I thought you were a cousin or something. My mom's from here. She's all about secrets. Maybe she had family she didn't tell me about. Then her boyfriend was around more and more. He was moving in, and he talked about his kids. Cross. Tasmin. I clued in, asked Zeke the names of the crew he was beefing with, and that didn't seem like a coincidence. Let's just say my mom and I had a 'come to Jesus' moment one night. She spilled everything, and now here I am, learning my real dad does actually give a shit about me, I don't have to feel guilty about hating the asshole who bankrolled me all my life, and I got siblings. Twins too. Jesus. Are you serious? Fucking twins, and they're my age." He shifted backward and motioned to Cross with a jerking motion. "There you go. We're caught up."

Zeke edged forward a step. "We heard about your arrest and came to the station to see if we could help," he told me. "Cops here are corrupt. If anything, we wanted to let you all know that."

Blaise motioned between him and Cross. "You and me, that changes everything on our side. I don't want to be enemies with my half-brother."

Cross was silent—studying, gauging.

Then, as if it were some cosmic sign, we heard Taz's voice behind us. "Bren? What are you doing?"

We waited. A full second, two, five.

Jordan cursed and shifted aside.

I turned, knowing she'd see guilt in my eyes, so I tried not to look. But her eyes weren't on me.

They moved past me, seeing Cross, and then went to the door and beyond.

Her eyes got big, real big.

"Cross? What's going on?" She moved forward, only stopping because my hand was still on his back.

He had tensed. He was all sorts of stiff, but he turned around, and as our gazes met, a flash of understanding passed between us.

I let him go, and in doing that, we opened the way.

Taz moved the rest of the way to her brother. She frowned at Blaise. "You're from Fallen Crest. What are you doing here?"

We all waited.

It was Cross' decision.

"Taz," he finally said. "This is our half-brother."

CHAPTER FORTY

TAZ LOST HER shit. And that was understating it.

She yelled, cried, sobbed, screamed, and folded into a ball. Then she started laughing, shaking her head, threatening her parents, threatening Cross. She turned to me a few times with fire in her eyes.

Blaise took off after five minutes. I was shocked he lasted that long.

Taz was in hysterics, and no one could calm her. The girls came in. Race. Even Z tried a hand. She shoved everyone away, turning and walking out with full heaving sobs wracking through her.

Race looked at Cross.

Cross looked at Race.

"I don't know what to do," Race said.

Cross held up his hands. "She lost it on me earlier. I'm sure all of this is from the divorce, me moving out, everything. But I don't think she needs her brother." He dipped his head forward. "It's all you, buddy."

Race grunted. "Asshole."

"Love you too." Cross chuckled.

Race looked back at me before leaving. "Did you want to talk? You mentioned it earlier."

I waved him off. "No. It can wait. Take care of your woman."

He ran a tired hand over his face. "Prom has sucked. Thank fuck it's the last one."

Z belched and raised a beer in the air. "Here's to that."

We found Jordan in the kitchen, leaning back against the counter with his legs spread wide. Tabatha was curled into him, her head resting on his shoulder, her arms around his waist. He had a hand stretched out behind her, resting on the counter. He'd been watching me. He lifted his head toward Cross and Z. He raised an eyebrow in question, but I just shook my head.

It was so fucking late.

I didn't want to have a meeting. I didn't want to check in with the crew. Yes, there were things to say, but the fight had left me. Channing was handling things. If I wanted to merely go to bed and cuddle with my boyfriend on prom night, I could. And the world wouldn't end the next day.

Channing was taking care of me, and for once, I was letting him.

It felt good. It felt damn good.

But that wasn't good enough for Jordan. He pushed off from the counter. Tabatha pouted, losing her half-standing rock to lean against, but he came over. "No meeting? That's it? All the shit went down tonight, and we're doing nothing?"

"Jordan," I sighed.

"Bren," he mocked.

"Hey." A reprimand from Cross.

"Don't *hey* me. Don't do that." Jordan stepped back, his jaw clenched. "It doesn't work like that. I've grown. I've done a lot of growing, but when I see one of mine get arrested, then I have to help tackle *another* one of mine to keep him from losing his shit at the police station, and now what? Then his sister loses her shit at the after-prom party and what? No more buddy system, but what else? We're all good? I'm not good. I'm pissed."

He pointed at Z, at Cross, at me. "I've been the rock this time. I've been steady, taking on all you guys. Even the one night it was supposed to be about me, it ended up being about you." His hands went up. "Which I'm fine with, I am, but I'm riled up, and I've been feeling threat after threat toward my crew, and now what? Nothing? Go to bed. Fuck your girl? I'm not down for that."

"Jordan," Z hissed, his hand on Jordan's shoulder. "Calm down. Are you listening to what you're saying?"

"Yes," he snapped, jerking away. "I want to bust someone's head in. That's what we do. Threat comes at us, we fight it off."

"No, man." Z shook his head. "You never say you're not down for fucking. Especially a hot girl that you love. That's, like, sanctimony or sanctuary, or whatever. I can't speak real good. I'm a little drunk."

Jordan ignored him, seething. "I need to do something to protect my crew."

"Jordan—" Cross stepped toward him.

"I need it!" His eyes were wild, his pulse pounding. I could see a vein bulging in his neck.

He was right. In the last couple months, Jordan had changed. He got a girlfriend. He fell in love. He moved from being the self-proclaimed leader and spokesperson to being the foundation. He was completely right, and because of that, because we could lean on him, we'd loosened the reins on our own shit. We were allowed to fall apart, because he wouldn't. Because he would be there, pulling us back in, and now, when we were done and sated and had run the gamut of our shit, he wasn't.

We'd cast him out, but no one was bringing him back in.

Cross looked at me.

There was no decision to be made. Jordan needed us, so that was that.

I murmured, "Let's go find Drake."

We piled into one of my brother's trucks so we had a bigger cab so all four of us could fit. Jordan drove. I was okay with that. He had the edge, not me.

We went to Drake's parents' house. No one was there. We went to the local motel. Nothing. We went to the other two smaller hotels nearby. We checked the hotels in Fallen Crest. There was one motel in Frisco, but it was half burned down. Still, we went. We drove past. It was closed down, no vehicles in the parking lot.

We did a swing through the motor home park. Frisco. Fallen Crest. Roussou.

We even ran in and asked at the hospital while we were in Fallen Crest. And as a last-ditch effort, we checked at the Roussou Police Department. They hadn't arrested him.

We never found Drake.

But we drove. And we drove.

We drove some more.

We drove the rest of the night, into the morning.

We drove until Jordan told us to stop.

When someone needed to eat, we stopped for early breakfast. When someone needed the bathroom, we made a pit stop. We went to gas stations, filled up on coffee, and hopped in the truck for another drive.

We did another full circle, going all the way out to Frisco, through the back roads into Fallen Crest, past Manny's, and we went the long route that circled back to Roussou. When we neared the city limits, Jordan swung into another gas station. This time to fill up with gas.

Silently, one by one, we all trekked inside. More coffee. Snacks. Whatever we needed.

When we got back on the road, no one said a word. This was for Jordan. We'd keep going until he was sated, and finally, four miles north of Roussou, he turned onto the shoulder of the road and swung the truck around.

"I'm good," he announced.

So we were going home.

No one made a joke. No one complained. No one did a damn thing. We were here for him in this truck, smelling, sweating, shivering (me), stomachs growling until we filled them, and now we were half sleep-deprived and half wired from the caffeine.

"Z, you first?"

Zellman yawned, sitting up. He'd had his legs up on the dashboard, his cup in one hand, a half-eaten hot dog in the other.

"Nah, man." He threw a lopsided grin over his shoulder to where Cross and I were in the back. "Let's take the truck to the lovebirds' house, get in mine. Tabatha took Sunday home in your truck. I'll drop you off."

Jordan didn't respond; he just drove us home.

When we got there, Zellman and Jordan went to Z's truck, and Cross lingered on the sidewalk.

No one said goodbye. We just dispersed.

"What's wrong?" I asked.

Z and Jordan heard, stopping.

Cross had his hands in his pockets, his head hanging down. "I, uh, I know I should go in there with you, but Taz. She's..." He gestured to his head. "She's been on my mind. I can't get her out, and I think... I don't know, I think it's a twin thing. I think she needs me."

My eyebrows rose. "You're going to your house?"

He shrugged. "Or wherever she is. If she's not at the house, I'll go to Race's. I got no problem sneaking in and crashing on their couch. He told us where the key is." He eyed me. "That okay with you?"

"Yeah."

I was surprised, because it truly was. I didn't know if Channing was in our house, but it didn't matter. I didn't feel alone walking in there—not the way I used to when I would avoid going home.

"I'll be fine."

"You sure?" He took my hands and pulled me in. His lips brushed over mine. "I love you."

I kissed him back. "I love you."

He walked backward first, then turned toward his truck. Z and Jordan, seeing we were fine, waved and got into Z's truck. A second later, they were gone. Cross was waiting for me to get in, so I did. Unlocking the door, I gave him a last wave over my shoulder and stepped inside.

I heard him drive away as I walked into the kitchen. Then the hairs on the back of my neck shot straight up and I froze, mid-step. But there was no one in the kitchen.

I whirled.

There, sitting in the farthest chair in the living room, near the fireplace, was Drake, a poker in hand.

"We need to talk."

CHAPTER FORTY-ONE

MY HEART WAS pounding.

Thump. Thump. Thump.

"Drake."

It just kept thumping. Loud. Strong.

Using the poker, he shoved himself out of the seat, and even across the room, he seemed to loom over me. He didn't look good. He had a different edge, harder, more desperate.

He moved toward me.

I backed up. "Stop."

He didn't acknowledge me, just put the poker down and resumed his path toward me.

"Come on." His tone was brisk. His eyes tired. His hair looked like he'd been raking his fingers through it nonstop, and underneath the edge, the desperation, the roughness, was exhaustion. He was resigned—I saw it now as he passed me.

He always had a purpose—everything he did, every move he made. Now, he was just trudging along. Life had weighed him down.

The round face he and his brother both shared was more haggard now, even since I last saw him at the store. His dark eyes looked almost washed out, and I hadn't noticed in the store, but he'd lost some of his bulk. He was thinning down.

He touched my shirt, tugging me behind him. "Come on."

I resisted. "Drake, what are you doing here?"

"I just want to talk. That's all. I'm not here to hurt you. I'm not here to threaten, to play games. It's over, Bren. All of it is over."

A spark shone bright from his eyes. Finally. He was here, the Drake I used to know. He'd been masked this whole time, but he was staring back at me, albeit bleakly, but he was there.

"Okay." I heard myself agreeing. "Where?"

Torment flashed for a second. "I want you to take me to your spot. You never let me go with you, and I know you've taken Cross. One night. One last night."

I still wavered. That was my spot. "Why?"

"Because I'm going to tell you everything, so you gotta give me something. You kept it from me all the time we were together. One last time, show me... Please."

The *please* did me in. My throat was raw. "Fine." I moved around him. "But I'm driving."

I caught motion behind me. He raised his arms in the air, his head falling back. "Fine. Yes. You drive. Such a hard bargain."

I rolled my eyes. "Guess whatever was going on really is done. You're back to pissing me off."

He grunted, following me out the door. "You don't say. You've always pissed me off." I caught his grin, unable to stop myself from joining him.

After we got to the woods and parked, I snuck looks at him as we walked. He was coming along quietly. Not a peep from him since we left the house, and as he fell in step behind me, his hands in his pockets, his head down, he looked amenable.

Was it that? Or was my first thought right? *Defeated.*

"This is it? Where you always used to disappear to?" He stepped around me, coming into my clearing. There was a bottle of whiskey hidden underneath some brush, along with a carefully wrapped blanket, but I wasn't pulling that out. That was for Cross.

I sat down, pulling my knees up to my chest, and I waited for him to sit beside me. He did, leaving a respectable distance between us. He mirrored my position for a moment, then let his legs stretch out. He leaned back, resting on his hands behind him.

That's when he saw. "Holllleeee...." His mouth parted. "This is where you'd go? To watch your old house?"

I lifted a shoulder. No way was I sharing why.

He cursed under his breath, looping his hands around his knee. "I was so fucking jealous of Shaw. He knew where you went, and he never told me. That fucker." He grunted, wincing. "I knew you two would get together the second I was out of the picture. Always too close. Wasn't natural unless one of you is gay or you're siblings. And you're neither."

"You told Race to try to date me."

I scowled. He laughed.

"I did. Alex reported the fallout. That was awesome. It was worth it, too." He watched me, his head tipped back. "Any way I can mess with Shaw, I'm taking it. Still. To this day. Little fuck. I never had a chance with you, not really."

Maybe. Probably. "We were good, until you left."

"No, we weren't," he said. "You just hadn't woken up yet about Shaw. I knew you would. Me leaving wasn't about you, but it was perfect timing. You and Cross, you guys were inevitable. I knew it. Everyone knew it. Even your crewmates. They knew it too." He paused a beat. "And speaking of, how'd they take it? I know you guys had that 'no dating' rule in your crew. I'm sure they must've been pissed."

I thought back to when Jordan had found us. Being mad was the last thing on his mind.

"Jordan found out the same day we took your brother to the hospital to get his stomach pumped."

Drake's smirk vanished. "Oh."

Now I watched him. "Do you care?"

His nostrils flared. "Do I care that you guys saved my little brother's life? Goddamn. What kind of monster do you actually think I am?"

Fine. Let's get into this.

I moved to face him and squared my shoulders. "One that sends his cousin to mess with my relationship. One that came back to set me up. One that's involved with a whole mastermind plotline that I can't quite get my head wrapped around." I paused and leaned forward, dropping my voice to a hiss. "Am I missing anything?"

He was riveted, growing absolutely still. "No. Keep going. What else do you know?"

"Did you tell the cops about District Weekend?"

"Yes."

I startled. I hadn't expected honesty so quickly. But I read his face again, and he'd spoken the truth. He really was going to tell me.

"Everything?" I asked.

His eyes darkened, right along with my thoughts. "Everything. Next question."

"Were the cops coming to arrest me?"

"Yes." A beat. "But not just you. I know what Alex thought, and he wasn't altogether right. There was an alliance between Neeon, his cop wife, and Broghers. They just want the crews out of Roussou. That's all. The TV thing wasn't going to interview students, but suddenly they figured a way to get all those waivers signed. And no, the TV people didn't know that part. No one could tell them, and they never questioned it. *Of course people want to be interviewed*—that's how they think."

"So the TV thing wasn't a plan to distract my crew?"

"No, it was, just not one set in motion by dear old Kenneth Broghers. My boss wanted you to get arrested so you'd be shipped off to juvie. When that didn't happen, it was strongly suggested to Principal Broghers that you be assigned as their assistant. You and your crew being distracted was plan B for my employer. The guy they have on the FC police force is the one who suggested the idea to Broghers' sister. He just cemented it when you weren't arrested that night." He turned to watch my house. "He was just doing his job."

His job.

"Did you burn the Frisco school down?"

"Yes."

I blinked. *What?* I hadn't expected that. Again.

And before I could continue my questions, he said, "And yeah, I got two punks from FC Public, gave them Alex's name, and told them to burn your school down. Said I had a cool grand for each if they did."

"You set your brother up?"

"You say set him up; I say more like removing him from the equation so my employer couldn't use him against me."

My mouth dropped. "You were trying to protect Alex?"

He didn't respond.

"He could've been beat up at school."

"I told my crew hands-off, and I knew you and your boy toy wouldn't feel right about it. I thought you guys would question him, just didn't realize it'd be the *next* morning. Jesus. You two just fuck and roll out of bed? You do the whole sleeping part after the job was done?"

Nope. Old Bren was rallying.

But.

I *wasn't* rising to the bait. I *wasn't* going to react.

He was answering questions. That's what I wanted.

"Was the intention to get drugs into the Roussou school?" I asked. "Is that why Frisco's school was burned down?"

"Yes and yes, but not the way you're thinking. My employer didn't have a seller in Frisco school. He does in Roussou, and he does in Fallen Crest. He wants drugs in both schools and only the schools. When Frisco students go back, he wants the drugs to go with them. He's already worked someone to handle distribution and selling there."

"So it hadn't started before then?"

He shook his head, yawning. "Nope. None of this started till a couple months ago." He glanced over at me, holding, waiting.

"When you arrived?"

"When I arrived." His mouth lifted up in a grin. "Always knew you were smart. You should be going to college next year, not doing nothing."

I gave him a hard look, but ignored that too. "The SWAT thing? Me getting arrested?"

His mouth thinned. "That wasn't me. I had nothing to do with that."

"Who was it?"

He didn't answer, not right away, and I could tell it took him effort. "That was Alex."

"Alex called the cops on himself?"

"No." He chuckled. "Alex was supposed to plant drugs on you. The guy in the FC police department called in the anonymous tip there was a shooter. He's the point guy behind all the joint task stuff with the two towns. They got there, and Alex hadn't put the drugs on you. Instead, he took 'em himself."

"The cop said he was DOA."

He rolled a shoulder. "My guess is that's the contact, and Broghers' sister went with it, arresting you. Any excuse to arrest you, she's going to take it. She's had a hard-on for you since you stabbed her newlywed husband." He flashed me a grin. "I warned you about them."

"How were you supposed to set me up?"

"I was just supposed to get in your head, cause chaos. Besides the District Weekend and the Frisco school, I didn't really do anything."

"And that day when I was getting a dress?"

"I'd met the contact. He was mad. Said I wasn't doing enough, but I'd never been part of this willingly, so what'd they expect? I saw you shopping and thought *fuck it*, she needs a heads-up. I knew what was planned for tonight, knew they'd take you in on something." His cheek ticked. "I *didn't* know they planned to use Alex for the drugs. I thought it was going to be the new Ryerson crew seller."

So there was one.

"Who's the student?" I leaned forward. "Who are the students for all the schools?"

He offered me a lazy grin this time. "Can't tell you that. I know your crew will go off. You'll either do the smart thing and tell your brother—let him and his scary buddies handle the sellers—or you and your crew will go bust their heads open. I gotta keep that quiet for now."

I opened my mouth.

"I'm saving it for the cops," he said before I could speak. "I'm waiting for my employer's contact to go off-shift. I need to make sure I get to the right cops, or things could get bad for me."

I suppressed a shiver. I knew what happened to narcs.

"Drake," I murmured.

I wet my lips.

There was one question left. And I didn't know if I had it in me to ask.

He waited, watching me, a smirk on his face. "Ask me, Bren. Say the words."

I closed my eyes. "Who is it? Who's behind all of this?"

I felt him leaning close. His mouth moved to my ear, and he said, "You know who it is."

He leaned back, and I opened my eyes.

"You've put together most of the players," he continued. "I know you know there's a connection. *You* tell me who it is."

I didn't say a word. My chest deflated. I didn't think I wanted to know, because of what else that would mean.

"It's not my dad, is it?" I whispered hoarsely.

"Nope. And by the way, they want to corner the high schools for drugs to avoid the Red Demons. That's the only connection with your dad, in case you were wondering."

Relief hit me hard.

Then I thought about common denominators.

Alex.

Drake.

The time.

When Drake came to Roussou.

A person in the Fallen Crest police force.

The ease and speed with which they'd done all of this told me they'd done it before. That told me they probably had money.

"Think, Bren. Who all was moving to town around the same time?"

Alex. Drake... Race...

I knew. I never met the person, but I knew he wasn't good people. I knew he'd already broken two families apart.

"Your uncle," I said.

"Bingo."

"Race's dad."

"Same guy."

My head spun. "How did you—how did you get roped into it?"

Race's dad had money, but I thought it was from his Harley business.

Drake laughed, the sound bitter. "How'd I get roped into it? I got into some trouble where I was staying. He bailed me out, literally. I racked up a gambling debt. My uncle paid it for me and said I could work it off if I came back here and whispered manipulative words in your ears. You're the Crew Princess, Bren. You're the heart of that world *and* the Normal world. Your crew. You guys are the guard dogs at school, and your brother is the pit bull of Roussou. Couldn't just take you out because your pops is connected now. Red Demons would go all out on one of their kids getting murdered."

I flinched.

A hard look was in his eyes. "And no, I'd never be a part of that. No. My uncle knew that couldn't happen either so fucking with you. That's the job I was given. Fuck with you, and both your crew and your brother go away, at least for a while, at least long enough to slip in and set something up. You were my job, but I got here, and I wasn't about playing my part for him. I messed around." A slow and sensual smile spread over his face. His eyes twinkled. "I had some fun, maybe too much fun, and then suddenly I got another incentive to play along, make some money, not fuck up and get in *more* trouble."

I frowned. "What?"

"I got a kid on the way."

A kid—Sunday. Sunday!

I scrambled to my feet. "You're the guy who got Sunday pregnant?"

He tipped his head back, watching me. "Really? That's what gets the biggest reaction from you? A teen pregnancy?"

I sat back down in a huff. "She told us it was someone from Fallen Crest."

He laughed, the sound smooth. "I know." He took a minute to crack himself up. "I told her to say that," he chuckled. "She and I were being nice to each other then, figured that's why she actually said it. I knew I'd be calling in the District Weekend party, and it might buy time for you guys to suspect those rich pricks for being behind it. Z having that in his head, it was only a matter of time before he went off."

Rich pricks.

A part of me collapsed inside. I knew where I'd gotten that phrase suddenly, and thinking on it, I remembered all the hateful things Drake used to whisper about Fallen Crest. I hated people from there, but even this year, I'd been proven wrong time and time again.

Drake. I'd gotten that dislike from him, and I hadn't even noticed. I'd never questioned. I'd blindly believed and adopted his mantra. Shame bloomed in my chest.

"You're not with Sunday anymore?" I asked.

"Nah. It was a week fling. That was it, but the kid is coming. She's keeping it, so there's my other incentive not to fuck up and get a knife in my back. And if I could make some money, a part of me was all about that."

"What changed?"

"Alex."

In an instant, his face transformed to dark and slightly murderous. "My uncle never should've fucking included Alex."

I spared him a look. "You gifted him to us. Remember?"

"I had to do that, and you know it. If I hadn't, your crew would've simmered. Your boy would've exploded one day, and I couldn't control that situation." His jaw clenched. "I like Taz. She's a civilian, and she never should've been hurt. My brother had that coming, and everyone knows it. And besides, I didn't gift him up. He volunteered. Those texts came from him, not me."

From Alex?

More shame, more regret, more...doubt filled me.

Violence.

Sunday was right.

We always went to violence first. Maybe violence needed to be the last resort? Like we'd been doing lately. It was a better feeling, not so dark, not so filled with hate, anger, all the stuff that gets in you and eats at your soul.

Maybe...

"Don't beat yourself up. Alex isn't all bad. He just has a drug problem." A growl worked its way up his throat. "A drug problem my uncle exploited, asking him to plant the drugs on you. It was the wrong fucking move."

Then I knew. I got it. And I got why he'd come to me first.

"You're turning yourself in to save your brother, aren't you?"

He stood, brushing some of the grass from his jeans. He looked down at me. "Yes and no. I found out what they did, and I was pissed, but I was going to go in anyway. It's all ending. Drugs were supposed to be planted on you, but the tip went in about a shooter, not drugs. My uncle's contact fucked up, went too big. Now there's heat on him even before me going in. It'd all unravel anyway. I'm just making it go at hyper-speed. I don't go in, they'll kill Alex. He's a loose end. They'd take me out too. I go in to save both our heads."

I nodded. "And you want me to get my crew together, go find Alex, and take care of him?"

"No. I want you guys to help take care of Sunday. My kid. If something happens to me, help with my mini-me." He bent, his hand resting on my shoulder. He squeezed and said softly, "I really did love you once, Bren."

He left, and I remained.

I didn't move for a long time after.

CHAPTER FORTY-TWO

DRAKE DID AS he'd promised.

He went to the police station, the Roussou one. I wondered if he'd changed his mind because the only dirty cops in Roussou were the ones who gave my brother information. Maybe. Who knew. But for whatever reason, he went there instead. I knew Drake had asked for immunity in exchange for his tale, but I didn't know if he'd get it. I hoped for that.

Either way, by noon, everyone had been apprehended.

Race's dad.

The dirty cop in the FCPD.

The sellers—leaving the Ryerson crew leaderless yet again.

I wondered if they were going to take the hint and just disband. And Alex went to rehab. I was losing count of how many times he'd been there. Maybe one day it would stick. I hoped so.

Zellman took the news identifying Sunday's baby daddy fairly well, considering the way Drake came out with everything.

As for me, I had one hell of an awkward dinner to look forward to.

Cross and I sat in his truck, parked at the curb next to his dad's girlfriend's house. We were still doing the dinner, and it was the first family-official meeting with everything out on the table— the affair nineteen years ago, who Blaise really was—and each person would have a support there for them. I had no doubt this wouldn't have happened otherwise. Significant others had to be there or Cross wouldn't have shown up.

Taz, on the other hand, was excited.

She and Race had gone inside, though Race was moving slowly. They hadn't seen us since we were just parking as they were already to the door.

Cross turned the engine off, sitting back. We both watched the house. Neither of us moved.

"Race isn't doing too well," Cross said.

I nodded. "I'm not surprised. Knowing your dad is a piece of shit is one thing, but finding out he's selling drugs is a whole other matter."

"You think he and his mom are going to be affected? Cops will seize their assets."

I shrugged. "Who knows? I hope not. The divorce was clean, wasn't it?"

Cross raised his eyebrows. "We could ask your brother's fancy friends. The one is in law school, right?"

"I suppose. I think they're still in town."

"How are things with you and your brother?"

Cross had told me everything that went down after I was arrested, while they were waiting to get me out on bail. I couldn't imagine it, but I wished with everything in me that I could've been there, seen everyone rallying for me. It brought tears to my eyes.

My throat swelled up again. "We're good." More than good. "I haven't seen much of him today, but he checked in with me. He and his guys were the ones who caught Race's dad. He'd gotten word and was in the middle of packing a bag. He was going to run."

Cross grunted. "Fuck."

"Yeah, but anyway, those friends are still here. Channing's spending time with them. They're going into business together, so they have things to discuss." I looked over at him, a wry smile on my face. "And by the way, they're all invited for another Monroe family BBQ this Friday, just like we had the other night."

Another car pulled ahead of us, but turned into the driveway. A black Maserati this time. It parked next to the Mercedes G Wagon. Cross and Taz's half-brother got out of the driver's seat, and Zeke Allen got out on the other side.

Cross nodded to them. "Think we should invite those guys?"

"I'm thinking Allen would shit his pants to have a dinner with the football guy."

Cross grinned, though it didn't reach his eyes. We watched as the two sauntered inside.

I wasn't going to ask how Cross felt about his brother. I knew he didn't know yet. Taz, though. Taz was in love. She'd been texting me half the day, asking about what clothes to wear.

"Taz asked me if I thought sunflower yellow was too poor for this dinner."

He snorted. "She asked me the same thing about her teal shirt. I told her not to give a fuck."

I smiled.

Taz was nervous. The twenty texts explaining how she wasn't going to drink any caffeine for four hours before the dinner was a testament to how nervous she was. She didn't want to arrive and have to use the bathroom immediately. She had it scheduled to use the bathroom past the halfway mark of the dinner, just before dessert would be served.

Then she'd sent a flurry of texts asking if I thought they were going to serve a multiple-course meal. And if so, how many? Three? Five? Seven? Surely, not a nine-course meal.

I'd stopped responding by then, but the texts had just kept coming. Plus one from Race.

Race: Sorry.

"You ready for this?" I asked.

Cross just sighed.

That was as good a response as I was gonna get. I reached for the door handle. "Okay. Let's do this."

The door opened for us as we stepped onto the patio, and though Cross told me his dad's girlfriend had come to the police station, I hadn't noticed her. She was beautiful—petite, with a heart-shaped face and little square chin. Wide eyes. Sun-kissed hair. It looked like it was naturally light brown, but she had a good mix of blond streaks. Half her hair was pulled back, and half swayed around the front of her face, touching just under her chin and dipping in to frame her jawline. Dressed in a white tank top, green cargo capris, tan sandals, and a low-hanging brooch that I was pretty sure could've bought Channing's house, she had a very Jennifer Aniston look to her.

"Hi!"

Oh, good gracious. She even sounded like Jennifer Aniston. She held the door open wider, but suddenly filled the space, her arms around me.

I froze in place.

She breathed me in. "Hmmm. You smell delicious."

Oh. My. God.

"Lilacs. I love lilacs." She stepped away, her arms opening for Cross.

He stepped back, stone-faced. "I'm good. Thanks."

"Right." She lowered her arms, running a nervous hand through her hair, and gestured inside. "Would you like to come in? Your father tells me absolutely no alcohol for you two."

Cross frowned. "You let your son drink alcohol?"

Another laugh, one that reminded me of sunlight and beach waves. "Goodness no, but I'm up on all the new trends, and allowing your teenagers a glass of wine is apparently a new *thing*. Can you believe that?" She held out her hand to me. "I'm Marie, by the way. Sorry. I just went right in for the hug. I'm bad with boundaries. Blaise gets mad at me all the time. He says I maul his girlfriends."

She winked. "Not that there are many. He's not the girlfriend type of guy. I once worried he didn't have a sex drive. He's always kept so quiet, I wasn't sure if he liked boys or girls, or both— because, you know, that's a thing too. A good thing. A healthy thing. An equal thing. I love all things." Her hand was still hanging between us. She didn't seem to notice. "And I ramble when I'm nervous. Your father told me not to share that I'm nervous, but I am. I'm human. What's your name, dear?"

I shook her hand, almost transfixed by her rambling. I didn't know what to do. "Uh. Bren."

"Bren!" She beamed at me, clasping my arm with her other hand. "A lovely name. You're so lovely. You could be a model. Has anyone ever told you that? They should, if they haven't. OH MY GOODNESS!"

I jumped back.

Her hands flew to her chest. "You're the girl Malinda told me about. I love Malinda. She came over a couple weeks ago, introduced herself, said she and I would be good friends. And we have been. She gives me all the gossip, because as you can see, I'm a little too friendly when you first meet me, but I promise I calm down. I get quiet, even. Believe it or not, people say they forget I'm there, but not right away. I always have the nerves. Do you have nerves? You probably have nerves. Cross, how are your nerves?"

Cross' dad appeared then, coming down a hallway. "Oh! Come in," he said. "Marie, honey." He swept a hand down her back and pulled her to his side.

Cross stiffened.

His dad didn't notice, busy extricating her hand from mine. "Let's, uh, let's not manhandle Bren. She has pretty strong boundaries." He smiled at me as he pulled her hand away, gently. "If I remember correctly?"

"You do, sir."

"Sir!" Marie burst out laughing, slapping a hand to his chest. "She called you sir. I'll be ma'am now." Her laughter faded, abruptly. "Oh, God. I don't want to be a ma'am. Please don't call me ma'am."

My lips pressed tight, and I just shook my head. "No, ma-—" I caught myself.

I was either extremely polite and formal, or I looked at adults with suspicion. There wasn't much of a middle ground with me. That was something I should work on.

"Uh..." Cross' dad moved back, his arm still around Marie's waist. "The food's almost ready, if you guys want to come in? We have beverages. Water? Milk? Juice? Soda? What's your preference?"

Without missing a beat, Cross said, "Beer."

"Beer coming up." He laughed, sounding forced. "Good one. Pick something appropriate for your age."

"Beer is. What do you think we had last night?"

"Well, it's not prom night, your girlfriend wasn't arrested, and you're in my house." He coughed. "Marie's house. Different rules."

Cross was eerily still.

My house. That's what he'd said first.

"I'll have water."

Marie looked at me, and I said, "The same, please."

"Perfect!" She clapped her hands twice before heading into the kitchen, leaving Stephen behind. Taz and Race had migrated over, and I could see she was still nervous too. Her entire face was pink—a light rose. Like the wine. She was doing deep-breathing exercises, her hand pressing against her stomach. Race had zoned out, for once not tuned into her.

Fuck this awkward stuff. Why not go for more awkward?

"Wanna chat, Race?" I motioned outside.

His eyebrows flew up. So did everyone else's, but Cross' dad looked relieved.

"Uh." Race coughed, glancing at Taz before moving forward. "Yeah. Sure."

Cross met my gaze, and his hand snaked out, grabbing my arm as I passed. I paused, just enough for him to run his thumb down the inside of my arm.

Then Race and I stepped outside.

They had a hanging porch swing, and Race sat there.

As soon as I sat beside him, a good space between us, he breathed out loudly. "Fucking hell. Thank you for this." He stretched his legs, his feet resting on the bottom of the porch railing. "I can normally handle tension—dealt with it enough in my life—but being with Taz's family on the day my dad was arrested..." He gave me a shaky grin. "Thank you."

I'd been feeling that same need to escape. I tucked my hands under my legs. "You know what I'm going to ask." That was my segue into the awkward conversation.

"Yeah." He grew quiet, turned toward the street, but I doubted he was seeing it. "I'm okay. I am. I'm just—*fuuuuuuck*." He leaned forward, his elbows resting on his knees. His head fell, and he caught it in his hands. "Fuck, Bren. Fuck." He groaned, sitting upright again. "I'm so sorry about everything. I know all of it. Drake called me this morning, said he'd talked to you and told me what he said. I—there are no words."

I felt my eyes widen. This was not how I thought it was going to go.

"Nothing happened to me," I said softly. "I'm worried about you. You're in our group. How are you doing?"

He shook his head. "I..." He coughed, his voice raspy. "I can't answer that. I'm here. I'm doing the boyfriend thing, but..." He fell quiet for a long while. "Can I say I'm relieved? Can I say I'm okay with him being in prison? Can I say...can I say I'm glad my mom is away from him? That he got what he deserved after what he did to her? Can I say all of that and still be a good person?"

I had no answers to those questions.

I sat. I was silent. I listened. That was what he needed.

"Can I say I wonder if he's going to share a cell with your dad? And if he does, what your dad will do? I mean, fuck. Drake told me the Harley business was just a front. They maybe sold a bike a year. The rest was drugs. How the hell did that even start? When did it start? Who's he connected to? Who was he getting that shit from? I mean, there's always someone, right?"

He turned to me, but it was a question I couldn't answer.

His voice came out hoarse. "I'm really sorry he was trying to target you, and I'm really happy it was your brother who got him. Good karma, right? Am I a piece-of-shit son for thinking all of this? What's my role now? Go visit him? Try to pretend he's not a piece of shit? Fuck. Who do I go with? My aunt or my mom? His ex-wife or his girlfriend? Or his ex-girlfriend? Who the hell knows about that one."

He fell silent again.

"And Alex," he added suddenly. "I'm not a fan of my cousin, but I think we know where he got the drugs last semester. Hard to hate him, knowing it was my dad who was supplying him. I feel half to blame."

I shook my head. "You aren't. You know that, right?"

"Does it matter? I don't feel like it does." He looked over at me. "How'd you handle it? Your dad went in for murder. I mean, how'd you handle that?"

I shrugged.

The situation was different. I *was* to blame.

I murmured, "Just get through it, I guess. Cross—he helped."

"Yeah." He turned back, gazing at that street but not seeing it.

We remained in silence after that, two friends sitting next to each other. We stayed until Cross' dad came to the door. "Food's ready."

As we approached the table, Taz's eyes were wide and wondering. She sat at one end of the table, the chair empty beside her, and she almost jumped up. I caught the concern and shame flooding her face a second later, but I just shook my head at her as I went to the empty seat beside Cross.

She bit her lip, and her eyes teared up. But she swallowed and gave Race a tentative grin as he slid into his seat. She leaned over, whispering into his ear, and he nodded.

Cross gave me a look, one eyebrow raised.

I lifted a shoulder. No, I didn't know how Race truly was. We'd have to observe him, because this wasn't a situation that resolved immediately so healing could begin. There'd be charges. Bail. If his dad got bail. The fallout in the community. School. Whether it would affect Race's college prospects or not. And his mom. Those were just the surface things, not the emotional undertones.

Cross leaned over and kissed my cheek. His hand squeezed mine under the table.

"Okay!" Marie brought over the last bowl and placed it in the middle of the table. A pan of flatbread sat at one end. The salad in the middle. Garlic bread. Spaghetti at the other end. A bottle of red wine. And around the table, cans of soda next to each of the other plates. The adults got the wine.

Pity.

"Mmmm... Dig in, everyone." She waved a hand over the food, taking her seat next to Stephen and pulling a cloth napkin to her lap. "I'm so happy you all are here." Her gaze found her son, who was sitting across the table, on the other side of Stephen and directly across from Taz. "And that you guys finally met, although I'm sure there are lots of questions."

Her face pinched, as if remembering who exactly these people were and how they were related.

No one moved for the food.

Cross' brother wasn't looking at his mom. His gaze was pinned to one of the food bowls, and like Race outside, I had a feeling he wasn't seeing that food either. Zeke was next to him, a smug grin on his face as he took in the scene.

Eventually, his eyes met mine. I sat back.

Here we go.

"Is it true Mason Kade is going to be at your house this Friday?" he asked me.

My eyebrows shot up. "What?"

He leaned forward, almost foaming at the mouth. "Tell it straight. How awesome is he as a person? If I could have his babies, I would, and I say that with pride being a heterosexual male. But man, if I went for the other team, I'd go for him. That dude is solid gold. Like pussy gold."

"Zeke!" Marie barked.

Blaise was fighting back a grin, but still not looking past the salad bowl in front of him.

"What?" Then that smug smirk just grew, and I realized it was a permanent fixture on his face. "Oh. Sorry, Mrs. DeVroe."

"Dude." A hiss beside him.

"Ah. *Miss* Devroe." He was trying to be polite, but coming across as leering. "I have a bit of a manwhore obsession with Mason Kade," he continued. "You know the Kades? Blaise's sister-in-law knows them—"

"Ohmygod!" I burst out.

"Dude!" Blaise admonished.

"Stop fucking talking!" Cross added.

"What?" Zeke frowned, looking around the table. "What? You do. You can't lie about that anymore. They showed up when you were arrested."

"She's not my sister-in-law. We're not..." But Blaise quieted, throwing Cross a furtive look. "Never mind. It's not like that. Shut it."

Cross leaned back, glaring across the table. "Talk about your shit, not others'."

"Yeah." Taz shot up in her seat. "Like, where's Monica? I have a few things to say to her."

"Who?"

Taz clarified, "Your girlfriend. Monica."

"I don't have a girlfriend."

"You banged a Monica for a couple weeks," Blaise pointed out.

"I did?"

"Boys!" Marie yelled.

Zeke just smiled at Blaise's mother.

Taz frowned. "She was my friend until the Monica Mutiny, her and Lila both."

"Lila?" Zeke was still frowning.

Almost bored, Blaise reached for some water. "The girl you banged *last* night."

"Petite little pu—" He caught himself, flashing an apologetic look to the head of the table. "Sorry, Mrs. DeVroe."

"Miss and..." She frowned toward her son. "Language, Blaise."

Blaise rolled his eyes.

"Miss DeVroe." Zeke didn't sound put-out, though. "Lila Jamison? You know her?"

"Yeah." Taz's mouth snapped shut with an audible click. "She was friends with me until she decided to go mutiny with Monica, because she want...wanted my brother."

Zeke looked at Blaise.

Taz realized her mistake. "My other brother."

Cross tossed his cloth napkin on the table. "Fucking hell."

"Cross," his father warned.

Cross shoved back his seat. "I can't. I can't do this."

"Where are you going?" Stephen stood up too.

Marie's eyes went wide and concerned.

Blaise still wasn't looking at us.

Zeke just seemed confused.

Taz blinked back tears.

And Race stood up with us.

Taz turned to him. "Race?"

"I can't. I'm sorry." He looked at me, his voice growing hoarse. "Not today, Taz. I'm sorry." He nodded to Cross' dad and Marie. "I apologize. It's, uh... My family received bad news today. I shouldn't—I should be with my mom, to be honest."

"We're going too, Dad." Cross' hand went to the back of my chair, and I was already pushing it back.

"Race," I called as Cross said goodbye for both of us.

He paused at the door, waiting for me.

"Let us drive you. Give Taz your keys." Because she was staying. I knew that the second Race stood and she didn't.

He looked over my shoulder, his jaw clenching, but he dug in his pocket and pulled out his keys. I took them, going back to the table.

"What are those?" Taz asked.

"You're staying, right?"

She slowly reached out, taking the keys. "Is it wrong if I do?"

My heart sank. I didn't want it to, but it did. I loved Taz. She was a good girlfriend, a loving girlfriend, and a good friend, but today, she was focused on her own stuff. Maybe that was okay.

I forced a smile. "Call us when you're heading back. We'll let you know where to take his truck."

I turned to go.

"Bren?"

I looked back. She was standing now, her hands gripping the table. "I don't know what to say. I can't... You know. You always know in these situations."

I laughed bitterly. "Right. Because my dad's in prison? Because of that?"

Shame flooded her face, tightening her features, and she looked down.

Yeah. That's what she meant.

I felt a knife going in under my sternum.

"Bren."

I paused again, reaching for the door handle. It was their father this time. He came over, smoothing a hand down his shirt. "I realize now that in light of everything that's happened, we probably should've canceled this dinner, but..." He peered over my shoulder. "I miss my son. I worry about my son. He's not really talking to me or his mother, and I'm... I'm worried about him."

I didn't know what bothered me the most.

Was it what had happened with Race's dad, yet he had come, trying to be here for his girlfriend. Or was it Taz, who was self-focused at this moment, having no clue how her sentiment hurt, or was it this parent who obviously cared about his children, but didn't seem to know how to have a relationship with them. One was too eager to please, too worried she'd lose her dad, while the other could barely stomach being in this house.

"He's living with us. He has my family."

I saw the hurt in his eyes and knew my words hit their target.

"You want him not to replace yours with mine? Show up. Come around. Be present. He's eighteen. Unless you hold college over him..." And I was guessing because that was my hang-up. "... you can't force him into anything. But for what it's worth, he came today. He didn't have to, but he did."

He nodded as I finished. "Okay. I will. I'll be around. I'll show up." He tried to smile, but it fell flat for some reason.

I didn't care to wonder why. I just turned and headed out. We needed a crew day, and I was already texting Zellman and Jordan as I got into Cross' vehicle. Race was in the back. Both of their phones went off, and Race pulled his out.

"I'm included?"

Cross smiled in approval as he pulled away from the curb.

I turned around. "Guest of honor, unless you want to check on your mom."

Race didn't respond. Not at first. "Just can't be the foundation right now. That's all."

I knew we all understood that.

CHAPTER
FORTY-THREE
Three weeks later

ONCE THEY ARRESTED Race's dad, everything unfolded.

The race to see who would get a deal began after that, and since Drake had gone in first, he got the best one. Race's dad didn't get as sweet a package, but credible sources said definite time was shaved off his sentence, or would be.

But all the Ryersons got jail time. Drake. Even Alex, since he confessed to knowing he was supposed to put drugs on me, though his time was minimal. And their uncle. Their uncle who did, in fact, go to prison where my father was.

One day, while we were getting ready to attend graduation, my brother had a visit with my father—my connected father who was now a member of the Red Demons. A day later, we found out two of the Ryersons had been attacked in jail. Drake got a beatdown. He'd spend four weeks in the hospital, we were told. And their uncle was in a medically induced coma.

Didn't take a genius to figure out the connection. I was glad. Sometimes, sometimes violence *was* needed. Sometimes it did have a place.

But this was the day of our graduation, and I was more focused on that.

"You ready for this?" Cross asked behind me.

I had my gown on, my hat in hand, but no. I was not ready. I hadn't even thought I would graduate.

"Bren?"

I straightened from my locker. The door was open, and I was staring inside at nothing. Empty. I'd cleaned it out two weeks ago, the last day the seniors needed to be in school, but it was habit.

I came to school. I parked. I walked inside. I went to this locker.

"Hey," he said gently, shutting my locker and turning me to face him. He shifted closer. We were told to wait in the hallway. Graduation would be out on the football field. We had to line up and go out there to our seats. There'd been a whole assembly about this ceremony, but for the life of me, I was blanking on how I even got here.

"I'm not prepared."

"What?" He inclined his head to hear me better.

I cleared my throat, but it didn't matter. My voice was still hoarse. "I'm not ready. I didn't think—"

I hadn't thought.

I hadn't planned.

I hadn't looked ahead.

All those years, I'd just stopped moving.

I was in the car, but the scenery was passing me by. That's what this last year had been for me, and it finally hit me. I had no plan.

"What are you doing next year?" I asked.

"Oh." His head tilted as he looked at me.

His eyes. They were gentle, knowing, but pitying at the same time. I didn't want the pity. I never wanted the pity, but this time, today, on this morning, I hung my head.

I was embarrassed. I couldn't do anything or push off this emotion because no matter how many times I hadn't wanted to think about the future, it was here.

I asked again. "What are you doing next year?"

He grimaced. "You want the truth?"

I snorted. "When do I not want it?" Wait. Except every time this conversation came up. "Yeah."

"All three of us got accepted to Cain University."

My head raised. "You did?"

They were leaving?

All of them?

I mean... I had assumed—no. I hadn't. I hadn't wanted to move forward. I wanted to stay in Roussou, keep the guys with me, and never deal with life. Stay. Hide. Fight. My mantra for so long.

"You're telling me now?" My voice was barely there.

He gazed at me with an intense expression, then suddenly something hard flashed. He let out a long sigh. "Yes. No, the plan wasn't to tell you today. We were going to let you get through graduation. We didn't know for sure your reaction, but we were going to wait until you asked."

My eyes narrowed. "I'm asking now."

"I know you are." He raised an eyebrow. "I was wondering if I should break the news to you when it's just me or try to put you off until later when Jordan and Zellman can participate in this talk too."

Jesus.

All three of them had planned this out.

I was mortified and ashamed all at the same time. I should've thought about this. I was graduating, for God's sakes.

"Bren." He moved forward, his finger under my chin. He tipped me up to look at him. "We are not leaving you behind."

Yeah. I'd still have three months with them...

As if knowing what I was thinking, he broke into my thoughts. "And I'm not talking about the summer. We are not going to die like your mother. We are not going to leave you like Channing did. We are not going to prison like your father. We are not a family you're going to lose."

He angled in, his hands falling to my hips. His forehead lowered, resting on mine. I felt his breath, warming me. "We are your second family, and you are not going to lose us."

There was a fist inside of me.

I felt it now, for the first time, but it had been there. Rooted deep in me. As his words washed over me, it relaxed.

"We have not pushed you because we know your fear. But yes, we made decisions without you. You weren't ready, so we did it for you." He tugged me even closer. "I hope, I really hope, you're okay with these decisions, but we did it with only love for you. We love you. I love you. Channing loves you."

"My brother?"

He nodded, moving both our heads up and down. His thumb snuck inside the opening in my gown since I hadn't zipped it closed, and he began stroking over my hipbone, under my shirt. "Heather loves you."

"Heather too?"

I was dying.

"Zellman. Jordan." A wry grin at me. "We did it behind your back, and I'm sorry."

"What'd you do?"

"Your brother's friends still have a house there. They're going to let us rent it at a discount."

What?

I stiffened, lifting my head.

They'd really gone the distance behind my back, using my brother for his connections.

"Well, I hope you guys all have a good time."

Together.

Without me.

"You're coming." He said it flatly, no emotion.

I narrowed my eyes. "What are you talking about?" I was already shaking my head. "I never applied for college. I know I didn't get in—"

"It's off-campus." His hands flexed, holding me tight and in place in front of him. "They relaxed their housing restrictions, and freshmen can live off-campus. We're going. And you're going." His eyes narrowed. "You'll get a job. Whatever. I don't care what you do, but you're coming. We're not doing next year without you. All of us decided. You come, or none of us go."

My mouth dried. My lips parted.

"What?"

I hadn't heard him right.

I'd expected a talk. I'd expected Jordan and Zellman to go to college. Or maybe Cross or one of them would stay behind. I—I was cursing myself. I just hadn't thought. I'd locked myself up and tried to throw away the key.

"I'm sorry."

"What?" His hand lifted, sliding around my neck. He tilted me toward him again.

I said it again, my hands hanging at my side. "You guys shouldn't have had to do this behind my back. You shouldn't have had to do any of it, wondering how I'd react. I'm sorry for that." I took a deep, but fucking painful breath. "I shouldn't have put you in that position."

His eyes closed for a second. "You really think I give a shit about that? I love you. I *love* you. You and me. We're still crew, no matter what happens."

His words were pretty and loving, and for the life of me, they couldn't wash away the sudden humility I felt.

That darkness in me, the firefly that liked to come out and keep me company, it had gone away. I didn't know when it happened—if it was after we saved Alex, or maybe before that. After I stabbed Principal Neeon, after everyone rallied around me, or maybe when I realized Cross loved me. Or maybe it'd just been a slow fading light over the year, through counseling, through letting others in. I didn't know.

I just knew I was standing here, feeling ashamed, but also in shock because I was alive.

The usual fear or panic or even anger that might've come after hearing the guys had made a plan behind my back didn't come. It just didn't.

"You okay?" Cross asked.

"I'm just embarrassed." They went to Channing about this. Heather too. "But also a whole bunch of other emotions too."

At that moment, Harrison walked by, head bent as he shuffled through notecards.

"Hey, Harrison."

He paused, his gown unzipped and his tie swinging to the side. "Yeah?"

"You're valedictorian, right?"

His eyebrows rose. "I'm surprised you knew that."

Cross frowned. "What the fuck?"

It wasn't a slight. I wasn't taking it as one. I nodded at him. "Where are you going to college next year?"

"Yale."

Cross was frowning at me. Harrison was frowning at me. After our talk at the buddy-system meeting, we hadn't spoken again, but it had meant something to me, and I was just now realizing it.

"Thank you."

His eyebrows shot even higher. "For what?"

That was for me, for now. "Just thank you. And good luck with your speech. I have a feeling it'll be great."

His eyes narrowed slightly, but he shrugged. "Okay. See you guys out there. I think they want us to line up now."

There was a slight breeze with a twinge of salt in the air. Hot, but not humid, and why I was noting these things was beyond me, but I was. I knew they were important because this moment was important. This was the day I decided to look forward instead of being paralyzed in place and gripping my loved ones so tightly they couldn't move forward either.

I was graduating.

There was the introduction.

They played songs, music that I wouldn't remember.

A speech from a faculty member.

A second speech.

We were all antsy, knowing this was a day we'd remember for years, but also wanting it to be done. I knew there were parties planned afterward. Both Jordan and Zellman had mentioned five different ones. Each of them would have their own party as well, the one their parents threw for them. Cross had refused when his mom offered to have one for him, so she was planning one for Taz next weekend. And Heather had asked if I wanted one too. I'd said no, but I knew they were planning something. Their friends were still in town. We never had that Friday BBQ, so I had a feeling whatever she was planning was going to replace it.

I waited for the speeches to get done, waited for them to say my name so I could walk across that stage and feel like I accomplished something, but the feeling felt cheap with me. I hadn't participated, not fully.

I hadn't embraced school. I went because I had to. I went because my crew was there, and even though I still wasn't the happiest with Taz, because she was there too.

I was forced to be part of the events planning committee, and that was the biggest of my high school activities. The crew had been everything to me, and here I was. A dying breed.

It was Wolf Crew. We were the last.

"And now a speech from our valedictorian, Harrison Swartz!" Principal Broghers began the clapping, stepping back from the podium as Harrison approached.

He ran a hand down the front of his gown, a nervous habit because his tie wasn't showing. Notecards still in hand, he cleared his throat. He took a deep breath. His shoulders rose.

He gripped the edges of the podium, and even from where I was, I could tell he was nervous.

Then—a real shocker—his eyes found mine.

My eyebrows rose.

Another breath from him, and he settled down.

He leaned forward into the microphone. "My name is Harrison Swartz, and I have a few things to say about our school..."

He mentioned students who'd won awards. He mentioned his favorite memories about winning the student council election, about what he'd learned being our class president. He thanked and noted teachers, a few janitors, some of the coaches. He congratulated a few of our sports teams who had won titles, set records, and gone to state to compete. He talked about the current year of politics, and then he paused, his eyes finding mine again.

His voice dropped, becoming more real, less smooth and polished. "I had a conversation with a person weeks ago that I had never spoken to before, and I never thought I would speak to." He nodded at me. "Bren Monroe."

I felt the attention. A few students in my row glanced down to me, and a few in front of me turned around.

"And it's not because of the obvious differences between us. Bren is very beautiful, and while I'm academically successful, I can admit that I'm a bit of a geek." There was a smattering of laughs. Harrison grinned, ducking his head a bit. "But that's not the difference I'm talking about, because in normal schools, that would play a part in our vast separation. In another school, Bren might've been considered one of the popular girls. In another school, I might've been considered well, like I just said, a nerd. That didn't happen here."

He paused again, clearing his throat. His eyes grew serious. "When she came up to me, it was the first time I'd spoken to her. She asked if I was going to be sick." He laughed lightly.

"I asked if you needed the bathroom," I said under my breath.

The people beside me heard and chuckled.

"I introduced myself to her, explained who I was and the reason I was at that particular place," he continued. "She thanked me for my service." His grin grew. "That made me laugh because here I was, the definition of a geek, and there she was, the definition of 'other'—and you can take that any way you'd like—but I never expected to be thanked for being student body president." His grin faded. "Then she proceeded to call me out. It was as if she could see inside of me and was reading my biases against her and her friends. She told me I wished there were none like her in our school, but she also called me out on worrying about what life would've been like if they *hadn't* been there too. She was right. All of it. I *did* have stereotypes. I didn't like having them in our school, but I benefited from them being there too. And then she stopped our conversation because she felt she was making me uncomfortable."

A beat. "She was. She had been, but after she moved on, I remained speechless for a moment. I never imagined my first conversation with someone like Bren Monroe would go that way. What she never found out was that she changed my mind. I realized they're like me. They have fears and insecurities and loves and likes. They're on social media, though I actually don't think Bren herself is."

He nodded at me. "I think by now, everyone has picked up on what 'them' I'm referring to, and while I know there are varying opinions on the system I'm talking about, I can only speak to how they affected my experience as a student in Roussou. Because in Roussou, I wasn't picked on. I wasn't bullied in person or online. I didn't have the typical jocks who might have called me lame or shoved me into a locker—that never happened here. And yes, there were scary moments over the years. Bouts of violence, but in a way, I always knew I was safe. I never walked my hallways worried about getting jumped. I never walked into a bathroom worried I'd get shoved in a toilet. *They* kept each other in check, and in doing so, they kept everyone else in check. We didn't really have popular people in our school. There's always a few exceptions, but in a way, we were all the same. We were equal. We were Normals. And I was one of them."

He paused. "I never told Bren that because of her, because of her group, because of her brother, we here were gifted an experience that no other high school was given. Roussou is not like other schools, and I am thankful because if it had been, I don't know if I would be standing behind this podium, giving this speech, and going to Yale next year. So, thank you." He stepped back, offered a small smile my way, and returned to his seat.

The clapping started. Then the cheering.

I had no words. He didn't have to share that moment, but he had, with me, with my crew, with all the other crews. Jordan and Zellman were hollering the loudest. I gazed over to where Cross was sitting beside Taz, and he'd already been watching me. His eyes flashed. I saw pride there, and I gazed down. He was holding his sister's hand, and she was crying, wiping away the tears with a Kleenex.

Race reached behind Cross' chair, tugged on Taz's gown, and she let go of her brother's hand and linked with Race's.

I hadn't asked. I didn't know what had transpired after Taz hadn't left the dinner to be there for him, but they seemed fine now. I supposed time would tell, but time would tell for everyone. Myself included.

Me and Taz. We'd figure it out. I knew her head was messed up right now.

Broghers returned to the podium, and the clapping faded. Everyone returned to their seats.

Line by line, we stood and moved to the end. One by one, we were called up.

Zellman went first. The cheers were loud.

I was next. The cheers were even louder.

Jordan wasn't far behind me.

Then Race. Cross. Taz.

Flashes went off. People whistled. They shouted congratulations, and then the time was done. Our tassels were moved from the right to the left. We took our diplomas, and at the end, we had officially graduated.

I was in the moment, for once. I felt everything and wasn't shutting it down—the sadness, the regret, the happiness, even the excitement, and I was blinking back tears when Channing found me.

"You crying?"

"No." I scowled, but one slipped out. "Maybe."

He laughed, and picked me up in a hug. "Congratulations, little sister. I love you," he whispered before setting me back down. Stepping back, he said, "I'm proud of you."

Then Heather was there, crying and hugging me.

Moose was next. Congo. Chad. Lincoln. Scratch.

There was a line, and I looked over, seeing Cross and Taz standing with their parents. The girlfriend wasn't there, and neither was Blaise. So it was just their family. And not far away was Jordan with his family, his little sister. Zellman was in a pocket of his own, his mom wiping her face and his grandmother. But he kept looking over at Sunday, who was standing with her parents, her head bowed, a protective hand over her stomach. She still wasn't showing, but I wondered if they knew by now.

"You okay?" Channing drew my attention back.

"What?"

His eyes were steadfast, his brow wrinkling a little. "You seem different today. What's going on?"

I shrugged. "Just...looking toward the future, I guess."

His face cleared of all concern, and he shared a quick look with Heather before smiling at me. "Yeah?"

I nodded. "Yeah."

His eyes were sparkling now. "Good."

I couldn't see myself, but I knew my eyes were sparkling back at him.

Good was good enough for me.

CHAPTER
FORTY-FOUR
One week later

"BREN?" HEATHER CALLED.

"Hmmm?" I was on the front porch of Heather's house. Well, it was still technically hers, but most of her stuff had been transported to our house. The official move was scheduled for later in the summer. When I went to Cain with the guys, Heather was going to sign the papers so her house would go to her brother. It was a big move. Those seemed to be happening everywhere now.

Heather opened her screen door as we both heard gravel crunching under tires. A black SUV was pulling in, passing Manny's and parking in front of us.

My stomach shifted, tightening, but Heather was all about these new arrivals. A wide smile on her face, she came out and let the door slam behind her. Her hands found her hips just as two doors opened. The football star got out on the driver's side, and the Olympic runner from the passenger side.

"Hey!" Heather shouted. "Where's Logan?"

"He's coming in a bit with Taylor," the runner said. "They were waiting for Nate and Matteo to get here."

"Matteo's coming? Great."

I side-eyed Heather, but she seemed genuine. She wasn't worried about me at all. These guys showed up, and I was mincemeat.

Jealousy flared, but I stomped it down. That was stupid. They were her good friends. I'd just gotten used to Heather's undivided attention over the year, and this was a two-minute meeting. I needed to get ahold of myself.

The female hugged Heather while the guy looked me over, almost exactly the way I'd just eyed Heather.

My eyes went flat. My lips thinned, and I scooted down in my chair, throwing up my feet on the railing. Whatever, dude. If he was trying to intimidate, he needed to pick someone else. I rolled my shoulders back and lifted my chin up. I was even willing to show a bit of teeth, but the way this guy's green eyes were cold and emotionless, and all the stories I'd heard about him, I didn't think he'd care one way or another.

I could see where all the hype came from, though that was a reluctant acknowledgment. The guy was gorgeous. So was the girl. Both with jet black hair, they could've been bookends. She had long slim running legs, and he was built—well, he was a wide receiver. Channing told me he'd had to slim down when he changed football positions. He still seemed like a giant, though.

"You're Bren."

The runner oozed warmth, and I turned to her, feeling myself standing without consciously planning on it. "Hi. Yeah."

She came at me, wrapped her arms tight, and squeezed.

Heather winced. "Uh. Bren's not—"

She stiffened, cursing under her breath. Pulling back, she grimaced. "Sorry. You're just..." She smoothed my hair and motioned over the rest of me as she forcibly took a step backward. "I'm Sam, and you're perfect, and I've been wanting to meet you for so long, but Heather's been wary. Anyway, I recently had a baby, and my emotions are still all motherly, and Heather talks about you as if she's your mother, and it melts my heart every time, but..." Her eyes raised to mine, and she slowed down.

She bit her lip, taking another step back. The footballer hooked an arm around her waist, pulling her to him, but they both stood, both observing me.

"Well..." I was full of piss and vinegar. "Don't I feel like an animal in the zoo right now."

"Bren!" Heather yelled.

The couple laughed. Both of them. They enjoyed that from me.

I wasn't sure how to take that.

"This is Sam and Mason," Heather said. "These are two very, very, *very* good friends of mine and your brother's."

I heard the warning in her voice and knew I needed to make myself scarce. I didn't adult well, and these people were too important to piss off the first time I officially met them. It was just my go-to habit.

"I should get going."

The guy spoke up, his eyes narrowing on me. "We heard you met Sam's mom."

"Mason," his woman said.

He ignored the reprimand. "What'd you think of her?"

I remembered that lady. I shrugged. "Not much."

Sam seemed to tense. Her face didn't show anything, but I sensed it. My indifference struck her for some reason.

His face got colder. "She said she knows your boy's father and woman. Said they're neighbors of hers. Said you might be around more because you and your guy are tighter than Sam and I were in high school."

I waited, my head tilted to the side. His words might've come off as just words. Maybe a conversation starter, but I wasn't getting that from him. He was warning me too, warning me that Heather had warned me.

That was interesting.

"Why are you warning me off from her?" I asked.

"Fucking Christ," Heather breathed.

The runner sent Heather an apologetic look. Heather sent one right back.

The two people not apologizing were the guy and me. I thought that was funny. He seemed perfectly content with what he was saying. Fine. Fuck it. He wanted to metaphorically push me around? Bring it, asswipe.

I took a step toward them and lowered my voice. "What is this? You're circling the wagons around your loved ones? Warning me not to mess with them or something? Do you know me?" My nostrils flared.

This guy's eyes were jaded and old, and he had seen and dealt with a lot. I saw all of that, felt all of that, and maybe that's why I was getting all riled up.

But then I wasn't.

Whatever the reason, I felt myself deflating into an odd serene feeling. No clue why. "You don't need to," I told him. "Everything you said is right, and though I haven't seen the lady again, I'm sure I will. It's inevitable since she seems to be the neighborhood watchdog. But you're wrong to worry about me. I'm not a typical high school punk. And I'm guessing she never confided in you either. That woman knew my mom, said she was friends with her. Why the fuck would I mess with someone who loved my mom?"

I heard Heather's intake of air.

She loved my mom. She'd said it. She and I had that in common, and it wasn't a connection a lot of people could claim. The right thing would be to cherish it, and since Mason had brought her up, since I was declaring all of this, I made the decision then and there.

I was going to seek her out and ask her to tell me about my mom, tell me more.

Finally, the guy cracked a bit and showed a sliver of emotion. He showed regret, but it was gone just as soon as it showed.

"Fuck's sakes," Heather said. "Where's Logan when you actually *want* an inappropriate joke to ease the tension?"

I flashed Heather a smile, but I knew it was sad. She'd been watching me, and she knew it was sad too.

"Bren." She reached for me.

I evaded her touch, but I spoke softly so her feelings weren't hurt. "You know me. I got default settings. I'm pretty sure Jordan is distracting Brandon so Z can sneak booze from your bar, but don't worry. After the last time, I reamed his ass. He'll leave money to cover. Jordan asked Brandon one night how much each bottle cost. Your brother didn't know the real reason he was asking."

Her eyes widened. "Are you kidding me?"

I shook my head. "Maybe you don't know us..."

"I'm sorry, guys. I have to take care of those little shits."

She stormed off, hurrying to Manny's in a quick gait, and the opposite of what I'd wanted just happened. I was going to be the one to go and handle them.

"Regretting your words?" the guy asked.

I looked at the guy again. "Maybe."

Another tug at his lip and the runner bit down on hers, looking down. Her shoulders shook silently.

Great. I was entertainment to them. This wasn't usually the response I got from adults.

"People older than me are usually scared I'll slip out a knife. You guys are laughing at me."

"Oh my God." The runner's shoulders stopped, and her head whipped up. "No! Oh no. We are not laughing at you. Just..." She turned, shared a look with her husband. "Mason's being protective of our friends. That's all. You can hurt Channing and Heather easily, and they're not usually people we worry about getting hurt. That's all."

That was... "That's insulting."

Both of them straightened at that.

"They're my family. Who's yours?" I shot back.

"They're family to us too," the guy said.

I directed my gaze at him, now finding my footing. "I don't care how rich you are, how famous you are, how close you think you are to my brother, to my future sister-in law. You fuck with them, betray them, I don't care what you do, but if the end result is pain for them, I will hurt you. I don't know how, but I will. That's *my* warning."

Anger flared inside of me, but it was mixed with other emotions like relief. These guys were doing what I did to protect mine. That was unnerving, but in a good way.

After that, the odd serene feeling came back, fluttering through me, calming me.

She quieted, watching her man.

He was watching me, and then he nodded and stepped forward. His hand stretched out. "Sounds good to me. I'm Mason. We're here for your graduation party, so congrats."

My graduation party. I'd forgotten for a few minutes. Shit. That meant more of these people were coming, because I knew Heather had closed Manny's down and invited nearly everyone in Roussou and Fallen Crest.

I was suddenly wary again, shaking his hand. "There's more of you guys coming? A Logan and Matteo?"

I'd met Logan, but it'd been brief. No interaction like this.

She tipped her head back and laughed.

Even he was grinning. "Logan's going to love you. He raved about how you were at the station."

"This is why Channing and Heather have kept us away from her. She's like us, Mason."

He grunted, but there was a small grin there. "Yeah. This will be interesting, to say the least."

I didn't know what they were talking about, but I'd never officially met Logan Kade. I'd heard about him. I hadn't heard of Matteo, but Nate sounded vaguely familiar.

I felt like I was wearing new skin.

Everything was changing, and I couldn't handle it.

"I think I'm going to go rescue my friends from Heather. It was nice to meet you both." I paused. "Samantha and Mason."

They nodded and moved aside as I went down the stairs, heading for the back of Manny's.

Another change for me? I truly meant that. I'd not been impressed with what they said, because words were empty to me. But actions and behaviors spoke to me, and them being worried about Channing and Heather, that said something to me. I liked it. I respected it.

"Come on, Heather!" I heard Zellman shouting inside Manny's. "I did a petition and got a thousand people to sign that you should give us free rum."

I was grinning even before opening the back screen door.

"Oh, really?" Heather huffed. "And who are these thousand signatures from? Your left and right hand alternating?"

Z was quiet. That gave her the answer.

"My God. Really? And why are you trying to sneak booze from here? You can get alcohol anywhere. Be like normal underage teenagers and sneak it somewhere else. At least work for your alcohol."

"That's what I was *trying* to do. You got in the way. And besides, your stuff's the best quality around."

I went down the hallway and was almost past the bathrooms and the office when a door opened. A hand shot out, grabbed my arm, and pulled me inside.

"Wha—"

A mouth was on mine, silencing me.

It wasn't any mouth. I knew that mouth. I'd felt it this morning, and I rose on my toes, wrapped my arms around his neck, and I opened mine in return.

All the weird stuff disappeared, and need, hot and yearning, need took its place.

Cross pulled back. "I fucking wish, but not here. Not in Heather's office."

I gave the room a quick scan. He was right. There was a sign positioned in the corner that said Chef Rules To Follow: Don't let anyone pasta away.

I shook my head. "That must've been a gift. Why would anyone choose to put that in their office?"

Cross dipped his head down, peppering kisses over my throat. "If we weren't here to celebrate *you*, I'd make up some excuse for us to ditch. I think we should have a day, just you and me, where we do that. Where we celebrate each other. You game? We could go somewhere. Alone. Just be. You know?"

It sounded heavenly. "I'm game."

We hadn't talked much the night before when he'd crawled into bed. He'd been at another family dinner, except this one had just been family. No significant others. The mom. The dad. Taz and Cross. I didn't think Blaise was included, and Cross had been quiet this morning. And then Heather had asked me to come early and help her pick out last-minute decorations since the party was for me.

I cupped the side of his face, my thumb running down his cheek. "How'd last night go?"

His arms tightened around me, and a shadow crossed his face. "It was what it was."

I waited, but he didn't add anything. Giving his chest a tap, I tipped my head back. "Hey. It's me. Talk. Let me in."

His eyes lifted. They were so hooded, so haunted, that my heart sank.

He closed them again. "Taz is going to Grant West, and what you said came true. My mom is leaving with her. She's going to buy a house there, settle in, get a job."

I waited, but nothing.

My hand flexed on his chest. "And your dad?"

"He's here." He looked up again. "What else is there to say?"

Kids went away to college. Parents stayed back. That was to be expected. I didn't think Cross was feeling the pain of that. It was the fact that his entire foundation was shifting under his feet. He had no home to come back to, but then I thought about it, and he did. It was me. It was here. It was Zellman and Jordan.

"Where's Blaise going to college?"

"Cain."

"Are you serious?"

He nodded, his face grim. "He was supposed to go somewhere in the east. Don't know why he switched."

"You think it's because you're going there?"

Cross was silent, and then shook his head. "No. My guess is there's some other reason he switched."

Cross hadn't said anything more about his brother, or his parents, or even his sister. I asked every few days, and he responded, but the answers were like this. He was letting me in, he just wasn't *fully* letting me in. There was an ocean of stuff in there about his family, but I'd be here when he was ready. And I knew it'd come out at some point. Everything did.

I smoothed a hand down his chest, hooking into his jeans. "After tonight. You and me. Yeah?"

He nodded, resting his forehead against mine. He breathed out, "Sounds perfect."

"I love you."

"I love *you*."

We could hear Heather walk past us, saying something about Zellman. Her words were muffled, but it was enough to remind us where we were.

"It's your party today," Cross said.

"It is. All of Heather and Channing's friends are here too. Or they're coming."

Cross sighed, separating from me. "It's going to be a long night."

It would. I patted his chest. "But hey, we have another party to look forward to at the end of the summer. Early screening of the documentary. Can't wait for that." I was being sarcastic and cheerful and yep, totally faking it here.

Cross' eyes widened in mock horror. "Who are you, and what have you done with my girlfriend?"

I laughed. "Didn't you know? That bitch graduated high school. She's long gone by now."

We moved to head out, and Cross ran a hand down my back. He leaned in, kissing the side of my forehead. "Never change, will ya? I really love this Bren."

I leaned into him, my insides warming and melting. "What are you talking about? I am changing."

"No." He stopped me, suddenly serious. "You're just removing some of the baggage, and the real you is coming out. You're brighter, shinier, and you're starting to glow, but you're still Bren." His eyes darkened. "I really need you right now."

My throat swelled, and I whispered, "I'll always need you."

He leaned down, and his lips found mine.

We stayed in Heather's office a bit longer.

EPILOGUE

Three months later

THE GIRL ON the screen sat on a stool in front of a black background, with a single light pointed at her. One camera. One producer. That was all.

Her hair was down, though she wore no makeup. A white top. Jean shorts. Black boots. A sweater had been placed over her shoulders because she was cold.

That girl was Bren.

That girl was me.

I'd been raw that day. This video, it wasn't what I wanted, but I used it. I turned it into something I wanted in the end.

I watched myself as I looked down for a moment, my hair falling forward, and when I looked up, I left it there. I had darkened my hair, almost black. I didn't know why at the time, but seeing it now, it blended with the background. Maybe that'd been my intention? A last attempt to blend in, not step forward? Or maybe I just wanted my face to stand out more.

I didn't know, but I liked it. My hair had grown longer too.

Maybe, just maybe, I was trying to become a new Bren. I was trying to put the old one behind—the one who wanted to stay in Roussou forever, who didn't want to grow up, who was so scared of the future she'd almost stopped believing it would come.

Maybe.

Either way, there I was. On a stool. Getting ready to pour my heart out. Then Becca asked me a question and my back straightened.

Becca's voice came from off-camera. "You asked to be interviewed. What made you decide to do this?"

"Because the other side needs to be told."

"And what side is that?" she asked.

"It was for protection. That's why the crews were started. Not to be a gang. Not for violence. Not for power. It was simply to push back against power."

"What happened back then?"

"A guy wanted to rape a girl. That's the root of the crews. A bad guy wanted to rape an innocent girl, and a group rallied against that bad guy. They wouldn't stand for it, so they fought back, and that was when the first crew started. The New Kings Crew. My brother's crew."

"There's been a lot of pushback by your school's administration against the crew system. They said you guys are violent and a danger to their students' safety. What do you think about those statements?"

Watching myself now, I didn't see how I'd tensed. I didn't see how I'd felt so sad hearing the same thing over and over again. Instead, I saw my head lift higher, my shoulders firm. I seemed more determined, fiercer, and I heard how strong my words came out.

"Ask the students if they've feared us."

"We have."

"What'd they say?"

There was silence for a moment, then, "They said there's an element of the crews that they fear, but they know you guys will protect them, and that's given them a sense of security." There was another pause. "Almost every single student did say they were glad they went to a high school that had the crew system. You guys didn't target them, you mostly kept to yourself, but if something were to happen, you were there to help."

Onscreen, I was nodding. That was nothing new.

"When our crew started, I was the first female to join one," I said. "People were cruel. People asked if I was the whore for the guys. If I was the group slut. It was the opposite. My crew set the precedent that we don't see gender. A female member is a crew member. That's it. Nothing more. Nothing less. *I* wasn't less.

Then another girl joined a crew, and I was told it was the same with them. Every crew is different. We don't all follow the same guidelines or rules, but the core of each crew is protection and loyalty. You protect each other, and you're loyal to each other."

"But you are dating one of your members, correct?" Becca asked.

I nodded. "There was a rule that there was no dating in our crew. And we followed that rule, until we fell in love."

"Did the others in your crew get upset?"

It was something we hadn't shared, but that interview was about being honest, being raw. So I'd shrugged and said, "Yeah. They were mad, but we worked through it. The whole crew did. There were lots of talks about the problems that could happen. There were talks about disbanding, or what would happen if we tried not to date. In the end, we *all* decided that the best result was to continue being a crew, for us to continue dating, and hope for the best. If the best didn't happen, one of us would leave."

"Did that ever happen?"

I shook my head. "No. We're still together."

"If there's one thing you wanted the world to know about the crew system in Roussou, what would that be?"

"Stop putting us in a box that only you understand. If you can't understand, try to learn. We're not bad. We're not good. We're not evil. There's no plan or agenda. The crews started to protect one girl. One. It was good in the beginning, and there is still good in the crew system." I turned, finding the camera straight on and ignoring the producer next to it. "The Roussou administration manipulated this entire documentary to do their bidding. Every student except myself, Cross Shaw, Jordan Pitts, Zellman Greenly, Race Ryerson, and Tasmin Shaw were coerced into signing a contract with local police that required them to be interviewed for this project."

A whispering buzz filled the room.

I remembered it then. Remembered Becca's shocked face. The camera guy who froze. Another director had come into the room. But I didn't hear the commotion I'd heard then. They had edited that out.

"There's a video online showing where police lined up students at a party," I continued on the screen. "They let students from Fallen Crest go free and arrested all the students that went to Roussou. Each student was given a deal. Sign up to join this documentary, be cooperative, and no charges would be brought against them. We were at the same party. People will say we weren't arrested, but it's because we weren't caught. We got away. There was another party of people arrested, and they got a deal cut. That's because those people were from the Ryerson Crew. Their leader at the time was working with a member of the Fallen Crest Police Station in a plan to undermine my crew and bring drugs into the high schools."

I took a break, but my eyes never wavered.

I never slouched.

I never adjusted.

I never flinched.

My head was held high because this was important.

I would show no weakness in this moment.

"The administration got what they wanted. All but one crew disbanded. My crew. We're the last, and we will have graduated and left Roussou by the time this documentary airs. I don't know what will happen with the crew system once we're gone. More groups might start up. The system might be done, and Roussou will return to being a normal high school. Either way, anyone who gives a damn has the right to know what really happened. Ken Broghers, Detective Broghers from the Fallen Crest Police Department, and our last principal, all worked together to force students be a part of this documentary."

A ghost of a smile crossed my face. "Not to say that some of those students wouldn't have wanted to be a part anyway, but the way it happened wasn't right. In fact, some would say it was discriminatory and coercive. But what's my opinion? I'm only a high schooler."

The rest of the documentary shared interviews with other students. All backed up what I'd said.

The new interviews gave more details about the party.

Tabatha shared her story about her cousin who was raped.

Sunday cried on camera, talking about how she wished she'd gotten pregnant a year earlier because she knew my crew would've helped. But now we were all leaving and going out into the real world, and she didn't think she'd get the same help or shelter out there.

She was right.

Video of Harrison's valedictorian speech was included.

And more student accounts.

They all had the same theme.

We weren't taken for granted. We weren't hated.

We *were* feared.

We *were* loved.

We *were* respected.

The documentary ended with a note that an investigation had been opened and charges were pending against Kenneth Broghers, Detective Broghers, and Robert Neeon.

The entire documentary wasn't just about us, which I was relieved to find out. They'd broken it up into a docuseries, and we were only the last half of episode three. The first half had been about Channing and Heather, how they were the bridge between the two towns. The first episode was about Mason and Samantha Kade.

Episode two was about Brett Broudou.

It wasn't a big documentary, but it had gotten some media buzz, mostly because of Mason Kade. It was picked up by ESPN and jointly ran on another cable network, so it wasn't going to change our lives. Knowing some attention would be brought to our school, knowing that our side had been shared, all that was good enough for me.

We'd moved on Friday.

The documentary aired two days later. They'd given us the entire series early so while the rest of the episodes would air in the next coming weeks, we got to watch all three in one night.

Jordan and Zellman threw a huge party. The girls were all here, along with Race and Taz. They'd both traveled from Grant West, which was a four-hour drive.

Taz had embarked on a full-blown effort to get to know her half-brother Blaise over the summer. That translated into him being invited, and though we weren't happy, we weren't surprised when he showed up with Zeke Allen in tow. Along with a few others.

Things were tense between Blaise and Cross. Neither seemed inclined to make the first move into whatever—either being enemies or becoming brothers, or just friends. Even with Taz, it'd been touch-and-go. Blaise seemed like he tolerated her at times, and other times, he fully avoided her.

Sunday and Tabatha spent much of the evening taking video and selfies with Blaise and Zeke, then posting them only to Lila and Monica's Instagram accounts. I didn't know the story there, but there was one.

"What are you doing back here?" Arms encircled me from behind. Cross pulled me against his chest, and I rested my head against his shoulder. Our hands caught, our fingers entwined.

I'd been standing in the far doorway that connected the garage and the kitchen. There was a clean line of sight into the living room, and for the most part, I'd had my own moment here. Watching that documentary had been surreal.

It was odd to watch my life on television.

My words were out there. I'd said them. This was a very different chapter for me. I'd gone on the record. I did a very un-crew thing, and I went after the administration on their terms. I used what they wanted to use against us, and I didn't know how I felt about it.

"Just getting a minute by myself," I finally responded.

This felt different. Not Cross and me, but being here. A new house. We were living with Zellman and Jordan.

"Almost my whole life, I've been hearing how bad the crews are. Almost all my life, I've had people wanting to get rid of us, and now they almost succeeded. I don't know how I feel about it. We weren't all bad."

Cross dipped his head down, brushing a kiss to my neck. "I know. We know it. And now..." He nodded toward the television, "You put that out there."

"A lot of people won't care."

"No, but..." He hugged his arms over my chest, rocking me back and forth in his shelter. "Maybe some will. You just don't know."

True.

I looked up. "Did you know the producers for that documentary are related to Nate Monson? They're his parents."

"I didn't." He paused a beat. "Who's Nate Monson?"

I grinned, folding my hands over his arms. "Well, according to Malinda—"

Cross laughed, squeezing me. "You've been spending too much time with that woman. She's a bad influence."

"Really?" I tipped my head up, grinning. "She drinks coffee with me and tells me stories about my mom."

"Like I don't know it was her idea to play ding-dong ditch."

"Technically, neither of us did that."

"No, you're right. You talked Taz into ringing the doorbell and running back to where you and Malinda were waiting in the getaway car."

"See?" I patted his arm, beaming up at him. "We didn't actually do it. We just assisted Taz in doing it. And besides, Malinda said she did that with my mom. I wanted to see how it felt."

"How'd it feel?"

Like harmless and silly fun, but I felt close to my mom that night. And I'd go again if Malinda suggested it. "It's a good memory to have now."

He frowned. "Wait. Who's Nate Monson again?"

I shook my head. We'd met him a few times, but Cross never really interacted with him. "It's just a funny connection. It's not that important."

We remained like that, standing in the back, him holding me as we watched the rest of our group. In that moment, I was content. And that was an emotion I was trying to learn how to be okay with—not to push it away, to let myself be happy. It was a work in progress, but with this new beginning, I was hopeful about this next year. I had my crew, so I was okay.

"Bren?"

Cross' arm tightened around me. We both stiffened at my brother's voice.

I frowned, disentangling from Cross. "What are you doing here?"

We'd invited them for the viewing party, but both he and Heather had chosen to remain at home, saying they were too old for college parties.

Everyone had quieted, seeing Channing walk into the house.

He didn't look happy. He looked concerned.

Dread began flickering in my gut. I'd literally just tried to work my way toward being okay with feeling some contentment, and then this happened—whatever this was that Channing brought to my new doorstep.

I stepped forward. "What's wrong?"

Channing's eyes narrowed, and he shook his head. "Nothing. Something good actually."

He was lying. I could see it.

Zeke came down from the stairs, a beer in hand. He stopped, saw Channing, and belched. "Is Kade here with you?"

Channing ignored him, his eyes steady on me. "Bren."

That wasn't his "something good" voice. That was his "come with me so we don't make a scene" voice. I started forward.

Cross came with me, but as we weaved through the group, nearing the door, Channing asked, "Can I have her alone for a minute? Just a minute."

Now I really knew this was going to be bad.

I met Cross' gaze as he moved his head up and down in the slightest nod. "Sure."

But he didn't sound so sure.

Channing's eyes fell to me. "Let's go outside."

I followed him.

He closed the door behind us, and right away, we heard a commotion inside.

Someone yelled, "Lights!"

The house went dark in the next second. Then we saw the curtains moving aside. They were all watching out the windows.

Channing swore under his breath. "Fucking college students."

I grinned. "Technically, none of us have started classes yet."

He rolled his eyes. "Right. Fucking high schoolers? That sound better?"

I didn't answer.

He took a breath, gesturing to the sidewalk. "Let's walk."

I was tempted to refuse, to make him spill whatever was wrong right then and there, but instead I fell in step with him, my hands going into my pockets.

We walked down the line of vehicles until we got to his.

"What's going on, Chan?"

He stopped just short of his truck and turned to face me. His head down, his eyes clouded, he said, "I am always here for you. You know that, right?" He put a hand on my arm, making sure I was looking him in the eyes. "I'm your older brother, and I fucked up when I was younger, but nothing—and I mean nothing—will keep me away from you. I will fight anyone if I think they're hurting you. You know that, right?"

Touched, I felt my throat swelling. I nodded. "Yeah, I know."

He stared at me, something weighing on him, and then he pulled me in for a tight hug. Holding me, he murmured against the side of my head, "I swear to God, if he hurts you, I will..." He stopped, swallowing as he forced himself to step back.

But his hands were still on my shoulders, as if he couldn't bring himself to fully let me go.

I was really starting to worry now. "What are you talking about? About Cross?"

"No. About—"

The passenger door of his truck opened. Someone I hadn't realized had been sitting there, had been watching us, had been waiting, stepped out.

"Bren?"

Everything swung around me in a circle. The vehicles. The house behind us. Even the fucking stars in the sky. Lightning bugs. The whole bit, because the ground got swept out from under me.

"Dad?"

Stay tuned for *Crew 3*, coming 2020!

For more young adult books, head to www.tijansbooks.com

ACKNOWLEDGEMENTS

A special thanks to all my usual team for this one!!

All my beta readers, proofreaders, my editor, my formatter! Thank you to all of the crew readers. I wanted to get this one out to you guys much earlier, but hit a few snags with other project deadlines and the characters weren't speaking to me. I'm an author who tries not to force characters so thank you again for understanding! Also, just a big huge hug from myself to all the Crew readers who were so amazing and supportive when I started posting little snippets of Crew Princess. I wasn't sure the reception I'd get, but you guys let me know you were more than ready for Crew 2! That is like air to authors.

And now you've read *Crew Princess,* I hope you're ready for *Crew 3.*

Make sure to keep an eye out in my reader group or on my website, because I have a few surprises coming next year from a few people in this book.

CPSIA information can be obtained
at www.ICGtesting.com
Printed in the USA
BVHW032143180820
586766BV00001B/42